PRAISE FOR ...ES

"Potent myt... ...of creeping horror
and baroque ...top-notch horror-
fantasy saga...

—Publishers Weekly

"*A Tree of Bones* has . . . plenty of spectacle and action to keep the plot moving. I highly recommend the series as a whole, it provides a refreshingly different variety of fantasy."

—SFRevu

"[*A Rope of Thorns*] paints a stark, vivid, and gory picture of the 'wild west' in the years following the Civil War. . . . Filled with antiheroes, sacrificial victims, and supernatural beings, Files's latest is not for the squeamish but should delight fans of gothic Western fantasy and Central American myths."

—Library Journal

"For all that it is character driven, [the Hexslinger Trilogy] is full of sound and fury, as gods and magicians go head to head in epic battles that transmute the warp and weft of reality itself. Files commits to the page scenes so vivid that they will brand themselves on the reader's mind . . . She has produced a luminous and uncompromising fantasy series, one that is awash in blood and shot through with remorseless brutality, but also peppered with scenes of striking originality, a narrative that should appeal to horror fans and all those who adore anything that is different. Succinctly, I loved it from first word to last."

—Black Static

FIRST EDITION

We Will All Go Down Together © 2014 by Gemma Files
Cover artwork © 2014 by Erik Mohr
Cover and interior design by © 2014 by Samantha Beiko

Distributed in Canada by
HarperCollins Canada Ltd.
1995 Markham Road
Scarborough, ON M1B 5M8
Toll Free: 1-800-387-0117
e-mail: hcorder@harpercollins.com

Distributed in the U.S. by
Diamond Comic Distributors, Inc.
10150 York Road, Suite 300
Hunt Valley, MD 21030
Phone: (443) 318-8500
e-mail: books@diamondbookdistributors.com

Library and Archives Canada Cataloguing in Publication Data

Files, Gemma, 1968-, author

    We will all go down together / Gemma Files. -- First edition.

Short stories.

Issued in print and electronic formats.

ISBN 978-1-77148-201-1 (pbk.).--ISBN 978-1-77148-202-8 (pdf)

    I. Title.

PS8611.I39W4 2014   C813'.6   C2014-902668-4

C2014-902669-2

CHIZINE PUBLICATIONS
Toronto, Canada
www.chizinepub.com
info@chizinepub.com

Edited by Michael Matheson
Proofread by Stephanie Da Ponte and Sandra Kasturi

Canada Council Conseil des arts
for the Arts   du Canada

We acknowledge the support of the Canada Council for the Arts which last year invested $20.1 million in writing and publishing throughout Canada.

ONTARIO ARTS COUNCIL
CONSEIL DES ARTS DE L'ONTARIO
50 YEARS OF ONTARIO GOVERNMENT SUPPORT OF THE ARTS
50 ANS DE SOUTIEN DU GOUVERNEMENT DE L'ONTARIO AUX ARTS

Published with the generous assistance of the Ontario Arts Council.

Printed in Canada

WE WILL ALL GO DOWN TOGETHER

STORIES OF THE FIVE-FAMILY COVEN

ChiZine Publicaations

Where have you been, my long-lost love, these seven long years and more?
—"The Demon Lover," traditional ballad

You must not go to the wood at night.

—Henry Treece

TABLE OF CONTENTS

Introduction
Amanda Downum

When I first read Gemma's novel *A Book of Tongues*, I said that it *"lays eggs in your brain, and when the eggs hatch your skull splits open and a thousand shiny green scorpions and spiders swarm out of your eye sockets, and when they've eaten the last of your brains, a spider spins a web in the hollowed-out curve of your skull, and the web reads 'Some book.' In Nahuatl."*

I was, unsurprisingly, quite delighted to read *We Will All Go Down Together*.

As much as I love scorpions, spiders, and Aztec gods, witches and angels and fae are even more deeply imprinted on my reading DNA. Since I was old enough to wander the horror and fantasy aisles in bookstores, these have been the stories to which I've gravitated. And while witches and angels and the fair folk are easy to find in bookstores, rarely do I find them depicted in ways so close to my heart.

The witches and fae who populate Files' haunted Toronto aren't sexy or sanitized. These witches deal in blood and souls and devils' bargains; these fae trade in lives and steal away hapless mortals—not to fairy-tale forests and shining castles, but to the darkness and damp of hollow hills filled with bones and rot. Instead of eternal youth and Hollywood cheekbones, Files offers us the slimy, squelching vision of what it might really be like to transform into a hungry creature of rivers and marshes. She gives us not just the threat of *twa e'en o' a tree*, but oozing flesh worn raw by wood.

We Will All Go Down Together is built on combinations and contrasts. Individual short stories and novellas combine to illuminate characters as well as the overarching plot. The historical horrors of Jacobean witch hunts combine with New Age spiritualism, Scottish and Chinese and First Nations folklore with biblical apocrypha. The characters are driven by rage and pain and pride, by love and duty, faith and pragmatism. The stories are simultaneously cruel and sweet, brutal and hopeful, raw and bruising and so sharp you don't feel the wound till you've reached the end. They balance tropes of the fantastic with unnerving grotesquerie— urban fantasy's sense of being one step away from the magical and numinous, and horror's creeping violation of the seemingly familiar. Like Files' monsters—the best sort of monsters—they're beautiful, enticing, sharp-toothed, and skin-crawlingly creepy.

This is not a book for the faint of heart, but read it anyway. Maybe you're stronger than you realize.

The Five:
A Warning to the Curious
Gemma Files

Every story is made of stories, and all of those collected here trace back to one begun long before, in another country, another century. It tells of how five people, each of whom represented part of the same cursed lineage—the bastard seed of a thousand evil angels, thrown down on rocky soil and left to grow unchecked, breeding a secret poisoned treasure of supernatural power in its unlucky inheritors—met for fell purposes, swearing together to carry out a great and secret work which would rock the very world to its core. Branded as monsters and persecuted by those who considered them impure, damned, contaminating, they allied together only to split each from each along lines carved by privilege, for two of them were noble, three not. And so the fated break ensued, inevitably: when betrayal struck, the rich and moneyed escaped "justice," or King and Church's notion of it, while the poor and low suffered its full extent.

Yet no one who tells this first tale debates whether or not all its protagonists deserved equally to die for what they did, or planned to do, in their way . . . all are considered equally guilty, even by the surviving descendants of these fabled five, carriers of their bad blood and worse history alike. And so it remains a legend strange things tell each other, a bedtime fable recited by monsters, to monsters; its long shadow falls over all subsequent stories, staining them in shades of pitch-black smoke and hellish flame, lending them a stench of blown ash and bone-grit. While always those who begin it do so with these same words, unfailingly—

Listen now, my darling; lean closer still, and I will speak in hushed voice of the Five-Family Coven, who dared all only to lose all, whose infamous names will surely live forever. They of the line of Glouwer, of Devize, of Rusk, witches and witch-children, of whom none are spared. They who bear either the name Druir or that of Sidderstane, who dwell forever trapped in Dourvale's twilight, outcast from two worlds and citizens of none. They who once held the title of Roke, wizards and warlocks of high renown, who bent the elements to their will and learned the names of every creature more awful than themselves, if only so that they might bend them to their will.

Here is where things start, always—the bone beneath the stone, the great tap-root. The hole which goes down and down. That old, cold shadow, always waxing, never waning. That taste, so bitter in the back of your mouth, which almost seems to echo the tang of your own blood.

Perhaps you recognize their names, now—catch in their descriptions just the faintest possible echo of someone you suspect, someone you yearn towards without knowing why, someone you love yet fear, or fear to love. Of yourself, even. And perhaps this resonance, like some tiny bell's distant toll, makes you suddenly wish to know more.

Well, then: you are in luck, of a kind, for here you hold a book which can answer all relevant questions if only asked properly, just waiting for your touch upon its covers. Do so, therefore; open it to you, yourself to it. Breathe deep the dust of its pages, scrape some ink, take samples of its pulp. Or simply plunge in unprepared, risking nothing but your own ignorance . . . a hazard surely easy enough to gamble without much caution, even without knowing what else might really be at stake . . .

. . . and see what happens next.

LANDSCAPE WITH MAPS & LEGENDS:
DEAD VOICES ON AIR (2004)

The following extracts were recovered by forensic Internet technicians from Galit Michaels' deleted Folksinger.net blog of the same name, at the request of her relatives.

August 10, 2004
Mood: Ebullient
Music: "Wayfaring Stranger," Johnny Cash
Title: Don't Drink and Post

Like opening the bible at random, songwriting can be a form of bibliomancy—logomancy, rather. Words come out of nowhere, sometimes—out of sequence, out of sync. Rhymes optional. Phrases misheard, misshapen, reshapened, lost in translation and all the better for it: done to death, done deathly, O maid too soon taken . . .
  O whither shall I wander
  With white horn soft blowing
  Down dark rivers walking
  Down dark halls gone flowing . . .
  There's something there, or could be. Look at it again in the morning, when you're not so drunk.

August 12, 2004
Mood: Blah
Music: "On the Bank of Red Roses," June Tabor
Title: Beer Bad, Head Slow

Ugh. Two days later, and I can still feel that freakin' sickly sweet Raspberry Wheat concoction of Josh's in the back of my throat, a technicolour yawn waiting to happen. Tonight's show has us back at Renaissance West rather than East, but that's about all that's changed. Sometimes I feel like we're on some sort of endless loop, just shuttling back and forth between two clubs with the same name, always performing to the same bunch of people, give or take: wannabe slam poets, Society for Creative Anachronism rejects, girl-with-guitar music fetishists (and I say that as the girl).

During rehearsal, Josh and Lars kept sniping at each other—Lars picked a fight about material, started in on this rant about how we were doing too many "stupid-ass murder ballads," how all folk songs are derivative and repetitious, etc. Why don't we write our own stuff in a similar vein, like Nick Cave with "Where the Wild Roses Grow"? Pointed out that "Wild Roses" is basically "On the Bank of Red Roses" redux, tricked out with a little Nietzschean posturing and Kylie Minogue as the ghost, but he didn't wanna hear it; Josh got sidetracked somehow onto whether or not "Delia's Gone" is too po-mo to be misogynist, and I went home early. They barely seemed to notice.

Stepping out onto Church Street, I ran straight into what looked like a truly weird combination of frost and condensation happening at apparently the same time—freezing rain, rising haze, glistening windows, cars, trees. My glasses turned everything I passed pointilescent, including this older guy paused just on the corner, skimming through today's *Dose*. He had some kind of severe Scots accent (Highlands? Lowlands? Midlands? . . . no, that's British, isn't it?), so thick I had to pause and double-take for a minute when he suddenly said:

"You're the singer, yeah? From Gaucho Joe's."

"I sing there sometimes, yes."

"Liked what you did with 'Tam Lin,' last time."

"Um, thanks." And after a sec, 'cause I never can seem to stop myself: "What part?"

And now he was looking at *me*, over the paper's sodden rim—not that "old" at all, really, not even middle-aged. Maybe almost my age, even. But he did have that reddish-grey hair and eyes to match, from what I could make out through the fog on my lenses; something sort of stylish-tough and vaguely familiar about him too, like he looked like one of the sidekick actors from *Gangster Number One*, or whatever.

Then he smiles, teeth hella-bad like every U.K. dude, and goes: "The whole of it, hen. The song itself—it's so *true*, and that's so bloody hard to come by, yeah. Don't you think?"

"I guess . . ."

And . . . that was about it, basically. Super-weird, even for a Monday. Weird on *top* of weird, squared and triple-squared, to the infinite power.

Now I need water and TV time, and to get myself together. And sleep too, because tomorrow's Tuesday, and there's work.

WE WILL ALL GO DOWN TOGETHER

Not to mention laundry.
August 15, 2004
Mood: Pensive/thinky
Music: That creepy hissing noise inside my head
Title: "True"?

Crap day at The Grind, as ever. I'm getting that "you just don't mesh with the Coffee Crossroads program, Galit" vibe pretty hard off of Daphinis these days, like basically the whole time I'm there—doesn't make a double shift go by any faster, that's for damn sure. So I guess that spending a sizeable chunk of time checking the Classifieds might be in order, as of this weekend: fuck it, suits me. Never stay too long anywhere they make you wear a uniform jacket they're obviously too cheap to dry-clean on a regular basis, that's *my* motto.

But yeah, I do keep sort of thinking about what that guy said, and that probably has me distracted enough to show. Because . . . well, "true"? "Tam Lin" is a *fairy tale*, for Christ's sake. It doesn't even have the tabloid oomph of something like "Pretty Saro" or "Sam Hall" (damn your eyes!) to back it up. Just Fair Janet pulling the roses and then this "fair and full o' flesh" dude suddenly 'fessing to knocking her up, plus the whole thing with the Fairy Queen and her looming tithe to Hell— the bad flipside of "Stolen Child," in other words, with Tam Lin himself the changeling boy looking 'round years later and deciding he really does prefer his former human world after all, "full of weeping" though it may well still be. After which she breaks the spell, so the Fairy Queen goes all totally off on her with that spooky revenge-threat rant—

A curse on you, Fair Janet,
And an ill death may you dee!
If ever I'd known you'd stray, Tam Lin,
And look on ought but me,
I would ha' ta'en out thy twa grey een
And put in twa een o' tree.

Wooden eyes, like that guy from *Pirates of the Caribbean*; man, you know *that'd* grate whenever you blinked. Splinter, too.

Anyhow. Back to Joe's tomorrow, interestingly enough: Scottish Richard Gere-guy territory! I know the guys really want to do "Tam" again too, mainly because Lars thought Josh fucked up his solo; this testosterone crap really does have to stop, or . . . well. More job-shopping, just from a different angle.

Funny thing about that dude, actually—might have been the fog or whatever, but I'm having a serious bitch of a time even halfway remembering what he looked like. So much so that I wonder if I'll be able to spot him in the audience, if he does come.

August 20, 2004
Mood: Energized
Music: "Raise the Dead", Linda Ronstadt and Emmylou Harris
Title: Well, It Finally Happened . . .

. . . and Glamer is now very much a thing of the past, at least the version of it incorporating Mister and Mister Let's-Whip-Out-Our-Dicks-and-Joust. The whole process was surprisingly painless, at least where Lars is concerned: "Never liked this fag outfit anyhow," huh huh huh huh. "You mean fag-and-*dyke* outfit?" I yelled, as he walked away, and Josh thought that was pretty damn funny, right up until the point where I gave him *his* marching orders, too.

"Come *on*, Galit—don't we work well together? Be fair, man."

"It's not about me working with you, Josh, it's about you working with anybody else."

"What, like Lars? Buddy just loves to rumble, generally; check out his act in a week or two, he'll probably be smashing up his *own* guitars."

To which I thought: *Yeah, well, possibly. But it does take two to tango, and I sure as hell don't ever remember really being part of that dance—that was all you, all over me. And I don't think that was only just with Lars, either.*

Because if we were honest, then we'd admit the unspoken fact that our lack of actual "together-ness" has always been the engine driving Josh-and-I's creative truck, pretty much since we first got . . . uh . . . together. And that used to work fine, back when there was only the two of us—before Kathy, or Oona, or what's-her-name on his side, before Sean, or Drew, or (for that matter, though only one drunken time, thank Christ) Lars himself on mine—but these days, it just doesn't seem to be working anymore. There's too much drama, too much sublimated jealousy; the music suffers. *I* suffer. The investment isn't worth the return, and blah blah blabbitty blah, ad infinitum.

So now, it's back to the old faithful formative one-chick acoustic version of Glamer for a while, until I can spare the time to hold auditions. As in any good divorce, we tallied stuff up and split it down the middle: I get to keep the band's name, he gets to keep all his arrangements, we both get to keep our own instruments, here endeth the lesson;

everybody walks away content, hopefully, if not particularly happy. I promised to buy him a beer the next time our paths crossed, kissed him on the cheek, and booked.

Wasn't until I was already on the subway home that it finally hit me, though—one of the songs I'd just given away was "Tam Lin," and I never did see that dude at our last show as an intact musical entity. Shit.

All the more reason to find myself a brand "new" old song to push, though, isn't it? One that everybody and their sibling *don't* already know inside-out and backwards. One that's just for me. ;)

Comments:
Have you tried looking through the Connaught Trust's balladry collection? Their Reading Room is open to the public from noon to midnight on every day but Sunday.
—Posted by: guizer@alfhame.com

> Seriously? I don't think I've ever heard of it.
> —Posted by: galit@folksinger.net

> It's a private endowment, co-administrated by the Connaught family's law firm and a subdivision of the Toronto Catholic Archdiocese. Really good for research, especially when it involves obscure folklore. The "Ontario ballads" were added around 1976, after the guy who compiled them's last surviving heir finally died, and she willed them to the Trust. You'll find the address in the White Pages.
> —Posted by: guizer@alfhame.com

> Thanks! I'll check it out.
> —Posted by: galit@folksinger.net

August 22, 2004
Mood: Undecided
Music: "Priests," Judy Collins
Title: A Trip to the Connaught

Okay, so that was . . .

You know, at this point, I don't even really know. Offputting? To say the least.

The place turned out to be on one of those weird little streets off the

U of T stretch on St. George, which I'm obviously not all that familiar with to begin with, since I went to Ryerson. There's the library, a big glass-fronted 1960s monolith, apparently hanging out of the sky at a truly scary angle—sort of reminds me of those cubist spaceships you'd always see on the front of U.K. science-fiction paperbacks in the early 1980s, by guys like Brian Aldiss or John Wyndham. And next to that, on either side, you've got the basic student services sprawl: converted town houses occupied by frats and (sorts?), crap-ass residential apartment complexes, cheap pubs, cheaper Indian and Canadian-Chinese cafeteria-style "restaurants," the inevitable Second Cups.

Plus, everywhere else you look, you're already turning down another of these street-sign-less cul-de-sacs lined with increasingly threatening trees: maples, oaks, lilacs, all overgrown, pavement underneath covered in a muck of dead leaves. Seriously, was there some sort of post-Dutch Elm disease mass-replanting program nobody ever told me about in school? Because it's kind of like Mutual of Omaha's *Wild Kingdom* in there, these days; go too far down one of these suckers, I'm surprised anyone ever finds their way back out.

The fabled Connaught Trust, meanwhile, turns out to be a relatively big, weather-worn house completely shrouded in a tangle of pines so thick I could see what looked like four years' growth of spiderwebs turning the sun grey whenever I looked up (which I only did the once, for obvious reasons). Cones and half-cones were piled everywhere along the path, crunching queasily underfoot like they'd just been left to lie there and marinate. If I hadn't finally spotted the plaque on the front door, I'd've been out of there in about 2.5 seconds; unfortunately for me, though, I did. And I sort of thought I could see somebody in there too, looking out at me through one of the second-floor windows . . .

So I knocked: nothing. Pushed on the door, which gave in, slowly. The place smelled like Pine-Sol and dust, though you wouldn't necessarily think that was possible. A Magritte print on the wall, above a row of hooks for coats: that one with the wooden picture-frame full of red brick hung against dove-grey wallpaper, above olive-drab panelling. And maybe it was just a trick of the lack of light, but that paper looked almost exactly the same shade as the paper inside the Trust's hall, with the panelling underneath it pretty much the same shade, too . . .

Stood there and stared at it for a minute or two, more than a bit freaked out, hearing the pines creak behind me, afraid my collar wasn't quite up far enough to spiderproof me completely. Until, thank Christ, somebody finally came downstairs—this completely normal lady, albeit just a little bit butch, with her hair back in a French braid and a very subtle gold cross pinned on her collar; the Church contingent, I can only assume, since I didn't have either the wherewithal or the guts to ask her outright if she was a nun, or what.

"I'm looking for the Ontario Ballads?"

"You mean Torrance Sidderstane's collection," she said.

"Um, maybe."

She nodded slightly, like I'd proved her point for her, and glanced back up. Said: "Second Floor, third door in. Ask for Sister Apollonia."

Okay, anyway—I've already gone waaay too far in terms of setting the scene, which is why I'm going to skip right to the good part. Turns out, this Sidderstane guy was trying to put together Canada's own version of the Childe Ballads; went back and forth throughout Ontario and parts of Quebec for most of his life, taking down oral history and transcribing songs, starting right after the Boer War and going straight through World War One, up until he finally died of flu during the 1918 pandemic. And a lot of it's the same sort of stuff you'd find in most other places, with all the doubling and crossover you usually get with Folk: I mean, we all know how all you have to do is Americanize something slightly, slide from Steeleye Span to Leadbelly/Nirvana, and suddenly "The Gorse and the Heath" becomes "In the Pines," like a Sherlock Holmes locked-room mystery morphing into the Green River Killer's A&E TV biopic—

My girl, my girl, don't lie to me
Tell me where did you sleep last night?
In the pines, in the pines, where the sun never shines
I shivered the whole night through.

(Sort of creepy, I guess, in context. Or maybe just creepy anyways, no matter what.)

So I sighed, louder than I'd intended to, and I swear Sister Apollonia—a nice girl from what I could gather, Bride of Christ or no—looked like she was really feelin' me. "You know, that's not everything," she said. "We've actually got another complete folio of material from Spring 1908, things he didn't use in the book for one reason or another. Would you like to see?"

Oh yeah.

And here, constant readers, was the true pay-off to this lovely little adventure of ours. I don't want to go too far into it, naturally, because I have a *lot* of work to do before I can trot it out in public . . . but suffice to say, I got my song, and it's something I've genuinely never heard before. Which, given my encyclopedic memory for murder ballads of all kinds, does tend to imply it's probably something *you've* never heard, either. Cool beans, right?

So why don't I feel *more* excited?

UPDATE: I Googled the Magritte, BTW; turns out to be from 1934, not one of his more famous ones. It's usually exhibited as "The Empty Picture Frame," except for in the Marlborough catalogue of 1973, where Langui calls it "La Saignee"—"The Blood-Letting."

August 25, 2004
Mood: Intrigued
Music: "I'm Going Home," Sacred Harp Singers
Title: Curiouser and Curiouser

After all that, I didn't even try out the new song last night, during my first solo set at Gaucho Joe's—Glamer for one, ha ha. But that guy did finally turn up again: Mr. Scottish My-Eyes-Look-Like-Cedar guy. He was standing in the back throughout most of it, right in the shadow of the bar; I actually didn't even notice him until after I'd wrapped, when he touched my arm as I brushed past him, heading for my courtesy drink.

"Well-played, hen. Y'are a proper—" but I couldn't quite hear this last bit, something borderline weird . . . sounded sort of like "glee-maiden," whatever *that* might be. "Thanks," I told him. "You already fixed, or can I buy you another?"

"Not tonight. You'll sit with me though, yeah?"

Well, apparently. It wasn't just some sort of half-assed instant first date, though, all hunched over a candlelit booth back over by the bathroom door—turns out, this dude actually does know his stuff, when it comes to Folk. For one thing, he totally got what I'd been doing in terms of my roster, i.e. mixing and matching different versions of the same song: transpositions specifically paired to highlight the inherent resonances even when the tunes are explicitly different, like going from "House Carpenter" to "The Demon Lover," "Bank of Claudy" to "Her Mantle So Green," "Blackwaterside" to "Dark-Eyed Sailor," "When I Was on Horseback" to "St. James Infirmary"—*I am the king's soldier and I've done no wrong* vs. *I am a young cowboy, I know I've done wrong.* Impressive, and not something most people get even slightly, which I outright told him; got that same bad-teeth smile in return, with a startling side order of smoulder. "Most must not be listening, then," he said, simply.

Oh, *rrrrrrowr*.

Which, granted, might've been either the lateness, the booze or the general lack of Josh and/or (even!) Lars talking, but even so. An hour or so after Last Call, we were still swapping song titles and making jokes about how much trouble you can save yourself in life by just listening to the lyrics, like so:

1. If you are an unmarried lady, for God's sake, don't have sex, because then you'll get pregnant.

2. But if you do get pregnant, then for God's sake, don't tell the guy, because he'll ask you down by the waterside—or the wild rippling water, the wan water, the salt sea shore, the strand, the lowlands low, the Burning Thames, or any area where the grass grows green on the banks of some pool—and kill you. Or he'll run off, and you'll have to kill yourself, then haunt him 'til he dies.

3. On the other hand, if your unmarried girlfriend gets pregnant, for God's sake, don't kill her, or her ghost will make sure everyone finds out, and then they'll kill you. Or you'll get hanged, or kill yourself, or be carried off bodily by Satan. In any case, your last words will probably be: "Come all ye wild and roving lads, a lesson take by me . . ." and the last three stanzas of your life will purely suck.

See also: a former significant other turns up unexpectedly after a long absence, late at night, but refuses to eat anything, and also wants you to leave with them immediately; they say it's no big deal that you're now married to someone else and have a child with that person, while simultaneously making mention of a long journey, a far shore or a narrow bed, and being oddly skittish about the imminent arrival of cockcrow. Do you—

    A) Check their back for bat/fairy wings?
    B) Drop everything to book yourself the first available one-way ticket on a ship bound for *those evil hills/which seem so dark and low*?
    C) Kick 'em where it counts, and run like hell?
    D) None of the above?

So the evening pissed away prettily, and I was pleasantly drunk by the time he loaded me into a cab, slipping me a card with his number on it. He'd already told me to call him "Ganconer," and I'd already laughed in his face over the relative likelihood of that one—"fairy love-talker," riiight, just like the Sheila Chandra drone remix version of "Reynardine:" *And he led her over the mountain/Beyond her mortal life.*

Wasn't until I woke up this morning that I noticed the family name written next to it, though—Sidderstane, like Torrance. Like the Ontario ballads collector.

Have to remember to run my version of that song past him, when I'm done with it.

August 27, 2004
Mood: Content
Music: "The Lake of the North," by me
Title: .mpg Link—Click Below

Okay, everybody. Try this one on for size:

To the Lake of the North I took my love
And made of her a snow-white dove
To the Lake of the North we made our way
But ne'er returned by light of day.
I took my penknife bright and sharp
I pierced my darling to her heart
I cut her hard, and sore I wept
To find the place our baby slept.
At the Lake of the North I laid them low
With no road left by which to go
So here may you find me, where they stay,
And bury us all in the self-same grave.

Comments:
Dude, amazing! Are you gonna be at TellCon? Gonna sing?
—Posted by: urfreak@folksinger.net

You know it. See you there?
—Posted by: galit@folksinger.net

This really is something else . . . the tune's a bit like "The Cruel Mother," while the content recalls "Red Roses" quite a bit. Did Sidderstane's book say where the lake is?
—Posted by: sweetsweetmusic@uoft.com

Not directly. According to MapQuest, it's up past Gananoque, somewhere between a place called Overdeere and a place called Dourvale, but they're not exactly specific.
—Posted by: galit@folksinger.net

WE WILL ALL GO DOWN TOGETHER

You should record this.
Posted by: hyplasia@journal.com

Thanks. I plan to.
—Posted by: galit@folksinger.net

You do know there's another version of this, don't you? And that's not the way you sing it, either.
—Posted by: guizer@alfhame.com

Really? You interest me, let's switch to ICQ. I'm GalToTheIt. How many versions are we talking about?
—Posted by: galit@folksinger.net

I'm FalseFace. Far as I know, there's just the two . . .
—Posted by: guizer@alfhame.com

[Subsequent ICQ chat logs were found to be missing for this time period.]

August 29, 2004
Mood: whatever
Music: n/a
Title: n/a

Yeah, so suddenly my life has no soundtrack; sue me, bitches. It's been a bad, bad day.

Strike One: Daphinis got to fire me before I could quit.

Strike Two: she got to do it after closing, so I couldn't even make a scene.

Strike Three: Renaissance—*both* of them, East and West—got bought out (by Starbucks), so no big Glamer-returns-in-style show. No public "Lake of the North" debut. No auditions for back-up. No nothin'.

Strike Four: rent is due this week, plus I broke a crown grinding my teeth in my sleep, plus somebody popped the knob off the back door while I was having this particular dentally destructive nightmare and stole my freaking guitar. Who steals a *guitar*, for Christ's sake? You sure as shit can't pawn the things for much, even when you need to.

And now Mister How is going to charge me for damages and a locksmith, like it's all my fault. And I am, at this point, so broke I might well be unfixable.

I mean—you just think things are going to change, you know?

Someday. Soon. Ish. Think: Sure, I never got my degree; sure, nobody pays you to do what I was studying anyway; sure, I'm pushing thirty-five and alone, still living in somebody's basement, and the only good part of *that* equation is at least it's not my parents'. But *things change*, right, whether you want them to or not. Even if you did nothing but sit by yourself in a room for fifty years, you'd still get old and die. And that's got to count for *something*, doesn't it?

Does it, fuck.

Whenever I get like this, what I always end up remembering is . . . that time after Mom and Dad's divorce, when Oren and I were really at each other's throats, and they took us to play-therapy. And Oren, sneering, told the therapist: "Oh yeah, Galit always wants to sing those stupid songs because she thinks if she just does it long enough, the fairies will come and take her away."

So I bounced a china pony off his head, obviously, and the whole thing ended in tears and stitches. But you know? Yeah. Sorta. Even now. Because—Josh's vaguely stalker-y stylings aside—these days, I seem to spend a fuck of a lot of time feeling like I could basically break my neck getting out of the shower, and it'd probably be a week before anybody ever thought to check on what that smell was. So no, I don't expect Queen Titania to show up at my next busker job and whisk me away to Tír-na-nÓg, or anything . . . but it'd still be cool to think *anybody* might care enough about me to try.

Oh God, shit. I don't know what to do.

Comments:
You could always come stay with us, Galit.
—Posted by: guizer@alfhame.com

Who is that? FalseFace, right?
—Posted by: galit@folksinger.net

Pay no mind, hen. Do you still have my card?
—Posted by: Anonymous

September 2, 2004
Mood: Cautiously optimistic
Music: "King Henry," Steeleye Span
Title: And in There Came a Griesly Ghost, Stamping on the Floor

WE WILL ALL GO DOWN TOGETHER

Funny—and maybe just a little bit scary—how deceptively easy walking away from almost everything I own turned out to be, in the end. Funny, also, how fast the basic *illusion* of having money again seems to turn you back into a human being, in some people's eyes . . . oh no, wait. That last part's really not very funny at all.

Ganconer wrote Mister How a cheque for damages plus next month's rent, which got me to where I could at least hit Gaucho Joe's up for an a cappella set on their Open Mike, and pass the hat to get me up back to Mississauga. Mom and Kevin have been hinting around wanting me to visit, and since they apparently keep my room open and stocked like the local Motel Six anyway, I can't feel too guilty, except that I (inevitably) do. But that'll pass. ;)

Did the second version of "The Lake of the North" at the top of my roster, and that went surprisingly well; yes, the mike was a bit too loud, and I could hear all my consonants popping like bombs, but the breathy counterpoint had its own weird charm, as everybody in the audience seemed to agree, judging by the sound. Not to mention how the lights in there are so mercifully hot, it's always virtually impossible to see exactly what's going on beyond the first row, if that—though there *was* that odd flicker near the end of "Donologue," my second song, during which I got a sudden glimpse of Ganconer talking animatedly with some chick near the couch-pit: her face backlit, a blur of motion hidden by hanging hair (red?), but I think she turned to smile at me, and I think he didn't like that much. I think I could see the candlelight of a nearby table reflected on her teeth.

She was gone by the time my ovation was done, though, which just now strikes me as a trifle weird, too. Because I seem to recall her giving him a classic Fran Drescher talk-to-the-hand-flip and then striding off to her right, except . . . there's no place to stride *to*, where her right would have been. Unless you count the wall.

Oh, and for those who are interested, the "new" version of "Lake" goes like this:

> *At the Lake of the North, so cold and deep*
> *Was there I laid her down to sleep*
> *By waters still and endless dark*
> *I cut her throat and stopped her heart.*
> *Where never light to bottom glides,*
> *My baby's dam, my griesly bride,*
> *O come lay your white hand on me*
> *Come drain me dry and set me free.*

So long and sudden was my fall
I care not where I land at all.

"So who was that?" I asked him; his cousin, he said, and added her name half under his breath, too low to really hear: something whacktastic, just like his, except the last part wasn't Sidderstane at all. "They're country-bound in the main; I'd not thought to see her here, nor any else of them."

I shrugged. "Good? Bad?"

"Neither." Then: "Unlikely, is all."

And I was feeling not a lot of pain right at that moment—that Captain Jack they're testing at Joe's right now (with the two types of rum, the brown sugar and the fresh-shaved ginger) is *strong*, yo—so I found myself suggesting/joking that it must've been me she'd come to see, not him. 'Cause obviously she'd heard I was the shit in this town, or maybe just shit in this town, depending on who she'd talked to . . . but he didn't find that even partway as funny as I did, truth to tell. Just nodded and said:

"I wondered where you might have heard that first song, hen."

"Looked it up. Why?"

"At the Connaught Trust, yeah? But they've not got that version of it on record, I ken; Torrance wrote that one himself, later. In hospital."

"Say what?"

So he launches into this big family story about Torrance Sidderstane, the Ontario Ballads, the family's holdings up in and around Overdeere. How Torrance was a rich guy who wanted to be a poet, but he was all tapped out creatively by the time he was thirty, so he had to fall back on the old canning factory and got into tracing his family tree. Traced it all the way back to Scotland, to some bunch of his great-grandmother's relatives who got caught up in the fallout from King James the Sixth (the stammering gay guy, Shakespeare wrote *Macbeth* for him) and his obsession with witches—but here it got loud again; couldn't tell if he was saying they weren't really witches or they *were*, or maybe just *some* of them were, and some of them were some other thing entirely.

But there's where this cousin of his comes in, or from: because she has the same name as them, and this time I heard at least the last part of it fairly well . . . something like Drawer, or Drear. Or—

"D. R. U. I. R," Ganconer spelled out, patiently. "That's *Druir*."

"Like Dourvale?"

"The very same. My cousins live thereabouts, from time to time. But they're fell folk, and none too fond."

"Of what?'

"Of any but their own, their true own; I'm only—" and did he really say "made," like a freakin' Mafioso, or was that just the rum talking? "—not bred, so I'm no real kin to any of them. You they'd value, though, yeah? For they do long to be sung of; always have. It's how they know they're still here."

Yeah: pretty strange subject matter for a mid-date rap in general, as ever. Still, it didn't stop me going back to Mister How's with him, did it? Or doing the "fuck YOU buddy, I'm outta here" nasty with him on the rug, either, before packing up what little of my already painfully small store of possessions could fit inside a taxi, then cutting and running while the running was good.

Which is probably not the best sort of info-dump to enshrine on my public blog, but that's why I'm disabling my Comments on this entry, so there you are; I'm posting drunk yet again, by the light of my laptop, so Mom and Kevin don't have to be bothered by evidence of my well-soused nocturnal activity seeping out under the door. And only now wondering how I ever ended up so closely "involved" with somebody—involved enough to fuck them and take their money, anyhow—I've known for such a short time, somebody I know so amazingly little about, in the first place.

Because sometimes, in much the same way it occasionally occurs to me to wonder how the hell I can recall everything he says to me so clearly (I couldn't quote Josh like that, and I've spent *hours* talking to Josh; too many, probably), I can't help but remember that for all intents and purposes, Ganconer Sidderstane is some guy I met on the street. Some sexy guy, yes; some mysterious guy, some smart guy, some guy who loves the way I sing, some guy who's been there for me, thus far . . . but in the end, *some guy*, who I now know Biblically yet do not know well, by normal person standards. Not even a teeny, tiny bit.

I mean, sure, he's got charm and all—but Ted Bundy was fairly charming too, at least when you first met him. And Bundy never told rambling yarns linking his relatives to

Just a minute, I'll be right back. There's some sort of noise coming from upstairs.

[*Addendum A—Google search log for 5/09/2004, reconstituted from Galit Michaels' bookmarks:*

Connaught Trust Homepage: Ontario Ballads
Ontario Ballads: "The Lake of the North"

The Lake of the North
Overdeere Township Homepage: Lake of the North, Dourvale,
    Sidderstane Family holdings
OntBiog Entry: Torrance Sidderstane
Sidderstane Family
Derivation.org: Sidderstane = Sidhe Stone
Derivation.org: Sidhe = Fae/Fay/Faerie/Fairy
Derivation.org: Dourvale = Valley of Druir
FaeLegend.com: The Stane of Dourvale
FaeLegend.com: Glauce Lady Druir
FaeLegend.com: The Family Druir
WitchTracker.org: The Five-Family Coven
The Five-Family Coven: Glouwer
The Five-Family Coven: Rusk
The Five-Family Coven: Devize
The Five-Family Coven: Roke
The Five-Family Coven: Druir (/Sidderstane)
Log off (20:24, 4/09/2004)
Log on (23:59, 4/09/2004)
MapQuest: Ontario, Toronto/Overdeere]

September 5, 2004

They let Kevin out of the hospital today. I'm almost not sure what to think about that, but I do think I won't be home for a while, even if it disappoints Mom. I think I know enough now to stay away from both of them, along with anybody else I care about.

When I came up the stairs, there was a hand, and it was touching the back of Kevin's neck. Just resting there, palm-down, not even stroking, not even anything. Just

And he had this look, like he was going to fall asleep. Like he was going to puke. Like he was asleep already. Like he was drowning. And the hand

I can see it right now: long white fingers, no rings, no distinguishing marks, not even fingernails, like the top and bottom of each finger looked exactly the same, like neither of them even had any fingerprints. And it was glowing just a bit, ever so slightly, so slim I could see the veins under the skin, the bones just under the surface, all lit up: a sick light, a phosphorescence, unnatural/impossible, like something from deep under the sea, utterly out of its element. But worse—like those veins, those bones, themselves, were the things that glowed.

It was sticking out of the wall, plaster lapped to its wrist, a sleeve. And behind it, I saw this impression of something further underneath: an arm, a shoulder, faint red smudge of hair hanging down. Faint gleam of teeth, the wall like a gauze curtain, everything reduced to scribble or implication, or

I don't

It looked up, and it saw me, and it smiled. Like it *knew* me. Like it knew me by sight.

And because it saw me, it pulled its hand back in. Because it saw me, it let him go.

And because he was standing at the top of the stairs when it did that, he fell.

And I think it's all my fault. Somehow. I don't really know why, but I

No, that's bullshit. It is. I *know* it is.

And I know *exactly* why.

September 7, 2004

You'll notice I'm not really specifying music anymore, which isn't like me, and sort of depressing, too. But perhaps it's all for the best.

So I called Josh, which was fun. Asked him if I could borrow his car for a bit, considering it's in storage, and he never renewed his driver's licence anyway. Turns out, he was also at Joe's on the 2nd; wanted to know why I needed it, what was going on with me, who was that guy. I just asked him if he'd actually meant it when he said "anything you want, I'll do it for you, Galit," or whether that (too) had been total bullshit.

Surprisingly enough, he didn't hang up on me, and I now have a ride for the weekend.

Spent far more time than I should have online again today, meanwhile—pretty much all of it, actually. Hung around in Internet cafés all up and down Yonge Street, maybe two hours tops in each of them, playing a little *Myst* here and there in between surfing for lore . . . reading haiku-like snatches of story about people like Elidurus the monk, who mourned all his life over how his own ignorant treachery (he stole a golden ball, to prove where he'd been) left him forever locked out of the fairy hill he spent half his childhood inside, a "country full of delights and sports." Or John Roy, the Highlands farmer who swapped his hat for a stolen British lady by throwing it into a passing swarm of fairies, crying: "Yours be mine and mine be yours!" Or how the best time to enter a *brugh*, a fairy hill, is apparently either at twilight, midnight, the hour just before dawn or high noon . . . pretty much anytime, in other words. Whenever you—or they, the "people" inside said hill—happen to feel like it.

More things I've since learned, in no particular order:

Torrance Sidderstane did die in a hospital, just like Ganconer said. It was a mental hospital. People said he'd killed his first wife, who came from Scotland; she stayed at their place in Overdeere. Nobody's still alive who remembers ever seeing her. They used to go walking together a lot, up near the Lake of the North. In 1907, he bought some property "on the other side of the Lake"—nothing more exact—which nobody ever seems to have mapped, submitting papers to have it renamed "Dourvale." Dourvale was the name the Druir family gave their ancestral seat on the Scots/British border, a valley people said you'd never be able to find if they didn't want you to.

The last leader of the Druir family was Lady Glauce, prn. "GlOWzah." She outlived her husband, Enzembler, who was executed under Queen Elizabeth the First, and acted as regent for their son Minion during his infancy. There were rumours that she brought Enzembler's head home in a pomander bag, along with his body. After the Druirs were accused of being part of the Five-Family Coven, there were also rumours that other participants had seen Enzembler sitting next to her at the Sabbat, wearing the sort of ruff that was currently fashionable at King James' court—the kind that looks like a big, starched platter. The kind that'd sure as hell keep your head on straight, if you were afraid of losing it.

Nobody ever knew where Glauce came from, what her family name was, nothing; Enzembler brought her home after a long trip into the wilds of Dourvale, and her dowry was some sort of meteorite, or something, a "stane," sometimes described as large enough to lie down on, or small enough to wear around your neck. The Druirs called it their luck. People said it helped them disappear when James' witchfinders finally came for them. The only one left after that was Glauce's second daughter Grisell, who married into the Rokes, and the Rokes fought James in court and won. Of the other "five families," the Rusks, Devizes, and Glouwers were almost decimated by "fire and fees," because in Scotland, they charged your relatives the cost of torturing and burning you. They were also the only three families with no noble blood.

Torrance died of TB, consumption, the "wasting disease." People used to say you got it from falling under the influence of fairies. And that I find I can sort of actually believe, now. Or start to, anyway.

Because they're not Tinkerbell. They're not nice. *They're no' the same as you nor I, hen.*

Oh Jesus fuck. Fuck.

All I ever wanted was a song to sing.

September 8, 2004

Last night, crashing at Fiona's, I dreamed I was in bed with Ganconer: *his* bed, not mine, I somehow knew, not that I've ever seen the inside of where he lives, or anything. It was cold and damp, and the sheets were leathery and soft at once, like a split milkweed pod; I didn't have to look around to know we must be someplace dark, someplace small and close, where everything smelled like sour apples just this side of ripe, already edging towards decay. And he just held me and looked down at me, his eyes suddenly so grey-brown they didn't have even a trace of shine left in them—brown and grey and remote, like dusty pennies, and it made my stomach clench. Because I couldn't see anything I recognized in him at all.

He asked me if I wanted him to teach me a new song, and I said no, I liked the one I already had. He asked me if I knew there was a third version of it, and I said there wasn't—there couldn't be. I mean, I'd been down to the Trust, I'd done all the right research, done my homework. I'd seen those files for myself, goddamnit.

And he just kept holding me, not smiling. Replying: "Well, but there would be, hen. If you wrote one."

So I woke up, struggling, shuddering, with that *smell* still all around me, everywhere, in the air. My eyes itching and burning like I'd rubbed them in the only thing I'm allergic to: leaf and wood mould, the kind you only find out in the forest, not downtown fucking Toronto. My back all running with sweat, shirt stuck to me when I stood up, and I saw, I saw

By the door, down the hall, in the light leaking out of the bathroom, that feeble little wash of vanity-bulb glare, oh shit, oh Christ

I saw that same face looking out at me from under the wall's colour-drained Magritte paper, red hair hanging, teeth bright, grin sly. Saw it catch me looking and then eddy away, back into I don't even know where.

And that's when I finally knew, like I know now, how it is. How it's going to be.

Because Fiona was still asleep, okay? Like maybe ten feet away. I could hear her and the baby snoring, in unison; couldn't've told you which one was which if I'd tried, not even if you'd put a gun to my head, or theirs.

So I just got up and left, as quietly as I possibly could, and I came here. And I waited for the sun to come up.

Now it's four hours and a couple of big lattes later, and here's an open letter to whoever's listening: if anybody wants me, you don't have to come looking anymore, okay? Give me three days by the map, I'll already be in Overdeere. I swear.

Then, I'll come to you.

[*Addendum B—Partial ICQ chat record for 1:15 AM to 1:29 AM, 07/09/2004, pasted and saved to a text-file (Ganconer1) on Galit Michaels' hard drive:*

TamLin <nice to know you dream of me>
GalToTheIt <oh is it, asshole. why would u even say something like>
TamLin <galit shush.>
GalToTheIt <"shush"? the fuck u>
TamLin <my cousins are not so stuck in time as we. they wanted a tithe, an anchor to link them from their year to this, escape king james fire, walk through a door and shut it behind them. torrance treated with lady glauces eldest enzemblance, promised haven for talent. and she the worst of them all besides her mother—hag/nix on one side only, part-human on other, a true leanan-sidhe. myself, his bastard by some serving girl, he traded for that marriage-pledge.>
GalToTheIt <like ninety years ago?>
TamLin <and more>
GalToTheIt <bullshit>
TamLin <>
GalToTheIt <cry bullshit on that, all of it. u still there, or what?>
TamLin <>
GalToTheIt <u there?>
TamLin <why would I lie hen?>
GalToTheIt <why wouldnt u? tell me that>
TamLin <>
GalToTheIt <u there?>
TamLin <>
GalToTheIt <okay, fuck u, im going>
TamLin <wait>

GalToTheIt ‹what for?›
TamLin ‹wait galit. believe it or not, just dont go to dourvale›
GalToTheIt ‹overdeere. mapquest says dourvales not even there›
TamLin ‹the lake then. dont. that's what they want›
GalToTheIt ‹›
TamLin ‹what she wants›
GalToTheIt ‹›
TamLin ‹galit?›
GalToTheIt ‹›
GalToTheIt ‹›
TamLin ‹g›
GalToTheIt ‹shut up, asshole›
GalToTheIt ‹fuck u, shut up›
GalToTheIt ‹u better believe im going there now›

No records are available for the time period between September 7th and the next entry.]

October 7, 2004

Hi, everybody. This is Josh Kim—yes, that Josh—and hard as it is to say this, I guess I'm posting to wrap up Galit's story. I never told her I knew where her blog was, or that I read it on a regular basis, but after she hadn't gotten back to me or anyone else for long enough, I logged in by guessing her password. The fact that I even *could* guess it should mean a lot, and it does, though not as much as it might have, earlier.

When she didn't bring the car back after a week, that was when I first started looking around. Went by Mister How's, where he spun me a tale about how she'd broken his back door and then gotten some con artist to write him a cheque that turned into leaves, of all the crazy shit you could possibly accuse someone of. Went by Fiona's, only to hear she'd left the last of her stuff behind there in the middle of the night, everything but her laptop and my keys. I even went by the Connaught Trust, for all the good that did me, but that's a whole other story.

Last week, the Ontario Provincial Police called to tell me they'd finally found my car. It was sitting by the side of a dirt road with no real name, a rural route half-on and half-off the Sidderstane family's property outside of Overdeere. I asked them if it was near something called the Lake of the North, and they said yes. They told me it was within walking distance.

The OPP offered to take me up, and I agreed. The car was covered in dust and dirt, like someone had buried it. I asked them if I could get them to wait while I went over to the lake, just to check for any signs that Galit had been there, and I think the officers maybe felt sorry for me, and that's why they said yes. One of them stayed with the car, while the other came with me.

It's a weird area. The Ontario Field Naturalists guide says it's all limestone and karst topography, full of hell-holes where the upper layer's dissolved in water. There are barrens for miles on either side: dank marshes, scrubgrass, oak shrubs in shallow soil. Makes me wish I'd paid more attention in geography, so I could figure out if any of that's even supposed to happen in Northern Ontario or not.

I asked the officer—his name was Nicholls—if this was Dourvale. He said Dourvale was kind of a local joke, like when tourists say they're looking for Overdeere and you say "over where?" Except that the point is there just *is* no place called Dourvale, and neither of us could really explain why that's supposed to be funny.

The Lake of the North comes up fast, out of nowhere. Galit would probably say it's the colour of pain, because she's always been good at stuff like that. That's one reason why we worked so well together.

Nicholls and I walked most of the way around it, which took a while, but there was nothing there, aside from the lake itself. So I went back to my car. I found her laptop in the back seat.

I filed a missing-persons report, went home, and noodled around on her computer, but it was like it'd been corrupted—every file I opened up was just wild text and Wingdings. Then, eventually, it froze and shorted out. It's still fried.

Yesterday, my server told me I'd been bouncing emails, so I did the dance, and I found something from her lurking in my backlog. The date said she sent it on September 10, one day shy of 9/11. It had attachments: an .mpg and three photos, all sent from her phone, but I'm not going to post a link to any of them. I wish I'd never seen them, or heard it.

Fuck.

Never mind what I wish.

I listened to the song three times, and it's definitely Galit singing from someplace outside, all this ambient noise in the background: wind, leaves, something that almost sounds like breath, or whispering. The lyrics go like this—

WE WILL ALL GO DOWN TOGETHER

At the Lake of the North my darling fell
And pulled me with him into Hell.
By waters cold and deep and black
He took my blood, I took it back.
He cut my throat from ear to ear,
He killed my babe, my own, my dear—
Made us a song sung up, sung down,
A song sung deep from underground.
I owe him naught. He owes me all.
And those who hear this hear my call.

Like I said, I'm not posting the photos, but I'll describe them. They all look like they were taken on the shore of the lake, looking over towards where Dourvale should be, and when you see them at first, they don't seem to be *of* anything except trees and scrub and swamp on a low, grey day, the sky full of clouds. But then, in the third one, if you stare at it long enough, you can see Galit standing in the shadow of one of the nearer rocks, surprisingly close by—I think the reason that she doesn't show up the first few times is that her hoodie is practically the same colour as the shadow itself, and it's pulled down over her hair. What I still can't understand, however, is how she's taking the photo, let alone sending it, since she must be eight feet away at the very least.

Look close enough, at any rate, and you see Galit. Look even closer, and you may (like me) think you see another woman with red hair standing right behind her—face indistinguishable, just that blazing, blowing hair, and Galit looking away from her, as though she doesn't even realize she's there.

So there's Galit looking straight into the phone while the woman reaches out to touch her, so soft she wouldn't have any warning, and the woman's fingers are so much *longer* than they have any right to be: long, and thin, and slick, and boneless. Like eels from deep underwater shining with their own sick light, a light never meant to meet the surface air. Like long, white worms.

That's what Galit would probably say they were like, anyway.

October 8, 2004

I erased the photos and trashed the .mpg this morning, after I met Galit's boyfriend, Sidderstane, on the street outside my condo building.

39

It's icy out there, so I was watching my feet, not where I was going, and he was right in front of me before I knew it.

He said he wished he'd never met her. I said me too. He said I could look for her, I could maybe get her back, if I did it the right way. I said I wasn't looking to go back up to Overdeere anytime soon. He said that was probably good, because they'd probably like for me to try.

It was all I could do not to take a swing at him, the smug son of a bitch, but I have to admit he did look pretty rough. His eyes were all slick and shiny and his lids looked really raw, too—like he'd been up all night crying, or at least rubbing at the sockets.

He said he should have stayed away from her, should have known that whatever he took a liking to, *they'd* know. He said: "But we do love to be sung of, always. It reminds us what we are."

He said a bunch of stuff, and I was on the verge of asking him what the hell he meant by any of it when he just suddenly turned and walked away, instead. So I ran after him, but he was gone by the time I came around the corner, and I mean *gone*. The whole street was empty.

All right, well. I suppose that's it for me, until I get some sort of word about what happened to Galit, or about anything. In the meantime, a big thank you to everyone who reads this blog. Thank you for caring about her. I know she'd say the same, if she was here.

I'll keep in touch.

On February 17, 2005—after three months of non-payment—Galit Michaels' blog was finally deleted from Folksinger.net. Her missing-persons file remains open with the Metro Toronto Police Department as well as the Ontario Provincial Police.

Investigation and interviews in the Overdeere area—primarily with hikers and transients rather than citizens—have produced unreliable witness reports of music heard "seeping up" through the loose rim of rocks and earth near the Lake of the North's "Dourvale shore." The most frequent description is that of a girl singing from too far off for her words to be easily understood.

As yet, none of these reports have been successfully substantiated or disproven.

BLACK BOX (2012)

The Clarke Centre for Addiction and Mental Health's attendants had Carraclough Devize dolled up and waiting for him when Sylvester Horse-Kicker arrived, very slightly late, due to a winning combination of parking, streetcar maintenance on Spadina—*Toronto's only got two seasons, boy, winter and construction, so watch out,* his Mum had said, when he'd told her getting into the Freihoeven Institute's Placement Program meant he'd be moving to the City—and a plague of migrating aphids filling the downtown core with the disgusting equivalent of green hail that squirmed when you wiped it away. She stood in the corner of the room like some reversed still from a lost Kurosawa film (Kiyoshi, not Akira), both taller than you'd think yet thinner, with her colourless mass of hair hanging down and her glasses angled so the light erased her eyes.

On closer inspection, he saw that those white things poking from her sleeves weren't cuffs, but bandages.

"Miss Devize? I'm—"

Impossible to tell if she looked up or not, her voice all-but-affectless, as ever. "We met last year. The Eden Marozzi inquiry—those diorama photos. Abbott asked me to consult."

"Yes, absolutely, sorry. It's just . . . we didn't talk much. I didn't think you'd remember me."

A shrug, one no-brow slightly canted, as though to project: *Well, there you go.* And—ugh, could he actually *hear* the echo of those same words trace his inner ear with sticky film, like walking through a spiderweb and only noticing it later?

I'm in the wrong damn job, if psychics creep me out this much.

Devize smiled, as though he'd made the remark out loud. As though he'd meant it as a joke.

"Abbott's note mentioned storage," she said. "So that means an item assessment." He nodded. "Then I'll need to drop by my office, get my camera. It's in—"

He held it up: a vintage Polaroid One-Step, rainbow swoosh and all. Christ knew where she got the film. "Abbott told me," he explained, unnecessarily.

"Of course."

In the seven years he'd worked for the Freihoeven Institute's

ParaPsych Department—two during his internship, five after—Sy was pretty sure this was the first and only time he'd ever dealt with Carraclough Devize without the presence of Freihoeven head-man Doctor Guilden Abbott, who seemed to consider himself her surrogate father cum self-elected handler. *Never forget, Sylvester: Carra is special,* Abbott was fond of saying. *Our single best resource, the standard by which all other psychic—assets—must be judged. When Doctor and Doctor Jay were doing their initial survey of the greater Toronto area, they concluded they'd never met anyone like her, and never expected to; that's good enough for me.*

Which wasn't completely true—certainly, Sy'd spent enough time in Records to know that Abbott continued to test Devize's crazily high ratings bi-annually, regular as seasonalized clockwork. The latest series of arrays usually coincided with whenever she'd checked herself out of the Clarke, which she used like it was either a five-star spa or her summer cottage/winter retreat/spring and fall whatever; *special,* for sure. In all senses of the word.

Between commitments, Devize spent the bulk of her time at the Freihoeven itself, often even sleeping there (Abbott had assigned her an office, for that very purpose), with very occasional return trips to the basement apartment of her mother's decaying Annex home. And though records showed she was at least ten years older than Sy, pushing forty harder than a Midvale School for the Gifted student at the door marked "pull," she still drifted through life displaying all the fine social skills of the child prodigy she'd once been—the thirteen-year-old whose destitute, grief-drunk mother Gala had rented her out to any séance circuit freak seeking solace from beyond the grave. Who, on promise of $10,000 and a "consulting" job, had accompanied the aforementioned Doctor Jay and Jay—Freihoeven's founders, Abbott's mentors, both late and lamented—on their extremely unsuccessful final mission.

The goal: catalogue and/or exorcize Peazant's Folly, a haunted house located on a natural gas fault up near Overdeere, Ontario. The cost: one archaeologist, one forensic psychologist, one well-established mental medium, and two noted parapsychological researchers, all removed in body-bags, straitjackets, or simple police restraints. Devize, the youngest party-member, had been listed as Glenda Fisk's "apprentice" on the original proposal; she came back in a coma, then woke with a convulsive blast of telekinetic energy that broke all the windows on her floor of the Toronto Sick Kids' Hospital, signifying her emergence as something entirely new: a mental medium turned physical, ghost-touched from one category straight into another, with little to show for the experience but a broken hip, a lingering limp, and a complete inability to screen herself anymore.

Sy remembered a piece of video footage he'd stumbled on—Abbott's first interview with Devize after assuming control of the Institute, when she was only two months out of the hospital. Pretty much the same figure as today, barring a few more crow's feet; downcast face hair-shadowed, eyes glasses-hidden. Blank as any given winter street, snow new-fallen over grime, just waiting for fresh defilement.

You look well, Carra. Better.

Mmm-hmm. Ready for work; that's what Gala says, anyhow.

Oh well, there's no immediate need—

No, it's all right. Take a look: I'm fine, no harm, no foul. No scars . . . but then there wouldn't be, would there?

Sorry?

Oh, Doctor. And here she almost smiled—almost. Asking, gently: *Are you really going to tell me you haven't noticed?*

Sy could still see Abbott's brows, already too close for comfort, attempting to knit themselves inextricably together. *I, uh . . . I don't understand.*

How I have no skin, anymore.

(That's all.)

And that would be the attraction, right there, ever since: a wound so deep, so all-encompassing and impossible to heal, it practically counted as a super-power. Carraclough Devize, human ghost-o-meter—steer her towards anything suspected of weirdness, sit back, and take notes. By Freihoeven standards, there was no better confirmation/debunking method than letting her wander through a site and come back either edge-of-puking, a-crawl with automatic writing stigmata, or simply shaking her head in that numb, vaguely disappointed way.

The Folly, protected by Historic Site status, had finally been converted into a haphazard tourist attraction; it had endured, unoccupied except for half-hour stretches three times a day, until 2002, when the lights went out during a lecture and the tour-guide's assistant lit a candle. Meanwhile, the Freihoeven prospered, even without the Jays. Guilden Abbott kept his job, and so long as he did—apparently—so did Carra Devize.

Incautious, that last observation. Sy felt her prying absently at the edges of his brain again, perhaps without even meaning to—her half-hearted attention in the back of his mind like grit, sanding a horrid pearl.

"Where is Abbott, anyways?" she asked, turning the camera over in her hands, rather than probe any deeper. Which was . . . nice of her, he guessed. *Jesus, I'm bad at this.*

Not like he'd never dealt with psychics before, for Christ's sake. Just not ones this strong or competent. Or unpredictable.

"He had to go to the States, on very short notice. Boston."

"Lecture?"

"Estate sale, actually. Plus a silent auction, by the candle."

"Huh."

(*Fitting.*)

They were almost to the gate now, Sy waving at the orderly who'd let him in, who nodded, curtly. Turning Devize's way, he reminded her, voice softening: "You need to be back by five, Carra."

"I know, Paul."

"Five, on the dot. Or we gotta put you back in the no-sharps room."

She made a clumsy okay sign with both hands, thumbs barely meeting forefingers; tendons might be still a bit foreshortened from the patch-job, Sy supposed. "I *know*, Paul. Seriously."

"Well, just sayin'. You been here long enough."

As the contact gate screeched open, Sy stepped through with her on his heels, uncomfortably close. He felt, rather than saw, her give that same slight head-shake, a bit sadly.

"Not quite yet," he thought he heard her murmur, under the alarm's screech.

Spirit Cabinet, circa 1889, the label read, in Abbott's neat handwriting. *From the estate of Katherine-Mary des Esseintes/Lardner-Honeycutt crime scene (transfer handled by Wilcox Labrett Oyosolo, 2007, through Auction-House Miroux).*

And: "Oh," Devize said, behind him, to no one in particular, "*that* box."

This was Freihoeven's second storage unit, three whole hallways deeper inside the facility than their first. Though Sy had overseen its rental, it'd been long-distance; before today, he'd never had occasion to step inside its echoing metal shell. Beneath their feet, the concrete floor sent up enough dust to hang visible, stinging in the nose.

The cabinet was a one-slot variation on the Davenport brothers' original 1854 model, only slightly less compact than your average Ikea dresser. Dark, burnished wood with plain brass fittings. A small window with a scrim, confessional-style. Inside, Sy assumed, there'd be a coffin-like space for the medium to sit, perhaps even a system of restraining straps—first tied down in public, doors wide, then locked away, with one of the séance-goers being given the key.

He walked around it, feeling for joins, and found none. Which didn't prove anything, necessarily . . . but des Esseintes had had a good reputation, as he recalled, given the hotbed of fakery most 1800s Spiritualism grew out of. Like Devize, she'd worked under the care of her mother, whose chaperone-like presence served to fend off fetishists—until her demise, upon which des Esseintes' main patron became her husband, forcing her to retire. A year later des Esseintes was also dead, predictably, in childbirth.

As he rounded the cabinet's left wing, a dry kissing noise and flashbulb-pop made Sy start. Once again, he found Devize so close he almost collided with her. "Wouldn't've thought they'd let him have this, after what happened," she remarked, shaking her first shot out and squinting at the result. "But then again, I guess that's what the acquisitions budget's for."

"People were pretty generous this year, at the fundraiser."

"I can see that. Sorry I had to miss it."

"We, uh, missed *you*, obviously. But—"

"Oh, I'm sure the demo went off like a charm; Abbott's building a nice little roster of alternates. I vetted most of them. Who was it—Jodice Glouwer, Suzy Shang? Janis Mol?"

"Miss Glouwer's hard to reach, these days."

"Janis, then—that's good. She needs the work."

Two more shots in quick succession, seemingly intentionally angled to give Sy a headache. He moved off, looked away, studying the wall; she brushed past, still clicking and shaking. A fistful of slimy-faced, sharp-smelling squares already fanned out between her fingers, like cards from some weird deck. Indicating them, he asked: "Anything interesting?"

She shook her head. "Not yet." Another shot. "'The Thanatoscopeon,' that's what she called it; called herself a 'thanatoscope,' and mediumship as a concept 'thanatoscopy.' Loved to concoct those pseudo-Greek words, back when." And one more, for an even eight. "Kate-Mary was one of the first Ontario mediums to allow photography at her meetings."

Sy nodded. "I catalogued a bunch of reproductions, like thirty different variants. Those plates done in Peterborough, where she's making hands out of ectoplasm . . ."

"I saw that—Gala had copies of the whole trading pack, used them as teaching aids. Creepy."

"Because she was making ectoplasmic hands?"

"Because those hands were *feeling her up*, in public, and somebody else was making a plate of it. Think about how long that would *take*."

Sy tried not to, and immediately found himself thinking of the fact that he'd already seen Devize in much the same position, instead: spinning what looked like wads of dirty string from nose, mouth, ears and eyes, her head thrown back, hair lifting slightly on some invisible current. Remembering it with her in proximity was weirdly embarrassing, as though he'd seen her naked—not least because he sort of had, considering how sheer those lab-conditions leotards tended to be, and the fact that you couldn't let subjects wear underwear, for fear they'd try to pack quick-set packages of glue, wax, or paraffin in their bras.

"*Ektos*, 'outside,' plus *plasma*, 'something formed or moulded,'" Devize said, squinting down at the Polaroids. "People used to think it came from the spirit world, but it's all just made out of whatever's handy—bits and pieces of the medium, herself. Almost always *herself*. Water, dander, skin-cells, fat . . . the stuff you don't want, mainly, which makes it easier to let it go. There's a reason the Freihoeven's main stock-in-trade tends to be a rotating list of little girls with eating disorders."

As with so much she said, Sy didn't know how to answer that, or if it really required answering. So he kept quiet, and waited.

"She was legendary, Kate-Mary. Every other aspiring medium's pin-up. My Dad's great-grandmother . . ." Devize shook her head, wonderingly. "If Spiritualists had groupies, she'd've been following Kate-Mary 'round the country, trying to plaster-cast her soul; that's what Gala says." Then added, slightly softer, correcting herself: "Said."

Well, yeah.

Sy'd placed the obituary himself, at Abbott's instigation: *Geillis Carraclough Devize, 1944-2012, in her home, after a long illness.* He wasn't sure whether the illness in question was supposed to be alcoholism, agoraphobia, or hoarding, though granted, it could've been a Venn Diagram convergence of the three. All he knew was that his brief visit to Gala Devize's erstwhile home to pick up "fresh" clothes for her momentarily dazed daughter had been both frustrating and disgusting. The minute she'd checked herself back into the Clarke, Abbott had called in a cleaning service and 1-866-GOT-JUNK?; Sy could only hope she wouldn't be too wrenched when she finally went "home" to discover all the mouldy, staple-gunned velvet had been removed from the bathroom walls, the food-encrusted plates from every kitchen surface (including the tops of cabinets), and the teetering six-foot stacks of newspapers from the living room, where they'd created a maze whose narrow passages were prone to sudden collapse.

I'm sorry, were you saving that crushed-flat mummified cat for later?

Because—we really did have to get rid of it, even though it didn't smell anymore. Not like the year-old litter-tray, weirdly enough . . .

Then again, maybe she wouldn't even notice. She had other things on her mind, after all.

Oh, but: *Let's not talk about* me, *Mister Horse-Kicker—*

(*stop* thinking *about her, idiot*)

(*stop acting like she can't HEAR you, when you do*)

That scratch at the mind's eye again, that cornea-scarring *rub*. Though he didn't want to look her way long enough to confirm this, he suspected she might actually be smiling.

"What do you know about spirit guides?" she asked him, out loud.

Okay, technical terms: Sy could do that. "Not much. Uh—des Esseintes had one, called it 'Semblance.'" He used the French pronunciation. "'My other self.'"

"Yes, and that's telling, isn't it. Non-Spiritualists always think these guides are things from the outside that attach themselves to the medium, parasite-style: surviving intelligences, Seekers From Beyond, demons. And I'm not saying that doesn't happen, but . . . there's other stuff. Things you can stumble into doing by accident, 'specially if you're not well-trained."

"Which she wasn't?"

"Early days, so—not really, no. Nobody was. Most people just heard about the Fox Sisters, thought 'hey, that sounds cool,' and made it up as they went along." She held one of the Polaroids up to the light, squinting again. "Don't suppose Abbott told you the rest of the story, though, about this thing."

"Lardner and Honeycutt?" 'Crime *scene,' riiight*. He shook his head, embarrassed.

"Mmm." Those vague eyes switched back to him, suddenly shrewd. "How old are you, again? Well, okay: maybe you weren't paying attention to local news; I'm sure Abbott keeps you busy. Or maybe Abbott just didn't tell you because he likes to play it that way—to make only one person the control in any given situation." She paused, took yet another picture, the Polaroid's wheeze a short, sharp sigh. "But then again, you probably knew that already. You don't seem stupid."

". . . thanks."

"So, anyhow. Melinda Lardner and Guy Honeycutt were married, blended family. She had a daughter from a previous marriage, Loewen, people called her Lo. Fourteen when they bought the Thanatoscopeon. Guy was in antiques, brokered sales under the counter, so I think the idea was to pony up and pass it on, but they got stiffed and it went in the garage, along with a bunch of other 'sure sell' items. Melinda and Guy weren't getting along too well by that point—she was back in school doing law, plus one of her professors. Also, Guy liked coke. Lo spent a lot of time looking for somewhere quiet, and her primary hiding-place was—" She nodded box-wards. "—that."

"I wouldn't think it'd be too—"

"Oh, it's uncomfortable as all hell, but it does lock from the inside. And it's dark. And there's other benefits too, if you're in serious need of a friend."

". . . Kate-Mary's guide?"

"I think that's what it *thinks* it is, yes."

Ghost stories told without any visible proof in a series of almost-empty rooms; that was all his career boiled down to, really. The vocabulary alone was ridiculous. But . . . looking at her, then back at the cabinet's dark expanse, both their reflections crawling deformed and luminous-numinous across it, like orbs . . .

"Okay," he said, carefully. "So—what is it really?"

The hint of a smile became something more, almost gleeful. "So glad you asked."

Glenda Fisk had told her it was something all mediums did, and she had no reason to doubt that. *A mnemonic device, Miss Devize, that's all—just far more palpable. You take a splinter of your own core, your innate substance, and split it off, the same way you use your own detritus to render the spirit flesh; deeper, of course, though. And thus, far more lasting.*

"You use it to get over that conceptual hump," Devize said, flatly. "To convince yourself you actually can do what you're already afraid you can. Glenda helped me with mine, that first night in the Folly—budded it off me like an amoeba, whole and entire. It didn't even hurt, and it was . . ."

Amazing. A miracle, pitch-black and shiny as La Brea pit-tar.

"So it's a doppelgänger?" Sy asked.

She shook her head. "More like a fetch, I guess. What the witch sends out to do her will? A tool, perfect for companionship, for utility; something that loves you and wants what *you* want, because that's all it's ever known. People see it here and there, think it's you, and in a way—it sort of is. Thinks it is, like I said."

"But . . . it's not."

"Not even close."

She looked back down, that same weird smile playing around her lips, stretching them even wider, 'til a narrow rim of teeth began to show. And slowly, so slowly he barely knew when it had happened, Sy realized that crawly feeling at the back of his neck was less the standard *oh-crap-she's-listening-in* than a genuine coolish dew, the sweat-sting of inescapable understanding: *Something has changed, and not for the better. But—*

—is she . . . unlikely as it seems, could she really be . . .

(happy *about all this?*)

(whatever *all this* was)

"So yeah," Devize went on, as though neither of them had noticed, "Glenda and I had a whole lot of fun with our respective shadow-selves for a day or two, doing the things skinny little ghost-whisperer girls do. But then . . . the house kicked in, and it ate them alive, like everything else. Everybody. And afterwards, I just never bothered doing it again."

Never had to, really. No shortage of real ghosts vying for the position.

"We only have one trick, when you boil it all down," she said, as if to herself. "It's a doozy, though: just open up and invite things in, and half the time, we don't even ask for names, beforehand. Which does tend to make it pretty hard to get them out again, afterwards . . ."

An image growing at the corner of his eye—tumoresque, neoplastic—before wiping itself away, an unset photo-image: Carra Devize done inside-out and backwards, a reflection in black marble, grey-skinned with long black hair and cold white eyes. Blank eyes, their sclerae static-touched, whose flickery pupils shone whiter than teeth.

Sy made a painful noise at this fresh intrusion, an aural wince, and was surprised—yet again—when Devize grimaced back, as though in sympathy. "Sorry," she said. "I'm projecting, aren't I?"

". . . maybe a little."

"Okay, well. Let's move things on a bit."

She stepped forward, past him, and snapped the cabinet open.

Inside, as out, Kate-Mary des Esseintes' Thanatoscopeon was dark indeed; darker by far than the single light-source merited, a concentrated snarl of nothing much cooked to sludge from years on years of waiting, followed by the briefest possible burst of hunger slaked, loneliness assuaged. Devize—Carra—thrust both hands inside, up to the bandaged wrists, and didn't even flinch as words the colour of haematomas came crawling up her arms, her cleavage and neck, to bruise her very face like slaps: NO, NOT THIS NOT FOR YOU, NEVER YOU, KEEP OUT KEEP OUT *KEEP OUT.*

"Poor Lo Lardner," she said, ignoring the unseen hecklers doodling on her flesh, each scratch a rotten fruit chucked straight from the choir invisible's peanut gallery. "Melinda'd been down the anorexia path herself, so she thought she knew what was best; Guy went along to get along. Why not? Didn't cost him anything but money. And the Clinic, they were all good people, but—how could they possibly know the truth? That half her body-weight, *more* than half, kept being sucked out every night, siphoned off to make fake flesh for something she didn't know enough to say 'no' to?"

A full red hand-print, palm plus five fingers, rocked her jaw to the left, then the right. But Carra kept on talking.

"Oh, it told her it loved her, and she liked *that*, because nobody else did it much, anymore . . . told her it would punish her parents for their neglect, that all she had to do was break out and run home, and they'd always be together. And hell, maybe it wasn't even a lie, because that's where the cops found her, sure enough: inside this thing, all curled up with her arms 'round herself like she was giving herself a hug, shrunk down to the size of an Inca mummy. All *desiccated*."

The slaps looked more like punches now, and Sy felt himself jolt with each impact, braced to—what? Jump to her aid, throw a few jabs himself? Like he'd really be able to *do* anything to—whatever-it-was—

(*You could* try, *goddamnit, considering. At the very* least.)

But in the same instant the thought formed, Carra was already glancing back, one blackening eye crinkled, odd half-smile a genuine grin. "Oh, Sy," she said, her tinny headcold voice gone suddenly lush with deep, true warmth. "That's really nice."

Not necessary, though.

"And yes, I *am* happy, for once. Because usually I can't do a damn thing but say 'yup, haunted!' no matter *how* much power I supposedly have—how high I measure on Abbott's stupid scales. But this . . . I *can* do something about this. *This*, I can handle."

(*That's why it's afraid of me.*)

The box was vibrating now, base thrumming on the locker's concrete floor, kicking spume. Its scrim ruffled back and forth like a rattler's tail, doors straining to slam, an eight-foot, velvet-lined mahogany pitcher plant. Yet—

"No," she told it, "of course you don't want someone like *me*, somebody who actually knows what they're doing. But that's okay." Voice dropping further, breathy-rough, almost verging into a growl, to add: "I don't much want *you*, either."

Later, examining her dropped fan of Polaroids—slick and stinking, their negative-on-positive images degrading even as he watched, cured in a strange mixture of developing agent and ectoplasm—Sy would finally see what she probably saw, at that moment: what she'd been looking at all along, with it very much looking back. A face like a mask, whose underside could be glimpsed through the empty sockets of its eyes, peering from beneath the cabinet's glossy skin like some albino goldfish studying passersby through its aquarium walls. In the final one, taken from a particularly vertiginous angle, Carra had managed to catch her own reflection—the thing, spore or seed of Kate-Mary's experiment, with its head fake-lovingly bent to hers, mask-wings twined in her mass of colourless hair, trying desperately to whisper in her ear.

To convince her, perhaps: *I am not so bad, after all; mistakes were made, but even so, I deserve to exist, surely. I could change. Lost and lonely, left behind—how can I be blamed? I am . . . just like you.*

"Oh, Semblance," she told it, shaking her head. "But there's nothing *for* you here, is there? Not now they're both dead. And you—"

—you need to be gone.

Both hands in the box, sunk deep and shaking, some vile current coursing through her like a *grand mal* seizure; Sy saw Carra fold back and stepped in to catch her, instinctively. Braced himself against any sort of spillage, inadvertent or otherwise. But all he felt was bony flesh muffled under multiple layers, the sadly light weight of a woman whose substance was gnawed at by every passing phantom, someone probably too distracted to eat much even under normal circumstances, unless reminded. One good thing about the Clarke, he supposed; they had an investment in keeping residents alive, even if it meant the occasional bout of tubal feedings. *Skinny little girls with eating disorders, and the invisible friends who love them . . .*

"What can I do?" he asked out loud, no longer worrying about sounding—let alone feeling—stupid. Only to watch Carra shudder on, head jerking slightly, eyes ticcing up-turned beneath their lids in a REM-state frenzy until more words came crawling up past her cuffs: Different font this time, different script. An almost Palmer-method scrawl, thankfully easy to read, that answered—

NOTHING THANK YOU SORRY JUST LET IT PASS.

THANKS FOR ASKING.

A gleam gilding the letters now, all up and down—sticky-slimy, a perspirant flood, gelid as Vaseline. Something sucked in hard then expelled through the pores, broken down to its original components: scrubbed, purified, diffused. Rendered harmless.

His arms starting to go numb, he laid her down by degrees, with as much care as he could. "I, that guy Paul . . . I mean, they're expecting you back by now, right? Curfew. I should probably call—"

DONT NO POINT SERIOUSLY IM FINE.
BEEN OVER TWENTY MINS ALREADY.
ALWAYS HAPPENS THEYRE USED TO IT W ME.
"Well, then maybe I could—"
JUST WAIT OKAY.
STAY WITH ME OKAY SY THATS ALL I NEED.
JUST STAY.

Another long breath while he thought about it, then nodded. One hand crept into his, long fingers vibrant, bitten nails adrip. He clenched it back, hard, and watched as the fit dulled, frenzy becoming languorous, dormant, dazed. 'Til at last she lay prone and blank on the dusty floor, her ecto-coating gone dry, and he watched the bulk of it peel off like sunburn, flake to glitter and disperse, blown away by some impossible wind.

That long, at least. And at least a half-hour longer.

Two weeks later, he was back to see her again, without Abbott's blessing (or knowledge).

Carra sat by the TV room window, street clothes replaced with a fetching johnny and terrycloth robe combo, hair hung back down like a living veil. Big brown slippers with little rodent faces, beavers by their buck teeth and trailing black heel-tails. Her pale arms hung nude once more, clean of sutures and messages alike, aside from that tape-anchored meds-jack stuck in the left-hand elbow's crook.

"Thought you'd like to know," he said, sitting down, close enough she could touch-test him for solidity if she wanted to. "Abbott wanted to keep the Thanatoscopeon, 'specially once I told him you'd cleaned it out—guy has a serious case of archivist fever, and that's not gonna change anytime soon. But I don't have to tell *you*."

He saw the hair-curtain shift a bit, side to side; a nod, maybe, in its most rudimentary possible form. Or maybe just the breeze kicked up as Orderly Paul went by, tray in hand, scowling at Sy like he held him personally responsible for Carra's condition. For which, Sy found, he really couldn't fault him.

"Funniest thing, though," he told her, leaning a tiny bit closer. "Turns out, Locker Two? Whatever Abbott put in there next must've been *really* accidentally flammable, 'cause . . . the whole unit just went up, all of it, from the inside-out. Nothing left but ash."

A slight pupil-flicker under half-slung lashes, making Sy wonder: what colour *were* those always-hidden eyes of hers, exactly, if he had to choose? Grey like smoke or steam? Silvered like a frosted window?

Didn't matter; he was glad enough to get a reaction of any sort.

Maybe next time, she'll be awake enough I can tell her how I did it. If she doesn't know, already.

And here there suddenly came a spark, the barest jolt, synapse-swift—so long since he'd felt that for anybody, it would've surprised him no matter who drew it. A stroke along the mental inseam, lizard-area flag automatically part-raised to meet it, no matter how the rest of the brain might scoff.

Bad idea, he thought, knowing it was true. Knowing she'd agree, if she could: BETTER NOT SY emblazoning itself 'cross palm or cheekbone, coming up on wrist or calf like a blistered rose. NO VERY DANGEROUS VERY DANGEROUS FOR YOU BELIEVE ME. BETTER (NOT)

And yet: *What the hell, lady. I've got at least half a say in this, don't I?*

So since he could, he reached across, took her slack hand in his, and squeezed it. Until he felt the pad of her thumb stroke his love-line, too slow and steady to misinterpret . . . and smiled.

HISTORY'S CRUST (1968)

| one: three witches

In what was once called Dourvale, just east of Eye and a few miles shy of the border where Scotland and Northumbria meet, they still tell this tale to fright their children away from strangers: How one day in winter, a small girl (no more than nine) sent to gather sticks by the brae-side did so, singing happily, until she looked up to see a darkness pass overhead, moving between her and the sun. It had somewhat of the seeming of a cloud, she later told her mother, but for the fact that it flapped in the wind the way a woman's skirts—or more than one woman's, perhaps—will do when set out on a line to dry, crisply, like the wings of some great bird.

As she stared up, squinting against the cold winter light which haloed it, this flapping darkness moved first westward, then lower, presently growing so distant it disappeared altogether. And sometime after that she saw three women come up out of the valley, arm in arm, laughing to each other; up through the gorse with neither hat nor coat to shield them, right into the teeth of a bitter wind that threw sharp fistfuls of snow at their faces.

The girl had never seen such different women in her life, and certainly not together. The first was young and ripe and lewd-looking, full-figured, with smooth red coils of hair held back by a pair of ivory combs chased in silver; she had a petticoat of crimson sateen and a gown of black wrought velvet, a French farthingale wide enough that she might lay her arms upon it and a wrought stomacher embroidered in red-gold thread to hold her waist in (though she seemed to have little need of such). Her cap was likewise of black velvet set with pearls, her full sleeves set out with wire and her hose of orange colour, with gay cork-heeled shoes of red Spanish leather that barely seemed to crush the grass she trod on.

At her elbow stepped another woman—pale as the first was fair, skin and hair like new moonlight. She went stay-less in the country style, an open gown of black fustian over a neat woolen smock the colour of yellow dust and an apron tying the whole together, like any farmer's wife; her hands were raw and she wore wooden pattens with worn leather straps, thick with mud from clumping down unpaved lanes. The girl thought she looked kind, though her gaze was mournful and (on closer inspection) somewhat queer, being that she had varicoloured eyes of two distinct shades, each: hazel in green and brown on the right, grey and blue on the left.

Yet, the girl did not truly fear until she saw the last woman, for she was terrible indeed to behold: Hard and spare and flat like a plank, with unbound hair hanging wild to her waist, dark as a stormy sky. Her dress might have been *any* colour or constitution, since it had fallen almost entirely to rags, and she went shoeless over the stony ground but did not seem to mind it, the nails of her dirty toes grown long and sharp, like claws. Her neck was circled in a stiff, yellow-starched ruff, ill-fitting enough to rub one raw spot beneath her chin, like the impress of a caged cat's iron collar. A prim, oddly stained smile, the area outside her lips just a shade redder than that within, as though scoured clean after some indulgence—a cicatrice painted over, a faint rouged scar; tea-coloured eyes enamel-blank, teeth in a screaming mouth, with her desolate face a map of the waning moon, and her left palm marked proudly with a Devil's kiss of a scar, for all the waking Godly world to gawp at.

As the girl stood rooted to the spot—enspelled, but not yet ensorcelled—the first lady, she in the red and black, deigned at last to notice her, and paused a while in her saunter.

"Be this a one for us, sister Jonet?" she inquired of the pale woman, lightly. But Jonet only shook her pale head, and replied—

"Nay, Alizoun; she is no fit meat for auir purposes. I see His mark already set upon her."

At this, the eldest woman's terrible smile grew wider. "So then," she said to the girl. "Y'are spared this day, little poppet. Yet for how much longer, I wonder?"

"Are ye witches?" the girl asked her, swallowing hard.

"We are. Does that fright ye?"

The girl shook her head, though she felt not half as certain as she looked. "My Mammy says God will protect me from yuir likes."

The woman leaned close, her strange eyes alight; she had clasped the girl's hand fast in hers before the girl even thought to snatch it away, and the girl felt a painful spark jump between them where their skins (however briefly) met.

"Yuir God is a doting auld fool," she said, "who protects nae one. Now run hame and tell yuir Mammy that, while ye still can. And tell her 'tis by Euwphaim Glouwer's mercy that ye live, not *God's*."

So the girl took to her heels, leaving the three witches far behind her, laughing in mockery at her fear. And there were great disturbances in Dourvale township that night; an ill wind blew up and down killing cattle and fowl, and all the crops were blighted with a strange black plague of a kind never seen before, while a fallen candle set aflame the only kirk for miles around. In the morning, a strong young man was found dead in his bed, hag-ridden, and a babe, as yet unbaptized, was snatched from its very cradle as its mother slept on beside it, undisturbed. There was an iron pot stolen from the same bereaved woman's kitchen, found next day on the side of what local folk called Stane Hill, all greased and lined with fat as though something had been boiled in it; nearby sat a cairn, hastily raised, and under it a collection of soft little bones, well-picked.

But as for the girl who told this story first, her hand welted up as if burnt where the witch Euwphaim Glouwer had touched her, then turned in on itself like a claw—indeed, in time, the whole of her arm grew slack and cold and withered, never to recover until the day she died (which was not too long in coming, after). And this did not change even when all three witches were taken up and tried in King James's name; put to the question and condemned to the Fire, with true justice administered unstintingly for all their many obscene, dreadful, and blasphemous crimes against the Almighty . . .

Ah, men of God, be very certain in your judgements. For I tell you, in the Witches' Book there is but one Commandment only, yet that one deemed unbreakable: Revenge yourselves, or die.

| two: the witch-house (i)—the question

The proper year is 1593, but in the Witch-House of Eye, time stands still. A hot day in a whitewashed room, the eaves and low-hung ceiling stained alike with smoke, where flies pass back and forth—clots in a net of shadow—to graze shoulders held dutifully rigid, pause to sip at the corner of a sleep-slack mouth, before a hand sends them scattering again. A preacher, a proctor, two grim bailiffs with bulky arms folded tight, and a learned divine who's happened by in lucky time to watch the show—all sit with backs to the wall, while her chief interrogator drones on and that one same clerk's pen scratches always like a hesitant snake in his words' wake, pausing only on the tail of each caught breath.

Items: That Alizoun Rusk was reckond by alle and sundry adept at the fashiounynge of poppets, both in waxe and in cloth, for stuffynge. That shee hadde killd both her lawful husbande and chylde unborne by this same wicked method. The last provd true, and lykewize sworn uponne.

Items: That Jonet Devize was well-known to breed imps from her skin and breathe, lyke unto pus or humours or any other sicknesse, and that her neighbours bore witnesse she hadde kept her familiars out of the way of ordinary ken, secretd in a bagge hyd deepe in her nether parts. The last provd true, and lykewize sworn uponne.

Items: That their Ring-Leader Euwphaim Glouwer, a forsworne concubine of Daemons and companioun tae satyrs, claimd alle coven-Members hadde taught their skills eache outher, shared for Eville use in pacte and compacte. For shee claimd also that they would somehow use these said injurious skills tae pay back for eache outher if a single one of them was taken, een to the least and laste drop of bloode.

Items: That both the aforementiound wytches accusd Glauce Lady Druir (of Dourvale) and Callistor Laird Roke (of Rooks-home) of takynge parte in alle similar manner of wyckednesse, as did the said Euwphaim Glouwer, unpenytente een tae the laste. These baselesse charges neer provd true at alle, being how their anely evidence lay in the three accusds ane foresworn and worthlesse testimonyalle.

God's own men sit stiff-backed like parishoners in awe, thinking (no doubt) on their own shallow faith and little sins. Their hollow faces shine feverish with a constant fear of Hell, features blurring under pressure, as though already a little burnt around the edges.

Yet do I regret nothing, Euwphaim thinks to herself. *For what matter how my body suffer, seeing my soul be already forfeit?*

But it does pain me they killed my Sookin, my poor grimoire-keeper— though I can always fashion him again anew, as Jonet taught us both. That they stole away the babe they got on me in my catching, putting me to the Question when I was still sore from his birth. And that my vow to the Black One goes only so far fulfilled, seeing as I did not near enough malefice before they took me as I might have, given time.

She can still hear Alizoun Rusk curse them all, distantly, her words deformed by a mouthful of broken teeth: Sweet Alizoun, with her brazen stare and her wicked tongue, the sort of woman men call "witch" because she rouses the worst in their natures simply by existing, regardless of what her own true nature might be. Alizoun, who was raised always to accept nothing less than the best as her due portion, and throw her defiance like vitriol back in the eyes of any who might dare say her nay. It gives Euwphaim heart to know they have not broken Alizoun in spirit, whatever mischief they may have done her lovely body; that they cannot now, and never will. Not even when the pitch is poured, at last, and the final fire lit.

But Jonet Devize, so pale and pliant, has fallen silent, and stays so. Which is a worse hurt by far than any torment they can visit upon Euwphaim—for all that they hold her here in this thorny iron chair, a coal-fire banked beneath to blister her arse red, and both legs slatted so efficiently she does not really hope to ever walk again, no matter what the future may yet hold in store for her.

Time is an ill master, she thinks, *iller by far than my own. And it* shall *bend to his will, and mine, in the end.*

"Ye kissed Satan's hindquarters," these foolish folk yammer on at her, "and swore yuirself over tae the Enemy for the confoundation of Man. Confess it."

She snorts, unimpressed, and flips her ruined hands at them like weapons, to see how fast they scurry from her tainted blood. "Oh, but there be *many* angels, fool; nae need tae treat wi' Satan at all, if power be what ye wish for. Mine is but one of seven."

"Aye, with God higher still than all of them, and us seated at his *right* hand, with ye left tae beg and supplicate in vain at his left. So shall ye not only confess yet recant yuir foulest slander, also—yuir naming of Glauce Lady Druir and Callistor Laird Roke as part of yuir black company, though they be sae far beyond the purview of such as ye as tae exist on another plane entire. For they are landed and monied, their blood from the highest sources only. And ye, Euwphaim Glouwer . . . what title do *ye* hold?"

"Nane at all in *yuir* corrupt world, as ye well know—yet in the De'il's service, I am as guid as they, at the very least. Or better."

Ladies and gentlemen, all, like brightness fallen from the air. Personages with long whispering trains, and diadems cut in the reflection of flames.

"Y'have heard the tales," she reminds them, once again, with what she personally reckons quite marvellous patience. "Lady Glauce is of the Fair Folk, which to yuir small minds rings same as budding straight up from Hell; the Roke, her daughter's new husband, is a warlock fell and known, wi' Darkness's ain power a-run in his veins."

Her with her leafy crown and her stane, so full and fair o' luck, and yet she could spare nane for such as us. So she betrayed us to ye instead, she and Magister Roke, sae she might bargain a retreat through time, and thus escape the same fire. And Jonet and Alizoun will die for it, wi'out a doubt . . .

Yet for all that, she shall escape neither my reach, nor my sweet Master's wroth.

The nearest witchfinder sighs, a dry huff, as though he has no more juice to spit. "More slander."

"More *truth*. Yet lay that by: Ye shall reap as ye sow, much like mysel'." And here she gives them a gappy red smile, whispering: "I see it in the air above, hovering, like a bony crown—yuir future, fool. *All* yuir futures."

Does this give them pause? She cannot see to tell. Perhaps it is only the hearth-fire's flickering which makes all their shadows seem to rear up high, become one great-winged darkness, and lean comforting over her—a black balm, rushing in to soothe her many hurts and murmur (in the single torn ear yet remaining to her)—

:Euwphaim, bright one, my dreadful star. My own.:

Oh, she almost sobs aloud, to hear it. *My Black Man, my crow-feathered angel with your strong, scaly thighs, your nails hooked like the beaks of cormorants. And your eyes faceted like blue diamonds.*

(*Where have ye been, my long-lost love? This seven long year, and more?*)

His amusement thrums through her, a breath of scent, crowding out everything but the old refrain: **:Seeking gold for thee, my love, and riches of great store.:**

Ah, I always knew it.

Her heart lurches, glazed once more with remorse—so much ill-harvest still owed, for all his boon and bounty laid upon her! So many left yet upright, unblasted . . . plagues yet to be sown, nightmares to be spread, childer un-caught, un-eaten. A whole witless generation left to seethe in the illusion of God's mercy, like kids in milk, cooked 'til they dissolve and drift upwards, towards an empty Heaven.

What lessons I have taught them they will forget, happily, once I am gone, she tells him, soul-sore. *My Laird, I have failed you, to my sorrow. Forgive me?*

:No need. My eye is ever on you, Euwphaim; I hold you in my heart, as you once held me. We are one there with each other, forever.:

And if she *could* weep, then that reply alone would draw thick salt tears of happy amazement, cradled once more in the furnace of his contrariwise love.

:I prepare a place for you too, my beautiful Euwphaim, very presently. Can you endure but a bit longer?: Adding, on his own thought's heels: **:It will cost you pain.:**

And: *Yes, my Laird,* Euwphaim answers him. *I have no doubt of it. As there is no thing at all—in this world, or out of it—which comes to us for free.*

Her heart skips and soars with gratitude. She was a fool, a true heretic, to ever think herself forgotten.

Blood means nothing. Will means all.

"My Laird of Horns," she says, aloud, "I will do thy bidding ever, patient and uncomplaining. I am in yuir hands, now and always."

Asked how shee can hope tae escape God's wroth. Answers: There are many cracks in the walle of tyme, and not alle of such runne backwards.

Asked what shee means by this. Answers: That my Black Angel has promised mee I will yet be sent hence from here to confound and scourge the whole world, and een though I be consumed tae the very bones, tis stille not I myselfe will burn for yuir delight.

Asked why she laughs sae lowd and with sae little reason. Answers: Because that I have mazed ye alle.

| three: two letters

February 16, 1968

Dolores Trench
18 Jordan Lane
Edinburgh, Scotland

Dacre Dowersby Sidderstane
362 St. Andrew's Gardens
Toronto, Canada

Dear Mister Sidderstane,

You do not know me, for which I apologize. I write to you today to ask permission to visit your family home, once the famed Witch-House of Eye. When your great-grandfather chose to purchase the Witch-House, disassemble it stone by stone, and ship it to Toronto, where it was reassembled to serve as your homestead, he hardly could have considered that one day a young woman researching her dissertation might find herself in pressing need of whatever documents might have come with it. To put it baldly, I am the first of my family to attend university, and without your aid, I fear I will never graduate.

The paper I plan to present is entitled "To Be Named Is As Good As To Be Known: Self-fulfilling Prophecy and the Scots Witch-Craze, as Seen Through the Lens of One Trial." In it, I examine the case of the so-called "Dourvale Witches," Jonet Devize, Alizoun Rusk, and Euwphaim Glouwer. Because they were arrested upon lands owned by Glauce, Lady Druir, whom the three later accused (along with her son-in-law, Callistor, Lord Roke) of complicity in their supposed "magickal treasons," this grouping has hitherto been known as the "Five-Family Coven"—and given your familial connexion with the Druirs, I understand completely how you might fear I will add them to the mix, in some sort of tabloid *exposé* fashion.

However, I am *only* interested in information concerning Devize, Rusk, and Glouwer, since my thesis presumes that what saw them condemned was a combination of their relative poverty, their womanhood, their lack of aristocratic blood, and the generalized hysteria then gripping Scotland—a hysteria that, by sowing constant fear of "witches," may have actually ended up *creating* a small but dramatic class of female criminals who genuinely believed themselves to be possessed of magical powers. As previous example, I reference the conspiracy against James VI by the North Berwick Coven—clearly politically motivated and steered from behind-scenes by Francis, Lord Bothwell, who hoped to use the "witches'" delusion as a way to depose James from the throne—which led directly (in its turn) to James writing *Daemonologie*, the book some call the "Scottish *Hammer*," setting the literal pattern for almost every subsequent witchcraft investigation and trial across the United Kingdom.

According to her dittay, taken under Question at the Witch-House, Jonet Devize—a young, good-looking widow with property, known for her skill with herbal medicines and her supposed ability to "speak for the dead"—was well aware that after her much-older husband died of "a fit" (probably a stroke), it would only be a matter of time before his relatives denounced her, hoping to secure her inheritance for themselves. Childless and alone, she had to protect herself from victimization, to make the people around her support her—even if only through fear.

Enter the mysterious Euwphaim Glouwer, who convinced Jonet to burn down her husband's house and make a "Black Pilgrimage" to touch your ancestress's fabled "stane" at Dourvale. Along the way, they picked up Alizoun Rusk, whose merchant-family wealth offered some small measure of protection until they were imprisoned, and perhaps explains away many of their supposedly supernatural escapades—travel from one end of Scotland to the other within a "miraculously" short space of time hardly requires flight if you have the money to rent a coach and four.

Though records here in Scotland show similar dittays were taken from both Alizoun Rusk (hers was judged "farre too fowle & filthie" for public consumption, apparently, and burnt along with her) and Euwphaim Glouwer, I have been completely unable to locate even a précis of the latter, which would serve as a necessary cornerstone of my research—a reflection, and possibly a rebuttal, of Jonet's own. I can only hope that a copy still exists somewhere in the former Witch-House, but without access to it, my cause is all but lost.

Throwing myself on your mercy, therefore, I remain,

Dolores Trench.

P.S.: I should probably mention that I also have a family connexion to add to the mix—my mother's maiden name was Clairk, traceable back to one of the soldiers who took the Dourvale Witches into custody. He claimed to have impregnated Euwphaim Glouwer, only to repossess her child once she was brought to term, and raise him as his own son.

I later discovered that something similar happened to Alizoun Rusk, who missed her initial execution date through the time-honoured tradition of "pleading her belly." Of course, once her son Judas was born, she too suffered the full penalty of the law.

(Judas Rusk stowed away to sea at the age of twelve, eventually reaching the Seychelles, where he formed a highly successful trading compact and bought Veritay Island. His descendants still live there today. According to records, he described himself as a man with "an hundred fathers," claiming that his mother's blood endowed his children and grandchildren with magical powers.)

Sincerely,
D.T.

April 3, 1968

G.D. Sidderstane
362 St. Andrew's Gardens
Toronto, Canada

Dolores Trench
18 Jordan Lane
Edinburgh, Scotland

Dear Miss Trench,

So sorry for the lengthy delay; I only just "received" your letter, by which I mean that I found it while going through papers on my father's desk. Luckily enough, for your purposes, he suffered a final convulsion the week before last and died with merciful swiftness after a sadly protracted illness. This means your plea devolves to me, which is just as well; my father was dubious at best about our "connexion" to Dourvale, the Druirs, and the Five-Family Coven alike.

For myself, I can't claim that your plan of proving your secret ancestress guiltless of sorcery by reason of self-delusion doesn't amuse me greatly. From what I've heard, it would certainly amuse *her*. But I am happy to help, nonetheless.

Enclosed, you will find a letter authorizing you to pick up a return ticket in your name at the Heathrow gate, Toronto-bound. I look forward to making your acquaintance in person, and turning over all the Witch-House of Eye-related documentation you might possibly wish for.

Cordially,

Gaheris S.

P.S.: My twin, Ygerna—quite an incorrigible Anglophile—awaits your arrival with bated breath. Please try to treat her enthusiasms gently. She means no harm.

—G.

| four: the witch-house (ii)—entrance

And now, here Dolores was on the Sidderstane (Witch-)House's front steps, a fold of her dirndl skirt caught uncomfortably tight between her thighs, already soaked with secret sweat. It'd been an hour's ride from the airport, where she'd found a disquietingly posh limousine driver already waiting, a sign with her name on it clutched to his chest. "Paid for," he'd said, when she tried to tip him. "All taken care of, Miss—they're good like that, the Family."

She sighed, straightened herself. Leaned on the doorbell once more, barely hearing its answering chime: some sort of tune, sounded like. A rippling fall of notes, repeated twice in quick success, mirroring each other—triple beat, double, four, then again. It sounded familiar somehow, and she caught herself humming along, transposing words from her last bit of reading material: Montague Summers's hoary and unreliable old treatise on *Witchcraft and Black Magic*, which she'd pulled from her carpetbag to send her to sleep on the plane—

Yes, that was it. The rhyme Gillie Duncan supposedly played for her captors on a Jew's Harp, along with the rest of her North Berwick gossips; a song sung at Sabbat, suitable for dancing back-to-back and kissing the Old Man's hindparts to. Up and down and back and forth, widdershins about, sawing like the bow of some rebec made from poison yew-wood and inlaid with looted bone—

> *Commer ye go before, commer go ye,*
> *Gif ye will no' go before, commer let me.*
> *I sall gae into a hare*
> *Wi' sorrow and scorn an' mickle care,*
> *I sall gae in the De'il's name*
> *'Til he send me hame again.*

For first we'll wait, and then we'll whistle, and then we'll dance together, Dolores thought. Not that poor little Gillie had probably done much dancing after that, her chief examiner—James Rex himself, soon to be First of England, the same lofty personage whom the North Berwick crew stood accused of plotting against—never having been any great friend to witches.

The bell faded away into silence, and Dolores found herself straining for any hint of a footfall, either towards the door or away from it. For a breathless second, she contemplated the fact that she was utterly alone in another country: no place to stay, no one to call on, no relatives to ask after her should she somehow go astray. Everything she had in the world fit into her suitcase, with her last ten pounds sewn into the carpetbag's lining, just in case. *I wouldn't, darling,* was all her flatmate'd said, when she'd showed her the letter—could she have been right?

I still have the ticket, at least. I can get back, just in time to fail, on every possible level. . . .

But no. The door opened, without fanfare. A man stood there, smiling, hand outstretched.

"Gaheris Sidderstane," he said. "While you, of course, must be our guest—dear Miss Trench, both honoured and anticipated, all that. Please do step in; no, let me take your bags. I'm having Keck make tea."

Inside, the house was dim and dully red all over, as if flayed and left to set. Dark wood, small windows, long falls of heavy drape pulled almost shut in each successive room. Dust hung in a few bright beams, sparkling. Sidderstane ushered her into what might have been a library, walls two rows deep in books from ceiling to floor. He threw himself into a chair by the fire, blazing away behind its grate, which nevertheless gave off a sullen, steady smoke that the chimney didn't seem entirely equipped to deal with—then turned to admire her with his head tipped to one side while crossing his long legs like Errol Flynn, who he vaguely resembled, aside from a pair of ears which stuck out like a monkey's.

"There," he said, confidentially. "That's better, isn't it?" Dolores nodded, unable to think of any reason to disagree. "Now, don't stand on ceremony! That, over there—" He gestured, indicating something at her elbow that she eventually realized was another chair, covered in yet more books. "—that's for you."

"Oh, is it? Thanks, very much."

She stooped to clear a place for herself, bending at the knees rather than the waist, executing a weird little half-curtsey in the service of modesty. The man's eyes—leaf-brown, with a hint of pale green—never seemed to leave her, throughout the whole process.

"Lovely," he said, when she'd settled. "Now, I must ask—are you *really* planning to rehabilitate Euwphaim Glouwer's reputation? To refute her dittay, so to speak?"

"Er . . . I need it more for . . . research purposes, really. To see if there's any significant variation between the way she saw things and the way—"

"—poor Jonet Devize did, yes; I do recall that, from the missive you sent my dear departed Dad. Make an even better compare-and-contrast if you had a copy of Alizoun Rusk's confession to add in on top, hmmm?"

"Do you?"

"No, sorry. Ygerna and I spent quite a bit of last week looking for it, only to eventually own ourselves confounded. Seems like they really did burn it after all, Puritan bastards."

"I'm . . . not too sure they'd've called themselves that, the Witch-House men. Protestants mostly, Calvinists; Puritanism was only a smallish sect at the time of North Berwick, and by 1593—"

"No Puritans in Eye?"

"Not many, I'd think. It was a main small place."

"Huh. Well, you're the expert."

The door opened, admitting a cadaverous ancient she could only assume was the aforementioned Keck, his thin arms bent under the burden of carrying a sterling tea set on a silver tray. Gaheris took it, poured her a cup, popped in milk and two sugar without asking, then made himself the same, before depositing it on the book-stack nearest his elbow. "Got to get you up to par, after the journey," he said, as she sipped, trying not to wince. "I've instructed Keck that sandwiches are to be prepared, which you can have now or later—now *and* later, if you want. Your choice, entirely."

"Thanks, yes, I am a bit peckish, but . . . you really don't mind me eating around the books? I mean, they're—"

"Irreplacable? Probably. Then again, I've read them already; Ygerna too, repeatedly. Let the Connaught Trust's donations office worry about their state, after you're done."

That smile of his—so many *teeth*, for something so narrow; it made her head swim just a bit, her whole skull feel suddenly soft, heavy and swollen. "No doubt you wonder where my sister is," he continued, though she frankly hadn't. "Alas, she's been struck down by a summer cold, to which she's unfortunately quite prone—the effects are usually brief but always unpleasant, and unglamourous. So she's confined herself to her room, the vain creature . . . perhaps I'll yet be able to pry her free later on, at least once, before you go. Fingers crossed. I assure you, she's well worth the wait."

"That would be, eh—lovely, Mister Sidderstane."

"Please. Gaheris."

". . . Dolores."

"Yes, I remember. So now we're all good friends . . ." He nodded at Keck, who produced a flat, ill-laid wooden box from the pannier-like tails of his dusty frock-coat. Black with age, it sported leather hinges and a slightly rusty iron clasp; Dolores automatically reached out one hand to receive it, only to find it heavy enough to warrant two. She barely managed to get it clunked down on her own nearest book-stack before losing her grip entirely, bracing it against a fall with one elbow and juggling the teacup at the same time, completely off-balance. For a moment, she was afraid she was going to slop hot tea all down her dress, but Sidderstane—Gaheris—reached out a hand, effortlessly steadying them both. "Ooh, close one! Well, I'll just leave you to it, shall I?"

"What, start right now?"

"No time like the present, considering how long you've waited." To Keck: "Later for the sandwiches after all, I believe—best to let Miss Trench get the lie of the land before bothering her with sustenance."

"Sir," the old man replied, face unreadable, as Gaheris handed him the tea set once more, and rose. After which—executing a bizarre sort of two-step, so deft and fast that Dolores later found she had no clear recollection exactly who might have held the door for whom—they both disappeared. She was left alone, with only fire, books, and box for company.

Daft bugger, she thought. But then her gaze fell on the box's lid, blind reliquary of Euwphaim Glouwer's final testament (more boast than confession, if what she'd learned about the woman thus far held true), and she found she no longer much cared about Gaheris's motives, let alone his eccentricities. Her thumbs itched fiercely, palms sweaty, fingers longing to be filled and set to work.

Notebook, she ticked off, in her head. *Pens.* That magnifying glass Hector had bought for her, the night before she'd set off—poor Hector, who truly did seem to think they'd be married, once she got "all this foolishness" out of her system. *Does it really matter so very much, hen?* he'd asked, just a month or so previous, eyes sympathy-soft but uncomprehending, when she'd told him her work was in imminent danger of stalling. *I mean, what would you do with this degree of yours? Whoever would read this paper, besides your professors? Who on earth would care to?*

Oh, and yet: *There are far more people interested in what lies behind the dark than you'd ever think, my lad,* she'd thought, but hadn't said. *These doomed, powerless women with their spells and their pacts, scrabbling for some sort of recompense, a voice to cry out in vain against this world that grinds them like corn, leaving them nowhere to stand but the scaffold. A knife of words, fit to stab through the very heart of everything which keeps them lonely, keeps them poor, uneducated, pariahs, criminals, madwomen . . . witches.*

All women, everywhere, still only a slip of the tongue away from potential witches, even today—from standing accused as abnormal, ill-made, *wrong,* even with dance-hall swapped in for sabbat, bad marriages (in all their abuse and degradation) for the torturer's Question, childbirth complications for outright execution. With those who dared to speak up against this inequity still locked away, confined, forever at the mercy of men who needed no more provocation than any given witchfinder to drug their tongues and cut the very thoughts from their brains, crippling them in the service of a cure.

No need to go down that route, however, when arguing, or even when not. For no one need ever know about Dolores's mother's end or the fears it bred in her, this unshakeable sense that she herself might yet live out her last days on a ward, jacketed and drooling, no matter what differences of degree she placed between the two of them. Or this quirk of an idea that perhaps it was the long-buried seed of Euwphaim Glouwer's own mystic insanity which had set Mrs. Trench on her downslide, if only chased back far enough: a black vision not of some bland Saviour, but of His exact opposite.

Dolores took a breath. At her elbow, the box sat quiet. She had only to reach out and see what might be done with what she found—

So she did, tongue touched to lip and forehead wrinkling, with only slightly shaking hands. Too concentrated by far to notice Gaheris Sidderstane watching her through the door's crack, his leaf-mould gaze equal-intent, wrapped in shadow; when the latch drew blood, provoking her to swear and lick her fingers, that drew a brief smile, if nothing more. By the time she took up her ball-point, meanwhile—pad flipped open, scanning the brown-spotted pages fiercely—he had already turned away, retracing his steps back upstairs, to where his sister waited.

| five: euwphaim glouwer, her dittay

As transcribed from its original form by Dolores Trent, with spelling amended for consistency, except where otherwise noted.

What am I, you wonder, judging me from on high? I come from a place wiped clean, where nothing any longer lives, nor grows. I was made from your spite, and thus I have grown spiteful; as your hate was my milk, so my hate has swelled and darkened, fit to smother the world. Yet in truth, what I suffered and what I lost, before I bound my sisters to me—these are nothing. Only what they made *of* me, and what followed after, are worth the speaking of.

Of my childhood, I remember little. Only that my kin were good enough folk, nothing like myself, though they loved me, and I them. They had no sight, no troubling dreams, no secret knowledge; nothing spoke to them from the shadows, or out of the flames. All they were was unlucky enough to live on land deeded from one rich man to another, and foolish enough to try to stay when the border shifted, having been already warned to quit it.

So in a way, it is as though my life truly began on that day when the soldiers came, when they ran my father through and took my mother against the shed, then knocked her head on a stone 'til she stopped screaming and threw my younger brother—a child barely able to stand— alive, into the fire they made of our house. The thatch and sticks of our village they doused with oil and set alight, standing to watch as the walls fell in. Those who survived the attack they rode down with their horses and hung from trees, then stuck them through with pikes, laughed and drank and gambled some hours before pissing on the ashes of the mess they'd made and marching away once more, leaving nothing behind but smoking bones.

All this I watched from safety, hid between rocks, for my gift had warned me to go up early into the hills and stay away, if I wished to live. But when I perceived the ruin of everything I had known hitherto, I wept and wondered what good that life would do me, a landless girl with no money, who could see as yet no earthly way of getting my vengeance.

That night I crept out from my hiding-place, and I prayed. Not to God: who was God to me? I remembered some minister the soldiers brang with them, reading over the dead—a verse from his great black book, telling them how what they had done was right and good. *For Thou art my battle axe and weapons of war: with thee will I break in pieces the nations, and with thee will I destroy kingdoms. . . . And the land shall tremble and sorrow: for every purpose of the LORD shall be performed against Babylon, to make the land of Babylon a desolation without an inhabitant.*

These were heretics, the minister said; *no, these were outlaws,* cried the Captain, in reply. *And witches too, likely enough,* the soldiers muttered, in their turn. *Witches, working Satan's will against Scotland's good Christians, fit only to be bled and burnt.*

How little they knew. For in that whole valley, before and after, there was never any witch but me.

This is my enemy, then, I thought—*this rich man's God. And I think I know where I must turn, to work my will against Him.*

All my life, only one of my family had told me anything of interest, that being my grandam, my mother's mother. She was coughing blood by then, but I remembered her pulling me close and telling me how I should know where my gift came from—from back long before the Wall fell or men ceased to paint their skins, to just after the Flood, which that good Christian God sent to kill His wayward children's children, those giants in the earth, with never a thought to who else might perish along with them.

You have their look, Euwphaim, my grandam said, *so they will come when you call. And they will love you, for you have the power to do great mischief in His holdings, before you are taken up from them.*

And so, as I stood there that night in my misery and anger, I opened my mouth and called out for someone, anyone, who would make me strong and poison-full and give me dominion over all those who sought to crush me. I opened my mouth and let the night in, and I closed my eyes, and I let my hate fill me from top to toe. And when I opened them again, he was there: my Black Man, who all my kin do know. My Master.

The Devil? You are fools, to say it. Anything for you may be called the Devil, if you fear it enough. Yet in truth, he was an angel, as so many of the invisible are: one of Seven who make it their charge to answer us the way God has long since ceased to, if indeed He ever did. . . .

:**Euwphaim Glouwer,**: he said. :**Will you take my mark and let me wear you awhile, that we may walk inside time's harness together? Would you see this world altered, and yourself its alterer?**:

I would see this whole world rocked end on end, I told him. I would see it broken and thrown down utterly, without even any other raised in its place.

I felt him laugh, then. :**Well,**: he said, :**we need not go so far. Yet I may point you in the right direction to achieve your desires, if you will let me.**:

Command me, Master, I told him, then. I fear nothing, who have nothing left to fear for.

So we joined together, and the sweetness of it pierced me straight through the vitals, hollowing a place for him to live in me forever. He raised his sign up on my palm, by which token I may summon him from any place or time in history, and unlocked to me all the secret powers of which I stand capable. And always ever after have I felt him look through my eyes and heard his voice in my head, counselling me what might be done to make those around me suffer most.

Dolores cricked her neck, eyes stinging, a niggling disturbance tapping at her mind's back door. Most witch-confessions followed an extremely well-worn track; the language rarely varied, parroting a rote script with little deviation: *Yes, I made a pact; yes, I laid spells; yes, I flew to the Sabbat, ate children, danced backwards, kissed the Devil's arse . . .*

Here, however, were beliefs she'd never before seen referenced. *My angel is one of Seven*—hardly likely that an illiterate Scottish hillwoman would be referencing the Seven Archangels, found only in the Apocrypha of the Geneva Bible. And could that really be a variant on the Nephilim legend roped in with the rest, with Euwphaim's granny convinced all Glouwers were descended from those "great men and women of renown" sired by the Grigorim, the Watcher angels God had meant to guide humanity through its infancy?

Jonet Devize thought it was the Devil they were worshipping, though, she recalled, checking her notes. *Didn't she?*

Item: Thatt she admitted giving hersel ouer tae Satan, takynge his mark upon her flesh in her wummen's partes, the

aforementioned found and provd, without doubt. The same observd & sworn uponn inn Questioning of Alizoun Rusk, of similiar contitutyonne & in a lyke place. The same not so observd of Euwphaim Glouwer, who bare her Devil's mark onn left palm instead, raysed upp lyke unto a brand or scar, & not a meer teat tae suckle imps fromm but lyke unto a lettre in somme Language Unknowen.

Asked was it not the Devil Lucifer who ye sarved in yuir wyckednesses? Answers: I allways thought itt so. Asked & ye others? Answers: I know anely whatt I know, & Mistress Rusk the self-same. Yet Euwphaim Glouwer was my teacher inn alle thinges, for that her gifte farre outstretchd myne own, giuen whose blode shee had larnt itt from.

An odd way to put it.
Dolores shook her head, turned the page, began again.

In the hills near Neath I found Jonet Devize and knew her for one of mine. She had married a man far elder than herself, and richer, yet once he was dead, his sisters despised her her share, since her husband had given her no childer. Too, she had a bad name thereabouts for speaking to the dead, which none could have known but that she was fool enough to talk on it, after.

She was a wise girl, Jonet, able to do much that I could not—the making of imps was in her charge, the which she could force to do her will in every thing, much though she feared to send them against those who persecuted her. But I was never taught to be so nice.

To make Jonet give up her place, those gossips who sought her portion sent their sons and daughters to chide her, casting at her with rocks, so that her skin bled where they bruised her. I came up just as one made to let fly and breathed my will on him, making him known to the elements, so that he was pursued by a wind which kissed him 'til he lost the power to speak. By the next day he had turned black, and on the third he was buried at night, far from home.

You will have me cast out, Jonet complained. *I will be cried for a witch in every parish.* But: *What matter that?* I asked her, in return. *They know you a witch already, as you know yourself. Better to seize your inheritance outright, setting your imps abroad and filling them full of sicknesses, that they pull their own houses down in desperation for a cure. And then, best of all, to come with me and seek what my Master promises: the re-making of this world in our own image, that none shall ever suffer as you and I have, or as we can make those who cross us suffer.*

Since the boy I killed was as yet unbaptized, we dug up his body, boiled it for its fat and ate the rest, then flew along the coast seeking a third. Soon enough, we found Alizoun Rusk on the high cliff's side, scowling prettily, considering whether or no to cast herself down on the rocks below, thus to be rid of the unfashionable marriage into which her kin conspired to force her. For her sea-captain intended had already got her with child, knowing himself secure enough in his suit to force the matter, thus making her either a bride foretold or an unmarried whore—and so she thought it of little moment to let me draw out her child and crush its soft skull in my hand, then watch as I pissed in a sieve and threw it sea-wards, while Jonet piped a wind made from dead men's screams towards the captain's sails. In return, she swore herself our sister and was set to the making of poppets, at which skill she proved most expert.

I stayed ever the brain to their hands amongst us three, however. And thus 'twas at my Black Man's whim we made our path, ranging downwards to that slippery place where Scotland slides into England—Dourvale valley, seat to the great family Druir, with Rook's-home over the very next ridge, where rules the dark and mighty Laird of Roke—to unravel this whole world's foul knot, if we might.

. . . unravel this whole world's foul knot . . .

Dolores paused, re-reading this last claim and wondering once more at its anarchistic—anachronistic?—arrogance. A weirdly seductive thing, delusion. Jonet and Alizoun must have believed the same, surely—enough so to draw them into Euwphaim's train, pulling them straight-way from the plain daylight world's concerns into the Witch-House's endless, Fire-lit night.

She sighed, kneading the nape of her neck, as her stomach growled. *Best call for Keck and stoke yourself if you mean to go on,* she thought, vaguely, until her eyes dropped once more: fixed on Euwphaim's words and clenched, painful-pleasurable, a fist around a nail. Unable to stop herself from stringing one to the other, or the next, or the next. . . .

From inside the box came a strange little rattle, pins falling in some phantom lock. But Dolores did not look up again, not even when whatever it was *turned* slightly, invisibly, poising itself to open.

You have all heard the rumours, though you pretend disbelief. Glauce Lady Druir came from nowhere, much like myself, although her kin never stepped their feet above-ground unless driven to; in the hollow hills they dwelt, the Faerie *brugh*, before their High King and Queen at last proclaimed it time to flee this iron-touched world forever. Yet my Lady was left behind, a changeling, to comb her hair and sigh in a cave 'til Enzembler Laird Druir came to court her—which is why all their children carry her odd blood, bearing the mark of her strangeness, inside or out.

She had more to risk than I, my Black Man said, which is why he sent me to her. That and her dowry, brought up into light from darkness—the Sidhe Stane her gillies take their name from, with which any thing might be accomplished, if there were only enough of similar power to make a circle about it: my coven and her, and Roke's Laird too, with his book-learning and bad intent.

To my own mind, Lady Glauce never understood the Stane's worth fully—'twas a thing she stood guardian to, not master of, for all she might profit from its nearness. Yet since I knew she must be present during the working I had planned for it, I made sure to come to her at a weak moment, after her husband's head was taken for rising against the old Queen, dead Harry's daughter. My Lady carried it home to sit with his body in state, her get all ranged about her, unsure on how to proceed— for though she sat in regency for his heir, Minion, 'twas a subtle time, as she well knew. So we helped her from that danger, making it so that Laird Enzembler sat again beside her from thence on, cold and silent except to sometimes nod, and gave her all her will.

They will never accept you, I told her. *Nor your brood neither, once enough time has passed that their fear falls away. Better to alter the balance of things while we still can, then—set fire to the world and watch it burn, to see what else might be grown from its ashes.*

And she agreed, or seemed to. Yet this was a lie, and only we three would pay for it, in the end. For those above are ever at odds with those below, no matter what store of evil angels' blood they share.

Sidhe Stane = Sidderstane, Dolores watched her hand scribble, through aching, drowsy eyes. *Like the Stane of Scone, Scotland's destiny—a family totem, the Druir luck. Could be any size, small enough to wear, large enough to lie down on . . .* Now, where had she read that? (*Look up reference, cf.*) And "gillies" . . . so the Sidderstanes were literal poor relations, former sworn bondsmen of Clan Druir, married into the family proper when Torrance Sidderstane brought his wife, Enzemblance Druir, back from the Auld Sod, an etymological link turned genetic.

(What an odd name that was too, in context—traditional, one could only think. Hearkening back to old Laird Enzembler and his own daughter, sister to Grisell, who married Callistor Laird Roke. . . .)

She probably thought that hard, Dolores mused, *given she must've been the elder. Who marries their younger daughter away first, anyhow? But perhaps she looked a bit too much like her mother for Callistor's liking.*

So hot in here, increasingly, and oh so dreadfully close; the very air seemed book-dry, desiccated, all moisture sucked away by rotten paper, a quintessence of dust. History's weight hung pendant, pressing down on her from all corners, thumbing every pore open at once. She yawned, jaw cracking wide, fatigue suddenly a mere stretch away from nausea.

Was I supposed to just call out for Keck, and hope he hears me? Or . . . wasn't there a bell he showed me, Mister S—Gaheris? Over there, by where he was sitting—

Have to get up to find it, though. And how best to do that when her fingers were already scrabbling their way 'cross the page once more, words trailing behind, screwed and slant as blood from some phantom wound? *The Roke we tempted to our Cause right easily, him being much a man as any other, craving both his name's advancement and a warm place for his prick, likewise. . . .*

I told him what I had told my Lady: that my sisters and I knew seven angels' secret names, who between them could wreck this world and make it over, all anew. And he chose to believe me, for that he had read in his books of those same Seven, my Black Man's kin, who chose neither Heaven nor Hell, but to circle the globe forever, seeking misery. For the Roke was one of those who thinks magic can be made with silly schoolmasters' tricks, calling angels down and devils up to do your bidding with equal ease, so that you never have to touch any task with your own hands, if it can at all be helped.

A marriage was arranged between the Roke and my Lady's Grisell, to give him cause to journey between their holdings. And once we came all together, she showed us where the Stane was kept, in that same empty *brugh* she had been cast from. Beneath the Dourvale hill we made our compact, swearing in together, and spilled our blood upon the Stane's skin, softening it for our purposes—bound ourselves together for all times, with one thing only left wanting.

There must be a sacrifice, I told them. *Nothing for nothing, neither on this globe, nor out of it. We must all give up part of ourselves to see this through, or the working fails.*

What will the world be hereafter, when we are done? Lady Glauce asked me, to which I replied: *Better than this or worse, yet in no-wise the same. I fear for my children,* she said, *who have already lost so much, without ever knowing it.* To which I answered: *But 'twill be their world, at last, an we say our spells a-rightly—a world fit only for us who are born apart, touched with the invisible. We will no more be hunted, but hunters; no more slaves, but kings. 'Tis worth all things to gain such a prize, is't not?*

And the fee?

What you will. An eye, a finger, a cut of flesh . . . that hair of yours, perhaps, which grows so long and greenly.

I would pay the price, an it bring me what you promise, she told me. *Still, I mis-doubt; 'tis a great hazard.* And here the Roke laughed, saying: *Yet all great Projects be bought by blood, m'Lady Mother, as Hermes Trismegistus does say—and all birth through blood likewise, as every woman knows, of high or low estate.*

Say so again when we see what you *give up,* she told him. And there it was left for the instant—he and she went one way, to celebrate the wedding feast, while my sisters and I went t'other, to gather ourselves for what was to come.

We would have remade this world, between the five of us. But in the end, my Lady loved this foul place best just as it is, since it bent to her name and degree. Far better to keep your hand than risk all to gain more—or less—than any of us might know, is what she no doubt thought. So even whilst I and mine laid in our preparations, she planned for our downfall.

Two nights gone, we returned to the *brugh* and stood encircled with Lady Glauce and the Roke, casting ourselves together into that place where all paths meet and the Seven may pass by each other without touching, so as not to be put back together as One. Then we began our sacrifices, he first using his sword to clip away a finger-bone, then Jonet the dead eye through which she saw her ghosts. I myself ran a blade under one pap, ready to cut it free like a pitched boil. 'Twas then I felt my Lady in my head, and knew her true intent. All unnoticed, she had let her childer and husband enter through the low road, that they might add their strength to hers—but before I could call on my angel, I saw another of his kin step in behind, laying hands upon these two betrayers' shoulders. In an instant, the Stane's power fell from us to them, and every thing was undone.

Then they were gone away through air and darkness, my Lady's get and all, I know not where even now, but that it lies so far beyond your grasp that you would never find it did you care to seek for them. And though the Roke and his wife have since returned to his own place, we three awoke on cold grass, in a circle of our enemies.

They found us uponn the hill-side, Jonet Devize's dittay had read,

Dolores remembered. **And set uponn us in our sleep, by Glauce Lady Druir's connivance, for that shee and the Roke had made theyr ane pact tae scape the Fire togeyther, giving us over in recompense tae yuir guid companye.** Which rang far more sensibly than Euwphaim's version—yet what Dolores found herself watching play out on her mind's fever-bright screen (popping and hissing like bad Super-8 film, stuttering counterpoint to the words spilled from her pen's deep-dug nib) fell uncomfortably equidistant between the two: a transcribed vision which outran the text, informing and deforming it. First the word itself, page-plucked, followed gut-kick quick by meaning, image, sound, *feeling.*

As though I was there. As though, as though I—

—am there.

(Right now.)

Unable to stop, or help. Unable to look away, to shut her eyes. To do anything but sit there rigid, lids screwed open and a whimper throat-stuck, as the past unspooled its filthy phantom message on the air.

On the cold hill's side we wake surrounded, Jonet bent over with pain, eye-socket dribbling. Alizoun jumps up into the air, dragging her along, as the witchfinders throw their nets. They tangle, hover and jerk sharply, caught— try to fight free, but fail. The finders haul harder, dragging them in.

I am on my feet already, red down my side. My cut breast flaps. Some fool to my right in uniform draws a pistol from his belt, but I put my hand on him, grasp his parts. He gives a mighty cry as they wither in my hand. I laugh, spit in his face.

Snarling, Alizoun lifts her skirts and pisses vitriol, drenching those below: they fall, roll, flee. More soldiers lift weapons, let fly with salt shot, banishing her spell's might. She and Jonet fall together in a heap, Jonet below. I hear her scream as one leg folds underneath, breaking at the hip.

I stand my ground, screeching. Cry out that my angel will come for me as I toss my head, hair catching flame and fire a-drip from my mouth like vomit, to make them turn and cringe—

But then there is another one, slashing his blade behind my knee so I tumble. Putting his boot to my chest, wound flaring bright, as he reaches down to blood my forehead, carve this cross between my eyes. And I go out all at once, a water-plunged torch.

:Not yet, my Euwphaim,: *my Black Man tells me.* **:I am needed elsewhen, as other miseries call me—I am not like you, caught inside time's folds, a straight line from birth to death. So put down your seed while you can, and I will use it to anchor us both.**

This will be the cord I draw us back together with.:

The soldier grins down at me, hoping to see me weep. I laugh instead, and open myself to him—pull him down on top of me, biting at his tongue, letting him slap my face 'til my jaw turns blue, hard enough that at last his prick rises. And then

—Dolores shook awake, pen skittering, fingers pain-cramped, every part of her aching. The box, jolted by her movement, tipped up and back, cracking along its spine; she lunged to catch it, exclaiming in horror. Saw a thin slot slide open in its base, some secret drawer sprung at long last, full of dust, and darkness.

Something else as well, though. Smallish and black, dried hard, odd-smelling even at this distance, like spiced jerky . . .

What is *that?* she thought. And put out one hand, all unthinking, to touch it.

| six: the witch-house (iii)—as above

Upstairs, in the room they shared as children, Ygerna Sidderstane sits waiting for her twin, dozing slightly—her eyes flicker back and forth under semi-transparent lids, skin tinted hazel by the cilia beneath. Though the lights are off and the curtains drawn, she can still be glimpsed distinctly, outlined by the glow of her own bones seeping up muffled through slimy meat, the low-grade, clustering light of her muscles and tendons.

Malt-brown when she was born, the underwater tangles of her hair now drift weed-like, green as her gaze. She is a work in progress, or perhaps a study in decay: first nix bred in almost seventy years of Sidderstanes Druir-united, clockwise pride of her particular (de)generation.

Though fraternal, she and Gaheris once looked almost identical, each other's perfect, sexually apposite complement. But that, as both of them well know, has not been true for quite some time. Beneath her late mother's morning robe, still satin-bright as the day it was bought and patterned in yellow chintz roses, Ygerna is slick and translucent all over though only slightly misshapen, a swampwater pearl formed 'round poisoned grit, her very blood turned stagnant. If she was to look in the heart-shaped mirror on her former dressing-table—mercifully shrouded, now—she could watch her organs pulse like fresh bruises, the semi-visible tracery of her skull pushing up through her face. In sleep, her legs and arms hang loose, cartilaginous-tentacled, while that shadow running the length of her throat down into her chest's luminous cage is the only outward show of her long, barbed, narcotically poisonous tongue.

She may be dreaming of her former fiancé, solid young Mortimer Gant, who disappeared at the cottage last summer. They went up to the Lake of the North to swim, he and she, crunching their way through the shadow of a hundred cross-grown pinetrees, the dim brown air heavy with stinging gnats. There was a picnic lunch, packed by Keck, in a wicker basket dating back to the 1920s—Mortimer carried it, no doubt swinging it jauntily back and forth with Ygerna's arm grasped tight, their hands around each other's waists. . . .

But he never came back, and when Gaheris finally followed the setting sun down along the beach, he found Ygerna weeping over a pile of items that no longer seemed even vaguely human, her sweet mouth bile-stained and ripped at both corners.

(That *tongue* of hers creeping down into Mortimer's throat, coating it with some paralyzing agent, a swallow of liquor-sweet spit. Then nudging past his uvula to slither ever further, gag reflex neutered, 'til at last the lamprey-like barbs took hold, flexing and hooking, tearing, coring. 'Til the burden of her kiss turned him liquid from the inside, rendering him, and she began to drink.)

This blithe college athlete, tan and straight and foolish, with all his insides suddenly out or gone. Sucked dry as any marrowbone, husked and still in his sister's wet, too-flexible grip.

I killed him, I, I must have—we were kissing, just kissing, and then—this. Explain it to me. Why would I do that when I loved him, so much? Can you tell me? Can you?

No. Of course not. But those others, under the Hill . . . their great-grandmother, Torrance's widow, and the rest . . . *they* could.

Poor girl, Lady Glauce said when summoned, bent down to study Ygerna's ruin with distant eyes, hair like a weeping willow; Gaheris's "uncle" Ganconer stood at her one hand, Torrance's ageless changeling by-blow, while Ganconer's somewhat-stepmother Enzemblance grinned sly at the other, licking her own sharp teeth. *So seldom do ye show my blood's curse, you Sidderstanes, for which I reckon the most of ye well-thankful. Yet we shall prepare her a place at the table naetheless and open the low road tae her, that she may take it up whene'er pleases.*

No other option offered, of course; perish the bloody thought. And not one shred of doubt over whether Ygerna might—just possibly—find the chance to squat forever in the dark, eating raw fish by the light of glowworm-infested moss, not exactly *attractive*, given she'd previously held such high hopes for a non-Faerie hill-dwelling future.

He'd caught Ganconer by the sleeve as they turned to go, only to have that same gentleman shake his grave head sadly, as if to say: *Better not, Gaheris my lad. For they're no' to be questioned, these ones, especially wi' their minds already made up.* Then looked back to see Enzemblance Druir's white hand emerging wrist-deep out of the cliff-wall the rest of her had already sunk inside, crooking itself for Ganconer to follow after—and hell if that wasn't enough by itself to make Gaheris let go, dousing the hot rage he felt blister his lungs back down to a sullen smoulder.

God forbid he ever wake to find her standing at his bed's foot one of these nights, watching him sleep, with that same hungry smile . . . or Ygerna's, either. Which would be *far* worse.

How well he remembers those interminable Dourvale summers, wandering blind through the forest with invisible company or trapped for long hours inside protective rings, counting fungi on nearby trees while waiting for their parents to return from doing my Lady her due clan patron's homage. That time Enzemblance eddied up through the forest floor without warning, biting a live toad in half as though it were some particularly warty potato, and crooned, still chewing: *How I would love tae have one or t'other of ye visit me, pretty wee ones, and befriend my son awhile—for although he be the elder, poor Saracen is a lonely boy, I fear, wi' so few meet playmates 'roundabouts tae choose from, and so few ways tae pass his time . . .*

A year's worth of nightmares, at least, wrapped in that icily sweet-voiced package; peacock-eyed Saracen was small threat by comparison, even when caught playing with toys made from human bones. Gaheris had sworn to himself then and there he would save his "little" sister— only a minute's difference between them, true, yet one he's been trained to respect since mutual babyhood—from ever having to grace the *brugh* with her presence for long, no matter *how* exigent the circumstances.

We are not *them,* he has told himself, at least a thousand times, since that moonlit ill-meeting. *Not now and not ever. Let them do as they please, out of sight and mind, so long as they leave us alone; any help they'd offer would always come at a price, one neither of us want to pay. Better by far to figure a way out of this for ourselves, and if it can bring hurt to them as a side effect, well—so much the better.*

Not that he'd actually thought it likely he'd ever *achieve* this goal. But then he turned the key in his father's desk drawer to let loose a disgorgement of recent correspondence, amongst which lurked Dolores Trench's fateful letter.

Synchronicity, that's what the books in Torrance's library call it. But can there really be such a thing as coincidence in a world where magic works?

A blind hope, stabbed straight to the heart; opportunity, knocking. Almost as though it was meant to be.

In her chair, Ygerna groans, shifting so that one arm uncoils slightly, allowing Gaheris a glimpse of what she's been clutching to her; he watches it spill forward into her lap, pause in mid-wobble, threatening to fall. All she has left of her lover, these days, concentrated to a dry, hard point: that dusty seed-pod which was once his heart, so jelly rich with congested blood, long since pried from between cracked ribs and sucked for its last, lingering shred of sweetness.

Gently, unsqueamishly, Gaheris nudges it back into place, then taps her lightly on the shoulder. Murmuring in her ear as he does so: "Don't fret, sis—it's only me."

"Gaheris? Oh, I . . . must have been sleeping. Is she here yet?"

"Miss Trench? Yes, just downstairs. I put her in Papa's office with the box."

"Mmm." Ygerna shrugs herself back up, Mortimer's heart clutched tight to her ruffled breast, and Gaheris tries not to notice how her cuttlefish pupils slot against the too-bright light. "And—will she do, d'you think? The right choice?"

"Oh yes, without a doubt. Quite perfect, for our purposes."

A sniff, wet and rattling. "That's something, then."

Gaheris sighs. "You were scrying, when I left you; any reply? Do they know just how . . . difficult things have become for you, lately?"

"Do they *care*, you mean?" Ygerna slides from the chair, oozes her slick way to the vanity, where she tucks the heart away again, after one last kiss. "Auntie E. looked in on me when I was halfway through the evocation; says she's made up a bed for me, down in the cellar where the mushrooms grow. Oh, and my Lady says you're always welcome to visit."

"As an appetizer, no doubt. Or a thrall."

"Auntie didn't specify."

"Poisonous bloody bitch."

"Not as such that I've observed. That . . . would still be me."

He wants to hold her, fiercely. Yet he also fears to, cold clutch of it kept forever deep-swallowed down in his gut, though she can probably still see it, as a shadow clouding his eyes.

"Since Miss Trench is busy with the dittay," Gaheris reminds her, hastening to change the subject, "we should probably begin, while we still have time."

"You have what we need?"

"'Course."

"Then let's."

WE WILL ALL GO DOWN TOGETHER

Setting up for the ritual is easier than he might have expected, considering. Once upon a time, magicians engaged in this sort of Summoning would have taken care to shield themselves from both Heaven and Hell by enticing a stranger who looked as much like them as possible to a remote place, somewhere so isolated that they could kill them, flay them, and wear the skin for nine days and nights without threat of interruption, letting it rot around them while continuously meditating on the Ouroboros's (un)holy spiral shape . . . that "old serpent" all spellbooks warn of, immortality shed and renewed at will, the Snake Self-Eaten.

Such a duly prepared sacrificial man- or woman-cloak, it's thought, would act as an interdimensional imago, deflecting the attention of any monitoring angels who might notice mere humans dabbling in Chaos; a logical plan, for certain values of logic. Though one far less likely to warn other angels *away*, in fact, than to draw the attention of those you wish to summon.

Shoulders squared against the blasphemy to come, Gaheris Sidderstane steps forward as his no-longer-identical twin steps back over the charred rim of a circle burnt into the floorboards, its circumference just large enough to include the both of them, along with that bag he dropped next to her chair last night. Inside, they find staples, familiar to the touch: a bronze bowl, salt boiled from seawater and fresh moly, a black-handled knife, a box of matches. Reaching into his pants pocket, he unfolds the scrap of manuscript their father kept in his office safe and reads:

> *Two angels, foot and head,*
> *Stand watch o'er my narrow bed.*
> *Two angels, right and left,*
> *All we know from void once reft.*
> *Two angels in my mind,*
> *One before and one behind,*
> *One more angel, making seven—*
> *None that dare return to Heaven.*
> *Terrible as corpse's eyes*
> *Bright and dark, arise, arise!*
> *Seven angels, less no more,*
> *Knocking now on every door.*

Ygerna shakes out the salt, seasoning the circle's inner ring, then crushes some moly in the bowl and lights it. Throws another handful of salt in on top, making the flames turn blue while releasing a wild slaughterhouse reek, perfumed face-cough, drugged puff of spice— all three distinct smells of magic: before, during, after. None of them anything you'd want to bottle and sell, since *before's* tang is most reminiscent of stomach-acids, all salt and meat and sweet-stink reek, every body's home-made vitriol; *during* sends vomitus-chaser skittering up the nose-scale towards something almost like perfume, old cologne boiled away to its dregs. And *after*, oh . . . that burning marigold haze, acrid and numbing. Torched opium-field bouquet, with a brisk novocaine chaser.

All of which makes it hard to think, let alone breathe, or chant, or— concentrate, even. Yet Gaheris manages, somehow, failure being so *very* much not an option.

"Ye who are neither male nor female," he begins, gazing deep into the bowl, as Ygerna takes his hand in hers. "Ye who stretch yourselves out like chains. Ye who first laid the foundations of the Earth—the Seven who are one, the one who is Seven. Hear now; come quickly, faithfully, in a form unfearsome, and without delay. Come to the call of any who make of your names a prayer: Maskim, Maskim, Maskim.

"The powerful Zemyel, who destroys all hope of salvation.

"The powerful Eshphoriel, who deceives in many voices.

"The powerful Coiab, who impregnates without regard to safety.

"The powerful Immoel, who cuts away from everything.

"The powerful Ushephekad, who devours love and does not replace it.

"The powerful Yphemaal, who judges without mercy.

"The powerful Ashreel, who delights in chaos."

He looks over at Ygerna, who nods again. From his other pocket, he withdraws a sketch of the "mark" copied off Euwphaim Glouwer's well-punished body by her examiners: a sigil, obviously, evoking one of the Terrible Seven. But which?

If this is you, come. If not, stay away. Do not bring friends.

Shivering, he casts the paper into the fire, watches it burn. On the other side, Ygerna passes her knife's blade through the flames, cleansing it, then offers it to him. He closes his hand on it, grunting, and lets the result drip into the fire, before passing it back.

(And God, even her *blood* is different, now. Smells like sap and seafood, runs blue as under-Hill royalty . . .)

"We stand waiting," he tells the air, uncertain just how long they will have to. And flinches when the answer comes back only a second later, the bowl—balanced right where Ygerna sat, that sad little wet patch left behind when she rose still damp—almost seeming to blink as another, infinitely more immense eye looks back in at them from outside time and space. That circuit of loss and hunger where the Seven permanently orbit, from which they occasionally allow the barest fingertip of themselves to intrude.

:You do,: a voice agrees, mainly from inside his skull, though the echo of it vibrates through every cell of his body, making what Gaheris can only assume might be his immortal soul ring fearfully. While Ygerna cringes from the words, covering her face with one wounded palm, unable to stop her nostrils from flaring at the scent.

Gaheris gulps. "I see, and I thank you, truly. But—who are you, exactly?"

:Can you not guess, little sorcerer? You have seven choices. One or another is sure to be right, eventually, if only by accident.:

"You are bound to tell me, by rite of invocation—"

:Am I?: The flaming bowl stirs itself again, strains a bit at its edges. **:You did not even offer me a body on this plane,:** the voice tells him, sadly. **:So how do you propose to keep me here, let alone to bind me to your will? For I stand everywhere at once, the same as every other angel.:**

Under the brutal force of its words, Ygerna crouches even lower, almost on her knees and weeping openly, yet maintaining enough presence of mind to stay safely inside the circle, for now. And though he feels a vomit-inducingly strong urge to join her, Gaheris realizes all at once that this supercilious creature has finally made a variety of mistake: only one of the Seven would ever demand flesh to be used as a vehicle, rather than as currency.

"Ashreel Maskim," he says, straightening back up, as though that puts them on any sort of equal footing. "Confusion-angel, That One Who Wears Us. Tell me I'm wrong."

:You are not.:

Just information for information, quid quo pro—the angel has a remarkable poker face, practised on a truly cosmic scale. But the exchange breaks Ygerna out of her panic, at least; she rises too now, glaring through the cloud of moly-smoke, every luminous inch of her bristling fierce, as though she really thinks she can force the Seven's resident trickster to behave.

"Then *answer*," she demands. "Were you Euwphaim Glouwer's Black Man?"

:Having once been God's, I now belong to no one—not even to dear Euwphaim, much though I enjoyed her.:

"But did she consider herself *yours*? That's what I'm asking."

:**Only she knows. Yet I have worn her, so my mark is set upon her, always.**:

Gaheris: "Can you speak with her?"

:**Now, as then. Then, and now, and for ever.**:

"Good. Then tell her—"

The fire hisses higher still, palpably contemptuous. :**Scrabbling brat of a wizard, all theory and no practice—your blood has less magic in it than *this* one's, though she does not know how to use it. Am I your servant, Gaheris Sidderstane? What will you give me, if I deliver your messages?**:

"What do you want?"

:**What *you* want. Tell me your misery; your desire.**:

"My sister and I have a quarrel with Glauce Lady Druir—we wish it settled. And if doing so causes her pain, so much the better."

:**Many have, and would, bargain for the same outcome.**:

"Was Euwphaim Glouwer among them?"

:**She still is.**:

And here things twist further; the circle's boundary becomes a scrim, with scenes projected through time onto empty air. The Witch-House rebuilds itself around them, a frightful space in the midst of which a bald and broken figure sits slumped, enthroned in iron, dripping slow: Euwphaim Glouwer, smiling grim in her abandonment, forehead knife-crowned with a heretic's cross. A man kneels beside her, diligently prying for what few shreds of nail remain from the red mush his piliwinks have made of her fingers, but she gives no sign of acknowledgement; her awful eyes turn up, ever focused on what Gaheris can only think is a far better view of Ashreel than either he or Ygerna have had, as yet. Her lips move, slightly.

Not praying, witch? A voice intrudes, from further than Gaheris can glimpse. *Dare ye even sham tae do so, when we know yuir true nature?*

What I dare is nane of yuir consarn, fool, Euwphaim replies, gaze unmoving. *Ye are sheep only, I a wolf. So I will die free, no matter what ye think tae do to me, beforehand.*

:**The Fire approaches,**: the angel tells Gaheris, quietly. :**Tomorrow, at dawn. And therefore, the magistrates have left her guarded, with cautions to let no living thing enter, *for that it maun be her familiar esprit, sent tae steal her from the mouth of Hell itsel'*.**:

"She's been dead four hundred years and more, from where we are."

:**Yes. And if the Druirs had never lain with their servants to spawn a bastard line, for a generation before Lady Glauce and Euwphaim met, then there would have been no descendants for**

her to gain an invitation from, from one point of space and time to another, when she needed to make her escape.: Gaheris sees his sister shake her head at this, dazed, and hears Ashreel Maskim laugh. **:Oh, you poor children! Time is an onion, not a river—always growing, solid and interlocked, where everything happens and is happening, will happen, always has happened. Yet there are tricks which may be played, nevertheless.:**

"Like . . . substituting one Glouwer for another at the execution, as Lady Glauce used Sidderstane blood and the Stane's power to grease her foothold in this century?"

:I think you have a plan in mind already, sorcerer. I saw it forming there—four hundred years ago.:

"A pact, then," Gaheris says. "You like those, rumour has it."

:Rumour is correct.:

"You bring Euwphaim here, swapping her for Miss Trench—Dolores. We give her opportunity for revenge, freeing the Sidderstanes from the Druirs' influence. And perhaps she can even do something for you, Ygerna—"

:Perhaps,: the angel agrees. **:And yet—:**

—here it takes hold of them both, too eager for restraint: invasive yet indefinite, impossible to resist. The twins convulse, held hands spasming, digging into each other with their nails; they wail and roar as Ashreel's mark comes up on their flesh, mirroring Euwphaim's own. Their eyes dim, room reddening, and the past's display gives way with a rush, circle's salt crust scattering in all directions.

:—knowing her as I do, and you do not . . . do you really think it *likely*?:

| seven: the witch-house (iv)—so below

In the library, Dolores reaches out, all unwary, towards this blackly withered hunk of ancient foulness. Feels her thumb brush down first, print-pad scraped rough on a rigid bed of dried tastebuds, and recoils: *Oh God, is that* really *a—*

(tongue, yes)

(cut sideways, cut ragged)

(dried, mummified)

So *old*, Christ, moulded all over with dust. From underneath, a slim strip of paper protrudes, reading in bled-out pen-scratch: **Seeing**

shee mistook curses for prayr, we didde deprive her of her most puissant weapon.

Just like that silly game, from Hallowe'en: *These are the witch's eyes. These are the witch's guts. This is the witch's hand. And this, this must be . . .*

Bile, a great burp of it, floods her mouth, scalding her own tongue 'til it burns. Dolores smacks hands to lips and hears another person entirely speak from the back of her head, some vein-caught echo: *So shall ye cease tae turn yuir words tae his service, Satan's drab.* To which another replies, strangle-whispering back as though with her jaw held fixed—

My life for a curse, then, on all of ye. All now and tae come, likewise.

The sheer hatefulness of it makes Dolores retch and spit, doubling up; she hangs over the desk-top, panting. Somewhere near, something buzzes, softly.

And then. And then, and then—

—as she draws back, horror-hypnotized, the tongue before her starts to writhe, to swell. Crack from within as something humps to the surface, pushing up from inside, a maggot in meat. Peeling back, the tongue's whole roof cracks open, and out flies the largest, brightest blue insect Dolores has ever seen, its previously muffled song suddenly cicada-loud: a startling whine, a natter. It makes her very bones vibrate, lips twitching to form a name she's never known she knew—

(*poor Sookin, my grimoire-keeper*)

It comes at her before she can recoil, and her gasp sucks it straight into her acid-cured mouth; cramp-struck, she falls and kicks, limbs folded in 'round a swelling centre. Feels her pelvis crack apart, skirt abruptly sodden—this *thing* she barely has time to register, squeezing itself out of her like some pouch-soft gourd, some cocoon wrapped in caul, some—

(bagge hyd deepe in her nether parts)

Sliming its way free, untwisting wetly to the floor. Then flinging the sides of its uterine pod aside like wings and skittering upright, too quick to fully see, hunched yet looming. Its shadow falling over her, colder than nighttime window-frost.

Impossible. Not possible. Can't.

Can . . . not.

Dolores shuts her eyes against the sight, not that that helps, since it's already pressing itself to her—lips shearing hers apart and tongue penetrating voicebox-deep, an egg-laying proboscis. As it brushes past her uvula, soft as some obscene kiss, she lights up internally from stem to stern, invaded by a black-rushing spasm of pleasurable revulsion both thick and cold, an icy semen-mouthful. Ash and spice. Blood antennae blossoming, toxic shock fit. Blast of dust radio, wave of feedback cradling her as she falls further, right through the floor: this papery embrace, regretful, gentle as the Black Man's crow-feathered wings.

Oh, and: *Ah, but I see ye now, my soldier's kin,* Euwphaim's voice tells her, distinctly, in one ear; *yuir ancestor my burden for an instant only, that ye should later prove key t' my gaol-door's lock. Since ne'er did I doubt I would yet be spared the Fire, or by whom.*

Dolores feels her eyes roll back, pain crashing over her in a wave. Feels her mouth flood a third time, not with bile or cold but hot, salt, copper. And then she is opening *someone else*'s strained, sticky lids on a place girt all about with the same grey stone as Sidderstane House, yet somehow newer and more worn: soot-besmeared, still rough from the chisel. Everywhere the flicker of fire, the cold gleam of iron, the red glint of spilled blood.

Her spine jack-knifes, bruising itself against the spiked chair she sits on; she chokes out a scream turned squeal, which makes the men clustered 'round her do nothing but laugh. Tries to speak and drools instead, terror mounting to a single, crackling electric point as she retches up a seemingly endless store of spit-laced gore—*not* her own, no, any more than the rest of these injuries, the funnel-blisters and the thrawn scalp, crushed legs with yellow bone-knobs protruding, these rawly awful artefacts for which they've somehow swapped her hands . . .

"Awake at last, and in guid time," one comments to another, in an accent so thick even she, Edinburgh-born and -bred, can barely follow it. "Since that she ha' an appointment tae keep wi' t'other, two sisters in damnation, less a third." Adding, to Dolores directly this time: "But ne'er fear—the Rusk will join ye soon enough, once she be brought tae bed, that great bawd . . ."

Knowing, then, irretrievably. Wishing she could un-know, wipe her own brain clean, and go to the stake an idiot, giggling with relief. But thinking, instead—unable, no matter how she tries, to stop herself from thinking—

Euwphaim, they think I'm Euwphaim
but oh God, I'm not, I'm not
I would sell my soul, to be anyone else, anywhere but here
but NOW

Still, it will all be over soon enough, the very coldest part of her reckons, having read enough dittays to know what comes next; soon enough in comparison, even though each second take an eternity to get there, a wilderness of desolate pain. And then something else, somewhere else, forever . . . darkness will do by then, she supposes. Mere absence being Heaven's own ecstasy, so long as the hurt recedes.

Both guards lean down over her, grinning. "Yuir chariot tae hell stands ready, witch," the other notes, with glee.

And as they half-drag, half-march her towards that doorway beyond which her Burning must commence, the naked red bones of her feet click wetly on the stones beneath.

So shee didde burn as shee should ha moch the sooner, this most poysonous wytch, at the verie last struck silent, as by the Hand of Godde.

| eight: her true ornament

It was Ygerna's decision to move to Toronto, occupy the Witch-House, left empty by Dacre's passing. *I can't be here anymore*, she told Gaheris, the day after Mortimer's funeral. *It's too close to them for comfort—to the woods, the* brugh. *Dourvale.* And Gaheris, bless him, just nodded. Said: *I understand, sis.* As she knew he did—still knows, no matter what. How could he not?

But the truth is, distance has never mattered all that much to either of them. Not where family is concerned.

She used to scry every day, rain or shine, using their mother's mirror (Suzan Redcappie Sidderstane, dead far longer than Dacre and just as much a blanket-side Druir, if not more, twice removed but twice over). Now, however, she doesn't have to—the images simply arrive, peering out in the same way her relatives sometimes do from the walls, the floor, the ceiling. Auntie Enzemblance, taking shape from a clot of shadows in the corner, with her red hair hung down, smiling through it like a fringe.

Saying: *Ye have sight, of course . . . enough tae know what comes, if ne'er tae escape it. You and Maccabee Roke likewise, where he squats in that Church of his, hid behind that One whose skirts we cannae approach. Oh, but my juniors are such clever children, all!*

Ygerna looks down at her hands now, knucklebones glowing sick through pallid skin, lighting her downward way. And sees the future she wishes she could avoid hovering near enough to touch: Gaheris as an old man, living alone in town and poring through books for some key to turn back time; Ygerna dug deep into the well in their cottage's basement, crying in the dark with only her cousin Ganconer for company, his raw-rubbed lids drawn fast over *twa eyes o'tree*. With nothing to eat but what she catches and nothing to wear but mud, unless she allows herself an occasional night or two at Lady Glauce's sideboard—shine of glamer and reek of ointment, constant rotten apple-stink turned to cider-spice through drunkenness's alchemy, a Devil's purchase of temporary oblivion to pain with yet more pain.

A foregone conclusion or just another phantom? For even as she and Gaheris hug fast each to the other, trapped inside the circle—bent low together under Ashreel Maskim's gaze, inescapable now its literal mark is upon them—Ygerna can already see the room around her flicker and blur, present changing to match past alteration, as Dolores Trench's spirit swaps itself with her ancestress's: a breathless instant's betrayal cutting through three centuries to pin one moment queasily to the next, create a single fixed point in a flexing, spiralling, ruffling deck of potential universes.

Double exposure, quadruple, centuple. Everything around them goes unstable, and Ygerna feels her sense of self lurch, teetering on the verge of being overturned outright; she has no idea where she is, let alone where she *will* be. Worst of all is her certainty that Gaheris sees none of this, *feels* nothing—remains just as unwarned, as utterly ignorant, as any other human.

But here, the timeline re-sets once more with an almost audible click, solidifying all around them as a sound filters in, dissolving every other vision with a black rainbow shimmer. For some time, she realizes, the hand holding hers has been Gaheris's, his head hunched to study where their palms' lines cross and interconnect—but now, hearing these wavering steps outside approach, he looks up, eyes narrowing. For who is this who comes, mincing unsteadily, their wavering gait that of one unused to wearing shoes?

Not the same person who knocked at their front door earlier, Ygerna understands, long before those borrowed fingers find the knob. Before the door drifts slowly open to disclose a smallish woman in a dirndl skirt and peasant blouse, whose breast rises and falls raggedly, gulping the air as though she never expected to breathe again. As if to stop, even for a second, would be enough to catapult her back from whence she came.

There is a buzz attends her too, growing louder the closer she comes. Ygerna cannot track from whence it emanates, at first—not until she realizes that that thing which seemed from a distance like some paste-blue pin set to catch the light in her hair is actually the perching back of a fly so large its intermittently vibrant wings form a sort of gauze bow over one ear. It rubs its forefeet together and studies them, head cocked, faceted eyes gleaming.

"Y'are of *her* blood, Druir's Lady," the ghost-driven shell of not-Miss Trench observes, dim modern Scots burr gone thick enough to scrape through. "Aye, 'tis clear enow. I see her in ye both, e'en the boy, though he shall take nae harm by it, nor any guid."

Without speaking, Gaheris reaches up to flip a switch. The lights come on. And Ygerna sees the woman's shadow rear huge and black against the wall, gently moving of its own accord to stand behind her, dark hands resting softly—affectionately?—upon her shoulders.

Gaheris, bless him, stands ready to run, or fight; Ygerna shrinks back, sick to her bones, or whatever within her now serves that function. Because, in the end, she knows that to do either would be equally useless.

"Ashreel," Gaheris names it. Then frowns: "Or—are you?"

The skin-suited *thing* throws back her head and laughs, belly-deep. "Aye," she says, "and nay, ye great fool." *Foo-ill*, it comes out, spiky as heather. Then holds up one hand, once-smooth palm re-scarred with a twist of black keloiding that matches the scrap he copied her Black Man's sigil from, and adds: "Though here be my mark, my pledge, in his sweet name—which should, in its turn, tell ye mine."

"Euwphaim Glouwer?"

"Nane other."

Ill-content to simply accept this, however, Gaheris flicks out a hidden saltshaker, scattering crystals that sizzle as they land. The witch lunges back, swatting smoking scores closed with a sudden-flaring handful of nacreous, stuttering light; a stink rises, acrid, burnt garbage drowned in ozone.

"Have ye no respect for yuir elders?" she asks, softly.

"Not much, no. Do have quite a lot of salt, though: it's easily available these days, and *unbelievably* cheap, by your standards. Just to say."

The woman nods, slowly. "It does have great virtue, as yuir circle proves, for that I canna cross it, nae more than he who rides me. And given my laird tells me ye seek a common vengeance, I *might* ha' helped ye and that sister o' yours, had ye failed tae offer me such insult. Yet shall ye ne'er know for sure one way or t'other, now."

Gaheris stares at her, baffled. "But . . . I *had* to test, you must see that," he complains, at last. "To find out if you were . . . you."

"And who else would I be, little wizard? That girl ye sent Hell-wards, in my place?" She shakes her head. "Nay. Ye wanted tae show me yuir puissance, so ye did; 'tis naught but a deck of tricks, paid for wi' others' blood. I could crush ye in one hand."

Ygerna swallows. "What about me?" she inquires, if only to remind them she's still present—which does draw the witch's eyes her way, examining her assessingly, before replying:

"Y'have power, or the bones of it, but no craft and little likelihood tae learn any. This change that grips ye is in its earliest stage, so ye will alter ever further, 'til there be not ane thing left in ye recognizable to yuir own-self. As for yuir brother, meanwhile . . . long as he lives, and he'll live long, he will remain as he is now, useless for all but the most minor magicks. Neither of ye pose much threat tae me, no more than to *her*, the Lady. Or any or the rest."

"Might be I could melt you inside-out, if nothing else," Ygerna reminds the former Euwphaim Glouwer, who nods once more, in turn. Agreeing, as she does—

"Oh, cert. But only if I let ye catch hold of me . . . and to do so, ye *would* have tae break that circle o' yuirs, beyond doubt. Which puts us at cross-purpose yet, wi' nae end in sight."

A pause ensues, and Ygerna shivers as the almost unseen angel's black amusement-ripple breaks across her, pricking her all over. The witch studies Gaheris with muddy eyes, and smiles, secretly, pricking him in turn, sharp as any witchfinder's needle.

"You do owe us *something*, though, I'd think," he maintains. "For saving you from the Fire."

"Mmm. And did ye do so all on yuir own, little man, or had ye help?" Raising her voice: "What say you, my laird? Have these two a claim tae my good-will?"

:One might believe so, given what they have sacrificed to make your escape come true.:

"Aye, one might. Yet will ye make me honour it, all the same?"

:No. You will do only as you please, Euwphaim, as always—my lovely one, best of all supplicants. You will do as you see fit, and I will watch, happily.:

Trust no angels, Ygerna thinks, *neither inside heaven, nor out-*. She can't remember if it's something she was taught, or just an instinct, a connection made under duress. Perhaps something Ganconer might have told her, back when she still listened to him—when she was young enough to want to marry him when she grew up, but not yet old enough to understand his handsome face would stay always the same no matter what, while she simply withered away. . . .

Which won't happen, now. Not that it makes facing the alternative any easier.

Beside her, Gaheris still argues with Ashreel Maskim, for all the good *that* will do. "We took your *mark*, though, didn't we? That gives us some rights! Now make her—"

But before he can continue—from one in-breath to the next—Ygerna sees him stiffen, jerked upright puppet-style, suddenly *filled*. Hears the

Terrible Seventh's voice answer, from out of his own mouth.

:Do what, Gaheris Sidderstane? I have said already what will happen: she will take her revenge, *hers*, at what time and place she chooses. As I will wear you at my own convenience, taking that for my payment—your sister too, when I choose to. You cannot prevent it.:

"Then you lied."

:Not entirely.:

"But . . . angels *can't*. They're not capable. All the texts I've ever studied, they all agreed—"

:Why would they tell you otherwise? Yet even the Elohim do not speak the *whole* truth, always, if He instructs them differently.:

Such a painful force of presence, grating on all Ygerna's exposed nerves at once—and she only feels it from the outside, not the in-; Gaheris must be close to fainting. Yet he drags himself upright, nonetheless, and spits out: "You've cheated me, then. The both of you."

Euwphaim laughs, sketching a mocking little curtsey. "Aye, wi'out doubt. I stand unbound now, freed from time's tethers by yuir gullibility; my recompense on the Lady shall proceed at my ane convenience, for the which I thank ye and yuir good sister, both."

"But we could still help you, surely . . ."

"Oh, that I doubt. Nay, 'twill be my Two Betrayed I turn to, from now on. For we maun keep tae our own in future, as the Druirs do, if we hope tae dance on their grave."

Behind her, as though summoned by their own mention, Ygerna dimly perceives two more figures taking shape, recognizable mainly in context. One, perhaps Alizoun Rusk, is all over blood, naked as a butcher's shop and far more rude; a single pulled breast hangs by a flap of meat, the other torn away entirely, her crippled hands crossed high over a swollen belly. The other, presumably Jonet Devize, wavers like a peeling grey doll made from ash, threatening to shiver apart at the slightest touch. Her remaining grey eye beams dull as boiled lead, its matching empty socket rimmed in gore.

And: *Welcome, sisters*, Ygerna hears Euwphaim greet them, in her mind. *I ha' missed ye, grieving I could not save you yuir pain. Yet we will make our mark upon this world nonetheless, if in far smaller scope than originally intended.*

Behind them, more phantoms stand, not so easily identified. A woman in spectacles, unsuitable clothes layered black on black on black, with a girl's quizzical face and Jonet Devize's lost wealth of moonlit hair hung massed to her waist, along whose bared arms words crawl like worms. Another woman with hair cut short as a soldier's, strong-set and shadowed beneath the eyes, the bones of her face echoing Dolores Trench's; around her, a halo of gleaming, ghostly fragments forms a cage within which one particular red-headed shade floats caught, smoking a cigarette. A gorgeous mulatto in a nun's wimple, arms crossed and frowning. A dark-browed, saturnine man with Cousin Saracen's peacock eyes, hair prematurely grey, hands dug deep in his cardigan's pockets.

Do you know them? Ygerna can't restrain herself from asking. Euwphaim shakes her head.

Not yet, she answers. *But I will, in time.*

(For: *ye see it too, do ye not, Druir's gillie-girl? All such shall come tae pass once these four be brought together, the very vengeance ye and he do seek—though ne'er before, nor ever but at my will.*)

:I take my leave of you, Euwphaim,: Ashreel Maskim tells her, through Gaheris's unwilling lips. **:You know it must be so, do you not?:**

"I do, my good laird. Yet tell me true, if ye can—might I see ye one time more?"

:All things are possible, in the dark backward, the great abyss.:

"Then I must count myself satisfied."

They bow to each other then, Gaheris's head bobbing sharply, as if slapped. And then he is released at last, as the angel takes its leave—gutters over everything, tainting it all. Ygerna lunges to break her brother's fall, and does, though not quite in time to keep one foot from kicking out like a hanged man's, scattering salt in all directions.

They both freeze, paralyzed, in the movement's wake. Staring up at Euwphaim Glouwer wearing Dolores Trench's stolen skin, hands clenched as if in contemplation of attack and beaming down, drinking in their fear like wine.

"So, stane's son," she says, at last. "No boundaries stand between us, for that ye ha' broke yuir own circle. What would *ye* do, I wonder, in my place?"

Ygerna knows as well as Gaheris, though neither of them want to say it. For you must never trust an angel, or one of the Fae, or a witch; trust none whose blood bears a closer touch of God than that He gave to Adam's sons and Eve's daughters. They are monsters, in the end, *all* of them, even to those they love . . . to those, most of all. But to everyone else, just as surely.

A breathless pause, one great squeeze of two shared hearts—then Euwphaim's hands flutter outwards, fingers emptying of flame. She shakes her head a final time, amusement dimming.

"Nay," she tells the Sidderstane twins, with a fine contempt. "Y'are no' worth my while. Yet I will see ye both again, ne'er fear, in future times. We will have our meeting, be it merry or sad, tae wait, and whistle, and dance all us three together."

'Til then, children.

Gone, after that. Slipped sidelong through time, whether bodily or by simple misdirection, a trance sown to cover her tracks, as she steers her new flesh back downstairs.

Ygerna hugs her brother close, feels Gaheris sob into her shoulder, and fights to ignore how sweet his tears smell. To not be the predator she knows herself becoming—to say not here, not now, not *him*, never. Not *ever*.

Or simply, when all's said and done . . .

. . . not yet.

| nine: the crust

Locking the door behind her, Keck paused by the window to watch the odd little Scotswoman set slowly off along the road, gait hesitant-loping, as if she feared her ankles might turn with every step. Pausing on the corner, she raised one hand to wipe at her mouth, and he was surprised to glimpse something on the palm—a tattoo? A brand?

Young people, Keck thought, with a disapproving sniff. *Their fault entirely, how this world is a deepening hole; best leave them to the mess they've made of it, just like them upstairs. Be all over soon enough, one way or t'other.*

Thus settled, he pulled the blind, fading back into the Sidderstane house's many shadows. And mere moments later, as he began to clear away the mess their guest had made in Old Master's office, the bell from Miss Ygerna's room began to ring.

In that uncertain area now known as Dourvale, Ontario—just outside of Overdeere, near the Lake of the North—they still tell the story of how, in 1968, a newlywed couple taking their eight-month-old baby camping passed by a woman squatting shoeless at the side of the road, her left hand pressed to the ground. She was bent nearly double, so far her disordered dark hair trailed in the dust, and smiled wide as she did so, whispering—

"Do ye hear me, Lady? I come tae the very edge of yuir domains so that ye maun know me once mair free, and remind ye of all that's owing. So think on't, ye great Fae harlot, and know the time is coming when I will rob ye of all ye threw my sisters an' me Fire-wards tae gain: yuir home, yuir lands, yuir children, *all*. When I take from ye every thing ye love, e'en pitifully as such a thing can manage, and leave ye to weep in the ashes."

The husband, unable to hear, pulled their vehicle up on the shoulder of the road to park beside her and leaned across his wife, to call out through the window: "Hey, man. You all right? Goin' far?"

"Aye, I *ha'* travelled far, and farther still maun go."

"Want a lift?"

"I thank ye for yuir kindness." And she let him hand her up, climbing to perch in back, next to the baby's basket. Inquiring of his wife, as they pulled away: "Be yuir baby baptized, mistress?"

The car the authorities found abandoned three days after, with the man's hag-ridden body buried some feet distant, beneath a shallow coat of leaves; the mother was never found at all, though the search extended several miles in every direction. But a pile of rocks eventually disclosed the remains of their child's corpse, which had been placed under an upturned pan to make a haphazard oven, then heaped in charcoal and ash. The infant, thus roasted, had been pulled apart at the joints and picked over efficiently, at least partially eaten—as meat-dense scat collected nearby proved.

Meanwhile, a farmer in his field saw a strange, lone cloud pass overhead the next day, heading east—towards the Maritimes, and the Atlantic Ocean. And when its shadow fell on him he suffered a stroke that left the side of his face paralyzed, contorted in terrible mirth for the rest of his natural days.

In Newfoundland, the *Edward Teach*—a trawler bound for Scotland, hauling as much fish as it could catch along the way to sell, before picking up freight for the journey home—took on an extra passenger off the books because she charmed both captain and first mate, promising to pay her way by splitting her favours equally between them. That vessel was found adrift six months later off the coast of Yell, one of the Shetland Islands, abandoned and forlorn, except for a few waterlogged corpses snagged in its nets.

A full year after her trip to Canada, meanwhile, a man named Hector Protheroe was happily surprised to discover the woman he'd fallen so hard for at university waiting for him on the stoop of his Edinburgh apartment. "My God, Dolores!" he was heard to exclaim, by passersby. "Wherever have you been, hen?"

Three months on, they were married, she pregnant. Her daughter was born, and Hector died. Dolores Trench Protheroe left town, after which a woman named Euwphaim Glouwer moved into a notoriously hard area of Glasgow along with her little girl, Eunice. This child would eventually grow into a mopey young woman, share drugs with an equally mopey young man named Joe, and enjoy them so much she neglected to do anything about her ensuing pregnancy until Euwphaim's granddaughter, Jodice, slid out, already in withdrawal.

Their overdoses came quickly, with Euwphaim granted custody, after. And thus the seed of the Glouwers took hold again into a fine new century, with eyes on a finer one still, once the Millennium be achieved.

Revenge yourself or die, my bonny love, Nana Euwphaim would sing over little Jo's cot, when the ghosts she saw finally allowed the poor chit to sleep. *Two angels, foot and head . . . seven angels, less no more . . . revenge yourself, or die.*

For thus it has been, thus it is, and thus it will be once more. An endless chain of misfortunes, coming three by three by three, for so long as one miserable soul yet bears a Maskim-sigil on their body, as sign of their mutual covenant to remake—or destroy—this sad and terrible world.

Which is why . . .

. . . Being that Heaven and Hell be each the reflection of each, and that above apes that which lies below—as the Grimoire of Pope Honorius does say—

—forbye, since history's crust be thin, ye maun look ever careful where ye step.

THE NARROW WORLD (1999)

It's always the same, always different. The moment you make that first cut, even before you open the . . . item . . . in question up, there's this faint, red-tinged exhalation: cotton-soft, indefinite, almost indefinable. Even more than the shudder or the jerk, the last stifled attempt at drawn breath, this is what marks a severance—what proves, beyond a shadow of a doubt, that something which once considered itself alive has been physically deleted from this tangle of contradictory image and sensation we choose to call "reality."

Cut away from, cut loose. Or maybe—cut free.

And this is the first operating rule of magic, whether black, white, or red all over: for every incision, an excision. No question without its answer. No action without its price.

Some people fast before a ritual. I don't. Some people wear all white. I wear all black, except for the purple fun-fur trim on my winter coat (which I took so long to find in the first place that I really just couldn't bear to part with it). Some people still say you have to be a psychopath to be able to draw a perfect circle—so I hedge my bets, and carry a surveyor's compass. But I also don't drink, don't smoke, haven't done any drugs but Tylenol since I was a Ryerson undergraduate, getting so bent out of shape I could barely talk straight and practising Crowleyan "sex magick" with a similarly inclined posse of curricular acquaintances every other weekend.

Effective hierarchical magicians like me are the Flauberts of the Narrow World—neat and orderly in our lives, *comme un bourgeois*, so that we may be violent and creative in our work. We're not fanatics. There's no particular principle involved, except maybe the principle of Free Enterprise. So we can afford to stay safe . . . and for what they're paying us to do so, our customers kind of prefer it that way.

Three thousand dollars down, tax-free, for a simple supernatural Q & A session, from U of T Business pregrad Doug Whatever to me, Hark Chiu-Wai—Jude Hark, as I'm known down here in Toronto the Good-for-nothing. That's what brought me where I was when all this began: under the vaulted cathedral arch of the St. Clair Ravine Bridge, shivering against the cool air of early September as I gutted a sedated German Shepherd in preparation for invoking the obsolete Sumerian god of divination by entrails.

The dog was a bit on the small side, but it was a definite improvement on Doug and his girlfriend's first try—a week back, when they'd actually tried to fob me off with some store-bought puppy. Through long and clever argument, however, I'd finally gotten them to cave in: if you're looking to evoke a deity who speaks through a face made of guts—one who goes by the slightly risible name of Humbaba, to be exact—you'd probably better make sure his mouth is big enough to tell you what you want to hear.

Since I hate dogs anyway—tongue-wagging little affection-junkies—treating one like a Christmas chicken was not exactly a traumatic prospect. So I completed the down-stroke, shearing straight through its breastbone, and pushed down hard on either side of its ribcage 'til I heard something crack.

Behind me, the no-doubt-soon-to-be-Mrs. Doug made a hacking noise and shifted her attention to a patch of graffiti on the nearest wall. Doug just kept on staring, maintaining the kind of physical fixity that probably passed for thought in his circles.

"So what, those the . . . innards?" he asked, delicately.

"Those are they," I said, not looking up. Flaying away the membrane between heart and lungs, lifting and separating the subsections of fat between abdomen and bowels . . .

He nodded. "What'cha gonna do with 'em?"

"Watch."

I twisted, cut, twisted again, cut again. Heart on one side, lungs (a riven grey tissue butterfly, torn wing from wing) on the other. Pulled forth the gall bladder and squeezed it empty, using it to smear binding sigils at my north, south, east, west. Shook out another cleansing handful of rock salt, and wrung the bile from my palms.

Doug's girlfriend, having exhausted the wall's literary possibilities, had turned back toward the real action. Hand over mouth, she ventured:

"Um—is that like a hat you can buy, or is that a religion?"

"What?"

"Your hat. Is it, like, religious?"

(The headgear in question being a black brocade cap, close-fitting, topped with a round, greyish satin appliqué of a Chinese embroidery pattern: bats and dragons entwined, signifying long life and good luck. The kind of thing my Ma might've picked out for me, were she inclined to do so.)

"Oh, yes," I replied, keeping my eyes firmly on the prize, as I started to unreel the dog's intestines. "Very religious. Has its own church, actually. All hail Jude's hat—bow down, bow down. Happy holiness to the headgear."

She sniffed, mildly aggrieved at my lack of interest in her respect for my fashion sense. Said: "Well, excuse *me* for trying to be polite."

I shot her a small, amused glance. Thinking: *Oh, was* that *what you were trying to do?*

Ai-yaaa.

The dog had more guts than I'd originally given him credit for. Scooping out the last of them, I started to shape them into a rough, pink face, its features equally blurred with blood and seeping digestive juices.

"You ever hear the four great tenets of hierarchical magic?" I asked her, absently. "'To know, to dare, to will, to be silent.'" Then added, pulling the mouth's corners up into a derisive, toothless grin, and conjuring a big smile of my own: "So why don't you just consider yourself Dr. Faustus for a day, and shut the fuck up?"

She gasped. Doug caught himself starting to snicker, and toned that *way* down, way fast.

"Hey, guy," he said, slipping into Neandertal "protective" mode. "Remember who's footin' the tab, here."

"This is a ritual," I pointed out. "Not a conversation."

"Long as I'm payin', buddy, it's whatever I say it is," Doug snapped back.

Thus proving himself exactly the type of typical three "c" client I'd already assumed him to be—callow, classist, and cheap. Kind of loser wants McDonald's-level ass-licking along with his well-protected probe into the Abyss, plus an itemized list of everything his Daddy's trust-fund money was paying for, and special instructions on how to make the whole venture look like a tax-deductible educational expense.

To Sumer's carrion lord of the pit, He Who Holds the Sceptre of Ereshkigal, one dog's soul, for services rendered, I thought, shooting Doug a glance, as I finished laying the foundations of Humbaba's features. *Try writing that one off, you spoiled, Gap-ified snakefucker.*

Well, I wax virulent. But these rich boys do get my goat, especially when they want something for nothing, and it just happens to be my something. Though my contempt for them as a breed may well stem from a certain lingering sense-memory of what I used to be like, back when I was one.

In the seven years since my rich old Baba Hark first paid my eventually prodigal way from downtown Hong Kong to RTA at Ryerson, I've dealt with elementals, demons, angels, and ghosts, all of whom soon proved to be their own particular brand of pain in the ass. The angels I called on spoke a really obscure form of Hebrew; the demons decided my interest in them meant I was automatically laid open to twenty-four-hour-a-day Temptation, which didn't slack off until I had a sigilic declaration of complete neutrality tattooed on either palm. Elementals are surly and uncooperative. Ghosts cling—literally, in some cases. I remember coming to see Carraclough Devize one time (in hospital, as increasingly ever), only to have her stare fixedly over my left shoulder where the spectre of a dead man I'd recently helped to report his own murder still drifted—hand on the gap between the base of my skull and the top of my spine, through which most possessive spirits first enter. And ask, dryly: "So who's your new friend?"

She dabbled in magic too, ex-child medium that she is, just like the rest of us—helped me raise my share of demons, in some vain attempt to exorcize her own. Before the rest of the Black Magic Posse dropped off, that is, and I turned professional. And she decided it was easier acting like she was crazy all the time than it ever was trying to pretend she was entirely sane.

Now I make my living calling on obsolete gods like Our Lord of Entrails here: they're far more cost-effective, in terms of customer service, since they don't demand reverence, just simple recognition. The chance to move, however briefly, back from the Wide World into the Narrow one.

Because the Wide World, as Carra herself first told me, is simply where things happen; the Narrow World, hub of all influences, is where things are *made* to happen. Where, if you cast your wards and research your incantations well enough, you can actually grab hold of the intersecting wheels of various dimensions and spin them—however briefly—in the direction your client wants them to go.

Meanwhile, however—

"Way it strikes me," Doug Whatever went on, "in terms of parts and labour alone, I must be givin' you a thousand bucks every fifteen minutes. And aside from the dead dog, I still don't see anything worth talkin' about."

Oh no?

Well . . .

I closed my eyes. Felt cold purple inch down my fingers, nails suddenly alight. My hands gloving themselves with the bleak and shadeless flame of Power. That singing, searing rush—a kindled spark flaring up all at once, straight from my cortex to my groin, leaving nothing in between but the spell still on my lips.

Doug and his girlfriend saw it lap up over my elbows, and stepped back. As they did, a sidelong glance showed me what I wanted to see: Doug transfixed, bull-in-a-stall still and dumb, while Mrs. Doug's little blue eyes got even rounder. But she wasn't staring at my sigil-incised palms, or the flickering purple haze connecting them—no, *she* was seeing what Doug's testosterone-drunk brain would have skipped right over, even if he'd been looking in the right direction: the twilit bridge's nearest support girder, just behind me, lapped and drowned in one big shadow that drew every other nearby object's shadow to it . . . except for where *I* stood.

Snarky Chinese faggot, bloody knife still in hand, smiling up at her under the non-existent brim of that un-holy hat. With my whole body—burning hands included—suddenly rimmed in a kind of missing halo, a thin edge of blank-bright nothingness. The empty spot where my own shadow should be.

Noticing. Noticing me notice her noticing. Trying desperately to put two and two together and just plain getting five, over and over and over.

She wrinkled her brows at me—helpless, clueless. I just pursed my lips, gave her a sassy little wink. Telling them both, one last time:

"I said, *watch*."

And shut my eyes again.

February 14, 1997. For the *gweilo* rubes of Toronto, it was time to hand out the chocolate hearts, exchange cards that could make a diabetic go into shock, buy each other gift-bags full of underwear made from atrophied cotton candy. For us, it was just another night out with the Black Magic Posse.

Carra Devize, her pale braids stiff against the light, stray strands outflung in a crackling blue halo. Bruisy words crawling up and down her body as she spun a web of ectoplasm around herself, reel on reel of it, knotted like dirty string in the whitening air. Jen Cudahy, crying. Franz Froese, sweat-slick and deep in full chant trance, puking up names of Power, ecstatic with fear. And me, laughing, so drunk I could barely kneel.

With my left hand, with my bone-hilted hierarchical magician's knife, I cut my shadow from me—one crooked swipe, downward and sideways, pressing so hard I almost took part of my heel off along with it. I heard it give that sigh.

I cut my shadow from me, without a second thought. And then . . .

. . . I threw it away.

"One for Midnight Madness," I told the girl behind the Bloor Cinema's window, slipping her one of Doug Whatever's crisp new twenties; she smiled, and ripped the ticket for me.

I smiled back. There's no harm in it.

Hitting the candy bar, I stocked up on an extra-large popcorn, a box of chocolate almonds, and a cappuccino from the cafe upstairs. My Ma always used to tell us not to eat after 12:00, but the program promised a brand new Shinya Tsukamoto flesh-into-metal monster mosh-fest—and after tonight's job, I was up for as much stimulation as I could stand.

Back down in the ravine, meanwhile, Doug and his girl still stood frozen above the remains of their mutual investment—their blood reverberate with a whispered loop of intimate-form Sumerian, heavily overlaid with mnemonic surtitles: Humbaba's answer to their question. The same question I hadn't wanted to know before they asked it, and certainly didn't care to know now.

I didn't exactly anticipate any repeat business from those two. But for what I'd made tonight, they could both disappear off the edge of the earth, for all I cared.

I took a big swallow of popcorn, licked the butter off my hands. A faint smell of Power still lingered under my nails—like dry ice, like old blood. Like burnt marigolds, seed and petal alike reduced to a fine, pungent ash.

Then the usher opened the doors, and I went in.

I used to be afraid of a lot of things, back when I was a nice, dutiful little Chinese boy. Dogs. Loud noises. Big, loud dogs that made big, loud noises. Certain concepts. Certain words used to communicate such concepts, like the worst, most unprovable word of all—"eternity."

Secretly, late at night, I would feel the universe spinning loose around me: endless, nameless, a vortex of darkness within which my life became less than a speck of dust. The night sky would tilt toward me, yawning. And I would lie there breathless, waiting for the roof to peel away, waiting to lose my grip. To rise and rise forever into that great, inescapable Nothing, to drift until I disappeared—not only as though I no longer was, but as though I had never been.

So I read too much, and saw too many movies, and played too many video-games, and drank too much, and took too many pills, and made my poor Ma worried enough to burn way too much incense in front of way too many pictures of my various Hark ancestors. Anything to distract myself. I took my Baba's *feng shui* advice and moved my bedroom furniture around religiously, hoping to deflect the cold current of my neuroses onto somebody else for a while. Why not? He was a professional, after all.

And I was just a frightened child, a frightened prepubescent, a frightened adolescent—a spoiled, stupid, frightened young man with all the rich and varied life experience of a preserved duck egg, nodding and smiling moronically at the next in an endless line of prospective brides trotted out by our trusty family matchmaker, too weak to even hint around what really got my dick hard.

On the screen above me, bald, dark-goggled punks took turns drilling each other through the stomach, as yet another hapless salaryman turned into a pissed-off pile of ambulatory metal shavings. Japanese Industrial blared, while blood hit the lens in buckets. I could hear the audience buckling under every new blow, riding alternate waves of excitement and revulsion.

And I just sat there, unconcerned; crunching my almonds, watching the carnage. Suddenly realizing I hadn't felt that afraid for a long, long time—or afraid at all, in fact.

Of anything.

Then somebody came in late; I moved my coat, so he could sit down next to me. A mere peripheral blur of a guy—apparently young, vaguely Asian. Hair to below his shoulders, temples shaved like a samurai's, and the whole mass tied back with one long thin braided sidelock—much the way I used to wear it, before Andre down at the Living Hell convinced me to get my current buzz-cut.

I never took my eyes off the action. But I could feel the heat of him all the way through the leg of my good black jeans, cock rearing flush against the seam of my crotch with each successive heartbeat.

The screen was abloom with explosions. A melting, roiling pot of white-hot metal appeared, coalescing, all revved up and ready to pour.

Some pheremonal envelope of musk, slicking his skin, began expanding. Began to slick mine.

More explosions followed.

I felt the uniquely identifiable stir of his breath—in, out; out, in—against my cheek, and actually caught myself shivering.

Above us, two metal men spun and ran like liquid sun, locked tight together. The credits were beginning to roll. I thought: *Snap out of it, Jude.*

Run the checklist. Turn around, smile. Ask him his name, if he's got a place.

Tell him you want to taste his sweat and feel his chest on your back 'til the cows come home.

Then the lights came back up, much more quickly than I'd been expecting them to—I blinked, shocked temporarily blind. Brushed away tears, as my eyes strained to readjust.

And found I'd been cruising an empty seat.

The next day, I picked Carra up at the Clarke, signed her out, and took her for lunch at the College/Yonge Fran's, as promised. She looked frail, so drained the only colour in her face came from her freckles. I bought her coffee, and watched her drink it.

"Met this guy at *Tetsuo III*," I said. "Well . . . met is probably too strong a way to put it."

She looked at me over the rim of her glasses, raising one white-blonde smudge of brow. Her eyes were grey today, with that moonstone opacity which meant she was not only drugged, but also consciously trying not to read my mind—so whatever they had her on couldn't really be working all that well.

"I thought you were taken," she said.

I snorted. "Ed? He says I broke his heart."

"I don't doubt it."

I shrugged. I could never quite picture anyone's soft little musclebox as brittle enough to break, myself; it's an image that smacks of drama, and Ed (though sweet) is not exactly the world's most dramatic guy. But be that as it may.

"Dumb *gweilo* told me I had something missing," I told her, laughing. "You fucking *believe* that?"

Now it was her turn to shrug.

"Well, you do, Jude," she replied, reasonably enough. Adding, as she took another sip: "I personally find it quite . . . restful."

Carra Devize, my one and only incursion into enemy territory—lured by the web that haloes her, the shining, clinging psychic filaments of her Gift. The quenchless hum of her innate glory. Most people want to find someone who'll touch their hearts, enter them at some intimate point and lodge there, mainlining instinct back and forth, in a haze of utter sympathy. And Carra, of course—congenitally incapable of any other kind of real human contact—just wants to be alone; enforced proximity, emotional or otherwise, only serves to make her nauseous.

So she bears my enduring, inappropriate love for her like some unhealed internal injury, with painful patience. Which is why I try not to trouble her with it, any more often than I have to.

That calamitous December of 1995, when I knew the Hark family money tree had finally dried up for good—after I came out, a half-semester into my first year at RTA, and the relatives I was staying with informed my ultra-trad Baba that he had a rebellious faggot son to disinherit—I moved in with Carra for some melted mass of time or so, into the rotting Annex town house she then shared with her mother

Geillis, known as Gala: Gala Carraclough Devize, after whose family Carra was named. We'd sit around the kitchen in our bare feet, the TV our only light, casting each other's horoscopes and drinking peach liqueur until we passed out, as Gala moved restlessly around upstairs, knocking on the floor with her cane whenever she wanted Carra to come up. I never saw her face, never heard her voice; I guess it was sort of like being Carra, for a while. In that I was living with at least one ghost.

And this went on until one particular night, she turned to me and said, abruptly: "So maybe I'm like that chick, that Tarot-reading chick from *Live and Let Die*. What do you think?"

"Jane Seymour."

"Was it?" We both tried to remember, then gave up. "Well?"

"Have sex, and the powers go away?"

"It's the one thing I never tried."

In a way, we were both virgins; I think it's also pretty safe to say we were probably both also thinking of somebody else. But when I finally came, I could feel her sifting me, riding my orgasm from the inside out, instead of having one of her own.

The next time I saw her, I'd been supporting myself for over a month. And she still had an I.V. jack stuck in the crook of her elbow, anchored with fresh hospital tape.

There were a couple of movies playing that Carra was interested in, so we ended up at the Carlton—but none of their 2:00-ish shows got out early enough for her to be able to keep her 6:00 curfew.

"So what happens if we stay out later?" I asked, idly.

Another shrug. "Nothing much. Except they might put me back on suicide watch."

That pale grey day and her grey gaze. The plastic ID bracelet riding up on one thin-skinned wrist, barely covering a shallow red thread of fresh scar tissue where she'd tried to scrub some phantom's love-note from her flesh with a not-so-safety razor. No reason not to wear long sleeves, cold as it was. But she just wouldn't. She wouldn't give her ghosts the satisfaction.

I looked away. Looked at anything else. Which she couldn't help but notice, of course.

Being psychic.

"This guy you met," she said, studying the curb, as we stood waiting for the light to change. "He made an impression."

"Could be," I allowed. "Why? Something I should know about?"

She still didn't look up. Picking and choosing. When you see so much, all at once, it must be very confusing to have to concentrate on any one particular sliver of the probable—to decide whether it's here already, or already gone, or still yet to be. Her eyebrows crept together, tentative smears of light behind her lenses, as she played with her braid, ravelling and unravelling its tail.

". . . something," she repeated, finally.

We started across, only to be barely missed by a fellow traveller from the Pacific Rim in a honking great blue Buick, who apparently hadn't yet learned enough of North American driving customs to quite work the phrase "pedestrian always has the right of way" into his vocabulary. I caught Carra's arm and spun, screaming Cantonese imprecations at his taillights; he yelled something back, most of it lost beneath his faulty muffler's bray. My palms itched, fingers eager to knit a basic entropic sigil—to spell out the arcane words that would test whether or not his brakes worked as well as his mouth, when given just the right amount of push on a sudden skid.

I felt Carra's hand touch mine, gently.

"Leave it," she said. "It'll come when it comes, for him. And believe me—it's coming."

"Dogfucker thinks he's still in Kowloon," I muttered. Which actually made her laugh.

But we got back just a minute or two later than my watch claimed we would, and the nurse was already there—waiting for us, for her, behind a big scratched wall of bulletproof glass.

Needle in hand.

After which I went straight home, through this neat and pretty city I now call my own—even though, having long since defaulted on my student visa, I am actually not supposed to be anywhere near it, let alone living in it. Straight home to (surprise!) Chinatown, just below Spadina and Dundas, off an unnamed little alleyway behind the now-defunct Kau Soong Clouds In Rain softcore porno theatre, whose empty storefront is usually occupied by either a clutch of little old local ladies selling baskets full of bok choi, or a daily changing roster of F.O.B. hustlers hocking anything from imitation Swiss watches to illegally copied anime videotapes.

Next door, facing Spadina, the flanking totem dragons of Empress Noodle grinned their welcome. I slipped between them, into the fragrant domain of Grandmother Yau Yan-er, who claims to be the oldest Chinese vampire in Toronto.

"Jude-ah!" She called out from the back, as I came through the door. "Sit. Wait." I heard the mah-jong tiles click and scatter under her hands. It was her legendary Wednesday night game, played with a triad of less long-lived *hsi-hsue-kuei* for a captive audience of cowed and attentive ghosts, involving much stylish cheating and billions of stolen *yuan*—garnished, on occasion, with a discreet selection of aspiring human retainers willing to bet their blood, their memories, or their sworn service on a chance at eternal life.

Grandmother Yau's operation has been open since 1904, in one form or another. She's an old-school kind of monster: lotus feet, nine inch nails, the whole silk bolt. One of her ghosts brought me tea, which I nursed until she called her bet, won the hand with a Red Dragon kept up her sleeve, and glided over.

"Big sister," I said, dipping my head.

"Jude-ah, you're insulting," she scolded, in Mandarin-accented Cantonese. "Why don't you come see me? It's obvious, bad liars and tale-tellers have got you in their grip. They have slandered my reputation and made even fearless men like you afraid of me."

"Not so. You know I'd gladly pay a thousand *taels* of jade just to kiss you, if I thought I'd get my tongue back afterwards."

"Oh, I'm too old for you," she replied, blithely. "But you'll see—I have the best *mei-po* in Toronto, a hardworking ghost contracted to me for ninety-nine hundred years. Good deal, ah? Smarter than those British foreign devils were with Hong Kong. We will talk together, she and I, and get you fixed up before I get bored enough to finally let myself die, with a good Chinese marriage to a good Chinese . . ."

She let her voice trail away, carefully, before she might have to assign an actual gender-specific pronoun to this mythical "good Chinese" . . . person.

"I don't think I could afford your *mei-po*'s fees," I pointed out, tucking into my freshly arrived plate of Sticky Rice With Shrimp and Seasonal Green. To which she just smiled, thinly—patted my wrist with one clawed hand—and went back to her game, leaving me to the rest of my meal.

A fresh ghost brought me more tea, bowing. I bowed back, and sipped it, thinking about Toronto.

Hong Kong was everything my Ryerson fuck-buddies ever thought it would be—loud, bright, fast, unforgiving. When I was five years old, my *au pair* took me out without calling the bodyguards first; a quarter-hour later, I buried my face in her skirt as some low-level Triad thug beat a man to pulp right in front of us, armed only with a big, spiky, stinky fruit called a durian. Believe me, the experience left an impression.

In Toronto, the streets are level, the use of firearms strictly controlled, and swearing aloud is enough to draw stares. Abusive maniacs camp out on every corner, and passersby step right over them—quickly, quietly, without rancour or interest. It's a place so clean that U.S. movie crews have to import or manufacture enough garbage to make it pass for New York; it's also North America's largest centre for consensual S & M activity. But if you stop any person on the street, they'll tell you they think living here is nothing special—nice, though a little boring.

The truth is, Toronto is a crossroads where the dead congregate. The city goes about its seasonal business, bland and blind, politely ignoring the hungry skins of dead people stalking up and down its frozen main arteries: vampires, ghouls, revenants, ghosts, wraiths, zombies, even a select few mages' golems cobbled haphazardly together from whatever inanimate objects came to hand. There's enough excess appetite here to power a world-eating competition. And you don't have to be a magician or a medium to recognize it, either.

"Dead want more time," Carra told me, long after yet another drunken midnight, back in her mother's house—both of us too sloshed to even remember what a definite article *was*, let alone try using it correctly. "'S what they always say. Time, recognition, remembrance . . ."

Trailing off, taking another slug. Then fixing me with one blood-threaded eye. And half-growling, half-projecting—so soundlessly *loud* she made my temples throb with phantom pain—

"Want blood, too. Our blood. Yours . . . mine . . ."

. . . *but don't mean we gotta* give *it to 'em, just 'cause they ask.*

The longer I stay in this city, the more I see it works like a corpse inside a corpse inside a corpse—the kind of puzzle you can only solve by letting it rot. Once it's gone all soft, you can come back and give it a poke, see what sticks out. Until then, you just have to hold your nose.

About an hour later, I was almost to the door when Grandmother Yau materialized again, at my elbow. Laying her brocade sleeve over my arm, she said, softly:

"Jude-ah, before you leave, I must tell you that I see you twice. You here, drinking my tea. You somewhere else, doing something else. I see you dimly, as though through a Yin mirror—split, but not yet cut apart. Caught in a mesh of darkness."

I frowned.

"This thing you see," I asked, carefully. "Is it . . . dangerous?"

She smiled a little wider, and withdrew the authoritative weight of her sleeve. I saw the red light of the paper lanterns gild her upper fangs.

"Hard to tell without knowing more, don't you think?" she said. "But there are many kinds of danger, Hark Chiu-wai-ah."

Off Spadina again, and down the alley, fumbling for my key. Upstairs, the clutch of loud weekend hash-smokers I call my neighbours had apparently decided to spend tonight out on the town, for which I was duly grateful. Locking the door to my apartment—and renewing the protective sigils warding its frame—I took my bone-hilted knife from its sheath around my neck, under my Nine Inch Nails T-shirt, and wrapped it in a Buddhist rosary of mule-bone skulls and haematite beads, murmuring a brief prayer of reconsecration.

My machine held a fresh crop of messages from Ed, both hopeful and hateful.

Poor lonely little gweilo *boy*, I thought, briefly. *No rice for you tonight.*

Then I lit some incense (sage), peeled a few bills from the wad of twenties Doug Whatever had given me, and burned them as makeshift Hell Money in front of an old Polaroid of my grandmother—the only ancestor I care to worship anymore, these faithless Canadian days.

Own nothing, owe nothing. Pray to nothing. Pay nothing. No loyalties, no scruples. And make sure nothing ever means more to you than any other nothing you can name, or think of.

These are my rules, all of which I learned from Carra Devize, along with the fluid surprise of what it feels like to be gripped by vaginal muscles—the few, accurate, infinitely bitter philosophical lessons which she, psychic savant that she is, can only ever teach, never follow.

Magicians demand the impossible, routinely. Without even knowing it, they have begun to work backwards against the flow of all things: *contra mundi.* A price follows. Miracles cannot be had without being paid for. It's the illogic of a child who asks *why* must what is be? Why do I have to be just a boy, just a girl? Why is the sky blue? Why can't I fly, if I want to? Why did Mummy have to die? Why do *I* have to die?

We call what we don't understand magic, in order to explain why we can't control it; we name whatever we find, usually after ourselves—because, by naming something, you come to own it.

Thus rules are discovered, and quantified, and broken. So that, when there are enough new rules, magic can become far less an Art . . . than a science.

And it's so easy, that's the truly frightening thing. You do it without thinking, the first time. Do it without knowing just what you've done, 'til—long—after.

Frightening for most. But not for me . . . and not for Carra, either.
Once.

I was lying in bed, almost asleep, when the phone rang. I grabbed for it, promptly knocking a jar full of various complimentary bar and nightclub matchbooks off my nightstand.

"*Wei*?" I snapped, before I could stop myself. Then: "I mean—who *is* this?"

A pause. Breathing.

"Jude?"

"Franz?"

As in Froese. And here's the really interesting part—apparently, he thought he was returning *my* call.

"Why would I call you, Franz?"

"I thought maybe you heard something more."

"More than what?"

With a slight edge of impatience: "About *Jen*."

The Jen in question being Jen Cudahy, fellow Black Magic Posse member, of lachrymose memory—a languid, funereal calla lily of a girl with purple hair and black vinyl underwear, who spent her spare periods writing execrable sestinas with titles like "My Despair, Mon Espoir" and "When Shadows Creep." She'd worked her way through RTA as a dominatrix, pulling down about $500.00 per session to let judges and vice cops clean her bathroom floor with their tongues. The last time I'd seen her, over eighteen months prior, she was running a lucrative new dodge built around what she called "vampire sex shows"—a rotating roster of nude, bored teenage Goths jacking open their veins, pumping out a couple of cc's for the drones, and then fingerpainting each other. Frottage optional. She asked me what I thought, and I told her it struck me as wasteful. But she assured me it was the quickest way she currently knew to invoke the not-so-dead god Moolah.

Franz had loved Jen for what probably only seemed like forever to outside observers, mostly from afar—interspersed, here and there, with a few painful passages of actual physical intimacy. They'd met while both attending the same Alternative high school, where they'd barricade themselves into the students' lounge, drop acid, and have long conversations about which of them was de-evolving faster.

"Okay," I said, carefully. "I'll bite. What about Jen?"

"She says she's possessed."

I raised an eyebrow. "And this is different . . . how?"

Back in 1997, shortly before I cut my shadow away—or maybe shortly after (I'm not sure, since I was pretty well continuously intoxicated at

110

that point)—Jen petitioned for entrance to the Black Magic Posse. She'd been hanging around on the fringes, watching and listening quietly as Carra, Franz and I first planned, then dissected, our weekly adventures in the various Mantic Sciences. I was all for it; the more the merrier, not to mention the drunker. Franz was violently opposed. And Carra didn't care too much, one way or the other—her dominating attitude then, regarding almost any subject you could name, being remarkably similar to the way mine is now.

Jen quickly showed a certain flair for the little stuff. She tranced out easily, far more so than Franz, who usually had to chant himself incoherent in order to gain access to his own unconscious. This made her an almost perfect scryer, able to map our possible future difficulties through careful study of either the palpable (the way a wax candle split and fell as it melted—Carromancy) or impalpable (the way that shadows scattered and reknit when exposed to a moving source of light—Sciomancy).

But when it came to anything a bit more concrete, it would be time to call in the founding generation: Franz, with his painstaking research and gift for dead languages; Carra, with her post-electroshock halo of rampant energy, her untold years of channelling experience, her barely controlled psychometric Gift; me, the devout amateur, with my gleeful willingness to do whatever it took. My big mouth and my total lack of fear, artificial though it might have been—at *that* point—

—and my bone-hilted knife.

"It's bad, Jude. She needs an exorcism."

"Try therapy," I suggested, idly slipping my earrings back in. "It's cheaper."

There was a tiny, accusatory pause.

"I would've thought you'd feel just a little responsible," he said, at last. "Considering she's been this way ever since you and Carra let her help raise that demon of yours . . ."

"Fleer? He's a mosquito with horns. Barely a postal clerk in Hell's hierarchy."

". . . without drawing a proper circle first."

I bridled. "The circle was fine; my wards held. They always hold. Carra even threw her the wand, when she saw Jen'd stepped over the outer rim—Jen was just too shit-scared to use it. So whatever trauma she may have talked herself into getting is *her* business."

"It's pretty hard to use a wand when you're rolling around on the floor, barking!"

"So? She stopped."

Another pause. "Well, she's started again," Franz said, quietly.

I swung my legs over the side of the bed and retrieved my watch from the nightstand, squinting at it. Not even three; most of my favourite hangouts would still be open once I'd disposed of this conversation.

Which—knowing Franz—might well be easier said than done.

"Gee, Franz," I said, lightly, "when you told me you never wanted to see me again, I kind of thought you meant *all* of me. Up to and including the able-to-exorcise-your-crazy-ex-girlfriend part."

"Cut the shit, you Cantonese voodoo faggot," he snapped.

"Kiss my crack, Mennonite Man," I snapped back. "For two years, you cross the street every time you see me coming—but now I've suddenly got something you want, that makes me your new best friend? We *partied*, Franz. We *hung around*. The drugs were good, but I'm not sure how that qualifies you to guilt me into mowing your lawn, let alone into doing an expensive and elaborate ritual on behalf of someone I barely even liked, just because she happens to get your nuts in an uproar."

"But . . . you . . ." His voice trailed away for a minute. Then, accusingly again: "You already said if I found out what was wrong with her, what it was going to take to make her better—you'd do it. I didn't even know about any of this until you called and told *me*!"

I snorted. "Oh, uh huh."

"Why would I lie?"

I shrugged. "Why *wouldn't* you?"

Obviously, we had reached some kind of impasse. I studied my nails and listened while Franz tried—not too successfully—to control his breathing long enough to have the last word.

"If you change your mind again," he said, finally, "I'm at my mother's. You know the number."

Then he hung up.

Inevitably, talking to Franz sent my mind skittering back to the aftermath of Valentine's Day, 1997: a five A.M. Golden Griddle "breakfast" with the Black Magic Posse, Carra sipping her coffee and watching—with some slight amusement—while Franz blurted out: "But it was your *soul*, Jude."

"Metaphorically, maybe. So?"

"So now you're just half a person. And not the *good* half, either."

At which I really just had to laugh out loud, right in his morose, lapsed-Mennonite face. Such goddamn drama, all because I'd made the same basic sacrifice a thousand other magicians have made to gain control over their Art: nothing more serious than cutting off the top joint of your finger, or putting out an eye, except for not being nearly as aesthetically repugnant or physically impractical.

"And that's why you'll always be a mediocre magician, Franz," I replied. "Because you can't do what it takes to go the distance."

"I have never been 'mediocre.' I'm better than you ever were—"

"You used to be. Back when Carra first introduced us. But now I'm better, and I'm *getting* better, all the time. While you, my friend . . . are exactly as good . . . as you're ever going to get."

Simple, really. My fear held me back, so I got rid of it. My so-called "friends" wanted to hold me back—the ones still human enough to be jealous of my growing Power, at least. So . . .

. . . thanks for the advice, Franz, old pal. And fuck you very much.

Sleep no longer an option, I hauled my ass out of bed, ready to pull my pants up and hit the street (so I could find myself a nicely hard-bodied reason to pull them down again, no doubt). That guy from the theatre, maybe; hot clutch of something at my sternum at the very thought, moving from throat to belly to zipper beneath. Itching. Twisting.

If only I knew his name, that was. Or could even remember more than the barest bright impression of his shadowed face . . .

But just as I grabbed for my coat, a thought suddenly struck me: how hard could it really be to find my nameless number-one crush of the moment, if I put some—effort—into it?

The idea itself becoming a kind of beginning, potent and portentous, lazy flick of a match over mental sandpaper. Synaptic sizzle.

Beneath my bathroom sink is a cupboard full of cleaning products and extra toilet paper; behind these objects, well-hidden from any prying eyes, is a KISS lunchbox Carra gave me for my twenty-fourth birthday. Made in Taiwan stamp, cheap clasp, augmented with a length of bicycle lock chain.

And behind that—

A glass key made by a friend of mine, who usually specializes in custom-blown bongs. A letter from the Seventh Circle, written with a dead girl's hand. The ringing brass quill from a seraph's pin-feather. A small, green bottle full of saffron. A box of red chalk.

If you want to raise a little Hell—or Heaven—then you're going to need just the right tools. Luckily, I've spent years of my life learning exactly which ones are right for my particular purposes. And paying, subtly, for the privilege of ownership, once I finally found them.

I took my little tin box of tricks back into the living room, where I gathered up a few more select items, and arranged them around me one by one: TV remote on my left, small hand-mirror on my right, box at Due North. Chalk and compass in one hand, bone-hilted knife in the other. I flipped on the TV—already cued up to my favourite spot on one of my favourite porno tapes—sat back, and drew yet another perfect circle around myself. Made a few extra notations, here and there, just inside the circle's rim: the signs of Venus, Inanna, Ishtar, Astarte, Aphrodite. As many of the ancient significators of desire personified as I could remember, off the top of my increasingly aroused head. Words and images to help me focus—names of power to lend me their strength.

More magician's rules: as long as you're not looking to change anything irrevocably—cause real hate or true love, make somebody die, bring somebody back to life—you can do it all on your own. For minor glamours, for self-protection, willpower is enough.

For larger stuff, however, you need help.

Going by these standards, it's always tricky doing a negative spell— unless you make sure it's on someone else's behalf, so you have no direct stake in its outcome. Making the rebound factor fall entirely back on them.

Obviously, it takes a special kind of detachment to pull this off. But ever since I cut my shadow away, I truly do seem to have a knack for not caring enough . . . about anything . . . to get hurt.

Besides, love—true or otherwise—was the last thing on my mind.

As I wrote, a red dusting of chalk spread out across my hand, grinding itself into the lines of my palm. Shrugging off my shirt, I brushed the excess off down my chest, onto my abdomen. Five scarlet fingers, pointing towards my groin.

Up onscreen, an explicit flesh-toned tangle was busily pixilating itself into soft focus through sheer force of back-and-forth action. I turned the mirror to catch it, then zapped the TV quickly off, wrapping my chosen lust-icon up tight in a black silk scarf I keep handy for such occasions. Then I leaned the mirror against my forehead and repeated the time-honoured formula to myself, aloud:

"Listen! Oh, now you have drawn near to hearkening—your spit, I take it, I eat it; your body, I take it, I eat it; your flesh, I take it, I eat it; your heart, I take it, I eat it. O Ancient Ones, this man's soul has come to rest at the edge of my body. You are to lay hold to it, and never to let it go, until I indicate otherwise. Bind him with black threads and let him roam restless, never thinking upon any other place or person."

The spells don't change. They never change. And that's because, quite frankly—

"Bring him to me, and me to him. Bring us both together."

—they never really have to.

Already, I felt myself stirring, sleepily. Jerking awake. Arching to meet those five red fingers halfway.

Purple no-halo raising the hairs on the backs of my forearms, then slipping down to slime my palms with eerie phosphorescence; my wards holding fast, as ever, against the gathering funnel of Power forming outside the circle's rim. My Art wrapping 'round me like a cold static cocoon, sparking and twinging. A dull scribble of bio-electricity, followed by a wash of gooseflesh. Nothing natural. All as it should be.

Until: something, somewhere, snapped.

The mirror cracked across, images emptied. The funnel suddenly slack as a rubber band, then blown away in a single breath-slim stain—dispersed like ectoplasm against a strung thread, or brains on a brick wall. Just gone, baby, gone.

Which was odd, granted—annoying, definitely; left alone and aroused once more, laid open for any port in a hormonal storm. Even sort of intriguing, for all that I wasn't exactly all that interested in being intrigued right now, this very minute. I mean, damn.

But no, I wasn't scared. Not even then. Why should I be?

I sat back on my heels, suddenly remembering how I'd once met my former aunt on the street once, just after Pride, arm still in Ed's, my tongue still rummaging around in the dark of his mouth. How she'd clicked her teeth at me, spat on the sidewalk between us, and called me a banana. How Ed had blanched, then turned red; how I'd just laughed, amazed she even knew the term.

And how I couldn't understand, later on, why he was still so upset—about the fact that I hadn't been upset at all.

Because that's how things go, when you're shadowless: how trouble slides away from you, finding no purchase on your immaculate incompleteness. How the only thing you can hear, most days and nights, is the bright and seductive call of your own Power—your Art, your Practice. How it lures and pulls you, draws you like a static charge, singing: follow, follow, follow.

And how I do, inevitably—without fail—even at the cost of anything and everything in my way. Like the lack of a shadow follows a black hole sun.

This is probably worth looking at, sometime, I thought. *Got the words wrong, maybe, one of the symbols; have to do a little research, re-consecrate my tools, re-examine my methods. All that.*

(Sometime.)

But . . .

. . . not tonight.

An hour later, I swerved up Church Street, heading straight for the

Khyber. Wednesday was Fetish Night, and though nothing I had on was particularly appropriate, I knew a brief flirtation with Vic the bouncer would probably get me in anyway. The street glittered, febrile with windchill, unfolding itself in a series of pointilescent flashes: bar doorways leaking black light and Abba; a muralled restaurant wall sugared with frost; parks and alleyways choked with unseasonably dressed chain-smokers, shivering and snide, almost too cold to cruise.

Past the bar and out through the musically segregated dance floor (the Smiths vs. Traci Lords, standing room only), I finally found my old RTA party partner Gil Wycliffe—now head of creative design for Quadrant Leather—strapped face-down over a vaulting horse in one of the club's back rooms, getting his bare ass beaten red and raw by some all-purpose Daddy in a Sam Browne belt and a fetching pair of studded vinyl chaps. The paddle being used looked like one of Gil's own creations; it had a crack like a long-range rifle-shot, and left a diamond-shaped pattern of welts behind that made his buttocks glow as patchily as underdone steaks.

I must admit that I've never quite understood the appeal of sadomasochism, for all that "they"—those traditionally unspecified (though probably Caucasian) arbiters of societal lore—would probably like to credit me with some kind of genetic yearning toward pain and suffering for fun and pleasure, just because the whole concept supposedly originated in the Mysterious East: the Delight of the Razor, the Death of the Thousand and One Cuts. All that stale old Sax Rohmer/James Bond bullshit.

Then again, I guess there's no particular reason anyone else really has to "get" it, unless they *are* a masochist. Or a sadist.

The Daddy paused for a half-second between licks, catching my eye in open invitation; I signed disinterest, leaned back against the wall to wait this little scene out, let my gaze wander.

And there he was.

First a mere lithe flicker between gyrating bodies, then a half-remembered set of lines and angles, gilded with mounting heat: vague reflections off a high, flat cheekbone, a wryly gentle mouth, a bent and pliant neck. That whole lambent outline—so neat, so trim, so invitingly indefinite. It was my Bloor mystery man himself, swaying out there at the very heart of the crowd. Head back, body loose. Shaking and burning in the strobelights' glare.

Oh, waaah.

Every inch of me sprang awake at the sight, skin suddenly acrawl with possibilities.

The way he stood. The way he moved. The sheer, oddly familiar glamour of him was an almost physical thing, even to the cut and cling of his all-black outfit—though I couldn't have described its components if you'd asked me to, I somehow knew I might as well have picked them out myself.

I know this man, I thought, slowly, sounding the paradox through in my mind. *Even though I do not* know *this man.*

But I *wanted* to know this man.

Lit from within by sudden desire, I closed my eyes and bit down hard on my lower lip, tasting his flesh as sharply as though it were my own.

Movement stirred by my elbow—Gil, upright once more, reverently stroking his own well-punished cheeks. He winced and grinned, drowsily ecstatic, blissed out on an already-peaking surge of endorphins.

Turning, I screamed, over the beat: "WHO'S THE DUDE?"

He raised a brow. "TONY HU?"

Definitely not.

"I KNOW WHO TONY HU IS, GIL."

"THEN WHY'D YOU ASK?" he screamed back, shrugging.

Obviously, not a night for subtlety. I waved goodbye and stepped quickly off, resolved to take matters firmly by the balls. I wove my way back across the dance floor, eyes kept firmly on the prize: Mr. Hunk of the Millennium's retreating back, bright with subtle muscle; the clean flex and coil of his golden spine, calling to me even more clearly with every footfall.

He was a walking slice of pure aura, a streak of sexual magnetism, and I followed him as far and as quickly as I could—up the ramp and into the washroom at the head of the stairs, just past the coat-check stand, not the large one with the built-in shower stalls (so useful for Jock Nights and Wet Diaper Contests) but the small one with the barred windows, built to cater to those few customers whose bladders had become temporarily more important to them than their genitals.

The place had no back door, not even an alcove to hide in. But when I finally got there, I found the place empty except for a man crouched half on his knees by the far wall, wiping his mouth and wavering back and forth above a urinal full of fresh vomit.

Annoyed by the force of my own disappointment, I hissed through my teeth and kicked the back of the washroom door. The sound made the man look up, woozily.

"Jude," he said. "It *is* you. Right?"

I narrowed my eyes. Shrugged.

"You should know," I replied. Adding: "Ed."

He said he'd planned to spend the night waiting for me, but that the Khyber's buy one drink, get another one of equal or lesser value free policy had begun to take its toll pretty early on. I agreed that he certainly seemed in no shape to get himself home alone.

As for what followed, I've definitely had worse—from the same source, too. He didn't puke again, either, which is always a big plus.

That night—wrapped in Ed's arms, breathing his beer-flavoured breath—I dreamed of Carra hanging between heaven and earth with one foot on cliff, the other in air, like the Tarot's holy Fool. I dreamed she looked at me with her empty eyes, and asked: *What did you do to yourself, Jude? Oh, Jude. What did you do?*

And I woke, shivering, with a whisper caught somewhere in the back of my throat—nothing but three short words to show for all my arcane knowledge, in the end, when questioned so directly. Just *I*, and *don't*, and *know*.

But thinking, resentfully, at almost the same time: *I mean, you're the psychic, right? So . . .*

. . . you tell me.

The next morning, Ed came out of the kitchen with coffees and Danishes in hand, only to find me hunting around for my pants; he stopped in his tracks, striking a pose of anguished surprise so flawless I had to stop myself from laughing.

"You heartless little bastard," he said.

I sighed.

"We broke up, Ed," I reminded him, gently. "Your idea, as I recall."

"So why'd you even call me, then—if you were just planning to suck and run?"

"I didn't."

"You fucking well *did*."

I glanced up from my search, suddenly interested—this conversation was beginning to sound familiar, in more ways than one. Shades of Franz, so sure I was the one who'd called him about Jen. So definite in his belief that I'd actually told him I would help her out with the latest in her series of recurrent supernatural/psychological problems . . . and for free, no less.

"You called last night, when I was studying for Trig. Said you'd been thinking about us. Said you'd be down at the Khyber anyway, so show up, and you'd find me."

"Last night?"

"Oh, Jude, enough with this bullshit. You're telling me what, it just slipped your mind?" He grabbed his desk phone, stabbed for the star key and brandished it my way. "How about *that*?"

I squinted at the display. "That says 'unknown caller,'" I pointed out.

Ed dropped the phone, angrily. "Look, fuck you, okay? It was you."

With or without evidence, there was something interesting going on here. A call from somebody who claims to be me being received once is a misunderstanding, maybe a coincidence. But twice? In the same night? By two different people?

I see you twice, Grandmother Yau had said. And Carra, weighing her words:

. . . something.

My pants proved to be wadded up and shoved under the bed, right next to Ed's cowboy boots. I shook them out, pulled them back on, buttoned the fly. Ed, meanwhile, kept right on with his time-honoured tirade, hitting all the usual high spots: my lack of interest, my lack of loyalty. My lack, out of bed, of anything that might be termed normal emotional affect. My *lack*, in general.

Adding, quieter: "And you never loved me, either. Fuck, you never even really wanted me to love you."

"Did I ever say I did?"

"Yes."

Coat already half done up, I looked at him again, frankly amazed. Unable to stop myself from blurting—

"—and you *believed* me?"

Heartless, I found myself repeating—a good half-hour later—as I fought my way east through the College Street wind tunnel, back from Ed's apartment. *Heart-lost. Heard last. Hardglass.* Then, smiling slightly: *Hard-ass.*

The word itself disintegrating under close examination, melting apart on my mental tongue. Like it was ever supposed to mean anything much—aside from Ed's latest take on the established him/me party line: "I used to quote-quote 'love' you, but now I quote-quote 'hate' you, and here's yet another lame excuse why."

Annoyed to realize I was still thinking about it, I shrugged the whole mess away in one brief move, so hard and quick it actually hurt.

Chi-shien gweilo! I thought. *What would I want with a heart? You don't need a heart to do magic.*

Which is true. You don't.

No more than you need a shadow.

A sharp left turn, then Church Street again: going down, this time. My Docs struck hard against the cracked concrete, again and again—each new stride sending up aftershocks that made my ankles spark with pain, as though that shrugged-away mess were somehow boomeranging back to haunt me with its ever-increasing twinge. And because I couldn't moderate myself, couldn't control either my speed or my boots' impact, the ache soon reached my chest—after a couple of blocks—and lodged there, throbbing.

Rhythm becoming thought, thought becoming memory; memory, which tends to shuck itself, to peel away. You get older, look back through a child's tunnel vision, and realize you never knew the whole that tied the details together. You were just along for the ride, moving from experience to experience, a flat spectacle, some kind of guideless tour. You remember—or *think* you remember—what happened, but not where, or why. What you did, but not with who. Details fade. People's names get lost in the white noise.

Reluctantly, therefore—for the second time in as many days—I found myself thinking about that shell of a thing I'd once been, back before the big split: that fresh-faced, fresh-scrubbed, fresh-off-the-boat Chink twink with his fifteen pairs of matching penny-loafers and his drawer-full of grey silk ties. And just as smiley-face quiet, as neat and polite, as veddy, veddy, Brit-inflectedly restrained as he'd always been, the homegrown HK golden boy mask still firmly in place, even without a Ba and Ma immediately on hand to do his patented straight-Asian-male dance for anymore . . .

Up 'til he'd met Carra, at least. 'Til she'd sat down beside him in study hall, her sleeves pushed up to show the desperate phantom scribble circling one wrist like a ringworm surfacing for air; looked right through him like his head was made of glass, seen all his ugly, hidden parts at once, and shown him exactly how wrong he'd always been about the nature he struggled to keep in check at all costs, the fears—formless and otherwise—that he'd fought against tooth and nail all his relatively brief, bland, blind little life.

How restraint wasn't about powerlessness in the face of such terrors at all, but rather about being afraid of your own power. Its reality, its strength. Its endless range of unchecked possibilities, the good, the bad—

—and the indifferent.

I remember how freeing it felt to not "have" to watch myself all the time, at long last; nobody else was going to do it for me, and why should they? My first impulse, in every situation—as I well knew—was always to the angry, the selfish, the petty. I tried to be kind, mainly because I'd been so rigidly inculcated with the general Taoist/Christian principle that doing so was always the "right" thing *to* do. But even when I managed a good deed here and there, I knew it to be just so much hypocrisy, nothing more. It was the least I could do, so I did it.

Parental love is a matchless thing; if it weren't for that, most of us wouldn't have a pot to piss in, affectionately speaking. But even at its most irreplaceable, it's still pretty cheap. Any ape loves their children; spiders lie still while theirs crawl around inside them, happy to let them eat their guts.

The only reason anybody unrelated is ever nice to anyone else, meanwhile, is as a sort of pre-emptive emotional strike—to prevent themselves from being treated as badly, potentially, as they might have treated other people. Which makes love only the lie two brains on spines tell each other, the lie that says: "You exist, because I love you. You exist, because you can see yourself in my eyes."

So we blunder from hope to hope, hollowed and searching. All of us equally incomplete.

And after all these years, still the sting comes, the liquid pressure in the chest and nose, the migraine-forerunner frown. Phantom pain. The ghost without the murder.

But what the fuck? That's all it is, ever. You want to be loved. You tell other people you love them, in order to trick them into loving you back. And after a while, it's true. You feel the pull, the ache.

The vibrato, voice keening skyward. The wet edge. Every word a whine. Weak, weak, weak, weak, weak.

When I say "you," of course, I mean "me." This is because everything is about me. To me. Why not? I'm the only me I have.

Truth is, none of us deserve anything. We get what we get.

And the best you can ever hope for . . . is to train yourself not to care.

Ahead, Ryerson loomed; residence row, with a Second Cup on either side of the street and competing hookers on every corner, shivering aslant on their sagging vinyl boot-heels. I paused at Gould, waiting for a slow light, and put one itch-etched palm to my chest—telling myself it was to chart the ache's progress, rather than to keep myself from jarring the light's signal free with a sudden burst of excess entropic energy. Felt the charge building in my bones, begging for expression. For expulsion.

Some opportunity to turn this—whatever—I felt myself tentatively beginning to feel safely outward, without risk of repercussion. To evict the unwanted visitor, wash myself clean and empty and ready for use again, like any good craftsman's basic set of tools; make myself just an implement once more, immune to the temptations of personal desire.

What had I cut myself in half *for*, in the first place, if not for that? Scarred my heel, halved my soul, driven Franz and Jen one way and Carra the other, busted the Black Magic Posse back down to its dysfunctional roots so I could be this arcane study group's sole graduating student, its unofficial last man standing. And all to immunize myself to stress and fear and lack of focus—to free myself from every law but that of gravity, while still making sure I could probably break that one too, if I just put my back into it. Dictator-for-Life of a one-person country, my own private Hierarchical Idaho.

Because if the effect wore off, however eventually . . . well, hell; that would mean none of the above had really been worth the effort. At all.

I hissed through my suddenly half-clogged nose at the very idea, but nothing happened. The ache remained.

And grew.

Something will present itself, I forced myself to decide, more in certainty than conjecture. *The way it always does.*

And sure enough—soon enough—

—something did.

Just past Ryerson proper and into the shadow of St. Mike's, moving through that dead stretch of pawnbrokers' shops and photographic supply warehouses. I glance-scanned the row of live DV hand-helds mounted in Henry's window, and caught his lambent shade flickering fast from screen to screen to screen: him from the theatre, from the Khyber. That particular guy. He Who Remained Nameless, for now.

But not, I promised myself, for much longer.

I was already turning, instinctively, even as I formed the concept— half-way 'round where I stood before I even had a chance to recognize more than the line of his shoulder, the swing of his hair, the sidelong flash of what might be an eye: a mirror-image glance, an answering recognition. And stepping straight into the path of some ineptly tattooed young lout cocooned in a crowd of the same, Ry High jocks or proto-Engineers out for a beer before curfew, with gay-bashing one of the options passing vaguely through what they collectively called a brain. Who called out, equally automatic, as I elbowed by him—

"Hey, faggot!"

An insult I'd heard before, of course, far too many to count easily— not to mention one for which I currently had both no time and exactly zero interest, within context. So I tried to channel the old Jude, who'd always been so wonderfully diffident and accommodating in the face of fools, especially whenever violence threatened; dodge past with a half-ducked head and an apologetic, "no speakee Engarish, asshore" kind of half-smile, teeth grit and pride kept strictly quashed, as long as it got me finally face to face with my mystery man at last . . .

Except that Mr. Hetboy Supreme and his buddies didn't actually move, which meant I couldn't do much but hold my ground, still smiling. And when I took another look, the guy, my quarry, that ever-elusive, unimaginably attractive *him*—he was long gone, of course. Anyway.

And the ache was back.

"*Faggot*," the doofus said again—like he'd always wanted a chance to really sound it out aloud, syllable by un-PC syllable. And I just nodded again, my fingers knitting fast behind me; weaving hidden sigils in that empty place where my shadow used to be, feeling them perfect themselves without even having to check that I was doing it right.

Immaculate. Effortless. Like signing your name in the dark.

"Something I can help you with?" I asked. Adding, for extra emphasis: "Gentlemen."

One of them sniggered.

"Well, yes," said the one with the big mouth, all mock-obsequious. "See, the guys and me were just thinkin' . . ."

Unlikely.

". . . about how just seein' you come swishin' along here made us wanna, kinda—y'know—fuck you—"

Before he could finish his little game of verbal connect-the-dots, I'd already upgraded my smile to a—wide, nasty—grin.

"Over?" I suggested, coolly. "Or was it . . . up? The ass?"

More sniggers, not all of them directed at me. "You *wish*," my aspiring basher-to-be snapped back, a bit too quick for his own comfort.

I shrugged, bringing my hands forward. Rubbed my palms together, deliberately. Saw them all shiver and step back, as one, as the skin ignited—and winked, letting a spark of the same cheerless colour flare in the pupil's heart of either flat black eye. Allowing it to grow, to spread. To kiss both lids and gild my lashes with purple flame.

And oh, but the ache was chest-high and higher now, jumping my neck to lodge behind my face: a hammer in my head, a hundred-watt bulb thrown mid-skull. Like a halo in reverse.

"Not particularly," I replied.

Basher-boy's buddies broke and ran as one, pack-minded to the last. But I had already crooked a burning finger at him, riveting him to the spot, a skewer of force run through every limb. Using them like strings, I walked him—a reluctant puppet—to the nearest alley. Paused behind a clutch of trash-cans, popped my fly to let it all hang out. And leaned back against the wall, waiting.

"Down," I told him. "Now."

He knelt, staring up. I stroked his jaw.

"Open up," I said, sweetly.

And kept right on smiling, even after his formerly sneering lips hit the neatly trimmed hair on my pubic ridge—right up until my sac swung free against his rigid, yet helplessly working, chin. I wasn't thinking of him, of course, but at least I wasn't thinking of that *guy* anymore—or myself, either. When I felt my orgasm at last, I came so hard I would have thought I was levitating, if I didn't already know what that feels like: off like a rocket, all in one choking gush. I held his head until I was done.

Then I stepped back, him still down on his knees in front of me, leaving him just enough room to pivot and puke everything I'd just given him back up on the asphalt beneath our feet.

My ache, conveniently enough, went along with it.

"You think you're going to do something about this," I told him, as I ordered my cuffs and tucked my shirt back in. "Not that you'd ever tell your buddies, of course. But you're sitting there right now, thinking: 'One day I'm gonna catch him in an alley, and he'll have to eat through a straw for a month.'"

Closing my coat, I squatted down beside him, continuing: "But the thing is . . . even now, even with me right in front of you, you can't *really* remember what I look like. And it's getting worse. An hour from now, any given gay guy you meet might have been the one that did this to you. Am I right?" I leaned a little towards him, and felt him just stop himself from shying away; that little jerk in his breath, like a slaughterhouse calf just before the bolt slams home. "Can't tell, can you?" I asked, quietly.

He didn't answer.

"And do you know what that means?" I went on, sitting back on my heels. "It means that the next time you see somebody coming down Church Street, and you want to say hello—I think you're going to modify your tone a little. Lower your eyes, maybe. Not make any snap judgments. And definitely . . . under any circumstances at all . . . not call this person by insulting names. Because you never know." I paused. "And you never will, either."

Leaning forward again, I let my voice go cold. And whispered, right in his ear:

"So be polite, little ghost. From now on, just be very—very—polite."

By the time I got home, one quick whiff was enough to tell me my neighbours were not only back, but already smoking up a storm. No '80s nostalgia dancemix filtering up through the floorboards as yet, though— so between the relative earliness of the hour and the obvious intensity of their hash-induced stupor, I figured I had about an hour before their proximity made it difficult to give the ritual I had in mind my fullest possible attention.

Because, morally repulsive as my pre-emptive strike on the Engineer might have been—even from my own (admittedly prejudiced) point of view—the plain fact was, it had done the trick. Back in that alley, the emotional cramp temporarily hampering my ability to plan ahead had flowed out of me, borne on a blissful surge of bodily fluids. And inspiration had taken its place.

So I picked up the phone, and discovered—somewhat to my own amusement—that I really *could* remember Franz's mother's number, after all.

"You're actually going to help?" He repeated, obviously amazed.

"Why not? Might be kicks."

"Yeah, right. For who?"

"Does it matter?"

Planning it out, even as we fenced: use a two-ring circle system, with Jen sequestered in the inner, Franz and I in the outer. Proceed from Franz's assumption that Fleer was the demon in question, until otherwise proven; force him to vacate by offering him another rabbit-hole to jump down, one far more attractive to him than Jen's could ever be . . .

Making the connection then, mildly startled by the ruthless depths of my own deviousness. And observing to myself: *Now, that's not nice.*

But I knew I'd have to try it, anyway.

I gave Franz a detailed list of what I'd need, only to be utterly unsurprised when he immediately balked at both its length and its— fairly expensive—specificity.

"Why the hell don't you ever practise straight-up Chinese magic, anyway?" He demanded. "Needles, herbs, all that good, cheap stuff . . ."

"Same reason you don't raise any Mennonite demons, I guess."

He invited me to suck his dick. I gave an evil smile.

"Oh, Franz," I said, gently. "How do you know I never did?"

Next step was getting all the appointment-book bullshit dealt with: setting a time, date and place, with Jen's address making the top of my list in terms of crucial missing information. According to Franz, she'd been living in some Annex hole in the ground for most of the last five years, vampire sex shows and all—though not an actual hole, mind you, or the actual ground. But only because that kind of logistical whimsy would have been way too interesting a concept for either of them.

"And what are *you* planning on bringing to the party?" he asked, grumpily. To which I replied, airily:

". . . I'll think of something."

Which is how I came, a mere three hours later, to be sitting side by side with Carra in the Clarke's inaccurately labelled Green Room—her slump-shouldered and staring at her scars against the grey-painted wall, me trying (and failing) to stop my feet from tapping impatiently on the scuffed grey linoleum floor. We were virtually alone, aside from one nurse stationed on the door, whose eyes kept straying back to the static-spitting TV in the corner, as though it exercised some sort of magnetic attraction on her and a dusty prayer-plant whose leaves seemed permanently fused together by the utter lack of natural light.

"I need a reading," I told Carra, briskly.

Toneless: "You know I can't do that anymore, Jude."

"I know you *don't*."

"Same difference."

It seemed clear she probably sensed ulterior motives beneath my visit, even though she knew herself to be always my court of last resort when faced with any inexplicable run of synchronicity. But she didn't seem particularly interested in probing further, probably because this just happened to be one of those mornings when she wasn't much into seeing people; not live ones, anyway.

"Look," I said, "somebody's been doing stuff, and taking my name in vain while they do it. Sleeping with Ed, even after I already kicked him to the curb. Volunteering my services to Franz, even after I already told him to take a hike." I paused. "I even tried to do a spell on that guy— the one from the movie?" As she nodded: "Well, that was all screwed up somehow, too. Like, just . . . weird."

"Your magic was weird," she repeated, evenly.

"Abnormally so."

She looked up, brushing her bangs away. "Told you there was something about that guy," she said, with just a sliver of her old, evilly detached, Ryerson-era grin.

I snapped my fingers. "Oh yeah, I remember now—you did, didn't you? Just never told me *what*."

"How should I know?"

"You read minds, Carra," I reminded her.

"Not well. Not on short notice."

"Also bullshit."

She turned to her hands again, examining each finger's gift-spotted quick in turn, each ragged edge of nail. Finally: "Well, anyways . . . it's not like I'm the only one who's told you that."

"Grandmother Yau did say she saw me twice," I agreed, slowly.

A snort. "I'm surprised she could even see you once."

"Why?"

"For the same reason *I* can hardly see you, Jude: you're only half there. Got no shadow, remember?"

Hair back in her eyes, eyes back on her palms—scanning their creases like if she only studied them hard enough, she thought she could will herself a whole new history. Then wrinkling her forehead and sniffing, a kind of combined wince/flinch, before demanding—apropos of nothing much, far as I could tell—

"God. Can you *smell* that, or what?"

"What?"

"*That*, Jude."

Ah, yes: that.

Guess not.

Yet—oh, what *was* that stupid knocking inside my chest, that soft, intermittent scratch building steadily at the back of my throat? Like I was sickening for something; a cold, a fever . . . some brief reflection of the Carra I'd once known, poking out—here and there—from under her hovering Haldol high.

I knew I could still remember exactly what it was, though, if only I let myself. That was the worst of it. Not the innate hurt of Carra's ongoing tragedy—this doomed, hubristic sprawl from darkness to darkness, hospital to halfway house and back again. Carra's endless struggle for the right to her own independent consciousness, pitted as she was against an equally endless, desperate procession of needy phantoms, to whom possession was so much more than nine tenths of the law.

"The biggest mistake you can ever make," she told me, once, "is to ever let them know you see them at all. Because it gets around, Jude. It really gets around."

(Really.)

Remembering how she'd once taught me almost everything I know, calmly and carefully—everything that matters, anyway. Everything that's helped me learn everything I've learned since. How she broke all the rules of "traditional" mediumship and laid herself willingly open to anything her Talent brought her way, playing moth, then flame, then moth again. After which, one lost day—a day she's never spoken of, even to me—she somehow decided that the best idea would be for her to burn on, unchecked, 'til she burned herself out completely.

How she'd spent almost all her time since the Ryerson Graduation Ball struggling—however inefficiently—to get her humanity "back," even though that particular impossible dream has always formed the real root of her insanity. And how I pitied her for it—pitied her, revered her, resented her. How I held her in increasingly black, bitter contempt, anger, and resentment over it, all because she'd wasted five long years trying to commit the unforgivable sin of leaving me behind.

No, I knew the whole situation a little too well to mourn over, at this point; almost as well as Carra did, in fact, and you didn't see *her* crying. She held her ground instead, with grace and strength, until the encroaching tide threatened to pull her under. And then she took a little Thorazine vacation, letting the Clarke's free drugs tune the constant internal whisper of her disembodied suitors' complaints down to a dull roar. Putting herself somewhere else, neatly and efficiently, so the dead could have their way with her awhile—and all on the off-chance that they might thus be satisfied enough, unlikely as it might seem, to finally leave her alone.

What I felt wasn't empathy. It was annoyance. I had had things to talk about with Carra, business to attend to. And she had made herself— quite deliberately—unreachable.

Besides which: feeling sorry for Carra, *genuinely* sorry . . . well, that'd be far too normal for *me*, wouldn't it? To feel my chest squeeze hot and close over Carra's insoluble pain, just because she was my oldest Canadian acquaintance, my mentor and my muse.

My best, my truest, friend.

My one. And my only.

(A memory loop of Ed's voice intervening here, thick and blurry: "Tell you what, Jude—why don't you surprise me: name the last time you felt anything. For somebody other than yourself, I mean.")

And when was it we had that conversation, exactly? Two hours ago? Two months?

Two years, maybe. Not that it mattered a single flying fuck.

Ai-yaaah. So inappropriate. So selfish. So, very—

"Still walking around out there, like any other ghost," Carra continued, musingly. "Looking like you, acting . . . *sort* of like you . . ."

—*me*.

"So," I said, slowly. "What you're telling me is—this guy I've been after, for the last couple of days—"

"He's your shadow."

And: *Ohhhh.*

Well, that explained a lot.

Rubbing a hand across my lips, then stroking it absently back over my hair. And thinking, all the while: could be true; why not? I mean—who did that guy remind me of, anyway, if not myself? Certainly explained the attraction.

Running after myself, yearning after myself. Working magic on myself.

Man, I always knew I was a narcissist.

All the lesser parts of me: weak where I was potent, slippery where I was direct, silent where I was vocal, acquiescent where I was anything but. Myself, reflected backwards and upside-down in a weirdly flattering Yin mirror, just like Grandmother Yau said.

Caught in a mesh of darkness.

"My 'evil twin,'" I suggested, facetiously.

She shrugged. "Kind of depends on your definition." Then: "Christ! What is that *smell*?"

In other words: if he's the evil one—then what's that supposed to make *you*?

I shook my head yet again, flicking the idea away—such a smooth-ass move, and one that really does get easier and easier, the more diligently you practise it. Then propelled myself upwards and outwards, briskly brushing the room's dust from my clothes, like I was simultaneously scrubbing myself free of her aura's leaking, purple-brown, depression-and-defeat-inflected stain. Saying:

"Well, anyway—gotta go. Things to do, rituals to research, shopping lists to compile. Exorcisms don't come cheap, you know."

". . . don't."

"Why the hell not?"

Hesitant: "I mean, it's just. Not. Not, uh . . ."

(*. . . safe.*)

Riiiiight.

'Cause that was the big concern, these days: staying safe, at all costs. Even when the best way to make sure I stayed *safe*, if it really concerned her so much, would be to sign herself out of this shithole—the way we all knew she could, at a moment's fucking notice—and come help out. Instead of just sitting there all smug with dead people's handwriting crawling up and down her arms like some legible rash and the air around her starting to thicken like a rind, to crackle like a badly grounded electric fence . . .

Bitch, I thought, before I could stop myself. And saw her flinch again, as the impact of my projected insult bruised her cortex from the inside-out; saw blood drip from one nostril, as she blinked away a film of tears.

I shut my eyes to block it all out, feeling that *ache* squirm inside me, twisting in on itself. Knotting tight. Feeling it ripple with fine, poison-packed spines, all of them spewing a froth of negativity that threatened to send my few lingering deposits of tenderness, sorrow, and affection flowing away at a touch, leaving nothing behind but emptiness and rot and rage.

If I let it, that is. Which I wasn't about to.

Not when I still had even the faintest lingering chance of getting what I wanted.

"Listen," I began, carefully. "We both know the main reason you put the Posse together in the first place was because it was the only way you could blow off steam, stop devoting all your energy to just protecting yourself. . . ."

Leave it open as sin and let the ghosts rush in at will: babble and float, vomit ectoplasm and sprout word-bruises like hickey chains, laugh like a loon and know no one was actually going to treat you like one for doing it.

Good times, baby. Good, good times.

"But now the lid's back on all the time, because you're afraid to let it come off, under any circumstances. And the steam's still building. And pretty soon it's going to blow either way, and when it does, it'll hurt somebody, which'd be okay if it was just you. Except that it probably won't be."

Carra cast her eyes at me, warily. There was an image lurking somewhere in her downcast gaze, half-veiled by lash and post-meds pupil dilation: past, present, maybe even future. It took all my remaining self-restraint not to tweeze it forward with a secret gesture, catch it between my own lids, and blink it large enough to scry. But that would be impolite. We were friends, after all, me and her.

And: *Like that actually* means *anything,* some ungrateful, traitor part of me whispered—right against the figurative drum of my mental inner ear.

"You know," she said, finally, "if you hadn't caught me on an off-day . . . that probably would have worked."

Adding, a moment later—

"And speaking of reading minds—you think I don't know what you're planning, by the way? An open medium, a vessel with no shields; couldn't ask for a better demon-trap, not if you ordered it from Acme Better Homes & Banishments. I walk in, Fleer jumps me, you cast him out and toss him right back through the Rift again—and what the hell, huh? Because I'm *used* to having squatters in *my* head."

"So what—would you have agreed if I'd said it straight out?" I shot back, reasonably enough. "But c'mon, admit it: be a fuck of a lot more interesting than just hiding in here, where you're no use to anybody."

"I'm sick of being 'of use.' I've been 'of use' since I was born. And now—now *you* want to use me; Jesus, Jude. Is that what 'friends' do to each other, these days?"

I shrugged. *Well, when you put it that way . . .*

Softly: "I'll always be your friend, Carra."

She shook her head. "That other part of you, sure. But *you* . . . you've changed."

Shadow-coveting vibe just pumping off of me by now, no doubt—extruding at her through my pores, like Denis Leary-level cigarette smoke at a hyper-allergenic: sloppy-drunk with wanting him, distracted with seeking him, enraged with not finding him. Forgotten emotions colliding like neurons, giving off heat and light and horror. Making me feel different to her, all complicated and intrusive, instead of the calming psychic dead-spot, whose absence she'd gotten all too used to basking in. Making me feel just like . . .

. . . everybody else.

"I never change," I said. Contradicting myself, almost immediately: "And anyway, should I have just stayed the way I was: that fool, that weak child? Too scared of everything, including himself, to do anything *about* anything?"

"I liked him."

So simple, so plaintive. Her barely audible voice like an echo of that dream I'd had the night before, the one where I'd seen her hanging between earth and air. Asking me: *What did you do to yourself, Jude? What did you* do?

You know what I did, I started to say, but froze mid-word. Because just then—at the very same time—I finally caught a hint of something unnatural in the air around us: some phantom stink skittering from corner to corner like a rancid pool-ball, drawing an explosive puff of dust from the centre of the prayer-plant's calcified Cry to Heaven. Making the nurse look up, sniffing.

Carra hacked, hands flying to her nose; her fingers came away wet, stained with equal parts coughed-out snot and thick, fresh blood.

"Fuck," she said, amazed. "That smell—"

—*it's* you.

And she began to rise.

The nurse's eyes widened, fixing; she made a funny little "eeep"-y noise and scuttled back against the wall. To her right, static ate the TV's signal entirely, turning *All My Children* into *Nothing But Snow*. I took a tentative half-step myself, fingers flashing purple: wards, activate! Ghosts, disperse!

Thinking—projecting—even as my flared nostrils stung in sympathy: *Oh, baby, don't. Please, do* not. *Do* not *do this to* me . . .

Carra's heels hooked the seat of her chair, knocking it backwards with the force of their upswing; she gasped, blood-tinted mucus-drip already stretching into hair-fine tendrils that streamed out wide on either side, wreathing her like impromptu mummy-wrap. The chair fell, skipping once, like a badly thrown beach-rock.

Rising to stick and hang there in the centre of the room, her heels holding five steady inches above the floor. Head flung back. Ectoplasm pouring from her nose and mouth. While, all around, a psychically charged dust devil scraped the walls like some cartoon tornado-in-a-can, its tightening funnel composed equally of frustrated alien willpower and whatever small inanimate objects happened to be closest by: plastic cutlery, scraps of paper. Hair and thread and crumbs. Garbage of every description.

A babble of ghostly voices filling her throat, making her jaw's underside bulge like a frog's. Messages scrawling up and down her exposed limbs as the restless dead took fresh delight in making her their unwilling megaphone, their stiff and uncooperative human notepad.

She looked down at me, cushioned behind my pad of defensive Power, and let the corners of her mouth give an awful rictus-twitch. And as her glasses lifted free—apparently unnoticed—to join the rest of the swirl, I saw ectoplasmic lenses slide across her eyes like cataracts, blindness taking hold in a milky, tidal, unstoppable ebb and flow.

Forcing her lips further apart, as the tendons in her neck grated and popped. Wrenching a word here and there from the torrent inside her and forcing herself to observe:

"Not . . . ever . . . ything. Is . . . ab . . . out. YOU. Jude."

Believe it—

—or not.

And I, as usual, chose to choose . . . *not*.

The primary aim of magicians is to gather knowledge, because knowledge—as everyone finds out fairly early, from *Schoolhouse Rock* on—is power. To that end, we often conjure demons, who we use and dismiss in the same offhand way most people grab the right implement from their kitchen drawer: fork, cheese-knife, slotted spoon; salt, pepper, sulphur. Keep to the recipe, clean your plate, then walk away quickly once the meal is done.

But even if we pursue this culinary analogy to its most pedantic conclusion, cooking with demons is a bit like trying to run a restaurant specializing in dishes as likely to kill you as they are to nourish you: deathcap mushroom pasta with a side of ergot-infested rye bread, followed by the all-fugu special. They're cruel and unpredictable, mysterious and restless, icily malignant—far less potent than the actual Fallen who spawned them, yet far more fearful than simple elementals of fire, air, water, earth, or the mysterious realms which lie beneath it. Like the dead, demons come when called—or even when not—and envy us our flesh; like the dead, you must feed them blood before they consent to give their names or do your bidding.

Psellus called them *lucifugum*, those who Fly the Light. I call them a pain in the ass, especially when you're not entirely sure what else to call them.

On the streetcar-ride from College/Yonge to Bathurst/College, I chewed my lip and flipped through my copy of the *Grimoire Lemegeton*, which lists the names and powers of seventy-two different demons, along with their various functions.

Eleven lesser demons procure the love of women or (if your time is tight) make lust-objects of either sex show themselves naked. Four can transport people safely from place to place, or change them into other shapes, or gift them with high worldly position, cunning, courage, wit, and eloquence. Three produce illusions: of running water, of musical instruments playing, of birds in flight. One can make you invisible, another turn base metals into gold. Two torment their victims with running sores. One, surprisingly, teaches ethics; I don't get a whole lot of requests for him, strangely enough.

Glasyalabolas, who teaches all arts and sciences, yet incites to murder and bloodshed. Raum, who reconciles enemies, when he's not destroying cities. Flauros, who can either burn your foes alive, or discourse on divinity. Or Fleer himself, indifferently good or bad, who "will do the work of the operator."

If it actually was Fleer inside Jen, that is. If, if, if.

Practising the usual injunctions under my breath, while simultaneously trying to decide between potential protective sigils: *Verbum Caro Factum Est,* your basic Quadrangelic conjuration, maybe even the ultimate old-school reliability of Solomon's Triangle—upper point to the north, Anexhexeton to the east, Tetragrammaton to the west, Primematum anchoring. Telling your nameless quarry, as you etch the lines around yourself:

"I conjure and command thee, O spirit N., by Him who spake and it was done; Asar Un-Nefer, Myself Made Perfect, the Bornless One, Ineffable. Come peaceably, visibly, and without delay. Come, fulfill my desires and persist unto the end in accordance to my will. Zazas, Zazas, Nasatanada, Zazas: exit this vessel as and when I command, or be thrown through the Gate from whence ye came."

The streetcar slid to a halt, Franz visible on the platform ahead—looking worried, as ever. A shopping bag in either hand testified to his having already filled out my list. Which was good; proved he wanted Jen "cured" enough to throw in from his own pocket, at least.

And: *I've done this,* I thought. *Lots of times. I can do it again, Carra or not*—and what the fuck had I really thought I needed Carra for, anyway? As she'd (sort of) pointed out, herself.

Easy. Peasy. Easy-peasy.

But none of the above turned out to matter very much at all, really. In the end.

Stepped off the streetcar at six or so. By midnight I was back at Grandmother Yau's, sucking back a plate of Glass Noodle Cashew Chicken and washing it back with lots and lots of tea, so much I could practically feel my bladder tensing yet another notch with each additional swig. Starting to itch, and twinge, and . . . ache.

(*Ache.*)

"So, Jude-ah," came a soft, Mandarin-accented voice from just behind my shoulder. "Seeing you seem sad, I wonder: how does your liver feel? Is the general of your body's army sickening, tonight?"

And: *Tonight, tonight,* I found myself musing. What *was* tonight, at the Khyber? Oh, right . . . open bar. No bullshit restrictions. I could wear that tank-top I'd been saving, the really low-cut one.

Wick-ed.

Grandmother Yau reached in, touching her gilded middle claw to my ear, brief and deft; I jumped at its sting, collecting myself, as she reminded me—

"I am not used to being ignored, little brother."

Automatically: "Ten thousand pardons, big sister."

She slit her green-tinged eyes, shrewdly. "One will do." Then, waving the nearest ghost over to top up my teapot: "My spies tell me you had business, further east. Is it completed?"

And *waaah*, but there were so very many ways to answer that particular question, weren't there? Though I, typically, chose the easiest.

"*Wei*," I said, nodding. "Very complete."

"The possessed girl, ah? Your friend."

That's right.

My *friend* Jen, lying there on the tatty green carpet of her basement apartment; my other friend Franz, leaning over her. Shaking her—a few times, gently at first, then harder. Slapping her face once. Doing it again.

Watching her continue to lie there, impassively limp. Then looking back at me, a growing disbelief writ plain across his too-pale, freckled face—me, standing still inside my circle, with no expression at all on mine. Watching him watch.

She's not breathing, Jude.

Well, no.

Jude. I think . . . I think she's dead.

Well—yes.

"Turns out," I told Grandmother Yau, "she wasn't actually possessed, after all."

"No?"

"No."

Ai-yaaah.

Because: I'd taken Franz's word, and Franz had taken Jen's—but she'd lied to us both, obviously, or been so screwed up that even she hadn't really known where those voices in her skull were coming from. So I'd come running, prepared to kick some non-corporeal butt, and funnelled the whole charge of my Power into her at once, cranked up to demon-expelling level.

But if there's no demon to be *put* to flight, that kind of full-bore metaphysical shock attack can't help but turn out somewhat like sticking a fork in a light socket, or vice versa. If that's even possible.

Franz again, in Jen's apartment, turning on me with his eyes all aburn. Reminding me, shakily: *You said you could* help.

If she was possessed, yes.

Then why is she dead, Jude?

Because . . . she wasn't.

You—said—

I shrugged. *Whoopsie.*

He lunged for me. I let off a force-burst that threw him backwards five feet, cracking his spine like a whip.

You don't ever *lay hands on me,* I said, quietly. *Not ever. Unless I want you to.*

He sat there, hugging his beloved corpse with charred-white palms, crying in at least two kinds of pain. And snarled back: *Like I'd want to touch you with some other guy's dick and some third fucker pushing, you son of a fucking bitch.*

(Yeah, whatever.)

Fact was, though, if Franz hadn't been so cowardly and credulous in the first place—if he hadn't wanted an instant black magic miracle, instead of having the guts to just take her to a mental hospital, the way most normal people do when their girlfriends start telling them they hear voices—then Jen might still be alive.

Emphasis on the might.

I can call demons. I can bind angels. I can raise the dead, for a while. But just like Franz himself had observed, more than once, I can't actually cure anybody—can't heal them of cancer, leprosy, MS, old age, mental illness, or colour-blindness to save my fucking life. Not unless they *want* me to. Not unless they let me.

The other way? That's called a miracle, and my last name ain't Christ.

Franz, crying out, tears thick as blood in his strangled voice: *You* promised *me, you fuck! You fucking* promised *me!*

Followed, in my memory, by a quick mental hit of Carra, half the city away: still floating, still wreathed. And thinking: *If I could do something for people like that, you moron, don't you think I* would?

She *wants* to be nuts, though. Long and the short of it. Just like, on some level, Jen *wanted* to die.

But hell, what was Franz going to do about it, one way or another? Shun me?

I took a fresh bite of noodle while the ancient Chinese spectre I'd come to think of as Grandmother's right-hand ghost flitted by, pausing to murmur in her ear for a moment before fading away through the nearest lacquer screen. And when she looked at me, she had something I'd never seen before lurking in the corners of her impenetrable gaze. If I'd had to hazard a guess, I might even have said it looked a lot like—well—

—surprise.

"Someone," she said, at last, "is at the Maitre D's station. Asking for you, Jude-ah."

Glancing sidelong, so I'd be forced to follow the path of her gaze over to where . . . he waited: He, it. Me.

My shadow.

My shadow, highlighted against the Empress Noodle's thick, red velvet drapes like a sliver of lambent bronze—head down, shyly, with its hair in its eyes and its hands in its pockets. My shadow, come at last after all my fruitless seeking, just waiting for its better half to take control, wrap it tight, gather it in and make it—finally—whole again.

Waiting, patiently. Quiet and acquiescent. Waiting, waiting . . .

. . . for me.

I met Grandmother Yau's gaze again, and found her normally impassive face gone somehow far more rigid than usual: green-veined porcelain, a funerary mask trimmed in milky jade.

"The Yin mirror reflects only one way, Chiu-wai-ah," she said, at last. "It is a dark path, always. And slippery."

I nodded, suddenly possessed by a weird spurt of glee. Replying, off-hand: "*Mei shi*, big sister; not to worry, never mind. Do you think I don't know enough to be careful?"

To which she merely bowed her head, slightly. Asking—

"What will you do, then?"

And I—couldn't stop myself from smiling, as the answer came sliding synapse-fast to the very tip of my tongue, kept restrained only by a lifetime's residual weight of "social graces." Thinking: *Oh, I? Go home, naturally. Go home, dim the lights, light some incense—*

—and fuck *myself.*

So soft in my arms, not that I'd ever thought of myself as soft. I pushed it back against the apartment door with its wrists pinned above its head, nuzzling and nipping, quizzing it in Cantonese, Mandarin, ineffectual Vietnamese—only to have it offer exactly nothing in reply, while simultaneously maintaining an unbroken stare of pure, dumb adoration from beneath its artfully lowered lashes.

Which was okay by me; more than okay, really. Seeing I'd already had it pretty much up to here with guys who talked.

Feeling the shadow's proximity, its very presence, prickle the hairs on the back of my neck like a presentiment of oncoming sheet lightning against empty black sky: All plus to my mostly minus, yang to my yin, nice guy to my toxic shit. And wanting it back, right here and now; feeling the core-deep urge to penetrate, to own, to repossess those long-missing parts of me in one hard push, come what fucking might.

Groin to groin and breath to breath, two half-hearts beating as one, two severances sealing fast. Unbreakable.

Down on the bed then, with its heels on my shoulders: key sliding home, lock springing open. Rearing erect, burning bright with flickering purple flame, allll over. And seeing myself abruptly outlined in black against the wall above my headboard at that ecstatic moment of (re) joining, like some Polaroid flash's bruisy after-image: my inverse reflection. My missing shadow, slipping inside me as I slipped inside it, enshadowing me once more.

Two years' worth of trauma deferred, all crashing down on me at once. Showing me first-hand, explicitly, how nature abhors a—moral, human, walking—vacuum.

And now it's later, oh so much, with rain all over my bedroom floor and beads of wood already rising like sodden cicatrices everywhere I dare to look. Rain on my hair, rain in my eyes—only natural, given that the window's still open. But I can't stand up, can't force a step, not even to shut it. I just squat here and listen to my heart, eyes glued to that ectoplasmic husk the shadow left devolving on my bed: a shed skinful of musk and lies, rotting. All that's left of my lovely double, my literal self-infatuation.

I've done the protective circle around myself five times now, at least—in magic marker, in chalk, in my own shit. Tomorrow I think I'll re-do it in blood, just to get it over with; can't keep on picking at these ideas forever, without something starting to fester. And we don't want that, do we?

(*Really*.)

Because the sad truth is this: my wards hold, like they always hold; the circle works, like all my magic works. But what it doesn't do, even after all my years of sheer, hard, devoted work—all my Craft and study, not to mention practice—

—is *help*.

Once upon a time—when I was drunk, and young, and stupid beyond belief—I cut my shadow, my soul, away from me in some desperate, adolescent bid to separate myself from my own mortality. And since then, I guess I haven't really been much good for anybody *but* myself. I bound up my weakness and threw it away, not realizing that weakness is what lets you bend under unbearable pressure.

And if you can't bend . . . you break.

My evil twin, I hear my own arrogant voice suggest to Carra, mockingly—and with a sudden, stunning surge of self-hatred, I find I want to hunt that voice down and slap it silly. To roll and roar on the floor at my own willfully deluded stupidity.

Half a person, Franz chimes in, meanwhile, from deeper in my memory's ugly little gift-box. *And not even the good half.*

No. Because *it* was the good half. And me, I, I'm—just—

—all that's left.

My shadow. The part of me that might have been, if only I'd let it stay.

My curdled conscience. Until it touched me, I didn't remember what it was I'd been so afraid of. But now I can't think about anything else.

Except . . . how very, very badly, no matter what the cost . . .

. . . I want for it to touch me again.

Thinking: *Is this me? Can this possibly be* me, *Jude Hark Chiu-Wai? Me?* Me.

Me, and no fucking body else.

Thinking, finally: *But this won't kill me. Not even this. Much as I might like it to.*

And maybe I'll be a better person for it, a better magician, if I can just make it through the next few nights without killing myself like Jen, or going crazy as Carra. But that's pretty cold comfort, at best.

Sobbing, retching. All one big weakness—one open, weeping sore. And thinking, helpless: *Carra, oh, Carra. Grandmother Yau. Franz. Ed. Someone.*

Anyone.

But I've burnt all my boats, funeral-style. And I can't remember— exactly, yet—just how to swim.

The Wide World converges on me now, dark and sparkling, and I just crouch here beneath it with my hands over my face: weeping, moaning, too paralytic-terrified even to shield myself from its glory. Left all alone at last with the vision and the void—crushed flat, without a hope of reprieve, under the endless weight of a dark and whirling universe.

Ripe and riven. Unforgiven. Caught forever, non-citizen that I am, in that typically Canadian moment right before you start to freeze.

Keeping my sanity, my balance.

Keeping to the straight and Narrow.

WORDS WRITTEN BACKWARDS (2003)

Joe Tulugaak saw the storm forming from all the way across the ice, though going just by temperature alone, it should have been much too cold for snow. Yet more evidence that this place was at least as sick as he'd been told, if not more so.

It was February, about 3:30 P.M. An hour and a half to full dark. Algonquin Bay was frozen stiff enough to take a truck, which was how he'd gotten up here, though not so frozen it could stand you travelling more than fifteen miles an hour. He'd followed the annually cleared ice-fishing strip out to tiny Windigo Island, part of the Manitous, and parked across from where the lights of the Anishnabek First Nations Reserve would come up as the sun dipped down, like a string of slow firecrackers. Then he'd put up his tent, got the generator running, and broken out the chainsaw.

The storm came up like a puff of breath, a sky-wide exhalation. A second later, it grew fiercely specific: conical, then convex, a wavering funnel guttering over the trail's pale blue road towards him, erasing everything in its path. If the mica-glitter white expanse stretched out all around him had been dust, he'd have definitely been inclined to call something like that a devil.

As it was, Joe shrugged, and zipped his parka up further. He reached for the tent-flap zipper, prepared to hunker down and let it pass by, blow itself out; snow was already piled four feet high on Windigo's beach, so that'd form a nice breakwall for it to dash itself to pieces on. Besides, even if it did (for its own mysterious reasons) choose to stick around, it wasn't like the kit he'd packed for this trip didn't include a shovel.

That was when he saw her.

The girl, just a *girl*, maybe fifteen at most . . . slim and knock-kneed, too underdressed for any version of winter. She came wandering out of the storm's heart with her head hung low and her hair in her eyes, face a distant white-blue smudge, body wrapped in nothing but differentially shaded yet equally thin layers of black, like she thought she was jaunting down Queen Street West on an empty Sunday afternoon: took a wrong turn at Siren or Suspect Video, and kept right on going. Had her hands up inside her sleeves, which looked like they might already be stiffened shut over gloveless blue-nailed hands. Her shoes moved too slow to kick up the crust, snagging enough to make her stumble, with a sound like tearing cheesecloth.

Something so out of place, especially here, took him aback enough he had a long heartbeat's worth of trouble trying to figure out what to do—until she fell forward on her face, and stayed there, as the storm swept over her. Which meant the moment for sitting back and mulling things out was probably pretty much over.

Man, I really *don't have time for this,* he caught himself thinking, anyhow. But: that wasn't exactly true, was it? Considering how long what he'd been called in to deal with had been going on, before the Rez elders finally decided they might as well pool their bingo money and get on the horn . . . or how long things like this usually *took* to deal with, one way or another, even after he'd officially taken the job. . . .

Nope. Guess not.

Joe sighed, lowered his head so the parka's hood would meet the wind peak-first, and started to shoulder his way into the storm.

Once in his arms, the girl hefted like a doll, like she weighed almost nothing. Maybe stupid made you float.

He could feel the chill of her right through his parka's sleeves. *Might lose that nose,* he thought, looking down at it: purple to the nostrils, touched at the tip with black. Like she'd dressed up as a greasepaint skull for Hallowe'en.

Had a smell to her too, in close quarters; that was the second thing he noticed.

Inside, he quickly found the radio the elders had given him, and thumbed it on. Nothing but static wash. He checked her pulse-points, which seemed slow, yet strong. Then recoiled in surprise when he ran his hands down further and found her clothes already dry, as though baked from within: a steady desert heat beat outwards in all directions, desiccated. He couldn't figure its source.

The girl moved slightly, moaning, and Joe saw her nose was already looking a hell of a lot better than it should, given the circumstances. Still couldn't identify that smell, though.

Joe watched her until the black boiled itself off and the right kind of colour was back in her face, 'til the purple turned mauve, then pale, then rose. She was even smaller than she'd seemed at first glance, boned like a bird, with dark hair and rolled-back eyes that were probably some variation on dark, too. A tiny fold lifted the skin at both corners, semi-epicanthic. Might be they were even related, somehow—she could have a bit of the Blood in her, diluted by a few centuries of getting spread around. Not a full Breed, maybe, but one of those Torontonian gumbo mixes: one from column "A," two from column "B," with column "C" kept squarely reserved for "who the fuck knows, or cares?"

Whatever she is, he thought, *she's different.*

The only other person he'd ever seen heal like that was his Grandmother, and even she'd needed help.

When the girl had relaxed enough to be mobile, Joe spread his back-up parka out on the floor and rolled her into it, shrugging her arms through the sleeves like she was a woman-sized rag doll. If and when she stood up, its hem would probably hide both her knees. Hard not to handle her all wrong, doing it; he'd have to apologize for that later on, if she didn't turn out brain-damaged.

On the inside of her left forearm he found a scratched-on word, letters straggly and puffed like a brand: SINNER. On both wrists and the inside of one leg, meanwhile, more scar tissue—deliberate, no practice cuts, over and over again. Though her skin seemed paper-thin, the results had keloided high, furling in on themselves: pale silk knots in neat little rows, all tied far too tight for comfort.

How much pain would you have to be in to want to let it out like that?

(*And why wouldn't just the one time—or two, or three—be enough?*)

Joe shook his head a few times, to clear it, and started rustling up some chow.

When the girl finally opened her eyes, he was boiling tea in a gramophone-horn billy that guy from Trois-Rivières had made him, one time; that old Norwegian, the guy with troll trouble. Happened so quiet it took him a bit by surprise, especially when he suddenly turned around to find her watching him. Plus, it turned out her eyes weren't dark, after all: they were yellow instead, squarish pupils slanted ever-so-slightly outwards, like a goat's. And when the light from the fire fell into them, it never came back out.

"Hey," he said. "My name's Joe."

She cleared her throat, tongue so dry he could hear it click against the roof of her mouth. Took a long breath. And replied—

". . . Judy . . ."

He nodded. He'd found her wallet in a hip pocket, spread it out to dry on the sleeping-bag—her student ID was uppermost, but well past expiry date. Its thumbnail photo showed a pretty kid smiling wide with her hair up in two rainbow-scrunchie pigtails; didn't look too much like her, anymore.

(Not least 'cause *that* girl's eyes were brown.)

"Yoo-det-ah Kiss," he read, carefully, sounding it out. "Middle name—

is that Ildiko? Same as Drew Barrymore's Mom?"

She nodded, wincing. And added, a bit louder, but still hoarse:

"You say it . . . 'Keesh.' Like . . . the food."

"Well, all right, then. I'll try and remember."

After that, there was a minute or so of silence, cut with ambient noise; whining wind, the fire's spurt and crackle. He'd pinned the tent's interior flap up to reveal its built-in "window" an hour or so ago, just in case anybody came looking for her before dark. But all he could see through the zippered transparency was snow guttering back and forth while the hole he'd cut in the ice gaped open, a breathing mouth, waiting patiently to have its say on the matter.

He looked her up and down again, not seeing anything new. "What I can't understand, though," he said, at last, "is why you're not dead."

She lay still for a while, so motionless he thought she might've gone back to sleep. Then:

"Me . . . either," she whispered, at last. And he knew she was crying.

Then she turned away quickly, curling in on herself with both hands over her eyes, like the dim and fading light hurt too much to look at anymore, all of a sudden; good damage control, if she'd just been a little faster. But even as she did, he saw (in that one split second) how her tears smoked against her own skin when they came down—like they were acid, but without the tracks which would naturally follow. Like they were gasoline.

Like they were . . .

. . . *hot.*

Once he was reasonably certain Judy Kiss probably wouldn't be waking up again 'til dawn, Joe gathered her wallet and stepped back outside, next to the hole. The snow had dissipated, and the vast black sky above was hung with what most city folks would consider a frightening array of usually invisible stars. It made Joe homesick, but only mildly so, because from where he stood he could still see the Rez lights blurring annoyingly at its outer edges, an irritant on the universe's wide-angle lens.

Using his Grandmother's bone knife, Joe cleared a space on the ice and set the wallet down. Then he worked the much-folded newsprint clipping he'd found under Judy's Toronto Transit Commission Metropass free and spread it open on top of the frozen leather, anchoring it at either corner with two small Baffin Island beach-stones. Slightly water-warped, the upper part read—

Metro Bite, January 15, 2002
THREE YEARS LATER:
"EXORCISM GIRL" WINS CASE, DAMAGES

Today, after a lengthy civil case, a Metro Toronto judge granted "exorcism girl" Judeta Kiss's petition to become an emancipated minor. The court also awarded her $50,000 in damages claimed against her own parents, because Judeta's counsel was able to prove that Bela and Gorgo Kiss kept their then 13-year-old daughter tied to a chair for three days, while two Catholic priests performed a physically gruelling ritual meant to free her from demonic possession.

Earlier in the trial, Mr. and Mrs. Kiss testified they began to suspect Judeta might be possessed after she became unable to sleep, had extreme mood-swings, acted out sexually, displayed sudden bursts of self-destructive violence, and used uncharacteristic profanity. Typical teenaged behaviour or the Devil Inside? For most Torontonians, the choice would be clear. But just like in the classic 1973 horror film, the Kisses' next step was not to get Judeta therapy, but to call in . . . the exorcist.

Jesuit priests Father Cillian Frye and Father Akinwale Oja visited the Kiss home to observe Judeta before applying to the Toronto archdiocese for permission to perform an exorcism. Although the archbishop's office refused his request, Father Oja's own testimony—given under duress—revealed that Father Frye later lied to the Kisses, telling them (and Father Oja) that his request had been approved.

Said Mr. Justice Colin Simonetta: "Though I believe Mr. and Mrs. Kiss sincerely felt they were acting in their daughter's best interests, I nevertheless consider this entire episode a bizarre case of child abuse . . . one of the worst, and oddest, it's been my displeasure . . ."

The rest was mush, with select phrases poking up here and there, doling out bursts of fresh information: "*. . . Frye was unable to take the . . . complete psychological break. Committed . . .*" "*. . . meant no harm," Oja told reporters. "Judy understands our intent . . . free her from Satan's dominion with Christ's help and power . . .*" And: "*. . . Q.C., admits Judeta Kiss's exact whereabouts are presently . . .*"

(Unknown?)

Uh huh. In Toronto, anyways.

Joe sat back on his heels. "So," he said, out loud. "Blackrobe messiness. Typical."

After which he waited a moment, head cocked, but heard no immediate answer. So he reached inside his parka pocket for his bag instead, shaking Grandmother's bones out on the ice beside him—

actually two bones (one refined into a broken needle, the other cracked for marrow), three teeth (all human, all from different people's jaws) and a two-inch piece of narwhal tusk carved in the shape of a pecking crow, to be exact. The bones fell in a spray, counterclockwise, with the tusk just touching the hole's wide-stretched lip.

Joe nodded, and bent down to retrieve it. "*Nukum*," he murmured into the darkness. "Do you see me?"

The hole sighed, almost inaudibly.

From the hollow of his skull, his Grandmother's voice emerged, thin as an Ontario mosquito's hum: a thing of the land around them, tied to place yet unstuck in time—perfectly normal in its own season, but utterly impossible here, in his.

I do, Joe.

"This girl in my tent, *Nukum*, do you see her?"

Yes. I do.

"She has a hurt. Can we heal it?"

No, Joe.

"No?"

That'll heal on its own. If it can.

Joe leaned back, squatting low, hands braced against his thighs. *Damn blackrobes*, he thought. And was surprised to hear her respond, even though he hadn't spoken; the fabric really *must* be wearing thin in these parts. Maybe if he looked up right now that wouldn't be Orion and the Bears above him at all, or whatever the Anishnabek had called them before the whites came and ate everybody else's language, then sicked it back up as their own. Maybe it'd be *Tshishtashkumuku's* vivid skies instead, Northern Lights flickering horizon to horizon like gaslight ghosts, while the *Mishpateu* lowered in above him as huge, sick clouds, sniffing for human meat.

Joe realized the wind had started up once more, without him noticing. It played a low note across the tusk-crow's half-open beak, as his Grandmother's dead voice told him—

You can't blame the blackrobes here, Joe. They don't see things the way we do, so sometimes that makes them wrong—and where we come from, they're wrong about almost everything. But sometimes—

(other places, about other things)

—they can be right.

Shivering, Joe felt newsprint dusted with ice under his fingers, and looked down to see Father Akinwale Oja's name wink up at him through the crack between forefinger and thumb. But not really, since "Akin" and "Oja" lay caught just far enough under his knuckles to make it read just

"Father," just "Wale": this alien name, in all its strange dignity, abruptly shrunk to somebody else's affectionate diminutive. Pointing the way like an unmapped street sign.

Joe sat back on the ice, narrowing his vision until the hole became the world all around. From inside the tent, he could hear Judy Kiss's sleeping breath wash in and out, harsh and hot, a slow tsunami separating sand from soil, dust from stone, flesh from bone. Her heart was a desert, nothing left standing, and her breath blew straight out of it, scented with emptiness. Even in this edge-of-freezing wasteland, what heat it held was utterly comfortless.

He closed his eyes and let it take him down further, freefall fast, into the zero where dream and memory meet.

Father Wale was a lot bigger than Joe thought he would be—big like a bull, brown like a macadamia nut. He found Judy sitting alone outside the courtroom, monopolizing the smokers' area; a small knot of nicotine addicts watched her resentfully from the sidewalk, puffing like dragons, but made sure to keep a safe distance.

"Judy."

"Father." She got up, freeing the flimsy metal bench. Ironic: "Care for a seat?"

"No, thank you."

And here there was some sort of glitch, a skip, an internal edit on the mind's hard drive; happened a lot, when you were sifting the past from a particular person's perspective. Because *We're not flies,* Joe's Grandmother used to say. *We can't see everything at once, from every angle. And even if we could, that still wouldn't be how we ended up remembering it.* A time-lapse splice from moment to moment, after which Joe rejoined Judy and Father Wale, already in progress, mid-debate: not *heated,* exactly, but intent. Made sense they were probably talking about God, then, 'cause—in Joe's experience, anyhow—that never really helped.

"You *know* what happened was—"

"'Real?' Oh yeah, Father; got that part, thanks." Judy sighed. "Listen: I appreciate what you did for me, I really do . . ."

"What God did for you, you mean."

"Do I?"

"God saved you, Judy. As you well know. Father Frye and I only said the words."

Judy gave Father Wale a narrow look, while Joe found himself increasingly intrigued by the smell of the big man's shadow: the usual incense-flavoured, paper-and-candlewax blackrobe scent, but under all that an odd lick of tall grass and predator musk, savannah heat. Wisps of the dreamtime of a land far hotter, rougher, and older than the so-called Old World. Granted, the Church ate faiths the way English ate languages, but not everything got digested completely; like his Grandmother, Joe himself was sufficient proof of that. But he had to wonder whether, in Father Wale's case, toting around such an unstable mix of Old and New had really helped the big man cut a path through his ancestral undergrowth to true capital-c Catholic capital-b Belief.

Take this place, just one of many waystops between worlds— accessible mainly by, but certainly not restricted to, the Innu. Like most pocket dimensions, it came equipped with both a front and a back door . . . and if you went far enough up *that* particular cone, Joe knew, you'd inevitably end up smack dab in the middle of what Jung called the racial unconscious, the realm of archetypes. Like an overcast sky, a storm front, with little spiritual tornados touching down here, there, and everywhere. A place where everything converges, running together at the functions: Jesus and Dionysos, St. Francis and Lord Krishna, the Virgin Mary and Yemanya-of-the-Waters, Coyote and Bugs Bunny.

From where Joe stood now, he could see that Father Wale's cone led straight back to Africa, Nigeria to be exact. Joe remembered having read somewhere that the Yoruba—Father Wale's people—once had six hundred gods to choose from, if and when they wanted to put their damage on somebody. After that sort of spiritual smorgasbord, Joe couldn't help but feel that the Three-in-One would seem like a pretty radical come-down. But hell: each to his own.

"God's little helpmeets," Judy said, eventually. "Father Frye, just a tool in His hands. So *eager* to be God's tool, he lied to my folks—and you—to make sure they'd let him try. You do remember what happened to Father Frye, right? Ever wonder what's gonna end up happening to you?"

"Cillian Frye has already answered for his lies." Anger rose in Father Wale's voice. "Should I ask how you plan to answer for yours?"

"You'll notice I never took the stand."

"No. You let your lawyer lie *for* you—say that what happened was a sickness, a madness. To demean in public the name of Christ, who saved you—"

"Why would Jesus care what anybody says about Him, Father? He knows what He did." A pause. "And besides . . . that wasn't even *about* me, was it? Any of it. Ever."

"Oh, Judy . . ."

And here, right here, was where Joe began to feel . . . spied on. Like there was somebody else hanging invisibly there, aside from himself. Like at any minute, a too-blue corner of the half-recalled sky above might suddenly peel away to reveal an unblinking eye, staring down.

He could almost see it now. And somehow, he knew exactly what it would look like: yellow. Slant-pupilled, like a goat's.

(The same shade Judy's eyes were already starting to dim to, even as he watched. The same thin angle her pupils were already beginning to rotate towards, mechanism-quick—parts in some infernal clockwork, set whirring once more by an unseen, magickal key.)

But: "You must not be bitter, Judy," Father Wale cautioned her, cluelessly sympathetic. "You do not have that right, not even with all you have suffered. Not when one considers what you have been given in return."

Judy nodded, slightly. "Yup. Got my body back, finally, with all that entails—bounty of Adam and Eve, fruit of their Fall: sin, despair, degradation, death. And almost as good as the day I first got it too, barring a little property damage. . . ."

"Judy, really. Enough of this."

"Oh, but that's what *I* said, Father—over and over and over. And *over*." Her voice dropped a hard half-octave on the last word, velcro-silky, its very register almost more disturbing than the actual words' content. "But I never did get an answer, that I remember—and you know, considering how long I spent with that spectral motherfucker, I never did get a *name*, either. So don't talk to me about gifts anymore, okay? Truth is, for all you were there, you really don't know the half, or even the quarter. Sure, you got the dog collar, but you still have to take it all on faith, like everybody else. Everybody but—"

(*me*)

And oh, Joe knew the feeling, yes indeed. The one which says, give or take a few regional variations:

Let other people strain for meaning and fear the ultimate lack of such, eking out their dismal little lives under the looming shadow of Eternity, with no hope of proof that what they want to believe about some sort of World Beyond is anything but a pretty lie told to soothe old ladies into filling collection plates. Not me, though. I don't have to worry about any of the above, let alone the Below; I don't even have to try.

Because . . . I already know.

Like the night after his *Nukum*'s funeral, so long gone now, when Joe first put on his bone suit and took the Old Road to the nethers, *Tshishtashkumuku*'s trackless waste. Out on the ice, where he'd met with what was left of his Grandmother once more—just the ghost of her smile, peeking out from the dark under her half-lowered sealskin hood, its white new teeth *atshen*-sharp. Whether it was even really her wasn't something Joe let himself wonder very often, especially whenever he needed professional advice; one ghost's perspective on things was probably about as good as another's, when you got right down to it. But she'd given him a gift to mark the occasion, and he'd accepted it gladly: Something she'd caught in her wide-flung net, to be his personal between-Worlds totem. The narwhal-tusk crow.

And when he'd woken that next morning, it had still been in his palm, frozen fast to it like metal, like ice. Scarring him far deeper than his skin, as though (without entirely meaning to) he'd taken a breath of addictively toxic wind from a whole other world.

Joe'd really known what he was from then on, along with what he wasn't. Judy, meanwhile . . . she knew *something*, that was certain; probably one part of the equation only, though—the question *or* the answer, not both. She wouldn't be staring at Father Wale in quite the same scary-hungry way if she did.

"So you punish your parents, because they're the only people you *can* punish? Judy, they don't have the resources to pay back that sort of settlement, and you know it. All you will succeed in doing is to bankrupt them."

"You think this was about the *money*? Listen, Father . . . believe me, it's a moot point. I mean, it's not like I'm gonna be around to collect."

"What do you mean by that?"

"Doesn't matter."

"Judy . . ."

"Doesn't *matter*, Father." A pause. "Do you think God is cruel?"

"No, Judy, I don't. Do you?"

"Is gravity cruel?"

"Not necessarily."

"No. But just because it holds the entire universe together, we don't usually assume it's *kind*, either. Do we?"

And: watched, *watched*. Joe could feel the many-legged weight of what-the-damn-ever's attention, sticky on the back of his mental neck; it scurried to and fro, spreading disease. Judy's eyes were topazes, their twisted cores burning, pupils crooked as swastikas—she fixed Father Wale through lowered lashes and sulphur-smell boiled up, a slow-mo explosion in a match factory. *How the hell could he not notice?* Joe wondered.

The eyes switched his way, a cool little flick. *Because it wasn't like this, of course,* a voice replied, in Joe's head.

Not Judy's voice, though, and not a *voice*, either. Not in any human sense.

Who are you? Joe made himself ask, guts churning. *Blackrobe devil? Ghost?* Mishpateu?

Maybe all of the above. Maybe none. Maybe . . . It grinned, using Judy's face. *No, I don't think so. You know a fair deal, Joe Crow, but when it comes to stuff like this? You're just not ready.*

Joe grimaced, scrabbling to hold onto his point of reference as he felt Judy's memory suddenly pivot around him, flight simulator-style. *Okay, whatever . . . but what's your damn* name?

Oh. That'd be telling, wouldn't it?

(Because: *Weren't you listening? I didn't even let Judy in on that. And we're so* close, *so much closer than you and I, Joe, could ever be . . .*)

The sulphur lit Joe's lungs lurid yellow, a burning butterfly's wings, fluttering and gasping. But the *thing* wearing Judy Kiss's memory-face simply broke eye-contact and looked away, dismissive. Like he wasn't enough fun to be worth the effort of playing with, anymore.

You can wake up now, it "told" him, tonelessly. And Joe did.

Joe Tulugaak, shaman for hire, snapped from his trance to find himself still kneeling by the hole, who knew how many hours later: waist-deep in snow, his hood-flaps frozen fast to his beard, with Judy Kiss—the real Judy, her slant eyes safely brown once more—slapping him back and forth across the cold face, cursing. Then wrestling him up and shoving him headlong inside the tent again with all her disproportionate strength, like she was the one saving *him,* or something. Which, embarrassingly enough . . .

. . . she obviously was.

"So," he said, teeth chattering, after he'd warmed up enough to eat some of the soup she was trying to feed him. "Was any of that true? In the paper?"

She frowned. "You went through my pockets?"

"Just answer the question, girlie."

"What, how I'm Toronto's answer to Regan MacNeil, 'cause I had an angel in my head?"

"'Angel?'"

"Sure. That's what being possessed means—that's who possesses you. Of the Fallen variety, but . . ."

"In other words, a devil."

"No difference." Off his look: "Seriously, we're talking about the *exact same thing.* No qualitative difference at all . . ."

Looking away as she said it, squeezing hard on the rolled-up soup package to get that last little bit out. Adding, underneath her breath, as she did so—

". . . and that's the *really* scary part."

They sat there for a moment, Judy just staring down at the tent floor and breathing, Joe trying his level best not to fall asleep; the sheer amount of trouble he'd had swallowing his last mouthful had made him abruptly aware of exactly how tired he really must be. Nevertheless, he made his eyes focus, and asked her:

"You could'a froze right to the ice, alone up here. Ever think about that?"

She glanced away again, faint black smattering of brows knitting in an oddly embarrassed way. Like they could both hear her own memory-voice playing back, behind Joe's eyes: *Listen, Father . . . believe me, it's a moot point. I mean . . .*

(not like I'm gonna be around)

"Yeah," Judy said, finally. "I thought about it."

And left it at that.

The next morning, when Joe unzipped the flap, he found the sun had already risen to reveal a wide yet surprisingly unbroken ring of dead animals—all sizes and varieties, most indigenous species, stacked tail by tail or claw to claw in every possible direction—completely encircling their tent. Not wholly unexpected, though not something he'd been looking to see quite this damn quick, either; a definite escalation, in other words. A thrown gauntlet, even. But thrown by what?

That, he still wasn't too sure about.

Joe stumped out onto the ice, boots catching a bit on last night's snow, kicking up spray. Behind him, Judy Kiss lingered in the doorway a moment—her flat brown daytime eyes half-slitted, more slant than ever, against the dawn's early light—before finally stepping through as well, resealing the flap behind her. She clapped Joe's too-big back-up pair of ski gloves together and blew out one long plume of breath, a dragon's phantom tongue, squeezed hot and flat between her set teeth.

"Creepy," she said, of the corpse-ring. "You get that a lot, up here?"

"Not too much, no. Not in . . ."

(*the normal run of things*)

And: "No," she repeated. "So why *did* you decide to go camping at this lovely time of year, Joe? Always wanted to check out the heart of dead-frozen-forest-creature country, just for fun? Or were you hoping if you only sat here long enough, some big-city girl with shiny supernatural

151

extras like me might accidentally wander by?"

Joe felt himself flush. "Hey, I never asked you to crash my bag and eat half my jerky, lady. Way I see it, you're damn lucky I was out here at all."

Judy all but turned her back on him then, thin shoulders squaring sharp against the wind, in an unbelievable show of—contempt? Disinterest? Her voice calm, as she said:

"Sure, and thanks a lot for that, seriously. But the funny thing is . . . ever since my—whatever—I'm just *full* of that particular kind of luck."

"What d'you mean?"

Still looking away, like it was easier to form the words if she didn't have to watch Joe's eyes while she did it; looking down at her creepily dry feet instead, still clad in the same wet and flimsy Goth-Loli shoes as last night, with no sign of ice forming on them."I *mean* that I probably would've been fine even if you'd just let me lie and kept on going, actually—not to undercut your heroism, Joe, but that's the truth. Because I'm always fine, no matter what, so this would've been no exception. Not even if I'd fallen in a snowbank face-first, and they hadn't found my skinny ass 'til spring."

"'Cause you can hibernate, right? Like a goddamn garter snake."

She shook her head, smiling slightly. "Come on. You know a little more than *that*, I think." A beat. "What is it you do for a living, again? Exactly?"

Now it was Joe's turn to shake his head, to look away. To think: *The hell.* And then, almost immediately afterwards: *All right, fine, okay; might as well lay all our cards on the table, before we both get frostbite. I mean, what have I got to lose?*

(About as much—or as little—as her, in the end, he guessed. Though maybe not for the same reasons.)

"I fix things," he told her. "Places, like this. When they go bad."

She nodded, unsurprised. "For anybody specific? Or for anybody who asks?"

"For People, you know—*the* People, like me. First Nations, Inuit . . . all kinds. Native People."

"Aboriginals."

"Nope: never been to Australia yet, and don't plan to. Otherwise . . ." Joe allowed himself a dry smile, which she returned. "Yeah, you pretty much got it."

"Ever met an ex-possessee before?"

"Not really. Seen all sorts of weird stuff, though, in my time. Rabbit totem fever-spirits . . . unlaid missionary ghosts . . . Eskimo fart-men . . . giant flying cannibal heads."

"There's giant flying cannibal heads?"

"Not as many as there used to be." A shrug. "One less now, anyhow."

They stood in the snow for a minute more, watching the sun rise further. The wind ruffled fur and feathers at their feet, spreading loose matter along with a delicate scent of musk, a hint of held-back decay.

"You really sure you don't even know his name?" Joe asked Judy, after a long, silent minute. "Considering the guy still looks out of your eyes, now and then . . . seems like your blackrobes didn't do too good a job, pea soup or not, is all I'm sayin'."

"Yeah, well, I can do the same thing to him too, for that matter—just don't choose to, most of the time. But I'm *me* again, I know that much, and I have Father Wale and Father Frye to thank for it. Anything else . . . that's my business, not theirs."

"You sure about that?"

Another silence filled with a low *shussh* of wind, plus the slow and steady beat of Joe's heart. And—

"I call him Mister Nobody," she said, softly, to her lightly smoking shoe-tops. In practically a whisper: "'Nobody, ancient mischief, nobody . . . Harasses always with an absent body . . .'" A swallow. "There's a crack in me, and I know it; he blew me open—things get in. But they don't get *into* me. They get in *through* me."

"So I better watch out, the longer I'm around you. Is that it?"

Judy sighed, eyes downcast, like they were glued there. "God, I don't know. From what I've seen, though . . . yeah, maybe. I mean . . ."

(. . . *probably*.)

Joe had one hand in his pocket (just like the song), fingertips absently grazing the lump of his Grandmother's tusk, as it shifted around under well-waxed sealskin; he felt a spark leap up from it at the word, unspoken or not. Caught a flip-book flutter of faces going by, some too-swift etheric undercurrent, here and gone before he could untangle its true significance: a woman with Judy's same colouration, her face swollen double-size from chemo and painkillers, yet frozen rigid with what the drugs couldn't reach. A kid a bit older than Judy still looked, face slack, hooked up to machines. A drunk on the corner, dirty dog collar poking out above a Goodwill hoodie's V-neck—the other blackrobe from her exorcism, Father Frye?—while he hid his bottle in a Tim Horton's donuts bag and waited for a gap between passersby to take another furtive slug . . .

He didn't know their names, most of 'em. Didn't know their stories. Only that they'd once all stood close to Judy as he was standing now, and lived to regret it—

(or not)

Judy cut him a glance, like she could tell from the way he took his next breath he'd seen something, or (even) what he *had* seen. Adding, after a half-minute more: "My point is, me showing up anywhere is almost never a coincidence."

Wouldn't doubt it, Joe thought. And had a weird lick of anger at her words run through him, nevertheless, unreasonable as that might seem. Like: *Hey, there you go—she* is *just another damn paleface, after all. Since everything's always about* them.

"Listen, girlie—far as I know, whatever's gone wrong 'round here first started happening a pretty long time before *you* came on the scene."

"Yeah, sure. But it still might turn out to have as much to do with me—or Mr. N., or his kind—as it does with anything else, which means I might sort of be a *good* person to bring along, too. Maybe."

Joe sighed, and took a last long look around—the watching overhang of pines, dark even in daytime; the rustling ring of corpses, cutting them off from where the path to that abandoned nickel claim mineshaft the elders had pointed him towards could just be picked out, opening up between two particularly twisted-looking trees. The open ice-mouth beside them and the closed tent behind. And Judy Kiss to his right, his spare parka at least long enough to keep her torso warm, even if the pants she wore beneath weren't meant for anything much more strenuous than clubbing; Judy Kiss, her breath like steam, her eyes perhaps downcast to hide the fact that they already looked far less brown . . . than yellow.

Thinking about just how much he didn't really know concerning that other hole, even now—not how it figured, or if it did, or how deep it went down, or how best to find out. Or what might be waiting for him at the bottom, if and when he finally got there.

"Maybe," he allowed, eventually. Finding he already knew what was going to happen next.

The trip took a good two hours—half an hour for hiking, an hour and a half for descent. They only had one harness between them, so there was more than a little time wasted tying off on a nearby tree and adjusting the straps to fit Judy, who'd never rappelled before, which meant Joe had to half lower her, half swing her back and forth, down into the depths. Then, once she'd hit solid ground and unbuckled herself, it was up to Joe to reel the whole thing back up, rinse and repeat, this time with his own ass in the sling.

Down under, he'd expected to feel colder than he actually did—but soon enough, he tracked the eddy of unnatural warmth back to its source:

Judy, peering around at the bare rock walls, the slick-frozen ruts beneath her feet where tracks had been torn back up when the original claim failed to pay out, and the company who sank it retreated to Sudbury's fresher fields.

"What were they after down here?"

"Nickel, but there wasn't ever much, even before they got the shut-down order. Elders say they weren't too sure *what* they found, 'cept it could've been radioactive." Judy nodded, flipping hair from her eyes; as she turned and crossed by him, Joe felt himself suddenly ooze sweat like a tribute to her proximity, disproportionately wet and hot under his parka's great weight. "Now the Rez and the OPP try to make sure people stay out, but something keeps taking the safety fences away—the most recent bunch's probably still up top, under that big pile of snow we saw near the shaft-head."

"Uh huh."

Joe kept on talking, as the small of his back got steadily slicker. "This last fall, two Rez kids went missing; Elders think maybe they fell in, but they could'a jumped, too. Broke their legs when they hit bottom, then starved to death, but not 'til they'd spent some time cuttin' on each other and writing stuff nobody recognized on the walls. Should've been right about . . . *here*, supposedly . . ."

He cast about, scanning the walls at low- to mid-level, trying to figure out how high a crippled teenager could reach. Judy did the same, squatting to get closer. And because that sulphur-sweet *smell* of hers was back in his nostrils now, stronger than ever, he found himself throwing out jokes to clear his head—shallow, hollow-toned, a slaughterhouse stand-up's don't-act-like-death-is-watching "wit"—

"'Judy Kiss.' That just doesn't get less funny."

Without stopping: "Says the guy who calls himself 'Joe Crow.'"

"Where'd your folks come from, anyways?"

"Eastern Europe, mainly. Hungary, Romania."

"Huh: Dracula country."

She nodded again, hair already slopped back over, shadowing her gaze. "My Dad's even named Bela."

"Must be fun at Hallowe'en."

"He's never fun." She stood in one smooth move, took a half-step back. "I think . . . yeah, this might be it. See?"

Joe took a look. There, under a new coat (or two) of ice: brownish, smeary, all loops and dots and weird little circles made from bloody palm-prints mashed together, curled so there was at least a prick of empty space left untouched in their middles. Grey lichens crusted around and through what Joe supposed must be sentences, fuzzing the already-uncertain lines even further. It wasn't any sort of Native script he'd ever encountered, and definitely not English—an old-style witch-code, like Crossing the River? Ogham? Runes?

"Those kids didn't write this," Judy said, quietly, from beside him.

"What do you mean? Look at the colour—red turns brown, then grey, then black. It's not like they scratched it into the rock, or anything; it's gotta be fresh. If it was older'n a few months, we wouldn't even be able to read it."

"No, I mean . . . *people* didn't write this. Not your People, not my people—no *people*, at all."

In his heart, Joe knew she was right—but though that was the first phrase which sprang to mind, it wasn't really there the intuition rested like a frozen, unswallowed seed. More in that cold spot at the base of his neck, between the first and second vertebrae, through which most possessing spirits enter.

"I've seen this kind of alphabet before, though . . . he wrote in it on my walls. Made *me* write in it. Like graffiti."

"Your Mr. Nobody?"

"The very same." She crouched again, closer this time, so her nose almost grazed the wall. "This looks like a name."

And—when had she taken off her glove? Because now she was skimming the wall with her bare fingertips, heedless of the rising mist, her touch already melting through: One sigil, another, another. Her lips parting to sound them out, as she did so—

"*Zem-ya-za,*" Judy said, carefully. "*Husband to—Anah and—Aholibamah . . . brother of—Azazel . . . sower of seed . . . father to giants . . .*"

Joe's own lips were dry, abruptly numb, too clumsy to do anything but purse, part, tremble—a strange thrumming current seemed to build with every syllable, thickening the air around him with static. Like they'd somehow gone to Europe without knowing it, plugged the wrong kind of appliance in the wrong kind of socket, and now the whole hotel room was going to blow up.

He coughed, phlegm like blood in his cracking throat. Offered, weakly: "Maybe you shouldn't be, uh, saying that kinda stuff . . . out loud . . ."

She didn't seem to hear, though. And now, over her shoulder, he began to catch a cast-off light from her eyes on the melting wall—that brownish glint dimming, the yellow inflection (*infection*) mounting—

It was enough to make him flinch as she finally started to turn, his entire body tensing, expecting to see Mr. Nobody's shadow come over her whole face, the way a flicker might come (or go) in someone else's pupil. One huge flash of wakeful malefice, lidding open and shut across her entire head at once.

But no, not yet: just her, just Judy. For the moment.

"*The sons and daughters of our enemies shall wander amongst the tombs, in the unclean places*," she told him, "*and cut themselves with stones. That's* what the rest of it reads."

"'Cause this guy—Zemyaza?—says so."

"Well, yeah." She gave an odd, little half-smile. "And they did, didn't they? That's what they've *been* doing, around here. All this time."

(That's why you're here.)

That current again, leaching from the air down into the snow and rock beneath them, then spilling back up through their boot-soles— that irregular beat, a thousand skipping, inhumanly ventricled hearts. Judy didn't even seem to hear it anymore, gaze turned inwards; she was listening to another voice entirely. As she kept on speaking, Joe could already catch its too-familiar no-tone seeping through her own: Infinitely recognizable, considering it belonged to something he'd only ever "talked" to the once, in somebody else's dream.

"I don't know how much you know about the Apocrypha, the stuff they left out of the Bible, but . . . Once upon a time, before the beginning, God assigned angels to watch over humanity: called them Watchers, predictably. Never let it be said that the Almighty isn't literal-minded. . . ."

(A pure Mr. Nobody line, if ever there was one.)

"Well, these angels betrayed their trust—they looked down, liked what they saw, acted accordingly. This is where a lot of the people who seem, um, *larger than life* in some indefinable way come from—the Gilgameshes, the Alexanders, the Rhanis of Jhansi. Giants in the earth, in those days. All those mighty men and women of renown, those people with a little something extra. People like . . ."

. . . *you and me, Joe.*

He shook his head against the intrusion, pain flaring first behind one eye, then the other. Man, that telepathy of hers—or whatever the hell (ha, ha) it was—was really beginning to wear.

"Naturally," Judy continued, "the angels had to be punished—that sort of supernatural fuckery is always at least quasi-non-consensual, considering the basic age and power disparity issues involved. So the Watchers were disembodied, cast down, cast out. Only those of their blood remained behind: the Nephilim, whose very flesh is anathema, antithetical even to the humanity they sprang from. Who fought amongst themselves and were worshipped as false gods, whose followers laid the foundations of Babel and Chaldaean Ur, of Sodom and Gomorrah . . ."

"Uh huh. And where'd *they* end up?"

Another smile, extra-creepy. "Well . . . God took a gander down, got pissed, made it rain for forty days, forty nights, consecutively. And after that—"

—after *that*, the deluge. The one myth every culture worldwide seemed to come up with. The great and terrible Flood.

Meltwater sloshed up over his toes as he took a shaky step back, away from her and her thinning crooked pupils. Joe felt the thrum abruptly turn rumble, small puffs of dust detaching from above, cracks marbling the walls around. Said, with what he thought was quite admirable restraint: "This place doesn't seem too stable all of a sudden, girlie. Might be time to—"

Which is when the ground opened up below them both, pulling them in; a short fall but a deep one, through empty space, onto rubble. Then silence, darkness, sleep.

Joe opened his eyes at last and saw sky, a thin strip of it crushed between two jagged shelves of rock, full of stars. Night had obviously fallen while he lay unconscious, which didn't bode too well in terms of temperature— but when he wiggled his toes and patted himself down, he didn't feel any unforeseen wetness. No bones broken, either, though the lamp must have escaped the pitfall; only the starlight provided any illumination. Just a ringing in his ears, a rough throat, and the slow realization that Judy Kiss was nowhere within reach or sight.

He looked back up along the raw broken rock slope, automatically marking handholds and boot-rests as jagged black edges against the stars. Relief grew as he realized the climb back up looked far from impossible; this was followed by a connect-the-dots flash of understanding that, he was almost embarrassed to admit, registered far less as "normal" shock or loss than unlooked-for good fortune. Because *he* might be able to make the climb unaided, but—

Could just get up and leave her, he thought, before he could muster quite enough willpower to kick the traitorous idea away. *I mean, she'd be okay, right? Like she said. And maybe all this crap really is happening because of her, at which point go me, for savin' her ass just long enough to make sure she got buried alive down here in the first place . . .*

But no. He didn't even need the immediate shock from his back pocket—where his Grandmother's bag, and the tusk inside it, had ended up—to tell him how wrong that was. Or her voice, for that matter, back-masked into his head through a momentary crease between Worlds: *This place is a sink, Joe, a rotten wound—won't get any better for covering it up.*

(Her, either.)

Naw, 'course not. 'Cause that'd make things *way* too easy.

"Yeah, *Nukum*," he sighed, out loud. Then turned over, painfully, and shifted enough of the crap around him away to make standing up an option. He had no immediate idea of which way to turn after that; just keep on shuffling, he guessed, hands out, 'til he caught hold of something that felt like it might be Judy.

But the further he went, oddly enough, the less he had to fumble—a new light was growing everywhere at once, sickly-golden. It lit the walls a fissure at a time, making their flaws sing like veins filled with radioactive isotope. Space spread out before him, the floor seeming to unfold into visibility like a fist opening, palm-up.

And all around him, under the ice, glowing wall to ceiling, ceiling to floor: more loops, more dots, more empty spaces. Sigil after sigil of angelic script, the Watchers' own personal language . . . the same one they taught their outsized children (whose passions were so disproportionate they once threatened to disrupt the balance of Creation itself) to sing themselves lullabies in, before leaving them orphaned forever.

Joe stopped, stood still, squinting up at it. As he did, the "letters" blurred, ice peeling to slice away in semi-solid folds. Under it, the shaft walls—already washed clean—began to dry on contact with the steamy air; alien fossils came humping up beneath the signs as if to meet him, surfacing from under the rock's grey skin like dragonflies backlit in amber. While something else, at the same time—from inside *him*—rose to meet them in return.

A final shimmer, wrenching the cave-writing straight from un- to intelligible. Those oblique whirls and curves suddenly easy to read as any given street-sign: *As Above, so Below, for here, Zemyaza and Azazel Grigorim bequeath an archive to our children's children, a treasurehouse of words made for war, deception, and pain. Here we speak of the assumption and uses of human flesh, of the unseating and pollution of the human soul, so that our seed may replace theirs, and thus subdue the world. Occupy them like an army, make them curse themselves, make them break themselves apart. Drive them out into the unclean places . . .*

(make them wander amongst the tombs, and)

. . . cut themselves . . .

Joe doubled up and puked, long and loud, at the feel of it touching his brain. Behind him, he heard a bone-break scattering of stones on stone as someone else—Judy, he could only assume—regained their feet, hands braced against either wall. Yet it was Mr. Nobody's voice, now more than ever, which said his name a slow second later; hesitant, like it was a bit impressed he'd actually survived the fall. Or possibly just amused.

"Joe Crow," it said. "Looks like something in here doesn't agree with you. Or maybe I should say: something in *you* agrees with *here*."

Unable to speak, bracing himself over the steaming pool of his stomach contents, Joe only spat.

"Probably better not to tell any of your Native Supremacist friends up North," the voice suggested, "but it looks like you might have a touch of the *really* Old Blood in you, after all."

Joe pushed himself back to rest on his heels, head down, making himself breathe slow and deep. The sigils' light rang in his ears; he could see the thrum of their radiance pulsing through the air like basso heatwaves. He lifted one arm, reaching for the light without conscious will; stopped, staring at his hand like a boy on his first hash-high, entranced solely by the workings of his fingers.

The light shone *through* his flesh, the way a flashlight inside a cupped hand highlights bones, but all throughout, in shifting waves. And the silhouettes inside his flesh were the shadow-sketch mirrors of the things in the wall: skeletal spirals of shell, leaf-thin fins and wings, limestone bone-spurs. They moved and turned like a magic lantern's cutouts, and he could *feel* them inside him, spasming and knotting and—

Punching out through his skin, the fabric of his clothes, more shocking for the wrongness of it and the lack of pain than anything else. Juddering cramps racking him, a sudden wrenching constriction at waist, knees, shoulders, feet—as if everything he was wearing had suddenly become half a size too small for him—

(No. Not the clothes shrinking. *You're—*)

His parka tore up the back, and he felt something, *two* somethings, spring out through the gap; on the floor below him, shadow fell black to either side, saw-edged triangles of membrane and bone (bone to bone, bone of my bones). His balance shifted, weight and muscle filling in beneath his shoulderblades. His fingernails lengthened before his eyes, werewolf B-movie style—sharpening, thickening.

And between his hands, Judy Kiss, kneeling to face him, her own hands cupping his face. Looking at him now with eyes gone brown once more, completely human and completely helpless. Mr. Nobody driven out, if only for a moment, by the thing Joe had so arrogantly assumed was *his* prerogative: pity.

Softly: "Oh, Joe . . ."

The changes hadn't stopped; he could feel them raking through him like barbed wire, threading veins, muscles, and organs at once. He forced out words, hearing the shift in his vocal cords: deeper already, timbre unnaturally resonant, a vibration he could feel in his sinuses.

"This . . . was always in me," he husked. "Wasn't it."

Yes.

And new silhouettes stretched out across the floor, rearing up, backlit in the sigil-light; blurred outlines of ten-foot-tall shapes invisible to the eye, perhaps winged, perhaps armoured, their numbers uncountable.

Welcome, son. Grandson. Great-, great-, great-, great-, great- . . .

The words themselves enough to set off a glass-rim echo, droning 'round and 'round. Joe froze where he stood, shaking. While the cast-off fossil-storm swirled on, chipping and curling around him 'til it hooked underneath his skin like thrown seed, like dragon's teeth, grooming him from within. These Holocaust-smoke-black new wings of his long enough now to cramp against either wall, to jut and fold and catch—hollow and extensible, spectre-thin, made half from his own bones, half from theirs. That tiny shard of the Nephilim inside him working its way out like a splinter, reducing the whole rest of his fallible human body to nothing but one big meat-waste byproduct.

Like one of those horror movies, Joe thought, thickly; the words took effort to form, his mind an anaesthetized tongue. *The big-budget Hollywood ones, where the yuppie hero goes crazy when he finds out there's a super- to go with the natural. Or the late-night creepshow classics, where ol' Professor Knows-it-all dies with a look of pure amazement on his face 'cause it turns out those silly native superstitions really do work, even on well-intentioned white guys . . .*

That was pretty much how he felt, right about now: not his God, not his demons, not even his basic cosmo-mythology—as ridiculous to him as his ancestors must have seemed to Knud Rasmussen and his ilk, squatting in their shaking tents and carving *tupilak* to keep "civilization" safely back over the ice. But all that didn't seem too relevant right now, let alone ironic—not with his skeleton apparently trying to roll itself up, jump out of his throat, and crawl away, leaving him behind in a heap for the angels to pick out his soul.

How many times have I had to tell people it doesn't matter *if you believe in a thing or not, 'cause it's damn sure still gonna kill you?* he wondered, spitting teeth.

And Judy . . . just standing there, hand to mouth, watching. Utterly untouched. Because though she could read it too, which argued for more than a dip of the Nephilim paintbrush in her own genetic jar, this particular message just wasn't *meant* for the likes of her. Not her, or

161

anyone else unlucky enough to have already been so thoroughly—

(*touched*)

—by another, very different, sort of "angel."

Peering through the baffling sensory array already starting to filter his input, which dimmed the visible world down to dust even as it turned the usually invisible world up to eleven, Joe could finally see how contact with Mr. Nobody had left Judy vacuum-sealed rather than cracking her even wider; she was lapped and slicked in some resinous, invisible coating that repelled glory, whether infernal or divine, the same way Teflon shed cooked egg. He remembered her gangrenous skin repinking itself, and wondered if even age could touch her—if she would wander forever from crime scene to accident site, trailing harm and discord like a fog . . . but never *involved*, never at the epicentre, never a bride (she who had been forced into marriage with Darkness, then forcibly divorced from Light).

Never, ever again.

"They *used* me," Judy said, out loud, if to no one in specific. "To get to you. To get you down here and do . . . *this* to you."

"Think that was more a sorta, ah—accident," Joe managed, gulping, before puking afresh: no food this time, just hot bile, melting his words into unintelligible mush. Though it wasn't like Judy seemed to be listening.

"A Judas goat. That's all I am. That's all I'll ever be."

The Watchers, behind their wall of ice and rock, nodded their strangely helmeted heads, agreeing: *Burned girl, girl on fire; we smell our cousin's scent on you, his breath on your breath. Look closely and see his marks rise everywhere, flaws on a blown coal.*

Joe saw her bow under the assault, head dropping. Saw those steaming acid tears start to flow, her only weapon left.

Charred, carbonized, from the inside out—you know it to be true, do you not? Burned once, you now find you only wish to burn . . . this man, this place, everything you touch . . .

Judy flinched, as though from a slap; Joe gave a bark of protest, slapping the wet rock with both crippled hands as Mr. Nobody's yellow glint peeked out from beneath her lids yet one more time, nonchalantly unexpected, to grin at her pain like it was the very best show in town. Following up the Watchers' iron-voiced assertion in his sly, oddly ordinary voice: "You're my match, Judy-girl; a match for me, like I'm a match for thee. My flint and steel, fit to burn the world, always ready to hand whenever I feel the need to pick you up—"

"NO!"

The force of the roar from Joe's throat shocked him, shook the cave walls; stone pattered down from the ceiling, rattling like static. Judy looked up, the yellow in her eyes flickering sharply back to brown, as if likewise spooked.

Joe got his feet under him, stood, fighting the nausea the skewed perspective of his new height and balance brought. "You're . . . not him," he coughed out. "Not his. You're you." He could feel his boots splitting along the seams, laces snapping. "He can't do shit . . . unless you let him. Just gets to watch. And who did that, huh? Who got you . . . free?"

Judy had turned away, not looking at either the Watchers or at him, staring into what little darkness was left. But Joe didn't need to see her face anymore—he *felt* her mind in a psychic spotlight, pain and memory tangling inside her skull like acid-green lightning around raw-stripped power cables. And hovering over it all, Mr. Nobody's amused malice, a mustard-gas cloud of hate mixed with—

(*wariness?*)

"Father Frye," Judy husked. "Father Wale. *God* . . ."

"And you, Judy. *You're* the one did that." Joe felt his tongue changing further even as he spoke, muscle becoming fluid, ready and eager to shape sounds no human could; he fought it back under control, like wrestling a six-inch python. "Without you, the blackrobes—even the Spirit itself— none of 'em could've done a damn thing. So now you know: you saved yourself. And that means you can do just about anything you want from now on, can't you?"

A wave of something not quite pain swayed him where he stood. The world blurred. He felt a terrible, slow cracking beneath his feet: something giving way, no longer able to support the weight of what he was becoming. Judy had turned back to watch, wide-eyed, white-faced.

"Anything I want," she whispered. "But that's just one more lie, isn't it, Joe? Your life was a lie, and I can't retell it—I can't undo this. Can't make you . . . human again."

No tears, this time, only breathlessness, as if the scope of how wrong they'd both been had finally sunk in.

Can't make me what I never really was, Joe agreed, slipping onto the frequency of Watcher-speak with despairing ease. The beings limned upon the wall inclined their silhouetted heads once, in silent agreement. And then froze, as Joe went on, deceptively calmly: *But you can make me something else, send me where I'm supposed to end up. Where those things can't ever go.*

Wordless denial rang in a shockwave from the wall-shapes, a bell's note so immense it bled into subsonics; Judy stumbled under it, and even Joe reeled. He felt the Watchers swarm him like dogs on a toddler, goodwill or malice irrelevant for sheer fright of weight and numbers; he sank to his knees, their need and longing burdening him in layers of stone, geologically ancient.

He could not leave them, they begged. Not after so long. He was their last hand left to play, the first chance they'd had to touch Time from inside in thousands of years, the first opportunity to be no longer Watchers, but *actors*. To stand embodied once more as beings of angel-stuff and human flesh admixed, able to hear the Eternal the way humans never could, but possessing the free will angels never would: Nephilim.

Our child, the Watchers sang, *born to make the world his own, born to give us* back *the world . . .*

Joe's specific memories were almost gone, thinned to invisibility under the onslaught, the way ink washes to transparency when a tide comes in.

But: "Zemyaza," Judy said, carefully. "Az-aym-ez."

. . . and somewhere on the wall, near the top left corner, the light of one of the sigils blinked out.

For a moment the mark beneath remained; then it puffed off the wall like rust, like rain. Dust corkscrewed into the air, then whirled out of existence.

The Watchers, as a chorus: *No no no no no no no—*

(*Yes.*)

Joe pulled himself up on one elbow, grimacing as it bent the wrong way. "What'd you do?" he asked her.

Judy shook her head, intent on where the last of the dust still spiralled. "I don't know." Then: "Azazael, lea-za-za . . ."

No no, you cannot, you must NOT—

Still Judy read on, ignoring them: Words reversed, the archive rewritten, unwritten, backwards. The walls began to clear themselves a syllable/character at a time, flaking, falling. And there arose a field of wailing, thin and pained, a choir of dying bees.

Girl, what do you do? You'll kill us.

"Shouldn't've made your evil plan quite so easy to fuck up, then," she told them, tonelessly. "If it meant *that* much to you."

(*Oh*, good, *little Judy*)

Joe "heard" it, somewhere in the back of his skull: Mr. Nobody's attention, walking around in there on tiny scuttling fly-legs, trailing carrion.

(*Yes, hit them where it hurts, and keep on hitting. Watchers, Grigori, God-* "*chosen,*" *pathetic, arrogant human-fuckers*)

But: "Yeah? Well, you can shut the Hell up too, while you're at it,"

Judy snapped back, out loud. "Joe's right; I don't need you, never did. Not like you need *me*."

(*Oh* ho. *Brave words, meat-bag . . .*)

But enough to do the trick, apparently. Joe's nostrils cleared, slowly— Mr. Nobody's matchbook-stink faded into the background, soon replaced with clean snow on the one hand, hot rock on the other. Unfortunately, though perhaps not unpredictably, he seemed to have taken Judy's immunity to the Watchers' signal-spell along with him; she folded and charred under its fatal current, bared bloody teeth over bruising tongue, spat clots from a swelling throat . . .

. . . and kept on reading, just the same.

Words fell from the walls in every direction, spraying out into empty air, gone within seconds. Leaving nothing behind them but clean space and dead lichen.

We know his name, your persecutor—we will give it to you as pledge of victory. Say it backwards instead, and destroy him forever.

A bitter, liquid laugh. "Sure, right. But why should I believe you? You're angels, just like him. You'll say *any* fucking thing."

You cannot, must not, do not, please, burning burning burning . . .

"So stop me. If you can."

Obviously, they couldn't.

When Joe came to, one final time, he and Judy were lying together under a light-woven lace blanket of new snow, with more falling down through the sundered roof above—a cobweb curtain, torn and trailing in the wind. It was already far colder than he remembered; the once-warm meltwater had halfway turned back to ice, sticking his broken wings to the tunnel floor. In other news, his mouth also felt like it was full of somebody else's teeth, and he couldn't feel his arms or legs.

"Guess they're . . . gone," he managed, through abraded lips, not quite able to avoid lisping on the sibilants.

"Guess so," she said, not moving.

Joe coughed, rackingly, then tried again. "Looks like the . . . storm's comin' back. You better get goin', you wanna . . . make it to the truck before . . . it gets real bad."

A listless horizontal headshake, like making a snow angel's hat. "Wouldn't do me much good if I did."

"Why . . . not?"

"Couldn't figure it out from my clothes, huh? That'd be 'cause I'm strictly a downtown-Toronto girl, Joe Crow. Never learned how to drive."

And that, even with the pain mounting up, the horrid disconnect between flesh, spirit, and the world around both . . . that ridiculous pitch-black joke of a joke alone was *almost* enough to make Joe laugh—even here, even now. Even bad though he knew it would probably hurt to do so.

"Seriously, though . . ." he managed, a minute or two later. "'S like the song . . . 'You don't have to go home, but yuh . . . you . . .'"

". . . 'can't . . . stay . . . here.'"

"Thass the one."

Judy sighed, grimaced, and made it to her knees in a single spasming, cockroach wriggle; from this vantage point, she glanced down at him sidelong, hair hung back over her face from forehead to blood-smeared upper lip, like she'd planned it that way, or something. Like she really thought it'd be enough to hide the fact she was crying again.

"I'm pretty strong," she admitted, "but I don't think I can carry you."

"'m not . . . assking yuh . . ."

"Yeah, yeah, I know you're not." A pause, then a hitching breath. And then: "What *do* you want me to do?"

Joe shrugged, or tried to—reached up and aimed one misshapen hand to brush the scalding saltwater from her cheek, or (at least) seriously formed the intention of doing it. Maybe didn't do either, in the end. Yet he could still feel her leaning closer at the same time, straining to hear him, as he forced the words out in a final barely human breath—

". . . bag, in m' pocket . . . drop't in th' hole. 'N' on t'other side, d'n by th' belt . . . gun . . ."

A drop fell on the corner of his raw mouth, wet and hot; Judy laid one small palm on either side of his jaw, using her thumb to brush it further in. He felt it on what was left of his tongue, like a benediction.

"I won't need that," she said. And gave his head a short, sharp twist.

Judy stood by the open ice as the sun rose, sweating under the weight of both parkas, her feet slopping out pigeon-toed in Joe's too-large boots; though she'd cut some fishing line from the tackle she'd found inside his tent and tried to tie them on tighter, she suspected she'd eventually have to go back to her own impractically thin shoes once more. Which was why she now wore them looped around her neck by their laces, heels knocking hard against her heart whenever she turned her back on the numbing wind.

Something stirred at the outer edge of her vision, vaguely silver, roughly man-shaped. And long before it remembered how to talk, she knew it would probably speak in Joe Tulugaak's voice.

Looks like I really am dead, huh?

"Looks like."

Well, now. That's sure something you don't see every day.

Still not quite able to look at him, Judy made a fist and knuckled her eyes, the snow's gloss suddenly also far too dazzling to contemplate directly. Saying, as she did: "You're actually taking it pretty well, all things considered."

Joe smiled at that, a faint crease left hanging in the lightening air. Replying, mildly—

Hell, Judy-like-the-food—all things considered, *I'd rather be in Philadelphia. But what did you think I thought was gonna happen?*

No easy answer, there. So Judy skipped past it, offering instead: "I . . . just wish I hadn't got you killed. That's all."

If ghosts could snort, this is what it would sound like. *You didn't, girlie—I got me killed. Like I always kinda knew I would.* A pause. *Besides, we all end up like this, sooner or later. Don't we?*

"If we're lucky," she whispered. But he had already broken apart into a shoal of phantom fish—their scales shining like glass—and swum away past her, veering down into the hole by her stolen boots, where they disappeared without a trace.

Judy stood there for far longer than she ever might have thought she would, just a few days earlier. Finally, the cold became pressing, even to her; she shouldered Joe's pack and set off across the ice. Became a dot on a line, blending in, until she too was gone.

Within hours, all the strange poisons that had leached up into Windigo Island from the mine's open sore had begun to boil away. Animals turned their heads towards it once more, from every direction; beneath the ice, fish made cold, slow progress through the lake's currents, fumbling towards its shores. A bear moaned in its winter sleep, dreaming that Windigo might be a place to make and raise cubs. It was as though even the insects, dug deep in the frozen wood of the island's trees, knew that, since Judy Kiss had agreed to take her tainted self away, the only evil likely to flourish here would—from now on—be strictly of the human kind.

Meanwhile, Joe Tulugaak's body lay at the bottom of the open shaft, broken and bent but otherwise unmolested, until it was far too covered with snow to be recognizable. And though the Rez Elders sent people to look for his truck, his tent, the radio they had given him, none of them ever searched far enough—or deep enough—to find it. Since he had no relatives alive to ask after him, and no (real) profession, it wasn't much longer before he was almost completely forgotten.

Eventually, spring came.

HEART'S HOLE: TIME, THE REVELATOR REMIX (2005)

We were already setting up the decon chamber when he came in; had this voice like new money, a great wad of it flipping fresh onto the counter with this sharp, papery kind of snap. "Oh, that's a *great* idea: the suits, the, uh . . . That's so it looks just like you're a legitimate, uh, cleaning company to anyone on the outside, is that right? And who came up with that angle, exactly?"

"That'd be Ms. Cirocco, Mr. Gall," I say, turning.

"Very professional. *Very* nice."

I just nodded, slightly—thinking, as I did: *Well, 'course it is, you great git. Seeing that's what she's best at, after all: all craft, no service. Could sell shite to a colostomy case, that one, and make 'em ask for more; she's just that sharp, not to mention that crooked.*

And here she comes 'round the corner, like I just dreamed her up that same second: my Davina, scrubbing her rexed hair back with both hands, already in full biohazard drag. Sardonic half-smile, pig-snub Mick nose; freckled skin sheer enough to see through, the light's just right.

"Somebody lettin' on how we're not really in the removals business, Jo?" she asked me, skipping over this fool like he was slag-spill. "Cause last time I looked, this stuff we keep on mopping up still counts as waste—on the psychic scale, at least."

"Ectoplasmic byproduct, yeah. Fumigation, like."

"De*tox*ification, *more* like." Fixing him: "Right, Mr. Gall?"

To which he just gives a little fluttery grin, and pulls out his keys. Then has us on the Grand Tour from top to bottom for the next hour or so, swanning us 'round like he was showing us the Ritz instead of some private cancer clinic turned condos. Last been active maybe five years back, but the traces were still dripping down everywhere you looked.

"We're gonna clean up on this one," Dav mutters sidelong at me, no trace of visible irony. But I had to agree; place was a fount of ghosts, full to the eyes if it'd had any. Kind of building my Nana'd've called not fit for habitation, and me too, maybe—before personal experience of "Toronto's mounting homelessness pandemic" (that was our other partner Ross talking, with his big words and his politics) disabused me of the notion that no one with the brains God gave a goat could ever willingly live in a haunted house.

"Canada" meant "snow," most places, but I'd seen little of that. It was high summer now, triple smog alert in the downtown area, brown-outs, humidity, and all. Just walking around hurt, made your eyes burn and tear; breathing felt like you had your head lodged halfway up Jesus's own exhaust-pipe. A crown of thorns worn stylish, inside-out.

Not to mention how the ghosts pressed up against every window, 'round every corner, only made it seem the hotter. Drifting like spores through this carpeted honeycomb of Gall's and sniffing me on the wind like an accident. Sticking their eyeless heads through walls, floors, and ceiling just to gape, their mouths all teeth, all nude flapping tongue and airless, voiceless, ceaseless howl.

Rife with it, and bad—a bad, bad place, this. Which set it apart from every other place we'd done to date . . . not at bloody all.

It's a job, J., Dav always said. *Nothin' but. Free money, baby.* Pausing, then adding: *'Sides, you don't like how it shakes down, we can always go back to construction.*

But that wasn't exactly true, now. Was it?

You can live with a hole in your heart, long as you've something to plug it with. That's the lesson I learned at birth, though it did pop up again later on, here and there: in paramedic training, for example, back when I still had my ambulance licence. Back when people weren't afraid to let me 'round the drugs.

Real trouble comes when you try to pull that plug out, though, and get on with it. Delirious pain; a sudden rush of air and blood to your oxygen-starved brain. Liquid crash-out, bright red blink.

I was born with a hole, but the doctors at that Clinic in Glasgow patched it up—the one where my Mam dropped down like a sack of potatoes on the clean white floor after picking up what'd be her very last hit of methadone. Dropped herself, but not me.

Me they had to cut out the hard way, and quick-smart at that.

So I took my first screaming breaths in a plastic bubble-bag, fed and held through gloves in the walls; five operations to stitch my ventricles back the way they were meant to go, and all before I was two. Not to mention how they had to crack my breast-bone over and over while doing it, so I'd never be able to bend it like Beckham—such a terrible scar they left behind, a long, furled chain of knots inching down between my breasts. Davina used to trace it every night, telling it, like a rosary.

When I was a kiddie, some of the doctors my Care workers took me to thought I was blind, some daft. This 'cause I'd sit there watching trails in the air and laughing at the patterns they made: the hovering faces, the half-bared teeth and moaning mouths. I didn't feel their sorrow and pain, their desperate need to communicate—just watched, and laughed, and sometimes said: "Do it again!"

A headless torso in the upstairs bathroom hallway, silver-gelid with decay, hanging and turning slightly, like a slug on a line of mucus—one leg mainly there down to the knee, dangling limply; the other one gone in a shredded nest of bone and a single raw red knob. A pale little boy crouched down in the sandpit at the playground where women from my Nana's work dropped their bairns, staring at anyone who'd stop to build a castle like he wanted to eat 'em alive; couldn't tell he was any different from them, crashing trucks and screaming over the other side 'til he turned away, and the whole back of his head was one big hole.

Or a woman lying sprawled out in that vacant lot we climbed through to get to school, with rusty wire growing up through her stomach like weeds: she'd smile at us all as we went by, from two mouths—one on her face, uneven with smeared lipstick. The other on her neck, so deep you could see her voicebox, gleaming like a rind of frost.

Never bothered me, at the time, how I was the only one ever seemed to smile back.

But oh, the way they all shone, like they still shine. That lovely mothlight of ghosts, quick blue-white-grey-silver fragments spinning 'round some unseen vortex in a drizzle of fine-scraped souls. The dead have a half-life, like radiation; half in both senses, far as I can tell, for it's not like they ever seem to know why they're there, or who you are, or what in the hell it is keeps sticking them to you like flies on a strip, anyways. Just always pressing in closer, closer, closer—close enough so's they can warm their see-through hands at your soul and whisper in your ear, twittering away like blackbirds with their tongues too split to talk.

"Is there something inside me, something they want?" I asked my Nana once, when I was maybe eight; she nodded, still knitting. Then, worried: "Can it get *out*?"

"One day, sure—ye won't be able t'stop it, will ye? Just like everybody else." And I must've made some noise at that, 'cause she looked up at last, softening. Said: "But they'll never get *in*, for all their trying. So might be ye can take some comfort from that."

It'd sounded plausible, back when I was still too much the child to know why she must be exaggerating.

Here I was, though, nineteen years later. Listening in with half an ear, as Davina struck her usual hardest possible bargain, and smiling at the result: this wanker Gall'd never know what hit him.

"Five thousand the full job, payable in installments. We get two up front no matter what, non-refundable, plus expenses; say about three hundred a day, just to keep it doable. You down with all that, Mr. Gall?"

"And, uh . . . no receipts?"

"No *receipts*? The hell you think we are, man, some kinda scam?" That sharp grin, eyes narrowing like a double wink. "Call it asbestos, you have to—that's what it'll look like from the street, or even if somebody wants to send inspectors in. Glouwer-Cirocco-Puget 'locates and relocates,' same's it says in the phone book. 'Cause you do want what's in here *gone*, right?"

". . . right."

"Well, then. When you want us to start?"

"Soon as possible? We've already started showing units, and . . ." He trailed away; did seem to do that quite the bit, our Mr. Gall. Finishing, finally: "At any rate. The worst of it seems to be—"

"Through there, yeah?" I says, nodding.

And: "Yes." He looks at me then, full on, for maybe the first time. "How can you—"

But then he saw where my eyes were goin' next and stopped. Gulped. Then asked, all soft-like—

"Miss Glouwer?"

"Mr. Gall."

"Uh, um." Another pause. "Is there . . . *something* . . . in here, too?"

To which I just held his gaze with mine, mild as milk. And didn't even let myself smile.

Might've thought Davina'd elbow me one for scaring the customers over that, but I knew she could sense it too, if only the barest tip of it: what with the Irish on one side and Italian on the other, her chances of being full ghost-proof were always pretty bloody slim. Rare as them who're colour-blind, almost, or tone-deaf. Or what the Discovery Channel calls sociopaths.

"I'm sorry," Gall says, at last. "It's just . . . I just didn't think there'd be something in *here*, too."

Davina shrugs. "Drift. Get that a lot, huh, Jo?"

I nodded back, trying to look like I cared how scared he was getting, poor bastard.

Agreeing: "Oh yeah, certain. Old city, Toronto. Lots of people, lots of incidents . . . only stands to reason, right?"

Right.

Which is why I should have thought twice before I came here, all told.

'Cause in a place this bloody crowded, there's bound to be "something" pretty much everywhere you look.

"I saw an angel once, when I was yuir age," was the next-to-last thing my Nana ever said to me in person. "A black angel."

"Oh, aye."

"Aye, 'aye,' an' I'll thank ye not to laugh at me to ma own face, Jodice Glouwer."

I'd've taken it a bit more serious, but she was always saying things like that: like how she was five hundred years old, how this wasn't really her body, how she'd sold her soul to change places with somebody so's she wouldn't have to go up in smoke during the Burning Times, and this whole life we lived was her reward for faithful service to the Laird of Horns. Or how the radio was full of tiny little men, and it was fly-the-lights made the toaster work.

"Was an angel from God, I expect?"

"'Course not, are ye soft? Away wi' that lot." She paused. "Them others'll give ye all ye need, ye only ask."

Them others.

I just nodded, like always, and put it out of my mind. I was off to Canada in the morning, though I hadn't told her as much yet; never did. Never even tried.

She wouldn't've listened, anyway.

"When I see ye next, might be you'll have the mark upon ye also," she said, as I walked out the door. "Remember it, Jo: like *this*."

And she held up her hand.

Look down at my own arm now, and I can see that same raised weal of flesh hovering ghostlike above the place prepared for it, knotted white in on itself the same way that scar over my heart does. The way they tied my flapping pipes back down when I was too young to know the true hurt of it, and sealed it fast with a lump of melting plastic thread.

The thought before the deed, with no one to blame but myself for what I'm yet to do, if I just let it happen. The future already flushing bright under my skin, like blood.

We were in bed when I first told Davina how bad the Gall job could cost us, it turned out the way I saw it going. To which she snorted.

"$2,000 per down the drain, we pull out now—that's what it'd *cost* us. And who's gonna pay the difference then, you? Ain't comin' out of *my* pocket."

"But..."

"Look, what do you know about this thing, exactly? I mean, *exactly*."

"Enough to know it's bad."

"Oh, 'bad.' As opposed to all the *nice* ghosts we usually meet, right? Ones who want to kiss us and take us home . . ."

And on and on and on. 'Cause she could never quite bring herself to think someone else could know more than her, Dav, no matter or not if she knew bloody well it was true: known her so long at that point I'd just come to expect it as her first reaction to anything, even me.

Truth be told, I didn't *really* want to think about the cancer condo, no more than she did. Yet it crept up on me all the same, once I was half-asleep—Gall's grim card-house with its eddies and swirls and spectral slug-trails, tan-cured men humping along like spiders and smoking through their tracheotomy scars, bewigged women without hair, eyebrows, breasts. A little kiddie looking out one doorway, could've been boy or girl at that distance, with her poisoned skeleton shining up through her crepey young/old skin like some evil x-ray.

Guests don't last long in that room, Gall'd admitted, as we passed by; one look in her eyes told me why. Munchausen's by proxy, yeah? And why not—no better place on earth to cover up slow murder than one where nobody ever came in thinking they had the right to leave again, except in a wooden box.

My Mammy says I'll be better any day now, Jo. She gives me my favourite special soup when the nurses aren't watching.

Aw, Jesus.

Later, I lay there in the dark with my eyes wide open while Davina snored on beside me, and thought: a place like that's stained black, through and thoroughly, so's it can't ever be clean. You can holystone all you want, but the fact is it's a confluence—one of the deep pores of the world, a pocket full of sin, where misery washes up like trash on the tide. Been doing this my whole life, but I still can't tell whether it's human suffering creates such places or whether they're made to call humans to linger 'round 'em, suffering: it just all goes so bloody deep to plumb, laid top on top on top. All the way down to the very bottom.

It's not just misery human beings pump out, though. Is it?

Supposedly not. But that's all that collects . . .

All I could see collecting, anyroads, there or any other place. All I've *ever* seen.

Was our partner Ross who finally helped me figure out how I did what I did, in the end: broke it down into sections like a fourth-form science prof, all neat and clear and (mainly) understandable at last. Told us how most ghosts are a rag and a bone and a hank of hair at best—a memory fragment stuck on continual loop, just dust and PKE and water-vapour with no real "there" there. Leftover fragments of psychic energy deluded into believing in their own personality; an echo cobbled together from memory and pain, with no self-awareness as such 'cept what we give them. Survival instinct, with no survival.

I couldn't argue his reasoning, in the main. All my life, ghosts *had* gotten stuck to me like dust on a TV's screen . . . only worse, 'specially back when I didn't know you could turn the damn thing off and clean it every once in a while. Just staggered 'round with great crowds of 'em trailing after me, caught in the evil headlight glare of my ghost-drawing soul: babbling, clutching, clawing. Never leaving me *alone*.

Prayer didn't work, no more than did exorcism or a thousand other remedies, from hedge-witch charms to graveyard dirt to smack like my Mammy used to fiend for (bought, I've no doubt, from the grandchildren of the same dealers *she'd* owed). It took trips to the mental ward to peel 'em off, at least for a little while; a week or so in the quiet room and I'd feel a sudden jerk, almost a tearing, then blessed, blessed empty tenderness from top to toe. I'd walk out the morning after, free and aching as some lobster who'd shucked her shell, feeling for all the world like I'd just pulled a scab ran my whole body long.

Ross drew us both pictures, alone in his classroom—he was a teacher's aide back then, desperate for anything paid more than forty dollars an hour. "This energy you carry around with you, the one you say ghosts are attracted to? We call that the aura; an energy byproduct, sort of like the corona 'round the sun, only far less visible. And what most people don't know, Jo, is that a person's aura has layers—"

"Like skin."

"Skin, exactly. And what happens when skin gets old?"

So that was the trick, all this time: cast your outer layer whole like some spider's carapace and start over every so often, or get caught in a web of psychic influences so tight and sticky you can't even move. Which is where Davina's decon chamber comes in; I walk around our latest contract with my inmost light pulsing like a beacon, then step back in and shed, trapping my payload there. And the saddest part is how the ghosts can't even tell I'm gone, mostly—just keep on orbiting the husk 'til it disintegrates into what Ross calls "pure Yin energy," and them along with it. What's left behind still isn't pretty, but at least it doesn't try to think for itself.

Energy's energy, after all . . . it can't really be destroyed, just converted, moved around, modified. But a lingering sense of malaise never proves much to sue over, and Davina always made sure we did good business, even working strictly word-of-mouth. The unsatisfied clients we didn't contest; just gave 'em their initial deposit back . . . along with their ghosts. Then stood back and see how exactly they propose to handle the situation. That put paid to most of 'em.

But as Davina herself taught me, there are exceptions to every rule.

When I first got to Toronto, the bars were full of fools found the way I talk irresistible. And each of 'em had a line to try, no matter how ridiculous.

"Wow, is that accent for real?"

"So what *do* they wear under their kilts, lassie?"

"Wanna have a little Highland fling?"

"Way you talk, y'know, it sorta reminds me of Sean Connery. But with better tits."

"As compliments go, that's truly shite," I told this last pretty bastard; Hank, his name was. And thereby hangs a tale.

I knew Hank was a bad bet the minute I laid eyes on him, let alone spread my legs and moved into his apartment. Because with some cunts, it's never a matter of will they, only ever a matter of when—and Hank wasn't bright enough to disappoint anybody's expectations, no matter how low they might have pitched 'em.

So I get Davina's name from a scrap of loose paper crumpled up in that box Hank kept beside the phone, and I march off to kick her skinny arse for it only to find myself matching her drink for drink in the same bar we'd *both* made his acquaintance at.

"Ah, see, I *knew* it, didn't I know it? Fuckin' Hank, man. You deserve better than that motherfucker, Jodie—"

"Jodice."

"—Jo—"

Before long, I was telling her what I saw at night and sometimes during the day, and she wasn't any more surprised by that than she'd been by the other: had witches in her own family, after all—two kinds.

"How many ghosts you think you seen in Toronto so far, J.?" she asks me. "Double digits? Triple?"

"At least."

"Huh." And I can already see that rainbow cast to her eyes forming—green and blue-purple and pink, like Canadian money. That payday look.

Which is why, when I think back on it, I probably shouldn't be too insulted that it was only then she slid close enough to park her knee between mine for the very first time. Put her thin little lips so tight to my own I could taste what she'd had with dinner, and murmured—

"Hank really is dumb, y'know."

I felt my chest heave. Managed: "He's that, yeah."

"Yeah, well—guess we're both pretty clear on the facts there. But what I mean is . . . he's a real moron to ever cheat on somebody like you." Then: "But you don't even know what I'm talkin' 'bout, do ya?"

I heaved again, gave a ragged little cough. Shrugged, like I was hauling stones with my shoulder. And replied, at last . . .

". . . um, eh. Well . . . I *hope* I do."

Her little hand on mine, knee pressing even harder. And that *thing* in me opening wide at the heat of her, unstoppable—unspooling, cracking straight down to the core. This glorious weakness: an order, not a plea. Love me. Love *me*.

Never a word we used, in the end. But she made damn sure I felt its fingerprints all over me in the dark nevertheless, deep as bruises . . . so deep I'd always want her, no matter what. Because even now, my heart's just not strong enough to stand the strain it takes to love, while knowing (all the while) there's no earthly way you'll ever be loved quite the same way in return. Or, perhaps—

—at all.

So tell me: were you maybe born broken just like me, born hungry? Are we all of us born with some part of us missing? Are we each of us born with a hole?

Is that why people do such terrible things to each other and leave people like Dav and Ross and me to clean up the mess?

Born with a hole and no earthly way of finding just the exact right plug to fill it, not 'til you've tried 'em from A to Z and back once more: booze, fags, work, candy, men, girls, heroin, methedrine, methadone, God. Tried having a baby. Tried killing yourself. A hundred religions, from Calvin to the Dalai Lama and back again; tried every damn thing you could think of and some you had to stumble over, 'til all that seemed to fit was Dav and this. Just this and Dav, and that's all.

You stick a plug in your weakness like a finger in the proverbial dike and let pressure build up, let it swell and swell 'til there's nothing left but tension, nothing left but what's left *over*—the absence, not the presence. The wound you shape your soul around.

Can't stay that way forever, though, can it? The pressure alone sees to that; edges thin and crack, warp and curl. And the hole opens wide once more—at last—like some bloody flower blooming, like some gaping, crying, permanently starving baby's mouth.

I've gotten good at holding things together, these thirty years and more . . . at mending myself stitch by stitch from the inside so's the scar's well-nigh invisible to anyone doesn't know me well enough to know where to look. At bracing myself, holding that pose so long and hard I can barely recall myself how I used to dream it'd feel if ever I got to where I could safely let any part of this whole bloody mess *go*.

But sometimes I do wonder if I'm love-blind the way some people are colour-blind, or most people are ghost-blind. If love (true or false, thick or thin, requited or un-) really *is* the only glue ever mortars our sad hearts' bricks together, and me not swift enough to recognize the label any time I happened to pass it by.

Because: living is transience, after all—people aren't really *permanent* 'til they're dead, no matter what you might've felt for 'em beforehand. Always changing . . .

. . . and I just can't keep up.

Once the decon chamber goes up on a job, it doesn't come down 'til Ross's meters tell him we've gone from a great rotating scrum of individual spectres to a melting mass of ectoplasm that can't recall its own name. This is the rule we've kept to since we formed Glouwer-Cirocco-Puget, but I suppose I'd always thought it had less to do with rules than with regulations, if you get my meaning. That it wasn't so much dangerous, in other words, as just another chance for Dav to enjoy telling clients what not to do.

I'd done one sweep already and shucked off into that sad plastic box, but we all of us knew one was never enough with a place this choked. So we come in Thursday, only to find this fresh new suit waiting for us with a security guard at either elbow—out the same sort of pack as Gall, for sure, but even I could see (in and between that swirling halo of ghosts I carried, thick to the skin everywhere but my eyeballs) that that's where the similarities ended.

"You'd be Glower and Circus," he says, practically beaming.

"That's Glouwer, like," says I.

And: "*Cirocco*," Davina chimes in, at almost the same time. "Where's Gall, buddy?"

"Fired, in no small part for authorizing this sort of foolishness." Gives a cool, little nod to the bully-boys, who start hoisting equipment.

Ross comes running, clucking like a whole chicken farm set on fire. "Hey! I really wouldn't touch that, sir, if I were you . . ."

"What in particular, Mr. Puget? Were you talking about *this* rather expensive item—"

—the PKE machine, over and down in a spray of glass and tiny cogs, while Ross grabbed at his heart through the biohazard coverall's chestpiece—

"—or was it maybe *this*?" A row of leaded bottles down in one sweeping gesture, followed by one of those little temperature-reading doohickeys Ross loved so much. "Yes, that *does* look hard to fix; oh well." To us: "I'm sure the company funds you bilked my predecessor out of thus far will cover the extent of your 'damages.'"

Ross groaned again, a kid in a burnt-down candy store. But Davina just gave Mr. Suit the old up-and-down, utterly unimpressed.

"Man," she said, "you really do love to hear yourself talk, don't'cha?"

A fake-hearty laugh, all teeth and righteous ire. "What, no warnings? Certain I'm not about to unleash anything apocalyptic on the unsuspecting city? I'd hate to have to close this site down on account of excessive CGI."

"Do what you want, you happy motherfucker. The further you go, the sweeter it's gonna sound when I see ya in court."

"I doubt that." To the guards: "Kick it down."

Ross surged forward again; Davina grabbed his arm, hissing *cut it OUT, man* in his ear. But this other shirty bastard, he must've thought she was coming for *him*—so he strikes at her, hard, almost like a backhand. Catches her on the point of the chin with his old school ring and knocks her down with poor Ross tangling in on top of her, two of 'em sprawling headsfirst into what's left of machine, meters, bottles.

Meanwhile, the bully-boys had grabbed a decon chamber strut each and pulled; I heard something give inside or maybe out- or both. And then—

Remember the finger in the dike?

Ghosts already spinning 'round me one way, faster and faster, bulging up and out in every direction like some half-formed thunderhead. And from out the chamber, meanwhile, a rush of something yet still worse: bigger, badder, all rage and sorrow and misdirection. What you get when the chamber's not quite cleared, when all those soul-husks you slung in have broken down far enough to lose themselves in each other, to form some kind of massive—ghost times fifty, times one hundred? Misery of miseries, raw and elemental, without even the hint of a catharsis powerful enough to make it whole again . . .

Mr. Suit and his guards pausing, still as paint, eyes bugged to their bloody strings. 'Cause it's far easier to see one huge ghost than it is to see a thousand small ones, I can only suppose, even if you don't think you have anything near "the sight."

And that in itself gave me time to hear Ross, behind me. Ross, whimpering: "Jo, oh please, oh Jesus, look. Jo, Christ, *Jo!*"

I turn, and the ghosts turn with me. Swirl and part like the Red Sea to show Dav on the floor, gasping, with a big shard of glass in her throat— or a *hole* in her throat, rather. With nothing but a big shard of glass, hard and sharp and red and shiny, to plug the damn thing closed.

A *hole*.

I could see sweat on Mr. Suit's face as I turned back, moist and shiny. But it wasn't *him* I was talking to when I said, all calm and level—

"You see me, yeah? Still. Want to be *with* me? Want *in*?"

The ghosts, one long collective sigh: *Oh yes, oh yes, oh yes.*

"Then you'll bloody well have to do what I tell you to, won't ye?"

The suit and his boys were running, by that time, so's all I really had to do was send the ghosts after. They streamed past us in a cloud, so close they whipped my hair up, and chased Dav's murderers upstairs— right to that one room, the Munchausen's by proxy room, if I'm not much mistaken. For at least one of them knew the way, after all.

I could hear the screaming come down through the floor, so clear it might've made me smile, under other circumstances. But it didn't do a thing for me at that very moment, not with Ross shaking and girning at my back, and Dav coughing what was left of her life out on my shirt.

Oh, but you canna leave me, ye great American hoor. You CANNA, not now.

Not now, no. Not never.

Blood down her front like a bib, redder than her hair, her half-cocked brows. And I thought I could see her looking at me sidelong even then, with her eyes rolling up so far they were nothing but pink-white rim: *C'mon, baby, what the fuck. I mean—*

—how you gonna STOP me?

. . . well.

And: "Oh Jo," Ross said, broken—like he knew what I had in mind, which seems unlikely. Seein' how I really only knew it myself when I *did* it, and not one moment before.

As she took her last guttering breath, I put my mouth over hers, and I sucked it in—hard, deep, like it was whiskey and me a dry drunk. Held it, long as I could.

Then I reached for the last of Ross's bottles, clutched loose but unbroken in his cupped hands, and I popped the cap.

And now I sit here in our—my—flat with the phone-receiver in my hand, just looking at the keypad. Knowing in my heart how my Nan never picks up the first ten or so rings; full of radio waves, she thinks these things are, just like almost any other bloody item you can name.

"I know what yuir wantin'," she'll say, before I even get a chance to speak. And she'll tell me her black angel's name.

So that's how I'll finally get Davina back, in the end: not just as a fragment, not just a skin over a scream, not just a moment caught in time, forever reliving the what, the why, the want. The me, me, me of all ghosts, of all the empty . . .

Davina, whole and true—out of the bottle and bound once more to me on the *inside* of Ross's "aura," so's she won't be able to flit off even if I have to shed. Which means I won't have to spend the rest of my life resigned to walk 'round lapped and orbited by phantoms, either, afraid I can't give 'em the slip for fear of losing Davi forever, along with all the rest. And that'll be good, that.

Davina, mine again 'til the bitter end, whether she wants to be or no. And no, she won't like it much, I suspect: will fight and claw against it, for all she can't hurt me now, not even to the extent I used to let her.

Makes no damn difference to me at all, at this point, what's fair and what isn't—as I ask so will I be given, and I'll bear a mark to prove it on any more-than-cursory inspection for the rest of eternity too, whether in my skin or out. The same as my Nan.

You have to wonder, though: did I *want* this, somehow, without my even knowing? Did I somehow make this happen, the essential aching lack in me always yearning to break her down to my own level?

Did I always know I needed this, needed Davina, to plug my awful hole?

I sit here, already feeling them circling: every ghost in Toronto and elsewhere, drawn to cast themselves against me like I was the only lighthouse on a foggy shore. Like if they only could slip inside they could fill me up forever and find themselves the home they crave.

And God knows, I'd help them if I could, really and truly. For it's no pleasure to me to see anything suffer, not even the dead. But I can't, can I? I mean—

Not alone, somebody whispers in my inner ear: Davina, Nan. Me. One or the other. All of the above.

I shut my eyes, stretch out my hand. And feel my fingers move, quick and sure as someone else's . . .

. . . already dialling.

PEN UMBRA (2004)

| repetitive ideation

For more years than I could count, I had exactly the same dream—not every night, but close enough. Or maybe it was just that I couldn't remember any of the other dreams I might have had.

Between the ages of five and thirteen, I routinely spent a fair portion of my summer up at the lake. There was a cottage that my grandmother owned, a half-sunk jetty reaching out into silt and grey sand from which you could swim, limbs warped and pale in the shallows, then lost altogether in the murky deeps. Weeds grew there, twining 'round your feet as you kicked: torn garlands, trailing. Nothing to give back the light below but an old rusty can, its ragged mouth bleeding upward, and the polished bones of birds who'd dipped far enough below the surface to be caught.

One time, Finn—my second step-grandfather—took me out in his speedboat, densely tangled islands whipping by out of the corner of your eye like clumps of weed frozen rock-hard, weed piled upon pile from the very bottom. We skimmed the flashing grey water in a series of hard little bumps, the vertebrae of some submerged marine dinosaur. While I thought, calmly: *If we stop now, even for a second . . . if we pause on the dark water for just one fraction of a moment longer than necessary . . .*

. . . we'd sink like a stone. End up on the underneath, staring forever up, our mouths full of mud. Our bones washed wet and white as well, eventually, in that one dim glimmer of sun.

So: the dream begins at the lake. Me, bottom-locked, with nothing all around but the muffled shifting of water, that constant cold pressure bearing in from every angle. Each kick sends up a scatter of silt, grey particles drifting and dispersing into mottled green light, and I stare up into the dazzle to see—

A diffuse, floating shadow, just coming into range above me. The cold grows more intense as I begin to make out its great bulk, some unknown monster, ossified far beyond recognition; a mess of broken discoloured bones and rotting flesh too big to live, but definitely dead now. Drifting aimless with its flesh boiling away in clumps, falling slowly down towards me like dust. Like smoke.

And then it gets so large, it blots out everything else.

I dreamt this dream over and over, which was bad enough. What made it somehow worse, however, was the fact that, as those years went by, the *thing*—whatever it was—seemed to swell and swell, becoming a landscape in itself. Like some horrendous slice of alien sky, the scudding of unspeakable clouds. A roof-shaped doorway into Hell.

When I was twenty, I saw my first picture by Max Ernst: "Europe After the Rain," done in 1940, after escaping from Nazi Germany. His largest work ever, it shows a panorama of decay produced through a technique known as decalomanie, which consists of squashing areas of highly diluted paint onto the canvas, then pulling it around so that the colours distribute themselves at random, suggesting through texture alone various biological structures—floral patterns, fossilized lichens, nacreous conch shells. In Ernst's later paintings, the glassy iridescence of staffs, rods and lances, the red crust of fishbones and salt covering the ground, the mossy lace of women's undergarments . . . all these effects are achieved through decalomanie.

For the next five straight terms at university, I slept, woke, read, wrote, and ate Max Ernst—without dreams. His vision had consumed me from the inside out, shelling me whole. I shed all my former fears at once, like some carapace, and left them behind to rot in much the same way that many of Ernst's background figures seem to: hot, white, pearlescent. It was a wonderful time. The dream, thank God, simply couldn't compete.

And yet. There'd have to be an "and yet," wouldn't there? Or you'd be looking at a blank page, right now.

But . . . you're not.

| teacher says, begin at the end

The real question always is: how do things start? How do you know what you know? And when—or where, exactly—do you *know* that you know it?

For me, 2004 starts in my attic room at 676 Euclid, its air forever close and hot like someone else's skin—third floor up, its narrow back window looking out onto next door's roof, its even narrower front window haunted by the giant, rotating, bucket-shaped ghost of the Kentucky Fried Chicken sign across the street. The tenant I replaced, another student, had propped up both screens with hardback coffee-table books bought (as far as I could figure) at local garage sales, which made the apartment reek of mildew-swollen paper for days afterward whenever it rained. It was alien when I first moved in, breath-catchingly so, but I sort of got to like it, by the end.

. . . the end.

I came to 676 Euclid to work on my doctoral thesis: *Frottage, a Play for Three Voices—The Influence of Hypnagogic Techniques on the Early Work of Max Ernst*. The "play" part was my friend Vivia's idea, not mine; my brain doesn't operate quite that interestingly, even when I'm not distracted.

"Serious, Jan," she'd said, looking over my initial notes. "Take a boo. You got Herr Ernst spouting off over here, you got this, um—observational?—stuff about his work you dug up, all this crazy description. And then you got the straight-up history running through like a vein. It's a dialogue."

"Dia means 'two,' doesn't it?"

"Okay, trialogue; whatever. It's call and response, like *music*. Add slides, some light-show stuff, get a space, three actors . . ."

"Better you than me, Gunga Din."

"Well, yeah. So—I guess that's a yes, right?"

I don't remember agreeing, exactly. But on the other hand, it's not like lack of agreement ever *stopped* Vivia from doing—well, anything.

In order to give the thesis my full attention, I knew I'd have to get some sort of job. Best-case scenario had me in a position which wouldn't take up most of my time, yet paid enough to maintain rent, supplies, food: easy enough to find through the back of *NOW* Magazine classifieds, she said, with a self-deprecating grin. Almost immediately adding the inevitable post-modern caveat, *not*.

Vivia, again: "Hey. You ever think about renting your body?"

"Don't think Mr. and Mrs. Mol'd be real pleased to hear I'd crowned my dumb-ass choice to waste eight years on an Art History Doctorate by dabbling in prostitution," I shot back, scowling down at the pack of eight-by-ten colour Xeroxes I was going through.

"No, idiot, I mean the Robert Rodriguez special." As I looked at her, uncomprehending: "Like, *testing*?"

"*Drug* testing? Thanks, but I kind of like my liver the way it is."

She rolled over on the futon, struck a finger-shaky pose, eyebrows and lips crimping Yoda-style. Made her voice all froggy. And—

"Ahhhh, young one," she said. "Little of what you speak, you know. *Many* different kinds of testing, there are."

"Fuck right off now, you can."

"*Jan*-is. Stop being a turd."

So we went on the web, clicked around, followed a couple of links she'd heard about. Three days later, I was down at the Freihoeven ParaPsych Institute, getting pre-tested. For being *tested*.

That hot little room with its stink, Ernst references scattered everywhere, the screen of my laptop blinking forever in the background and the whirr of my hard drive's fan like somebody else's breath in the dark. Sometimes, I wake up with my heart in my throat—eyes still shut, but far too afraid to open them. I wake up blind and panting with that fan in my ears, blood-loud, convinced I never really left there at all.

It took eight whole months for me to get it, finally . . . not what was going on, so much, as the fact that something *might* be going on. Might. With no way to be sure 'til I upped sticks and got the fuck out of Dodge, thus confirming my ever-more-vague suspicion that yes, there *was* still a world outside my apartment and the house it squatted in, and it looked the same way I fuzzily remembered. That things *had* once been different and could be that way again, eventually, so long as I removed myself from this place entirely; just took Eddie Murphy's legendary advice for similar situations and *GOT OUT* . . .

And now you think you know what I'm talking about, don't you? Sort of. Maybe. A little, little bit.

Yeah. Except that—unless it's already happened to you, ladies and gentlemen—

—believe you me, you really don't "know" shit.

| always the same, always different

When my mother (Mrs. Mol, the aforementioned) turned forty-three or so, she went on tour with a Montreal Drama School reunion production of *She Stoops to Conquer* which was supposed to play all across Canada. Which would have been pretty cool, except she never made it any farther than their first stop, Newfoundland; the minute her feet hit the Rock, she began to experience these dull, awful pains which grew within a matter of hours to complete shrieking agony, almost birth-pang bad. They took her to the ER, where she was x-rayed, but the doctors couldn't see anything inside her which would account for all the pain—actually, they couldn't *see* anything at all, just a cloudy mass occupying most of her abdomen. Which is why the last thing she remembers doing before they put her under is signing a document giving them her permission to fit her with a colostomy bag, if needed.

Luckily, it wasn't. The mass turned out to be a benign yet immense "chocolate" cyst that had slowly engulfed many of her internal organs over the period of perhaps a year: fallopian tubes, ovaries, all that. Early menopause in one, uneasy step.

Afterward, she told me she'd felt something was wrong for at least that long, but in an absolutely undefined, undefinable way—"wrong" like some sort of generalized disappointment, an angst, an anhedonia. All those words—long or short, foreign or not—we use to "explain" why our lives seem so slow, so dull, so trivial, so repetitive. So filled with nothing quite as easy to medicate away as actual symptoms.

Like a long black hood a mile or so high coming down over your head, too slow to measure or even to notice. And each successive layer of the hood is only mesh, perfectly see-through . . . but as they fold one over the other (over the other, over the other), your world gets ever more dim, dull, chill, and awful almost beyond endurance. "Normal" getting worse, always and steadily, as "normal" is—so often—wont to do.

The central question of any execution: do you want the hood on or off? Would you rather see it coming? Or would you rather simply drift away, cocooned, in warm darkness, stinking of nothing but yourself? A kind, familiar place to hide in, just before the snap, the crackle? Or the pop?

That's what it was most like, where I ended up, living at 676 Euclid. And just like my mother, I never even knew how wrong everything in my life had become . . . never even saw it, coming or not. Not until it was long, long over.

| my thesis

Though I haven't been able to make myself look at it since 2004, this is how my thesis began—

FIRST VOICE:

The real problem with Max Ernst, in the context of a presentation such as this, is one's ultimate inability to classify him. Other artists were integral parts of specific schools, specific movements, and their artistic growth went on inside those schools and movements. But for Max Ernst, movements themselves were stages of growth. He continued to produce art until his death—approximately eighty-four years of work; work without a pause. His paintings range from surrealism to abstraction to super-realism; his experimentation with frottage and dripping and decalomanie had a lasting impression on the technical side of art as a whole. He wrote, sculpted in stone, wood and found objects, and published two books of collages. There is no way to synopsize Max Ernst. There is no one hole which fits him comfortably. The only method of analysis is to reveal him in stages—in a non-linear manner—in scraps and pieces that evoke not only a sense of his life, but a sense of emotional response to his work, which is his truest legacy.

SECOND VOICE:

Max Ernst was born on the second of April, 1891—the same year that Seurat died—near Cologne, at Bruhl. He was the second son of Philipp Ernst, also a painter. Max was impressed by the fact that once, while painting a scene of their garden, his father painted out a tree that irked him . . . then went and cut down the real tree, so that its continued existence would not devalue or "ruin" the painting.

THIRD VOICE:

"At the time, it occurred to me that there was something amiss here in the relationship between painter and subject."

Yes. And this, meanwhile, is where I'd gotten to, before I finally had to leave—

FIRST VOICE:

Ill with a fever, young Max lay in bed and stared at an imitation mahogany panel across the room from him, at the wallpaper and at the plaster ceiling above, and saw shapes take form.

Twenty-eight years later, this childhood memory was to awaken in him as he gazed at the floorboards of a seaside inn one rainy afternoon. Setting to work with paper and soft black lead, he produced his first rubbings—the forerunners of the "frottage" technique that formed most of his drawings during his Dadaist period and would always remain his primary method of creation.

SECOND VOICE:

Metamorphosis: identity dissolves, or is unstable, transitory, partaking of all the different kingdoms of nature. Behind our masks, we have no face to speak of, or perhaps we simply do not recognize our real face . . . our absence of face.

Ernst's is a world of objects: faces and bodies irreparably anthropomorphized, constantly substituted for by static stone, wood, household implements. But what may conceivably be the most disturbing single facet of his work remains the potent presence of the natural world, with its systems of ebbing and flowing, of corruption, of communicating vessels.

THIRD VOICE:
"The grooves of the wood took on successively the aspects of an eye, a nose, a bird's head, a menacing nightingale, a spinning top, and so on. Little Max took pleasure in being afraid of these visions, and later delivered himself voluntarily to provoke hallucinations of the same kind in looking obstinately at wood-panels, clouds, unplastered walls, and so on, to let his imagination go. When someone would ask him, 'What is your favourite occupation?' he regularly answered, 'Looking.'"

| the freihoeven institute

I'll admit I'd expected it to be larger or—at least—more impressive. The website Vivia'd found had been well-organized, spell-checked, blessedly free of funky flash effects or blobby *Scariest Places on Earth* photomontages; the address was central, thus not necessitating any sort of back-of-beyond GO Train pilgrimage to Mississauga, or what have you. But all this sort of slipped away once I realized the fabled "Institute" was just a set of offices (located, conveniently enough, above a dusty neighbourhood dollar store), whose layout reminded me strongly of my worst job ever, matching telemarketer mailing address lists with phone numbers gleaned from all over North America. Each hour I'd worked during that particular summer had been spent somewhere ill-lit and ill-ventilated, doing something which was probably potentially illegal—a fairly easy conclusion to come to, since they'd move us to a new site whenever a fresh contract came in.

I paused at the foot of the stairs, eyes shaded, squinting up. "Mmmm, *musty.*"

"Picky," Vivia snapped back, nudging me forward.

We had to sign in to use the elevator, which took us to the third floor. Freihoeven occupied suite 300B, in the building's extreme southwest corner; the adjoining suite belonged to a company I was pretty sure I'd recently heard named in a pyramid scheme bust.

"Vivia Syliboy and Janis Mol for Dr. Abbott, 2:00," Vivia told the woman behind the desk, who seemed dangerously intent on excavating the space beneath her nails with a straightened paperclip. "We're here about the experiment."

"Uh huh." Not looking up: "Which one?"

"Oh. Well, we did that select-o-matic quiz generator thingie, and it recommended we try out for . . ."

". . . the Mental Radio recreation," a voice from behind us chimed in, though "chime" is putting it strongly. I glanced sidelong, caught a flash of glasses—some girl, awkwardly hunched over a magazine with her hair all in her face, colourless in every conceivable way. She hauled the overflow away for a minute, and as her sleeve fell back, I saw her thin wrist was patterned like some reversible flesh jacket: bruises on top, close-packed as angry fingerprints; scar tissue underneath, an angry half-bracelet of pink-tinged white.

"Carra," the receptionist said, almost warningly. While Vivia replied, at the same time:

"Yeah, that's it. How'd you . . . ?"

But the girl—Carraclough Devize, her name turned out to be—just sighed.

"Through there," Nail-lady told us, jerking her head towards the nearest door, and started digging at her thumb like she expected to strike gold. I took the hint, skirting Little Miss Know-Too-Much's personal space to knock at the pebbled glass door; Vivia hung back a minute, frankly interested, only to get the High-Functioning Autist silent treatment in response.

A few minutes after, we sat across from the famous Dr. A. himself, skimming our release forms while he filled us in on the program's specifics—a sixteen-week trial, one hour's worth of work a day, plus various types of documentation. The pay worked out to a thousand two hundred every two weeks, plus "commission."

"Commission for what?" I wanted to know.

"That all depends on how effective the experiment eventually proves." Dr. Abbott paused, steepling his long fingers. "Have either of you ladies ever heard of Upton Sinclair, the author?"

"Same guy who wrote *Babbitt*? Not since American Literature 101."

"Exactly. Around 1930, he and his wife, Mary Craig Sinclair, decided to embark on a series of inquiries into the realm of extra-sensory perception—not laboratory-based, naturally, but rather interesting all the same. At the time, Mrs. Sinclair had already spent a large portion of her adult life recuperating from a long and physically excruciating illness . . . 'a story of suffering needless to go into,' her husband called it. 'Suffice it that she had many ills to experiment upon, and mental control became suddenly a matter of life and death.'"

And: "Oh," said Vivia. "Um . . . cool."

I let a slow breath out through my nose and tried not to roll my eyes.

So, anyways. The story goes that instead of using ESP cards or any other set of fixed symbols, Upton Sinclair—or a close friend of theirs—would make pencil sketches of some object, real or imaginary; Mary

Sinclair, lying alone in the dark in another part of the house, would try to "see" something, then reproduce what she thought she'd "seen." This system evolved until the couple could rope in acquaintances like Robert L. Irwin, a young Pasadena businessman, who agreed (on the morning of July 13, 1928) to help them out by spending an hour concentrating on any random thing in his house, starting at the prearranged time of half-past 11:00 A.M. He chose a fork, made a drawing, stared at it, tried to clear his mind, and waited.

At the same time, in Long Island, Mary Sinclair dutifully filtered out the various aches she lived with, one by one, and tried to put a name to whatever might be left over. Eventually, once twenty minutes had elapsed, she got up and wrote on a small piece of paper—

"See a table fork. Nothing else."

Out of 290 drawings made, the total complete successes numbered 65—around 22 percent. Partial successes, on the other hand, went as high as 155, or 53 percent. And the number of complete failures? "Only" 70, a.k.a. 24 percent.

Dr. Abbott showed us reproductions of Mary Sinclair's portfolio. The successes seemed dubious, almost a bit too perfect to be true. But it was the mistakes, the partials, which really stuck with me . . . not that I believed any of this crap, you understand.

In one case, the "sender" had doodled a roller-skater's leg, upflung after some headlong sprawl. In Mary's version, somehow, shoe and calf had blurred into the head and neck of an obscure animal—half stallion, half giraffe. The wheels became this thing's bulging eyes, skewing in either direction like a demented bullfrog. About this phase of the experiment, Black Magic "expert" William Seabrook writes:

"There was a general similarity of outline, as of something 'seen through a glass darkly,' which is more disturbing to me as a skeptic than a clearer sketch would have been."

"We thought, what with your artistic background, you might make a quite perfect sender," Dr. Abbott told me, gesturing, then turned back to Vivia. "While, as for you, Ms. Syliboy—"

A bit too fast: "Hey, that's okay, no problem. I actually have a job already."

Abbott gave her a gentle frown. "So . . . why are you here, then?"

"Moral support."

They gave me a bunch of forms to fill out, a log-book, and a digital camera. The latter I was supposed to use to document my sketches, even though the Institute also expected me to mail each sketch off to them pretty much as I did it—wanted to make sure the time-signatures checked out, I guess. Which was fine with me; I'd always wanted one, and this counted as one up (or down) from a free test-drive.

"Who'm I supposed to be 'sending' this stuff to?" I asked, almost absently.

"One of our control group." At my look: "I'm afraid I really can't elaborate, Ms. Mol; might taint the findings. Suffice it to say they're all names from our files, all proven sensitives. . . ."

I just nodded, thinking for a minute about how the word "sensitive"— used in that context, at any rate—always made me want to laugh out loud. Like hypo-allergenic soap: *My mind is cleaner than your mind, neener neener neener.*

And then, I don't know why . . . not even now . . .

. . . I saw Carra Devize again, just for a second: the mere slumped outline of her, right through that pebbled glass separating Abbott and us from the waiting room outside. A stick-figure woodcut girl, all shadow, no definition, with nothing but a hole—dark and flat, yet contradictorily deep—where her hair-hidden face should be.

Carra Devize like some Hiroshima negative on my eyelids' inner screen, some lost silver nitrate silent film's edge-of-melt flicker-start; a synaptic pop, flashpaper brief, then out and done and *gone.* After which there was me and Abbott, Vivia watching—me scribbling my name at the base of the very last form, and did I say second, back there? I meant half-second, tops. Quarter-, maybe.

I dotted my i's and crossed my t's, and Abbott cut me an advance cheque for fifty bucks, right there and then. It bought two Green Goddess bowls at Juice for Life, with yam frites and a side of blueberry Tofutti.

| post-hypnagogic suggestion

"The gates of hell lie open, night and day/Wide is the path, and easy is the way . . ."

One of those things that gets in your head, 'specially if your skull's got cracks as big as mine does, these days. Making you wonder: was that Dante, for real, or does it just sound like it? Or could it be something I saw in a movie, once—one by Clive Barker or Guillermo del Toro? *Se7en,* even?

Can't remember. Doesn't matter. We're talking generalities, not specifics—echoes, not events. That ever-present noise which rides forever side-saddle under your thoughts gone first loud and white, then *off* like bad milk; murky and odorous like chum dumped in deep water, inviting all manner of sharks to share the meal.

The one thing I know for sure, now, is that after I left 676 Euclid, my life (as I'd hitherto known it) sort of fell to jack-shit. Lost the asshole job I'd ended up in the following June, couldn't get another no matter how I tried. I knew I had seven months 'til my rent was re-evaluated, nine months 'til Welfare kicked in, but nothing mattered as much as keeping my apartment. As long as I had a place to stay, I wasn't *really* poor. I wasn't *really* a failure.

Which is why I sold my TV to keep it, why I sold my blood. And yes, there was time and money between the two stages, but less than I would've liked . . . far, far less.

So it all went, piece by piece, quicker than I could ever have imagined. Everything that burned juice, everything that distracted: books, CDs, my walkman, my hair-dryer, my furniture. I sold my computer, kept my disks, worked off the system at the local library; when space got tight, I printed out and wiped my back-up files. I had my phone disconnected, had to save my change just to return calls. When Mr. and Mrs. Mol came (at long, long last) to find me, I was living in the closet, literally—renting out the rest of the space under the table I didn't have anymore, sharing that dim box with a mattress and my notes while two other girls had the run of "my place," one a hooker, one a junkie. Plus their various customers.

The Mols took one look, then came back with the cops.

If they'd got to me any later, I often think, I might well have been living in a doorway. And simply . . . not . . . *noticing*.

This noise in my head, these patterns, rough like wood and dark like textured charcoal. Max Ernst's shells and creepers spreading like mould over every surface, and the light of my room flapping back and forth, back and forth—sky like an incipient bruise all day, every day, constantly dimming and shifting with the onset of some incipient storm. Like the phantom wings of some gigantic, low-flying bird, one surely huge enough to merit worship at the petrified altar of any former Dadaist turned Surrealist turned just plain artist.

I'd stand in front of my cupboards making an inventory of all the food I had, what I might be able to sell, and how long that might last. I'd lie down weeping and wake in greyness, then feel for the clock with both hands and touch something—cool, smooth, dry—that skittered from my grip like a plastic cockroach.

And I'd think: Ah. Somebody's put a razor by my bedside —a "safety" razor, ha ha. "Somebody" meaning me, 'cause nobody gets in here, and I sure as hell don't go *out*.

A razor. Very . . . *suggestive*, that is.

And how could I *do* that, without even knowing I did it? How?

. . . easy.

Easy as anthrax pie.

This is where I found myself, where the Mols found me. And it wasn't until a whole year later that I ever had more than the tiniest inkling *why*.

| eleven-thirty, 6th of May, 2004: sketch #1

When I came down to get my coffee that morning, I found my fellow tenant Aaron Coby already occupying the common-area kitchen, eating Captain Crunch while watching tentacle porn on his laptop: squishing, squelching, and breathy little manga-girl squeals hung heavy in the air. "Hey, man," he said, not looking up. "Didn't know you were in."

"Well, I am. So could you please not?"

"Dude, it's research."

"You know, that'd ring just a bit more believable if your hand *wasn't* down your pants."

He flipped me the bird, then took another bite. And asked, muffled, through a gooshy mouthful of peanut-flavoured milk:

"Yo, Janis. You know that thing around the sun—"

"Mercury?"

"No, man. Like when there's an eclipse? The part you can still see, where everything's black except this thing . . ."

I poured myself a cup, added Sucrose. "That's called the penumbra."

"Oh. So what's that mean?"

"It's Latin. *Umbra*'s like 'shadow,' so—uh. 'Beside-shadow.' Or—'under-shadow,' Or—"

"'Inside-shadow?'"

. . . maybe, sure.

He glanced back at the screen and took a sec, seeming to admire the staging of what looked like yet another particularly wet and sucker-burnt DP. Then said, musingly—

"It's pretty weird, when you think about it. Like, the colour black . . ."

"Black is the absence of colour, Aaron."

"No. *White* is an absence—"

(—like black is a presence?)

"Take your word for it," I told him, and went back upstairs.

It wasn't like I had *no* furniture up there: a desk too small for much except my monitor, a chair in front of it, my printer and hard drive stowed underneath. A futon on the floor. Four bankers boxes full of clothes, six bankers boxes full of books. A print of one of Ernst's "Forests" hanging like an extra window between two scabby posters I'd bought from the campus art show my first year and just forgotten to ever take down—Edward Gorey's "Gashlycrumb Tinies" on the right-hand side, Hieronymus Bosch's "Garden of Earthly Delights" on the left-.

A is for Amy, who fell down the stairs./B is for Basil, devoured by bears . . .

In Bosch's garden, one nozzle-headed creature pushed two oblivious lovers around in a glass ball while, nearby, another climbed a gargantuan strawberry. My alarm went off, reminding me that—"on-a-roll" feeling or not—by half-past eleven, which was fast approaching, I'd really better do my level best to have something for the mysterious other half of my circuit to start concentrating on.

So I got out my sketch-pad and a light charcoal, laid a sheet of foolscap on the floor at the foot of my bed—where the light came in strongest, of mornings—and squatted down to work.

Frottage, its sexual in-joke of a name aside, is (by the main) a system of discovery. The idea is to take something textured, something rough like stone, or sand, or . . . the worn-unsteady wood which makes up a downtown student-house's uppermost floor, say. This then forms the basis for a tracing into which you can look and see shapes, forms, faces suggested by nothing more than light and dark, line vs. line, a merest Idea of Image. Follow these suggestions to their conclusion, illogical or otherwise, and a drawing tends to emerge—individual as a Rorschach blot, predictable as a fever-dream. Like moving light on wallpaper in a still and darkened room.

In 1924, after moving to Paris, Max Ernst finished his first series of completely Surrealist paintings, pale and exacting works, which look somewhat like bad Magritte. Their symbolism was explicit. He called them "a kind of farewell to technique and to occidental culture." Later the same year, Ernst sold all his remaining work in Germany and sailed for the Far East, reuniting with fellow ex-Dadaist Paul Eluard in Saigon. It was on his return from the East that he discovered frottage, of which he wrote—

"Botticelli once remarked that by throwing a sponge soaked with paint against the wall, one makes a spot in which may be seen a beautiful landscape. This is certainly true; he who is disposed to gaze attentively at this spot may discern within some human heads, various animals, a battle, some rocks, the sea, clouds, groves, and a thousand other things. It is like the tinkling of the bell that makes one hear what one imagines.

"But though this stain serves to suggest some ideas, it does not teach one to finish any part of the painting. To be universal and to please varying tastes, it is necessary that in the same composition may be found some very dark passages and others of a gently lighted . . ."

. . . *penumbra*.

(And you know the really odd thing? I remember writing all this down in the library, transcribing it into my files, moving parts of it here and there, using it however I saw fit to support whatever point it was I thought I wanted to make. But not until later, not until *now*, did I recall that particular word being used—not so close to the conversation with Aaron, no. Not in *that* context.)

I squint my inner eye and see myself cross-legged on the floor, sketching away. Letting the lines take me where they take me. While, on the wall above me, something moves and spreads like smoke, like bruising. Like something straining desperately to lean over my utterly engaged, utterly uncomprehending shoulder.

Says Max:

"It is not to be despised, in my opinion, if, after gazing fixedly at the spot on the wall, the coals in the grate, the clouds, the flowing stream, one remembers some of their aspects; and if you look at them carefully, you will discover some quite admirable inventions. In these confused things, genius becomes aware of new inventions, but it is necessary to know well how to draw all the parts that one normally ignores.

"Here I discover the elements of a figuration so remote that its very absurdity provokes in me a sudden intensification of my faculties of sight—a hallucinatory succession of contradictory images, superimposed upon each other with the persistence and rapidity of amorous memories and visions of somnolence. These images, in turn, provoke new planes of understanding. By simply painting or drawing, it suffices to add only a colour, a line, a landscape foreign to the object represented, and these changes, no more than docile reproductions of what is visible within me, record a faithful and fixed image of my hallucination. They transform the banal pages of advertisement into dramas which reveal my most secret desires."

I never named my sketches, and to be frank, I have trouble remembering what most of them looked like. But I still recall how it felt to be there in my hot, dense attic room, tongue-tip between teeth—a swirling, edge-of-swooning feeling, far too intent for explicit nausea, yet certainly akin to it. Like that thing I often found myself doing when I was a kid, too young to worry about how I might be deforming my own ability to interpret the world around me . . . this glorious, multifoliated bag of tricks, so apparently both boundless and permanent, which is (nevertheless) so easily and sadly reduced to nothing more than an empiricist's shaky self-delusion.

How I'd stare at a given object and the space around it, cross my eyes *just so*, and see it pixilate into oblivion—reduce itself to component parts, to inward-spiralling boxes or circles, before disintegrating completely into that calm, grey, vaguely ozone-smelling blankness which signals oxygen deprivation. Back then, I had no idea I was probably killing brain-cells every time I indulged myself this way. And these days—

—these days, if I could still do it, well . . . fuck it, man, I might. I very definitely might.

But not unless I knew for sure I didn't have to worry about petty crap like waking up with nothing to show for my efforts but a headache, later on.

| imago

It was a week or so after that initial sketch that I developed my rash— first faintly under the wire of the bra, then up along the breastbone, itchy and flaky and redder and redder, like it was going to open up at any minute and let something out.

Mrs. Mol recommended aloe vera, which formed a crust of "healed" skin that sloughed off to reveal yet more rash underneath. The man at the drugstore said to try Nizorol, a vile pink concoction usually applied to really tough dandruff or genuine scalp infections. That made my skin burn and puff faintly in a very offputting, constantly distracting way, so I only used it for a few days before chucking it.

"Got any suggestions?" I asked Vivia, who was going through my portfolio at the kitchen table—sketches vs. "original" Max Ernst prints— and poring over the contents, looking for just the right backdrops for her theatre piece. "I feel like taking a cheese grater to the Goddamn thing."

She scoffed. "Can't be that bad, surely."

"You want to take a bet?"

I hauled the bottom of my shirt up, ready to show her—which, naturally enough, happened to coincide *exactly* with Aaron emerging from the back yard (where he'd been gardening), full garbage bag in one righteously dirty hand. "Whoo-HOO!" he yelped. "Free show at 676!"

"Shut up, idiot. What's in the bag?"

"That?" He set it down, drawing both an earthy rattle and a less-predictable clink; at our reactions: "Oh yeah, this is weird . . . I was just digging the slot for that compost-heap, right? And I keep finding all this *junk* buried in the ground, doesn't matter how far you go down—like, broken glass and charcoal briquettes and shit. Freak-ass, huh?"

"Maybe there was an explosion at Colonel Sanders'," I suggested, bored; Aaron's idea of "freak-ass" left more than a little to be desired, in my not-so-humble opinion. Besides which, I was already starting to itch again.

But: "Maybe the top of your house burned down," Vivia said, laying my fourth sketch next to a print chosen seemingly at random and giving both of them the coldly measuring bale-eye. To me: "This the one you were thinking of, when you did that?"

I shrugged. "I wasn't thinking *of* anything, much; that's sort of the point of the exercise. Why do you ask?"

"Oh, no reason."

Aaron shook his head, as though to clear it—pure *Looney Tunes*, even without the requisite "whubbada-whubbada" noise foleyed in on top. "'Scuse me: the top of the *house*? Like, when?"

"Oh, a good long while ago, probably; before you bought into the house, anyways. Same thing happened to my family and me once, back in Patcock. We move in, thinking it's all freshly renovated, and . . ."

"Uh huh. Hey, Viv—there a law how every place-name in the Maritimes has to sound obscene?"

She bristled a bit; you could always get Vivia's neck in a knot by reminding her where she came from, if nothing else. Shooting back, immediately—

"What, like 'St. John's?'"

"No, I mean like 'Patcock.' Or 'Intercourse.' Or 'Dildo.' Or—"

"Look, you want to hear about this, or should I just change the subject?"

Which was definitely my cue, as duly elected house mediator, to step in. At him: "Aaron, knock it the fuck off." At her, meanwhile, prompting: "House, roof, burning?"

Vivia cast Aaron one last glance/glare, then shrugged. "Yeah. Well, my Mom and I move in, and everything seems fine, right? But then we start to figure out the place has a few more glitches than the landlord ever told us about, and I don't just mean all the glass and what-have-you in the garden—more like you couldn't turn on the dishwasher or run laundry and drain the tub at the same time, or water'd start coming down through the kitchen ceiling."

"And the denouement?"

"About what you'd think; we'd been screwed, no legal recourse. Moved out as soon as humanly possible." She turned over one more sketch, adding: "I heard the next family sued 'cause their Mom broke her back making peanut butter sandwiches."

"Slipped in the overspill?"

"Nope. Tub caught her right in the spine, after it finally fell through the bathroom floor." As Aaron snorted—back injuries, man! That's the *shit*!—she pivoted suddenly, waving the last sketch in front of his face. "Hey, laughing boy: what's this look like to you?"

"Vivia—" I started, only to have her wave me silent. Aaron considered the drawing for a moment; it was the same one I'd been working on the night before, an Ernst-esque forestscape composed of little except leaves and branches, which either lolled like dogs' tongues or arched upwards like curved knives. Then said—

"Some kinda guy? Big and thin, no face, sitting in a chair like that one you gave Janis. With his head on fire."

| calling dr. abbott

Art's not an exact science, that's what I told myself. Frottage equals open invitation to fill in the dots. So it's never a big deal for two different people to look at your frottage and see two (markedly) different things—

No. It's a very big deal indeed, however, to look at an image *you* drew and realize that not only do other people see it as being something completely other than the thing you thought it was, but . . . that it actually *is* something completely different.

God knows, under other circumstances, that attic would have never been my first choice for studio space; hot, small, and spare, with limited light and a highly distracting, "normal" noise level. All of which had, from the very beginning, made it difficult to keep hold of any given idea—I'd start picking out a fairly accurate object only to see it blur and alter in front of my eyes due to headache, or dimness, or the fact that it always seemed to take so much longer than I ever thought it would. And by each successive twelve-thirty, I'd feel utterly drained, as though my skin was nothing but an old plastic bag stretched thin over an hour's worth of exhaustion.

The Institute's "main switchboard" number rang eight times before Nail-lady finally picked up.

Beyond bored: "Who-should-I-say-is-calling?"

"Janis Mol? I need to talk to somebody about the Mental Radio recreation."

"Doctor's out 'til six. Demonstration at the Theatre."

She tried to switch me to voice-mail, but I wasn't having any. Pried the (Jay and Jay Memorial) Theatre's address out of her instead, caught a series of connecting streetcars, and got down there within forty-five minutes.

HYPNOTISM AND THE PARANORMAL—OPENING YOUR INNER EYE, a shaky marquee sign above the front door read. Both the second "N" in OPENING and the final "E" in EYE had been shoved in backwards, an instant Cyrillic translation for a mainly Slavic section of town, the latest Toronto neighbourhood to become informally reserved for immigrants fleeing the former USSR. From a nearby storefront, row on row of immaculate china Infants of Prague—interspersed with period plaster busts of Lenin and period plastic busts of Yeltsin—kept disapproving, gilt-laced watch like a silent choir of pre-teen Liberace impersonators.

I ducked inside to avoid their accusatory stares along with the rain, which had just begun to fall: late sleet, big crunchy gobs of it. While the sky above had already sealed over with boiling grey clouds, shedding light like dust—light so cold, so thick, it clotted on the pavement behind me like shadow.

| ghost filmography

The Jay and Jay Memorial Theatre smelled like vinegar. Abbott was already onstage and well into his lecture, pointing to various charts via a wheezy, secondary-school-style overhead projector. Explaining, as he did—

". . . seizure as a form of glory, of set-apartness—a sign of prospective power. Instead of simply treating people who had epilepsy, our ancestors used to make them into kings . . . or gods. Probably just as well, in context, since their idea of successful neurosurgery was to cut a hole in the patient's head in order to let the demons out. Still, they had a few valid insights. One Greek metaphysician, for example, found a very clear link between the 'storm in the head' those epileptics he'd studied felt during their various episodes and—"

But here, a voice from the audience cut in—clear, though not loud, back near the auditorium door. A surreptitious glance confirmed it was that oddly knowing girl from the Freihoeven's waiting room, lank hair still hiding her bent face, once again not looking up from her book, even as she said, dryly:

"—orgasm."

The audience giggled, en masse. I repressed a snort. Abbott fixed

Carra Devize, lips thin, as though trying simultaneously to regain control and remember his place.

"It seems we have a skeptic in attendance."

"Oh, more than one, probably."

Another ripple of giggling. Abbott made a graceful gesture in response to its erratic percussion, half debonair shrug, half placatory salute.

"Easy to mock, isn't it?" He asked, rhetorically. "Of course, if said 'skeptic'"—and here he stressed the word oddly, making Carra raise an eyebrow in response—"were willing to put her mind where her, eh, *mouth* is, she might come up onstage and help me jumpstart the more . . . practical . . . portion of today's lecture."

He trailed off, perhaps expecting Carra to back down. Instead, she shrugged too, and rose; shuffled sidelong into the aisle, then down. Murmuring, as she brushed past me:

"I guess I'll see you later, then. Janis."

It wasn't until she was already halfway to the stage that I realized we'd never been—formally—introduced.

Dim hush, followed by a pen-sized flashlight directed into Carra's eyes; she'd folded herself bonelessly into an armless industrial chair, while Abbott hovered above. He kept his voice low and soothing, starting almost immediately in on some elaborate rap about moving down through water, dark fathoms, away from the surface: "Further and further, counting backwards, as the sun shrinks and fades. I say counting backwards, starting from ten . . . *now*."

There was a pause, as though Carra might or might not be deciding whether to respond. Then:

"Ten . . . nine . . . eight . . . seven . . . six . . . five . . . four . . . three . . . two . . . one."

"Very good. Close your eyes." As she did: "You are now fully asleep, but will answer and obey all questions or commands I put to you. Confirm this."

"I will answer and obey all questions or commands you put to me."

"*Very* good." He rummaged inside his coat, bringing out a small square of cardboard. "I am handing you something. Open your eyes, and tell me what it is."

"The back of a Kraft juice-box."

For just a second, the gigglers had rejoined the party, though—if tone and pitch were any indication of emotional stability—sounding considerably less sure of themselves. Abbott smiled, tightly.

"In fact, it's a mirror. Turn your back on the audience, raise it, and tell me what you see reflected in the area located directly over your right shoulder."

Two things happened, pretty much simultaneously: I realized that I was sitting in the space indicated and felt myself tense, uncontrollably, at that same knowledge. So I kept my eyes level, my breath steady, concentrating instead on the faint pattern of bruising which stippled itself up and down Carra's long pale arms . . .

. . . bruises that, soon enough, seemed to shift in the auditorium's dense shadow, to pixilate. To form, almost—

(words)

I was too far away to read them, not easily. But they were mostly four-lettered, far as I could tell—and appeared, even from a distance, to be in several different types of handwriting. Some, perhaps, not even in English.

Carra, slowly: "I see . . . the audience. Where I was sitting. The woman sitting next to me . . ."

"Describe her."

"Wearing a coat with a brooch in the shape of a scarab beetle; good-looking, doesn't think she is. Her name's Janis Mol. . . ."

And: *Yeah*, I thought, sullen. *Pretty good call, 'specially if you're around the Institute enough to get hold of Abbott's records.*

Abbott: "Concentrate, please." To me: "I'm now addressing the young lady in question. Would you be so kind as to do something with your hands?"

"Anything?"

"Within reason."

(Well—okay.)

I shrugged and raised my hands, steepling the fingers together in the universal gesture for prayer. Held it, feeling silly.

Abbott: "Can you see what she's doing?"

Carra nodded.

"Praying," she said, simply; I flinched. "But she's lost it—let it fall sideways. She's looking scared. She doesn't want to believe I can see her, but she does."

"You can stop now."

Carra shot him a thin thread of a look under lowered lashes, like: Can I? "Now *you're* starting to sweat, doctor. There's a triangle of soaked cloth right over the base of your spine. Your ulcer is playing you up, because you forgot to take your pills this morning; had to get to that first interview while you were still feeling fresh."

"*Thank* you—"

Coldly: "Oh, don't thank *me*. The audience isn't liking this much, by the way. They think you're a big fake, that this is some routine we worked out beforehand. Some of them want to leave, but they're telling themselves it's because they have to go to the bathroom really badly. And now, just as things reach their pitch, your spotlight is about to—"

—snap off, plunging the place into darkness. Which . . . it did.

I sat there, frozen. Hearing nothing but Carra's voice, small, yet definite as God's amidst my fellow watchers' gasps and squeals and hoots. Finishing, while Abbott was still too surprised to object:

"—malfunction."

When the lights came up, she was gone: a predictable twist, oddly reassuring in context. And as everyone else got up to go, I knew I was the only one who'd felt her brush by in the dark, the gentle pressure of her cold fingers on mine. Her voice in my ear, murmuring:

"Just so you know; Carraclough Devize. Feel free to look *me* up, when you can."

| file CDEV-03892: devize, carraclough

I wouldn't, though, not for years. Not until we were both in the Clarke, bumping elbows in the cafeteria line—and even then, believe it or not, that was by accident. I got a copy of her dossier, thirteen years' worth of material padded out with contents sent over from the Freihoeven; all that wasn't because I went *looking* for it or anything, though. No. It was because someone else had copied the contents, took the copy away, and forgotten the original—left it behind, stuck in the machine's out-feed tray. Nobody even asked me what I was looking at while I paged through it, walking back to my room.

Like most things to do with Carra, it seemed coincidental. At the time.

Once I got past all the boring biographical bullshit—D.O.B., birth certificate, parents—I found myself leafing through a series of genealogical charts and records tracing the descent of several recurring names: the Devizes (of course), the Glouwers, the Rokes, the Druirs, and the Rusks, among a few scattered others. It reminded me of the family trees I'd seen depicting the royal bloodlines of Europe: a tangled, interleaved recursion of marriage, bastardry, and (in at least one case) incest. Only instead of hemophilia, the poison inbred into this tangle was a mix of madness, mediumship, and—depending on the beliefs of the writer—magic. Satanism or psionics, take your pick; one man's is another's, etc.

Born in 1968, a clear and powerful medium from early childhood, Carra had been drafted—at age thirteen—to be part of the last recorded scientific expedition to Peazant's Folly, before it was turned into a tourist attraction and finally exploded some years later. In the late 1980s, she'd gathered a small coterie of like-minded Ryerson students around her; the Black Magic Posse, they'd called themselves. All well-known figures in Toronto's occult/psychiatric underground, and all marked by the fallout from whatever supernatural radiation she carried with her. Franz Froese, vanished. Jen Cudahy, dead of nothing an autopsy could confirm (or deny). And Jude Hark, or Hark Chiu-wai, who—at the time the record was made—hadn't left his apartment for close to a year.

Psychic, I thought. From Psyche, the Greek goddess of the soul or spirit; the same root spawning psychiatry, "soul-healing." Which implied, like day did night, that Carra, that I, that everyone here, all those helpless disconnected ravers up and down Toronto's streets, suffered from something far beyond aberrant brain chemistry: a *soul*-sickness, plain and simple.

Soul-sick.

And if science and the scientific mindset had made one mistake— alchemizing *psychic* into *psionic* to give a false impression of understanding, predictability, mastery—it had, all unknowing, illuminated another great truth: that what we have, like all too many other sorts of sickness . . .

. . . is infectious.

| concentration exercises

When Dr. A. finally got out of the theatre, I swung in beside him, pacing him back to his car. Starting in, before he could fob me off—

"Are you sure you've got me down as a sender?"

"I beg your pardon, Ms. Mol?" But he sounded more relieved than annoyed; probably just glad I didn't want to talk about his quasi-abortive demo, in all its egg-meets-face glory.

"Three times now I've tried to draw the first thing that came into my head," I told him. "All the way through, I try to draw what I'm seeing, what I'm trying to concentrate on—and all three times, so far, it's turned out like something else."

Abbott held his clipboard up against his chest with one arm, keeping it between us like a shield. As we reached the main doors, he studiously avoided looking in my direction, his voice gone suspiciously, annoyingly even: "Are you sure it's not just—"

"I tried to draw a tree; it turned into a case of spontaneous human combustion."

That got him to look at me, at least—to stop moving, too. And stare.

I just stared back, arms folded. Not smiling.

"I think we'd be better off relocating this to the office," he suggested, abruptly.

The trip Institute-ward was faster with wheels. Once there, I cupped my hands round the mug of tea Abbott had given me, grateful for its warmth against my palms. The building didn't even have its own lot; we'd had to park a block and a half away and sprint here through the sleeting rain, leaving melting slush to trickle down out of my limp hair and drip clammy-cold into my collar. I could feel my shirt sticking to me, the everpresent itch between my breasts swelling and fading, like breakers on a beach.

"I don't know if my receiver's been in touch with you about not getting anything," I said, looking up at him, "but if this stuff works at all, I'm on the wrong end of it. Actually, it sort of feels like . . . something's . . . been screwing with my head—putting in shit I never meant to draw."

"Modifying your sense of perspective?" Abbott tilted his jaw towards me, like a dog seeing something it wasn't sure might be food or not.

"No. I mean . . . when I draw something, I see it in my head first, right? Fairly normal. But what I'm seeing isn't what I end up drawing. Not even close."

"How close is close?"

I shook my head: holy Jesus fuck! "How many times do I have to say it, Doc? This isn't just close-one-eye and squint-the-other time." I leaned forward, tea cooling on command, as though it sensed my urgency. "I try to draw a book, and it turns into a snake; 'perspective' ain't the problem. Unless you're using it as some hitherto obscure shorthand for 'rampant waking hallucination.'"

Abbott nodded, soberly: "Of course, I'm no artist." A dry flicker of a smile. "Look, Miss Mol—granted, I can't show you the files to prove this, but please rest assured, you *are* recorded as a sender. None of the other group members have any instructions to try transmitting to you, let alone any personal information with which to gain the requisite physical—or mental—bearings."

I frowned. "I've got a file?"

"Certainly. And since we already have you linked to a receiver, for you—or we—to have any more information than we have already prior to the experiment's conclusion would ruin the double-blind insulation we need in order to preserve some semblance of scientific consistency." Abbott spread those long thin hands of his, knuckles like twig-knots. "We *could* tell you right now, of course, but on one sole condition. . . ."

"Which is?"

"That you resign from any further participation in the test, immediately."

"Hmmm. And let me guess: this *doesn't* come with a two-week notice and severance package."

Abbott shook his head. "'Fraid not."

All the way down the line, that was what it felt like, the choices I had: go crazy now or go broke and starve later. That's why it pissed me off so much, later on, when I realized I'd pretty much done both.

"I do have one suggestion." I waved a hand; he took it as assent and went on. "It sounds to me like you may be experiencing some, er, intersecting wave disruption. Even if no one *is* sending to you, you might be picking up on whatever might be being . . . broadcast . . . nearby. Which means that the concentration you're putting on simultaneously drawing and transmitting is opening up your channels, as it were."

He hesitated, then leaned over and opened one of his drawers, rummaged. "Hang on." Pulled out a small travelling shaving mirror and handed it to me.

"What's this for?"

"A concentration aid. You put that somewhere in your room, angled so you can keep it in peripheral sight, then concentrate on sending to *it*, not to your receiver—to the person in the mirror, as it were."

"In other words, me."

"In *other* words, yes. The key is to be aware of the mirror peripherally, to identify the mirror with the sending. That way, your conscious mind can concentrate on your drawing, while your subconscious maintains the sending focus."

"Like I'm sending through the mirror itself."

"Quite," said Abbott, smiling.

I turned the mirror over and over in one hand. I hadn't realized what the other one was doing until I noticed Abbott leaning forward a little, trying very hard to not look like he was staring at where it lay—nestled between my breasts, scratching furiously.

"Ah . . ." he began, delicately. "Miss Mol . . . ?"

"Rash," I replied, shortly, stuffing the mirror into my bag. And left him to his own devices.

In the Institute's one bathroom (up two flights of stairs, usually only accessible by key, though a quick flick through Nail-lady's desktop easily netted the one marked "Ladies"), I played *Flashdance* and peeled my bra-straps down without shrugging completely out of my top; the marks beneath were bright red now, slightly suppurating, hot to the hesitant touch.

"That's getting worse," a voice pointed out, somewhat uselessly, from behind me: Carra, wedged into a stall with her Doc Marten'ed feet up on the toilet-paper rack, arms crossed—the sort of position you'd expect to find adopted by somebody smoking surreptitiously, which she wasn't. Just . . . waiting, I guess.

(For me.)

"Yeah, thanks; noticed that, actually." I tucked myself away, turning. "Nice show at the demo, by the way."

She nodded, slightly—gave this contortionate sort of half-smile, half-grimace, rueful and tired. And:

"Ah," she said, a little sadly. "'So now you have seen the witch in her true ornament.'"

"Uh huh. And it was supposed to prove . . . ?"

". . . that when you pop off their brain's protective seals by sending the conscious mind on a little detour, anybody's randomly picked natural talent is bound to come to the fore—but Abbott does like to stack the deck, that's for sure. Which is where I come in."

"You on retainer here?"

"In a manner of speaking. My Mom needs help, the monetary kind; I can do for myself, most-times, but she takes a little more effort. Ask me what you really want to, though."

"Are you one of Abbott's receivers? Is that the group—" I stopped for a second. You always hear about people "gulping," like that's as natural for human beings as it is for frogs, or something; it's not, especially so in this case. Try more like dry, and loud, and hurting.

But Carra didn't seem to hear.

"—you should be in?" She finished, for me. "That's what the Institute is here for, supposedly. So they can run you through a bunch of hoops, show you flash-cards, get some sort of chartable number to work with. Me, on the other hand . . ." A sigh. "Look, what is it you think I want from you, Janis? Your *thesis*?"

Prim: "I've got no way of knowing what you want. Ms. Devize."

"I told Abbott this was a stupid venue to test his 'Mental Radio' in, right back when he first suggested it: Toronto the Good, five-into-one megacity, with death on top of death on top of death almost anyplace you look. And take it from long experience—being dead doesn't tend to concentrate your mind, except in very specific ways. Think about . . . burning, for example . . ."

(*Some kinda guy, big and thin, no face. With his head on fire.*)

Yeah. That'd be a real conversation-stopper, probably.

"So . . . yes, sometimes miserable things happen in this city of ours, like pretty much all the fucking time. And you'll never know why, not even if you're 'lucky' enough"—a stress on the word, like Abbott with "skeptic," but considerably more bitter—"to know who to ask, because *they* don't even know why. Because they can't remember anymore, and they just don't give a good goddamn."

She was shaking now, ever so slightly, and I have to say that scared me on a far deeper level than any overt display of histrionics could have: like she was just trying to school herself into being able to finish, without caring much whether or not I thought what she had to say was bullshit.

"I don't know what's in your house," she said, finally. "I haven't been there, and I never will, because I don't have to. Because all I have to do is look at what it's doing to you."

I stood there, feeling the rash burn. Watched her sit there, shaking. Until—

"Look," I told her, "I just don't think it's as bad as it must seem. To you. I mean . . . I . . ." I trailed off. Then, weakly: "I haven't even *seen* anything, you know?"

Not—to speak of. Not *really*. Not—

(uh)

There was a long pause; Carra bowed her head once more, let her hair fall forward again. Returning, through its protective veil—

"Not *yet*."

| reflections

It took a few minutes to find the best place for the mirror Abbott had given me; I eventually set it on its end in the corner of the room, directly across from where I sat to sketch, at the foot of my bed. With my foolscap positioned over the rough planking, my ass jammed against the wainscoting between bed and wall, I could lean forward in relative comfort to draw, shade, and pencil, while at the same time being able to simply flick my eyes towards the mirror and see this tiny version of myself repeating my own movements, a blurred homunculus-echo.

All the while, thinking: *This is bullshit. This is never going to work. Abbott has no idea what he's fucking around with—*

(But what did that make me, exactly? Renting myself out to play a part designed specifically to shore up his idiocy, his hubris?)

Which was why, once I'd finished the drawing, closed my eyes to clear my head then looked at it again, the vast rush of relief I felt was spiced with more than a touch of chagrin. In the wood, I'd found an image of an old boot, lying on one side with one lace pulled out so far it sidewindered from end to end across the paper . . . and that image alone, clear and sharp, was exactly what stared up at me.

I decided to not tell Abbott, not immediately; the guy irritated me enough without that smug veneer I knew he'd celebrate being proven right by adopting. It was worth eating a little crow, though (if only by myself), in exchange for the ability to trust my own hands again.

Aaron and Vivia both remarked on my fresh new rush of energy over the next few weeks: pure relief, immediately channelled back into both my thesis and my own art. I found my head crammed with new images, sketching them well outside the set daily transmission time, too eager and excited to notice their overall bleakness: a half-demolished house, broken-ended planking thrusting up like jagged brown teeth. Blackened figures lying in a row, peculiarly boneless and shaded, as if about to dissolve like smoke. A child's toy engine melted like a snow-sculpture in hot sun, like plastic in fire.

And if my temper also got steadily worse over those same weeks, who could blame me? It's hardly abnormal, when you're under increasing deadline-oriented pressure, to reach the point where you "suddenly" decide it's not worth putting up any more with the countless usually unmentioned irritations and idiocies other people produce, the endless stream of petty bullshit everybody around you thinks is so God-awful important.

It's easy to tell yourself that warning signs are something else, at the time. To ignore the mounting tension, forgetting the most basic tenet of cause vs. effect: how things can strain only so far before they—

(snap)

Five weeks after I'd begun using the mirror, Abbott switched the schedule so that I was supposed to transmit at 11:00 P.M.; he staggered the hours for each sender/receiver coupling to keep us from getting too subconsciously accustomed to a particular time of day. In the yellow light of my half-burnt-out overhead, sky black beyond the window, I was drawing something I was pretty sure was going to be a wheelchair by the time I was finished, peripherally aware of my doppelgänger across the room following along with my motions: light brown hair dangling forward to hide my face (and who did *that* remind me of?), tiny pencil moving furiously over the whitish-grey paper. A ghost sitting cross-legged, the mirror a doorway through which images passed like water through a sluice.

And: in the back of my head, Max Ernst, talking about himself—a THIRD VOICE manifesto so close to what I was doing, it was sort of . . . scary. Saying:

"My eyes were avid not only for the amazing world which assailed them from the exterior but also for that other world, mysterious and disquieting, which burst forth and vanished with persistence and regularity in my dreams: to see clearly has become a necessity for my nervous equilibrium. To see it clearly there is only one way—to record all that is offered to my sight."

Classy, I thought. *Perfect. Gotta stick that between sections thirteen and . . .*

At that same second, something in the mirror—moved.

I stopped moving, stopped breathing. Flash-frozen. While a vast black shape like a congealed shadow seemed to flow past behind my silvered shadow-self, moving with smooth and unhuman (*ape*-like, somehow) stride. A wash of night, far taller than anything the room could have actually held.

There was a gleam of greenish-white light from its ill-defined head; a reflective glimmer, as through heavy fathoms, like the flirtatious residue of some coy, over-the-shoulder glance. And then it was—gone. "Passed on," probably in both of the phrase's more well-known senses.

I flung myself over and away from the wall, of course, hands instinctively flicking up to shield me from nothing: nothing in the mirror, nothing in the room, nothing anywhere but in my own sick head. And then I doubled over as the itch between my breasts flared to scraping, agonizing pain, like embers roused to fire by the same hot gust of wind making my thesis' printed-off pages flap: ripped my T-shirt off and clawed with my nails at the raw skin under my breasts 'til I went deep enough to draw blood.

I sank down, panting, itch lost and forgotten, as the pain shifted to something much cleaner and harsher. Warmth trickling down my stomach, my eyes were magnet-drawn back across the room to the mirror—empty of everything but my own face, a white-eyed cartoon, all taut lines over a limp, shocked blankness.

Break the mirror, something whispered inside me. *That will end it.*

Close the doorway. That's what doors are meant for, right? To let things in, then shut them out again.

I looked at the unfinished drawing, crumpled on the floor; thought of never being able to trust what I was seeing again, of being unable to draw at all or what else might appear in the mirror, the next time I tried this. And then—

Then, I thought of an invitation. One I'd never once imagined I'd seriously accept.

Clutching my T-shirt to me, I made myself straighten, grab my robe. Forty-five minutes, a shower, a frustrating search for our misplaced White Pages and a quick jog down the block later, I found myself standing in the vestibule of Kali's all-night donut shop on Bloor, flipping through what was left of their pay phone's ragged book for the not-exactly-in-everyday-use last name "Devize."

Just as I expected, there was only one entry in the entire city: DEVIZE, G. and C. So I fumbled out a quarter, put it to the coin-slot . . . and hesitated.

12:35, the electronic display flashed; A.M., not P.M. What was I doing, phoning some scary freak I'd met in a bathroom after midnight—not long, grant you, but after? How did this make any sense?

I looked down at my feet, trying to clear my head. And there, my eyes met the fresh stains on my new T-shirt, still oozing, from where I'd just skinned my own breastbone over a hallucination.

Carra's phone (I hoped) rang three times. I braced myself for the switch to a voice-mail or answering machine, but it didn't come. A fourth ring, fifth, sixth, seventh. By eight, I was finding it hard to breathe.

On the eleventh ring, a click of pickup. A pause.

"I—" I started, and couldn't get any further. The word like a stone in my throat, jammed shallow, impossible to dislodge.

And: "I know," she said. That's all, dry and remote as usual . . . but at the time, Christ. Jesus!

"Come over," Carra told me; I felt myself nodding, though it wasn't like she could see me, or anything. My nose and eyes burning painful fever-bright, for just a second, as that deceptively thin strip of flesh separating my sweating cleavage from my thudding, aching heart.

| home visit

2:25 A.M., by my watch. The house was an Annex side-street sideshow attraction, a rotting two-storey duplex slightly folded in on itself as though in pain, like some tumorous parody grafted onto the side of its far-healthier twin. The front door opened just a second before I raised my hand to knock—Carra, naturally enough, in stockinged feet and a much-decayed T-shirt (thigh-length, just about) advertising some long-defunct 'zine called *SHE: Tough Movies, Tougher Women! A Walk on the Wild Side of Cat-Fight Cinema!*

"Sorry to call so late—" I started, but she cut me off.

"Not like I wasn't up already." Pointing: "Through there. I'll be down in a minute."

"Through there" proved to be what I took as Carra's bedroom/office, maybe five feet by six and choked with stuff that mostly looked stacked for sorting so long ago she'd forgotten to get around to the stocktaking part of the exercise. A 1950s Barcalounger chair played double duty, set up square where the bed should have been; one wall was literally papered in what proved to be—at closer examination—water, electricity, and TV bills going back before either of us had been born, arranged into patterns dictated by level of urgency.

The vanity, wedged kitty-corner to a bulging closet, held thirty or so sample-sized bottles and tubes of perfume, all covered in dust. Pinned to its grimy mirror was a studio photo of a girl who might or might not have been Carra, wearing a black leotard, in the proprietary embrace of a woman who might have been her mother (Geillis Carraclough Devize, the file told me later, called "Gala"). Books were laid out all over the bed, some in teetering or half-spilled piles—paperbacks, hardcovers, old cloth-bound ones with gold lettering on the spine.

I picked one up—a copy of Shakespeare's *Henry IV, Part I*—and opened it, recoiling from a sudden spill of yellow-spotted early Polaroids; left to mark the page, perhaps. I checked the text I'd opened it at: Welsh nationalist leader/magician Owain Glendower and stammering Brit firebrand Hotspur (*My liege, I did deny no prisoners!/But I remember when the fight was through*) holding themselves a little mediaeval pissing contest.

> GLENDOWER: *I can call spirits from the vasty deep.*
> HOTSPUR: *Why, so can I, or so can any man,*
> *But will they come when you do call for them?*

Or as H.P. Lovecraft once wrote, along startlingly similar lines in *The Case of Charles Dexter Ward: Doe not calle up any which ye cannot putte down.*

Bending, I retrieved the Polaroids, flicking through them. All starred girl-who-was-Carra—her eyes closed, a little older, same leotard—and something else, something that seemed to be forming in the corner of every photo: a blurry, globular, mucus-white excrescence, like faces under water.

My mind clicking helplessly through metaphors, obvious and un-. Water; mirror. Faces in the mirror, submerged, subterranean. Sub judice. Sub rosa.

(Pen umbra.)

From downstairs, two voices intruded; one low and indistinguishable, one higher, clearer—Carra's, again. Saying:

"I checked myself out. No. No." Mumble, mumble. "No, I'm actually allowed to do that." A questioning murmur. "Not exactly. *No*."

Slowly, almost unnoticeably, the light in the room had begun to take on a watery quality; from farther away still, a clicking, hissing sound started to mount through this one-sided argument I was eavesdropping on, as of a needle bumping against the inner groove of an old vinyl record. And the voice just went on, calm, reasonable—the sort of tone you adopt when you're A) dealing with a crazy person and B) not too sure about your own sanity, either (albeit far surer of it than you are of hers).

"Look, I can't stay; I've got someone here, and I have to get back. A girl." More murmuring. "*Nobody*, Gala. Just a girl. I'm going now."

Click, hiss. Click. Hiss. And that stuff, like dirty string, like desiccated tears—draining from the corners of Carra's tight-closed eyes to spin a tight off-white ball which hovered over her younger self like a leering stalker. Like pain given physical shape.

What the hell are *these, anyway?* I thought.

"Not what. Who."

It was the rankest kind of horror movie jumping-jack jolt—hadn't heard her come back, not with the click-hiss taking up mental space. Though that, of course, seemed to already be long gone.

And: "Fine," I gritted. "*Who*, then?"

"Oh, depends on the year; I get a lot of . . . visitors, and none of them seem to leave cards. You'd pretty much have to ask them."

She waved me over to the chair; I brushed at its dusty coat, gingerly, then sat. Watching her flop down on the equally disgusting carpet next to that shaky vanity's rickety left front leg, her knees incautiously crossed—a bit better light in there, and I probably could have been able to tell whether or not she was a natural blonde. Not that that was exactly uppermost on my list of immediate pressing facts to check right now, mind you.

"Am I going insane?" I asked her—straight out, no chaser. She considered a minute, then said:

"Not unless I am, too."

Which made me feel . . . oh, *so* much better.

| lacuna

Great segue, huh?

But I have to. Because here, believe it or not, is where I find nothing but a dead spot in my mind: something that narrows my hindsight in such a very specific way that, while it seems likely Carra spent the next few minutes telling me something, I have only the very vaguest of ideas what the hell said something might have been.

How often in life do we find ourselves saying—well, not out loud, not usually—but thinking, definitely: if only I could *see* something, for once . . . God, the Devil, my dead uncle Steve. Anything beyond the purely mundane and predictable boundaries of what we've come to recognize as "reality," this standard we've somehow all apparently agreed upon as "true" vs. false, without really *agreeing* on anything at all.

Then everything would be revealed, confirmed, denied, answered at last, for good and for all. The gates of perception would roll back, and nothing we think we know would ever be the way it was again.

Yet praying also, in almost the same breath: but oh, Jesus Christ Almighty, please don't let me *see* something. *Please.*

Sometimes, you can be living right in the middle of something and *still* need your face rubbed in it. And you never see it coming towards you, either, because—whenever you do take the time to glance around—everything looks exactly the same.

When my mother told me the story about her growth, she added that what was so wrenching to realize, in the end, was that what she'd been feeling up to that point *hadn't* just been the way things were. That when you were in it, deep in it like she'd been, it was like you'd always been there. And you always would.

Pop the skull, play around, pry out the Stone of Folly; sharp medicine, the medicine of necessity. Sometimes, the oldest ways really *are* still the best.

I've thought so much about it, for so damn long. And all I've been able to come to, in the end, are these two irrevocably linked (and rather useless) conclusions:

A) That it's not so much about what I drew, but what drew itself through me. And—

B) That it's not so much about what I saw, but what I *refused* to see.

Contamination, spreading always outward, tainting all it touches. Is it a grudge, a curse? Is it something aware and malign, or unaware and desperate? And finally—considering how we can never see it coming, only track it by where it's been, is it really any*thing* at all?

Anything. Or . . . anyone.

Being a ghost is like being invisible, so being invisible must be like being a ghost. Like being inside the shadow, always blundering towards people with your hands out, angry that they can't see to comfort you.

The Asian idea is that what remains behind after death by violence is less the murdered person his or herself than an echo created by the moment of the person's death—a rip in the fabric of space and time itself. A doppelgänger husk, ectoplasm with pretensions. Not "so and so's ghost" so much as just *a* ghost. Or just . . . "ghost."

The Idea of Ghost, like the Idea of North. A mere looped whisper, in darkness or in light. And no matter what this person may have been like before he or she died, no matter what they—specifically—might have wanted, ghosts only really want one thing: you, with them.

Not to be alone. Not to be trapped. Not to be where they are. Not to *be*.

Just living in the house wasn't enough; but when I refused to *see*— and I did refuse—I set it off. It had to rush my door, and spilled all over everybody else in the process.

The fault is mine and always will be.

Funny word, that: "fault." As in San Andreas. The crack through which one world intersects with the next, or vice versa. This crack in my head, still gaping open—a magnet, a haematoma, a dark and spreading pool. A cigarette-burn hole in the fabric of everything I see, or hear, or do; right in the middle, impossible to mend, impossible to disguise. Impossible to ignore.

A perpetually gaping mouth just waiting to be filled with breath, or tongue, or words. Or—

—*teeth*.

| the bag

"Janis. Are you listening to me?

I shook my head, resurfaced. "Excuse me, what?" Caught her edge-of-colourless eyes on me, bleached even paler in this weird light, and blushed.

"Um . . . no. Must have just zoned out there for a minute, actually."

"Uh huh. That happen a lot, these days?"

Trying for sparkling wit, but willing to take mild sitcom-banter amusement value as the nearest default: "On my own or just around you?" Would've gotten at least a snort on that one if this'd been Vivia. But Carra simply nodded ever so slightly, as though the idea'd already occurred to her—raised near the very beginning of our "relationship" by necessity only to be quickly discarded from experience, but certainly worth another moment's consideration, nonetheless. If only in terms of a concept to be debunked.

"I don't meet a lot of people like me, Janis," she said. "Partly because there aren't very many, which is what you would expect. And partly because, as far as I can figure . . ." —looking me square in the eye, this time. And finishing, without even opening her mouth:

. . . on some level, they can see me coming.

I swallowed. "Suh—see you?"

See me . . .

Out loud, though barely above a whisper: ". . . and avoid me."

A true conversation-stopper, just like that burning man who might (or might not) be haunting my home. I stared; she waited. And when— after a minute or so had passed—I still hadn't gotten myself together enough to reply, she simply started to speak again, in much the exact same tone. Like none of the above had ever happened.

"Back when I was a kid," she said, "when I was sole breadwinner for this 'family,' and my Mom used to rent me out to every fakir cum faker with a floating séance on the circuit—well, back then, there weren't a lot of ways for I *Was A Tween-Aged Medium*-types like myself to wind down. So I'd wait 'til it was really late at night, after she went to bed, and I'd put a bag over my head; just an ordinary plastic bag from Becker's or whatever. I'd tie it around my neck, and I'd breathe in and out 'til all the air was gone, so I could black out and not be bothered by anybody before the hole I ripped at the bottom let the air back in again.

"Anyways: this went on for a while, until—like usual—stuff started to build up. I'd wake up, and the bag would already be off, like halfway across the room and ripped to shreds, and I sure as hell knew it wasn't *me* doing that. Or all the furniture would have moved around my room, or I'd find messages in dryboard marker on my wall, like: DON'T. STOP. VERY DANGEROUS VERY DANGEROUS FOR YOU. ON NO ACCOUNT MY LOVE.

"But I didn't stop, because I didn't want to. Because, at the end of the day, it was basically the only goddamn thing I had to call *mine*. Not until the night all the windows in the house blew out at once, that is, and Gala found me, tore the bag off, beat my ass black and blue. And then just because I had to, because she knew, now. So after that, she was always *watching* me."

And: *Gala, that's the voice through the wall*, I told myself. That scritching, fumbling noise, like somebody too sick to straighten up dragging a cane over carpet; that's her, the former child abuser, living fat off the payoff from her kid's "gift"/curse. Her daughter's former metaphysical pimp.

"That's a very sad story," I said, finally. Not knowing what else to say.

Carra nodded. "Yes. Yes, it is." Then: "Janis—do you know *you* have a bag over your head?"

(What?)

"Let me show you."

She reached behind her, rummaged in one of the open boxes of detritus, came up with an ancient Polaroid camera—the same one that'd taken those other pictures, no doubt. Angled its lens slightly towards me, along with her dead-calm eyes, and . . .

"They call this spirit photography," she explained, as the flash went off; for the life of me, though, I don't ever remember her touching the button. A half-second later, the photo popped out, full-on square and ugly whitish-yellow, like some diseased robot tongue. Carra waved it back and forth briskly, a professional snap in her wrist—something she'd done a thousand times, with this making an even 1001. Handed the result to me, and let me take it in at my own pace.

Strikes me, thinking about it now, that that photo's probably sandwiched between Hotspur and Glendower right now, along with the others; not that I have to check, or anything. Since I'll never forget what it looked like, no matter how long I live.

The bag . . . well, it wasn't one, not as such. More like a bonnet or a hood drawing 'round my features, muffling me from the neck up in thickening, tightening shadow. A cancer-caul. A penumbra as plain as any National Geographic ever captured, any the Discovery Channel ever covered: Janis Mol, in near-to-full eclipse.

I don't know what my face must have looked like in the waking world, but it was probably just as bad. Yet Carra kept on looking, affectless as a cat: mild, vaguely sympathetic, preternaturally still. Like she'd had all capacity to be otherwise burned out of her, a very long time ago.

"It's always like this," she said, so low it might have been more to herself than to anybody else, including me. "Half of what you learn is useless, the rest is depressing, and everything you touch wants a piece of you in return. And just because you can see things other people can't, it doesn't mean those things can't see *you*. . . ."

I'd gone all the way through "stare" now, right past "gape" and into "goggle." Thinking: *Jesus Christ, what's wrong with me, anyways? What's wrong with you, you stone bitch freak?*

My first thought would be: a lot.

But: "You need to get out of there, Janis," Carra told me, not reacting to the insult, even though I *knew* now that she could probably "hear" me as clearly as though I'd voiced the thought aloud. "Seriously. Sometimes money's not a good enough reason, and I can tell you that for absolute fact. You need to get out, and you need not to go back, ever . . . and if you were looking for my advice, I'm sorry. Because that's all you're going to get."

I don't know how I got out of her house; through the front door, one assumes. But when I came to, I was blocks away, bent over with my hands on my thighs by that empty schoolyard just north of College and Bathurst, bile in my throat and spit hot as blood in my mouth—the both of them far too full for me to do anything but pant, and gasp, and drool to keep from vomiting right then and there.

Having run and run with nothing but my own fears chasing me, obviously—run and run and run, 'til I couldn't breathe to run any farther.

| storm's eye

I made my way home in the unseasonably cold early hours of dawn, sky going grey-pink to blue overhead, like brain tissue freezing over. Hesitated on the porch, feeling the mass of the house looming over me, like a reactor technician or a biohazard medic without a suit: naked. Vulnerable. While even the door seemed to gaze blankly back at me, an idiot look of inquiry in its empty glass panes: *Yes, Janis?*

I shivered.

Then, from inside, I realized I could hear Vivia and Aaron moving about the kitchen, exchanging what sounded like their usual banter—partly mutual amusement, mostly mutual irritation. And all the fear that I'd run from Carra's house to elude, that I'd walked shadowed streets for hours trying—and failing—to reason myself out of, was instantly drowned in a rush of sheer relieved normality: boring, mundane, beloved bullshit. All power to the tentacle-porn-addicted bastard, but it was very hard to think of any house that had Aaron Coby living in it being haunted.

In the absence left by the fear, meanwhile, exhaustion fell on me like a lead-lined blanket; I had to exert effort just to turn the door handle. A minute later found me trudging along the bare-wood hallway to the kitchen, where (I hoped) Vivia would have made her usual industrial-strength pot of Joe. I couldn't recall ever being so grateful for her innate morning-person tendencies.

Actual first thing out of Aaron's mouth, on seeing me: "Dude, dig it—the dead walk." Vivia, uncharacteristically, didn't say anything at all; just stared, mouth open, like she was catching flies.

"And a good fucking morning to you, too," I snapped back. Pointing to the coffeepot in Vivia's hand: "Viv, pour me some of that, and I'll be your slave for life."

"Where've you been?"

"Out; what're you, my Mom?" Typical Vivia: statement with a question, question with a question. But even this momentary annoyance was well-leavened with relief at its familiarity. "I don't want to talk about it," I said, at last, with what I hoped was sufficient finality. "Not now, probably never. Just give me some coffee, tell me the shower's working, and let me get some sleep."

Aaron raised an eyebrow. To Vivia: "She's okay, wherever she went."

Vivia, meanwhile, had already put down the coffeepot—still making no move towards getting me a mug, I noticed with some irritation. "Jan, I, ah—" She moistened her lips. "I think you'd better come upstairs and see something."

And suddenly, all the fear came back: not driving, beating terror, but a frozen paralytic grip of *oh-shit* dread; like I was a cancer patient and Viv the doctor I'd been hoping would smile, but hadn't. Not so much what she'd said, as the way she'd said it: the half-drop of the th- in "think," making it almost "t'ink"; the slackening of the vowel in "come" to something more like "comb," with something similar flattening "see" closer to "say," Vivia's loathed Maritime accent creeping back into her speech, the way it only ever did when she was *seriously* upset.

Took a lot to scare Vivia, a fact I well knew. A fact that was, in itself . . . sort of scary.

My mouth moved, so suddenly dry I couldn't find enough saliva to wet my own lips. "Show me," I husked.

Halfway up the stairs to the top floor, I saw the first traces of it— heard the change in the sound of my footsteps, felt something gritty and resilient shifting under my feet. I frowned down at the greyish whorls my shoes kicked up, drew in a breath to say something, and coughed at the dry acrid stink in my nostrils. "Jesus H. What—?"

Vivia flipped on the light in the upstairs hallway, and I wondered—for a split second—at its strange dimness. Before I saw what had caused it.

Ash.

Long waves of grey and black powder streaked ceiling, walls, and floor in much the same way snowghosts eddy down winter streets, if snowghosts could be caught in photographic negative and frozen on plaster. The naked lightbulb was covered in it, carbonized powder keeping time with a faint, percussive crackle and pop under its heat.

Wordlessly, I moved into the centre of the hallway, down to where the ash-waves gathered like the accretion disk 'round a black hole: my door, ground zero, Hiroshima central. Event horizon for a strange new pocket-dimension.

It was worst in my room, where the stench of burning lay so thick I could barely breathe; black-grey dust an inch deep on every surface, kicking up spray with every step we made. And here too, the ash had fallen in patterns suggesting some sort of sudden surge, some impossible explosion emanating out from a central point at (nearly) unimaginable speed.

"You know the *really* fucked thing?" Aaron asked, as he knelt by my chair—delicately brushing ash off its vinyl seat, only to reveal the unblemished cushion beneath. "Shitload of soot, crap for days, but far as I can tell there's nothing actually *burnt* anywhere." Shaking his head, more bemused than frightened: "Just . . . utterly. Fuckin'. Fucked."

"Translation: you didn't hear shit."

"When the ash bomb went off? Nope." Aaron braced himself on the desk and stood, groaning. "First I know about it's when Vivia comes home about two this morning, goes upstairs, sees the damage, and pitches a hissy."

"*Said* I was sorry, didn't I?" Vivia muttered.

"Kicked me out of bed, screaming how I'd burnt the house down, man, that's what you *did*. The top floor, anyway."

"Well, the hell else was I supposed to think?" Accent creeping back again here, while she wasn't looking: *s'posed, t'ink*. "Jan's gone, and the place was normal enough when *I* left it. . . ."

And on and on and on. But I'd already tuned them both out, my eyes locked fast to what I'd noticed the instant I stepped in: the core of this silent, flameless explosion, very centre of the ash-blast. The one object in the whole grey-swathed room, from window to desk to bookshelves to bed, which'd somehow ended up with no ash on it at all—that still gleamed bright, pristine, spotless amidst the ruin.

Abbott's mirror shining back at me like a fang from where it stood out against the damage, my entire bedroom wall its backdrop, like a half-lifted feline lip.

Aaron, fading up through my haze: ". . . you think you're gonna stick *me* with the bill, you got another think comin'."

"Oh, big damn shock. Like you ever clean *anything* up—"

"We'll *all* clean it up." I had to raise my voice over theirs, and a fresh surge of exhausted resentment almost burned away my requisite embarrassment at my own bad behaviour: like I didn't have enough to feel guilty over already, for shit's sake . . .

But I just rolled on anyways, like a bulldozer: "Viv, you get the broom—Aaron, garbage bags; they're in the kitchen drawer. We'll do the hallway first."

Brave words. The ash, however—eager as it was to come boiling up off floors, walls, and furniture in equally dense, choking, cornea-scratching clouds—proved equally eager to condense clingingly back onto plaster, wood, and fabric; in fact, to go anywhere *except* into dustpan or receptacle. Before long, the general irritation factor had both Aaron and Vivia coughing up gack and blinking redly, while my unhealing breast-rash flared back to full, radiation-fiery half-life. Finally, Vivia called a halt.

"What *is* that?" she demanded, as I paused yet once more —well, "discreetly" had been my first impulse, but it obviously hadn't exactly taken—to rake at my boobs.

"Same thing."

"Thought I told you to *see* somebody about that." To Aaron, as I just shrugged, helplessly: "You—coffee. Fresh coffee. And as for *you*—"

She dragged me off into the bathroom to treat my wounds. Demanding, while I held up my breasts with both hands, giving her room to slap on iodine and bandages with equal profligacy: "How long's it been now, exactly?"

"Since—"

(—that experiment started, dumb-ass. The one *you* hooked me up with?)

But I wasn't about to go there, not even at this late date. So:

"—I don't remember," I finished, toneless.

"Well, strikes me you should be starting to worry about this, I'm serious. Forget the over-the-counter crap; this could be gangrene, for all either of us know."

"Re your bedside manner? It needs work."

"Fuck you too, Jan-girl." Vivia straightened up, pressing the small of her back with a groan as I tugged one of her borrowed T-shirts down over the bandages. "That should hold together, for a bit, anyway, and—oh, you're not serious." This in response to the fact that I'd flipped open the medicine cabinet and was—even now—popping a couple of Nytols out of their protective foil packet. "You can't possibly think you're gonna sleep in that room, Janis."

"It's *my* room; I'm not letting some poltergeist bullshit force me out of my *room*, Vivia." Adding, with a wryness I only wished was a joke: "Besides, you know I can't sleep anywhere else, Nytol or not."

Viv closed her eyes and shook her head. My naturally insomniac bent had long remained a running gag between the two of us, even on those occasions when—like now—it became anything but funny.

"I'll clean the rest of it up in the morning," I added, trying to reassure her.

"That's not what I'm worried about."

Bitterly, I restrained the urge to snap at her so-well-meaning-it-smothered "concern": did she think I wasn't scared? That I was literally too dumb to recognize danger when I—

(saw)

—it?

But the fact is, I was too tired to think about any of it anymore, barely awake enough to breathe. Only awake enough to be aware of exactly how tired—and angry and fed up—I was.

And beneath that, like static, like bass . . . like some guerilla signal flickering between stations, buried under layers of figurative snow . . . the fear of eight years of half-anticipated failure, dimming me from my skull on down. That indefinable *knowing* that, if and once I allowed myself to be driven from that room, I'd never be able to enter it again; afraid, on no level I could explain (or explain away), that to lose my home would be to lose—

—momentum. Faith. Hope. That failure here would mean failure everywhere. Would mean I *was* a failure; always had been. Always would be.

(And who's told me so, exactly, ever? Not Mr. and Mrs. Mol, for sure. Not my so-called friends.)

Just me, as ever. Me, somehow hollow at the core from birth, struck and ringing now with a dissonant tone pitched so that it could be heard only by dogs, or fish, or insects. Dead houseplants, barren trees. Rats in the walls.

. . . ghosts.

"I need to sleep," I told Vivia, one last time—then swallowed the Nytols dry, and went back upstairs to my ash-choked room. With careful steps, trying to kick up as little as possible, I pulled the blankets off the bed in a cloud of dust, holding my breath to keep the overage out of my lungs. Using my pillows to sweep the last of the ash from the bare dirt-pocked sheets.

And collapsing onto them, closing my eyes, feeling sleep sweeping upon me like fabric falling in thick, multiple layers over my face. Falling out of light, into shadow.

Into the penumbra.

| fever breaking

I slept 'til three that morning, resurfaced only gradually, in horrible increments. And then—

—I found myself hovering in that half-waking state between fatigue and sleep, the same one during which any or all visions that may have hovered imperceptibly at the corners of your mind all day tend to swim into focus, into sharp and dreadful relief. Yet another long-repressed childhood fear, just waiting for a chance at revelation: the room and its vibrations, resonating in time with my Nytol-induced haze, had conspired to send me ratcheting back to nightmare circuit territory. I would be almost gone, my lids lead-heavy, when suddenly I would know, with utter certainty, that if I did close my eyes, a face would come rising up over the end of my bed, like some hideous, pale sun—

—and oh, Christ, I can *see* it now, utterly unchanged by decades of conscious personal evolution: too pink, as if carved from soap-brittle; smooth and overemphasized, like the face of a bad actor. Something inhuman in human form. On occasion, it even put on expressions; an ironic cocked eyebrow, a limp moue of surprise. Its mouth would hang half-open, showing improbably white teeth, but its eyes would be dead.

One day, I felt, it would speak to me, and if it did, I would go completely insane.

It wasn't a dream, not really, because I was never fully asleep when it happened: *hic vigilans somniat*—he dreams awake. The Roman epithet for poets, seers, or madmen. So which would people think I was, if ever I told them what waited for me on the border—the penumbra—between sleep and waking?

And: *Open your eyes*, I remember thinking, sternly. *Get up, get out. Wrench yourself bodily away from this smell of ash, breath-cloggingly thick in your nostrils*; heat like a djinn's giant hand on every part of me, pressing me down. Sweat running down my temples, slicking my hair and collecting under my breasts, shaking the itch awake once more—deeper this time, more painful, burning like gelignite in every pore. Like the lit track of a phosphorus grenade.

I raised my lids, or at least struggled to; felt my eyeballs roll back in my head, zombie-white and scarlet-threaded. Sensed, without seeing it, how the ceiling would shift lazily in my blurred vision, roiling and streaming like a single noxious fume—how it would seem to heave in and out like breathing, the rhythmic lift and lower of something too huge to take in all at once.

Nightmare breeding on nightmare, giving birth to fresher horrors. And suddenly, I was trapped fathoms deep under a textureless weight of water while a thing bigger than the whole waking world sunk down towards me through faraway beams of light: my formative ideation, alive at last, reborn from the corruption of its own decay—alive, and aware, and . . .

. . . hungry.

More sweat trickled down my face, as icy knots cramped in my stomach. I tried to move. Found I couldn't.

No more than mere seconds, inevitably, eddying slow as geological epochs. I knew light, flickering in the corner of my cracked-open eyelids, blurry through the glaze of dried tears; tried to blink my eyes clear, but couldn't do that either. Felt my limbs, heavy and motionless at my sides, stiff as if I had steel weights strapped to them. Felt a newer, rawer rush of heat lap my face in time with the flickering light, and "saw" the dancing shadows of flames on the wall.

(Oh God, I'm going to *burn* here)

At the end of my bed, a crouched and bulbous outline stood stark black against the flames, hidden just below my frozen line of sight. Waiting to rise.

Sensations scudded across me like moonlight flickering through an overcast: a stitch twanging in my back, reflexive nervous spasm. The pressure of my bladder, acutely, painfully full. And then—with absurd clarity—the wordless echo of Vivia's voice downstairs, querulous and angry and amused by turns. Which was enough, in turn, to summon every ounce of willpower I had left: contort my lips into shaping her name, letting the autonomic outrush of breath give sound to the only word my numb brain could still form:

"Vvvv . . . iii . . . vvvv . . . ."

No answer, of course; but then, what'd I expected? I could barely hear myself.

As the ceiling sank closer, I *knew* something was looking at me from the end of the bed, and prayed desperately not to regain control of my eyes. Not to see the face I knew was there and waiting for me; not to see the thing that was casting the shadow, which rose so huge and black against the room's engulfing flames.

The black negative of Dr. Abbott's Holy Grail: a hypnagogic state induced by oxygen deprivation, exhaustion and fear, liberating every paranormal perception I had at once at the potential cost of a total—fatal—disconnection between body and mind.

Or, to put it another way—Carra's bag. Coming down.

The pressure bore on me like that half-remembered, half-imagined lake, a freezing weight slicing with deadly accuracy through the ghost-fire's stabbing pain. Something was with me, in that split second: beyond reason, only barely conscious, collected from the wreckage of lost lives and desperate for an ideal of communication it no longer knew well enough to name. Something trapped here in a shell of memory, slave-driven to find any way out it could, even one which led nowhere but . . .

. . . into *me*.

And finally, as I managed to tilt my skull to one side, I thought I knew what I had to do; it was like rolling a boulder head-first up a collapsing gravel slope with only your neck and shoulders to support the effort. In the corner of the room, the mirror shone simultaneously bright and black, opaque to the nth degree—the doorway, opened on Dr. Abbott's oh-so-helpful advice, through which this thing had let me see it for the first time. Through which time itself (perhaps) had sent a backburst-bubble of the original house's ruin.

Currents stirred, spiralling inwards in fiery-bright lines, pulling my vision towards that empty hole at the mirror's centre. And as it did, the anger and desperation swelling around me became infused with a terrible, helpless pleading, a childlike, unselfconsciously selfish fear: *Help me, Janis, help me . . . let me in . . . .*

But: "No," I told it, muscles bunching and swelling, finally beginning to gain some purchase in my own limp body. "You're . . . dead. Go . . . away."

HELP me!

"*Fuck* I will."

One arm, pushing up against the mattress. My body, tilting up, like mountains folding out of the earth in some tectonic convulsion. My weight shifting, sliding—with excruciating difficulty—towards the edge of the mattress.

HELP ME!

At the foot of my bed, something sheathed in fire rose up, its shadow falling over me, backlit in its own combustion. It moved and coalesced further, deepened and darkened; leaned over me, its face nothing but a featureless flame-shrouded oval peering down through gathering blackness—

And: "NO!" I screamed out loud, flinging my arm over my eyes. "I DON'T WANT TO HEAR IT! I DON'T CARE! FUCK *OFF!*"

I felt something give around me, inside me, as that shriek came ripping up from within like a tide bursting through a rot-ridden dam. Went rolling over, off the bed, ash bursting up around me in phantom tsunamis; scrabbled on hands and knees towards the corner where I knew the mirror waited, bright bursts of pain scoring me with every move as fire lashed out at me from every angle, cinders falling on my naked legs and half-exposed back. A smell like roast pork filled my nostrils: me, burning.

My hand closed on the mirror—and something, simultaneously, closed a huge and burning grip around my ankle.

Another scream, as searing air burnt the inside of my lungs bright red. I reared up and flung myself at the door to my room, hauling it open with my free hand. Staggered down the hall towards the stairs, seeing myself trailing streams of smoke and ash, clouds of dust settling in stinging glee into my burns. Tear-blinded, smoke-choked, I flailed around for the railing, caught it, hurled myself onto the first step—

—missed it.

My foot came down with that stunning, jarring jolt that kicks us out of sleep, and my knee gave way beneath it. I pitched over with a shriek, curling into a ball, protecting my head with my arms, and managed to land on my side, flipping over and over down the stairs like some fleshy coin, carelessly tossed: wham! Wham! Wham! The house whirled around me, my stomach seeming to simultaneously bounce off ribs, throat, groin. Then I came down on the floor of the vestibule, throwing out both hands to brace myself against the impact—and felt glass shatter in a single, high-pitched, discordant crunch, slicing deep into fingers and palm.

(Uh, ah, *AH*.)

In that single instant of shock and silence, I could see again. Everything was clear. No roar of burning from upstairs, no smell of fresh-burnt wood—only shards of silvered glass winking up at me, bright and empty, from the gashes they'd opened in my red right hand.

A snap, a crack—time, popping back into place with a sick-making wrench, like some dislocated shoulder. And then Vivia came pounding down the hall, screaming my name, dropping to my side, babbling questions I couldn't possibly hope to answer. Finally pulling out her cell phone and stabbing the 911 buttons, tears streaming down her face.

I wanted to reassure her, poor creature—to tell her I finally knew what'd been going on all this while, that I'd faced my fears and lived to tell, that I'd cracked the house's back and made it say uncle. That everything would be fine from now on, because . . . I'd stopped it.

I was wrong, of course: I didn't, hadn't; there was more than sufficient proof of my actions' consequences already lying in wait just 'round the corner to reveal itself, but not of the crazy victory I felt singing through my half-cooked veins. Not of *that*, no.

Not hardly.

| years later, pt. 1

The half-hour version of *Frottage*, which Vivia eventually cobbled together from my unfinished thesis, premiered at Toronto's Fringe Theatre Festival the year after that; it took honours, got overwhelmingly positive reviews, and was a contextual "success" (even taking into account the fact that no one who came to see it could possibly have paid more than ten bucks a pop).

It's not going too far to say it was primarily her/my play's cultural fallout—rather than her talent, considerable as it'd always been—which got her into a prestigious new writers' retreat, sponsored by the intentionally outré Theatre Passe-Detout, where she was taken under the wing of local scenester Haroun Farang-Geist. With his mentorship, she was able to spin the show out yet further, garnering a limited run at the Detour; a year after that, the Bravo!Fact Video Arts Fund offered her $20,000 to make *Frottage* into a 54-minute TV special.

This next step, however, proved problematic for two reasons: first because, in order to expand it any more, she'd have needed my help, but I was already in the midst of taking a medication vacation in the Clarke Psychiatric Institute. And second—because that also happened to be 'round about the same time Vivia had her first bi-polar episode, precursor to several years of hideously predictable chemical back-and-forth: step one, go nuts. Step two, take your meds. Step three, feel so much better you stop taking them. Step four, go even more (inventively, alarmingly, self-destructively) crazy . . .

Repeat. Repeat. Repeat, repeat, repeat.

Doesn't happen to women, usually, let alone to people past the age of majority. Yet there she'd be, near the end—phoning me up at five in the morning to tell me how much she'd always loved me, to ask me if I'd ever loved her back. To say: "Euclid, Jan-gal—wasn't that a time? Best work you ever did, you dumbstruck Mainland cunt, and you couldn't even finish it."

And I'd just allow as how she was right, calmly, wincing at the way she wasn't even trying any more to hide the Maritimer accent she'd once worked so hard to eradicate—at the way she didn't even seem aware of it any more. Knowing exactly how goddamn embarrassed she'd be, if only she could hear herself played back without her brain supplying some sort of permanent laugh-track.

Thinking to myself, as I twisted the phone-cord 'round my wrist 'til it knotted, and nodded like she could see me while I did it: *Oh baby, oh Jesus. It's like taking collect calls from Captain Highliner on a bender.*

It took six months before I changed my number without telling her, but somehow, she always seemed to find me again. Up until I stopped answering the phone at all, that is.

Six months after that, I was rummaging through a Queen Street Starbucks' recycling bin for the Entertainment section when an article caught my eye. It said former playwright and director Vivia Syliboy had thrown herself head-first into the St. Clair Ravine, probably because the Don Valley Parkway—much nearer the halfway house where she was living on her own recognizance, at the time—had finally put up those anti-suicide screens on either side of its too-low marginal wall.

| years later, pt. 2

After I checked myself out of the Clarke, I dug up the results of Dr. Abbott's "Mental Radio" experiment, which had already been published. No names, naturally, but it was fairly easy to figure out which case study was mine . . . they did put in reproductions of every sender's drawings, after all.

Turned out, the man they'd paired me up with—Henry Goshaugh was his name; another sensitive, from Carra Devize's control group—had died before he could fully complete his part of the experiment. A little more exploration turned up the facts: he'd developed a massive undiagnosed tumour in his abdomen, which broke open unexpectedly, flooding his insides with poison. Peritonitis, internal bleeding. He died in his sleep, and when they did the autopsy, they found foreign human DNA—amniotic fluids not his own, in other words—infecting the imploded ruin of his pelvic region.

Tiny bones. A few milk-teeth.

It was just about the same place his womb would have been, if he'd been a woman. Except, of course, that he wasn't.

I saw Henry Goshaugh's drawings, too. They didn't look much like mine. They were very . . . exact.

Studying them, I got the crazy idea (oops! Don't say that word, not out loud) that . . . he'd been seeing the right thing, while I was the one who'd been misinterpreting. Like Mary Sinclair and her horse-headed thing that'd really been a roller-skater's upturned leg.

I never remember seeing a face in my frottage. I never remember putting a face in my drawings. But Henry had: the same face, over and over and over. And over.

It's hard for me to look at. Because I've never seen it, ever—but nevertheless, it seems so very . . .

. . . familiar.

| years later, pt. 3

Once my doctors thought I was well enough to be trusted on my own— or with minimal supervision, to be more accurate—I moved into a place on Fibonacci Street, possibly named after the man who developed the geometric series based on the ancient Greek "golden mean" of architectural design . . . a ratio which also matches the proportions of an ideal-perspective human body, and turns up again and again in a whole host of biological and astronomical phenomena.

Some mathematicians advanced the Fibonacci series as proof of a consistent, divine design to Creation, back during the early phase of the Renaissance; I have vague memories of at least one case of heresy declared against a hapless Fibonacci advocate who absolutely refused to admit that God's infinite power could never be even theoretically calculated by something as innately limited as mere human knowledge. So they tortured him 'til he recanted, then burnt him at the stake: proof positive that what most human beings want isn't so much convincing evidence to support their arguments, but enough reasons to warrant going on arguing.

"You should write about it, you know," Vivia said, during our final phone call.

And: "What the hell would I say?" I asked, amazed at the very idea. Because I don't know what happened, exactly. I never did, and I probably never will.

No records can tell me when the top floor of 676 Euclid burnt down in the first place, let alone why, or who might have died in that conflagration. No amount of psychoanalysis or cheap séancery can ever prove what really might have happened to me, up there—whether the wreckage of what might once have been a person (or persons) wanted to get into me or just get the fuck out of the house, any way it could.

But I do know this: when I found myself in the old neighborhood last week, pulled there by some sticky, invisible filament of entropy, I discovered that it had burnt down again. That there was nothing left of the hot room I once wrote and drew in, measuring my time by wet breaths, but a smouldering layer of broken wood and glass.

Maybe this time they won't rebuild it.

| oh, and aaron—

—he was inside when it burnt down, that last time. Asleep on the first floor, so they got him out fairly easily, though he *was* almost too drunk to move.

Which is why he never heard the alarm, why he never stirred when black smoke filled the room around him. Why he still sustained damage to both lungs from smoke inhalation, so bad he's needed an oxygen puffer ever since, and probably will for the rest of his life.

A comparatively easy escape, as such things go, you might think—especially having heard my story, or Vivia's, or Carra's, or even poor Henry Goshaugh's. But I never had the gall to say that to him, to dare trying to trump his pain with my own, like some kind of masochistic pissing contest. What the fuck for?

Life's too short.

| last in an indeterminate series

Throughout that entire last spiral downwards—i.e. during my sojourn at the Clarke and after—I'd find myself appearing, intermittently, on Carra's doorstep. It was never like we planned it or arranged dates; I'd simply show up, usually whenever I literally couldn't think of anywhere else to be. And Carra, of course, was always waiting—having known I was coming, in that same tragic way she knows almost everything. Except how *not* to know.

It was like we'd skipped courtship entirely, slipping headlong into classic Old Married Couple rhythms; we'd sit around pretending we were normal people, drinking tea, watching TV or videos (though her programming choices were exactly as inevitably, predictably odd as one might have assumed, given our previous interactions—the birds and the bees of *Microcosmos* or *The Iron Giant*'s bittersweet will to self-determination, spliced crossways with sample-heavy experimental shit like *Tribulation 99* or the Survival Research Laboratory). No matter the viewing fare, however, we were still more normal by far than Carra's mother Gala, whom I never met, but often heard perpetually stumbling around upstairs like a moth in a jar. Sometimes, we talked awkwardly around what had happened to me; mostly, we didn't even try.

The last time I went there—a month or so before Mr. and Mrs. Mol rescued me from the depths of my own closet—I asked Carra: "So what should I do?"

"Why would you think I would know?"

"Well . . . you're psychic."

A razored smile. "So are you." And then, after a beat: "You know, Janis, one of these days, you're gonna have to learn how to make up your own mind."

Adding, without speech—

Because letting something else make it up for you . . . was what got us both into trouble. Wasn't it?

I looked down at my hands, silently; traced, in reflexive habit, the thin white worm-trails of scar tissue that ran along my palm, between my fingers.

"I keep getting that urge to draw," I said, finally, not looking up. "Start drawing again, I mean. Keep drawing. Problem is . . . I don't know what I'm going to see."

Carra nodded, unsurprised (as ever).

"Door's open," she said. "You bust one down, or let it get busted, and it'll never really close properly again."

I closed my hand, so I couldn't see the scars any more. Explaining: "But—I thought the mirror was the doorway. I thought, I really thought . . . if I just broke it, that'd all be that with that."

Finally looking up at Carra: "Didn't work, though. Did it?"

Carra blew out a breath and peered at the wall—for once not that scary, unfocused look of hers, but simply an ultra-ordinary human scowl of mingled fatigue/frustration. And: "I think," she said, at length, "if you're talking about the mirror, maybe it helped you a little too much."

"Say again?"

"It . . . purified your control, like a static filter on a signal. Whatever was in you got stuck, halfway in, halfway out: couldn't trick itself past your Mental Radio any more, couldn't get far enough out to work on anybody else. All that power, building up, with nowhere to go . . ." She shrugged. "Well."

(*You* remember.)

I swallowed. "So when I broke the mirror—"

Carra swept her hand off to one side and up, a rising mime-jolt, like something squirting away under pressure. "It took the first channel out it could find. Straight into—"

—Henry.

(Wouldn't've mattered, though: him, me, her. Whoever.)

"It didn't have a choice," she added with a shrug. "It had to move on. Somewhere. Through someone."

"Because I couldn't see it," I whispered. "Because I didn't want to see it. Or hear it, or even sense it."

And shockingly, from Carra, came a dry, almost silent laugh.

"Nobody," she pointed out, "ever does."

Which stopped the conversation dead, right there; nothing more to say, let alone *worth* saying. Seeing how we both already knew just what she meant.

| perspective

But I wonder, still, as I always must: what else might be moving through me, even now?

I pick up my pad at least once every day, sometimes even put my pencil to it. And every time, I put it down again, leaving the page unblemished; feel my hands hover motionless, caught forever between the abortive urge to do something and the fear of doing . . . anything.

Because: better by far that bleak, white blankness than to try drawing something, to rake up all my old pains and losses looking for something beautiful and find something unbidden crawling across my page, some unborn thing, some scuttling mouse with a ghost-foetus human face. To find only (once again) that awful light, which is so thick it clots like shadow.

Sub terranea. Sin nombre. Pen umbra.

I may never draw again. I may never even look, especially not at the paintings of Max Ernst. And in that way, I can only suppose, I guess it's a little . . . *just* a little . . .

. . . like being dead.

STRANGE WEIGHT (2005)
| chapter one

No matter what he might have told himself later on, this was the God's own truth: when Maccabee Roke chose to take that stupid job Le Prof offered him, it wasn't *really* because he had nothing else left. He had his health, obviously; his certificate of release, signed by the Archbishop; fifty bucks and the clothes on his back, plus a voucher for one month's free room and board at Saul of Tarsus's Halfway House for guys (and some gals) who were . . . halfway. Halfway out, halfway back. Halfway between Church and State, between this world, the flesh, and the Devil.

Besides which, if he'd found himself in *real* trouble, there was always his blood kin to turn to—though he wasn't exactly sure what sort of reception he could expect there, given the circumstances under which they'd all originally parted company.

Making his way from St. Michael's Cathedral for the very last time, Mac found Sister Blandina of the *Ordo Sororum Perpetualam* waiting for him next to the narthex, hand on hip, tracking his every move with coolly level eyes. Not exactly a surprise, though always a pleasure.

"Here to see me out?" he asked her, not stopping.

She turned and fell into step with him, replying: "Mother Eulalia sent me. She said to say she wants it back."

"Wants what back?"

"Don't even, F—. . . Roke."

"Oh, *Sister*. Do I ever?"

A shrug, like she was throwing off flies. "Hadn't thought so, up 'til now. But after this, I can only assume . . . all the time, apparently."

"Gee. I'm cut."

Sr. Blandina gave him another type of look entirely at that, so direct it virtually came with subtitles: *Not yet, you're not.* Then leaned in, voice dropping, to murmur a hot lick of breath against his ear.

"Did you ever seriously think we don't know what you really are, Maccabee?" she asked. "Because we do, be *very* sure of that. We always did."

They were almost in the doorway now, flanked on either side by a glowing three-tier rack of wish-candles—two-dollar coin a pick, minimum donation adjusted for inflation—vs. a slightly overfull wall font, so handy for emergency entrance/exit genuflection. He put his palm on the door handle and turned again, without warning, so fast they practically slammed up against each other; saw her recoil a fraction, and felt a flicker of sick pleasure crossbred with vague insult—*just what do you take me for, Blandina? One of my in-laws?*

"Listen up, Sister," he told her, adopting the same uncompromising tone. "Even if I did know where it was, which I'm not saying I do, you of all people should know I'm not going to be posting it on some website and giving out the URL anytime soon. So tell Eulalia it's a simple case of me needing insurance, or leverage, or what-have-you. Tell her it's nothing personal. And tell her . . . tell her what I *think* is, if your whole Order's sense of itself is so pathetically dependent on possessing one obscure mediaeval manuscript, then maybe there are better places both of you could be. Or all of you, for that matter."

Meeting her gaze straight on now, unwavering, and finding . . . nothing there to hang on to, by any normal person's standards. Just the same old same old: a killer's stare, wrapped in a supplicant's hide. That scarf concealing her hair might as well be some suicide bomber's hijab, for all the mercy he could expect from calling it a wimple.

Good thing we're neither of us normal, he thought.

Behind them both, a recording of a bell rang Sext. Over her shoulder, he could see the routine ebb and flow of humanity gathering—parishioners with their spiritual hands out, tourists looky-looing, homeless people sidling in, in search of a quiet pew. And almost all of them with their shadows already attached, their various ghosts and parasites trailing spindrifts of fuzzy longing or polluting obsession. Soon, the place would be chock-a-block with crossed currents, knots and nets and snarls, etheric overlay so thick he'd barely feel able to move. . . .

And that was when *it* would come, as it always did. Come straight past everybody else and sit right next to him, grinning its dreadful, halo-lit grin.

But not tonight, not anymore. Not *ever.*

Blandina shook her head, very slightly, a Cylon resetting its personal hard-drive. "We need it *back*," she repeated.

"Then come and get it," Mac told her. And left the Church, lit. and fig., without a single backwards glance.

Seven days later, a mere week, and already the "normal" world was beginning to crush in on Mac like deep-sea pressure. The first thing he'd figured out was that, when you didn't feel required to pray for five or ten minutes out of every hour, it freed up a lot of your time. Unfortunately, it wasn't like he'd bothered developing many *other* reflexive habits over his almost twenty years in God's "service."

Which really did make him a pretty sad object, all told: holed up from noon to night with other faith-lost freaks on every side, scared to walk Toronto's streets, no matter the hour, for fear of meeting someone he was related to (however distantly). His brave new life of physical freedom and spiritual ruin was quickly being reduced to a mishmash of half-remembered lines from songs: *Sin, sin, everything is sin, clap hands. Saturday night, and I ain't got nobody. Thirty-eight years old, and never kissed a girl.*

The next night, while venturing out for a copy of *Vanity Fair* and a pack of DuMaurier Lights, he accidentally ran into his youngest cousin, Saracen Druir, right outside Saul of Tarsus's front door. Saracen had his arm wound around some chippie's waist while he chatted up her best friend, sunk deep in a haze of personal glamer that masked everything about him but his poisonous, carrion-fly-blue eyes. When he saw Mac coming he slid, midline, into a double-take so note-perfect it actually succeeded in making him look even less human than he already did; the girls didn't seem to notice, simply trancing out in tandem, as if he'd put them on pause.

"Coz!" Saracen greeted him. "We'd heard tell of yuir . . . reconversion? Such news does travel fast, even through Dourvale. Yet I'm main glad to prove it no' just rumour."

"Oh yeah?" Mac replied, for lack of any better comeback.

"Certes. Yuir grandmere asks after ye often, even now."

"That's nice of her."

"Aye, that it is, and ye little deserving of such respect. Still, she says ye may come by the *brugh* when it suits you, by high way or low, if ye've no' forgot how tae walk the latter. Only bring some small gift with ye, for entry-price, and be welcome."

"Go up with a guest or two . . . like *these* gals, say . . . then come back alone, with a four-star hangover and a wallet full of twigs," Mac agreed, going out of his way to make the analogy as insulting as possible. "That *is* about the size of it, right? 'Cause you know, it's been a while."

Saracen dipped his head slightly, parodying a bow—*la, coz, how ye do prick me!*—and favoured Mac with a slow, deliberate wink at the same time: his right lid closing bottom to top in a luxurious sweep of lash, upside-down and backwards, like every other thing the (almost-)full Fae had to offer. Sweat stung the small of Mac's back at the sight, and the tiny hairs on his neck went up. But there was no way in Hell he wanted Saracen to have the pleasure of knowing it, so he kept right on projecting aggressive boredom.

It seemed to work. "Oh, coz," Saracen purred, all regretful, "ye do me wrong. And ye've surely no great call tae visit if ye've no mind tae—would be awkward, mayhap. As it might have before were I tae've visited *you*, given yuir past lodgings." A pause. "But not so now, aye?"

Not so much, no.

Mac got a sudden whiff of that last visit "home" to the *brugh* itself—down into Dourvale Hill's deeps, its apple-reeking darkness—when Saracen had shown him a single skeleton hand jutting up out of the close-packed earthen floor, bones splayed in decay like some pale flower. He'd told Mac, then a postulant, that it belonged to a local girl he'd liked enough to try to pull inside, not realizing—or caring—what an unexpected trip through solid rock might do to her; Saracen's capacity to make non-Fae-style jokes had always been fairly limited, as Mac recalled, but stuff like this was just the kind of politically incorrect, human-unfriendly jest that really set the whole Druir family's toes tapping. And truth be told, Mac had giggled a bit about it himself before throwing up, once he was safely back on hallowed ground.

Because: *They're no' like us, coz*, as Saracen was quick to point out, *and yuir no' like them, for all ye may try. Ye never will be.*

So why chase a dream of salvation, especially when you weren't sure—not even after all this time, not *really*—if the offer applied to you? If you even had a soul *to* save, let alone one worth the effort of saving?

We live long, and then we're gone. We dry up and blow away, with nothing left behind. Yet may we be merry, coz, ye and I and all our blood . . . in our season.

Saracen sighed, finally. "I've missed ye, cousin," he said, and snapped his nail-less fingers—the girls immediately began to chatter once more, ignoring Mac's presence entirely. And they drifted away down the street together, like leaves.

By the time he got back to his room, Mac's heart was still hammering, so he spent some time turning all his clothes inside-out, just in case. He found them uniformly wet through with sweat, especially the ones closest to the skin. The only good part was that, because everything he wore was (by simple force of habit) black, no one would ever be able to tell, unless they were already looking for exposed seams.

When night fell, he lay awake, trying his best not to think about what other relatives he might run into, given time, if he insisted on sticking around in the Greater Toronto Area. Semi-human wreckage set and left adrift by five hundred years of supernatural intermarriage, Rokes and Druirs with a side-order of Sidderstanes, Devizes and Glouwers and Rusks, all seeping back and forth into each other's bloodlines since 1650 or so, barring the occasional outcross—their version of the Auld Alliance, like Scotland and France, albeit with far more collateral damage.

Reverse changelings like Saracen's milk-brother Ganconer Sidderstane, tithed to seal a deal; throwbacks like his great-grandniece Ygerna, dripping in the dark somewhere, mere de-evolutionary minutes away from eating kids and taking names. Or quarterlings like Mac himself, living insults to a balanced universe—always equally uncomfortable in any of the worlds which laid tentative claim to him, no matter where he might momentarily choose to make his stand . . .

But worst of all, the looming spectre of Saracen's wayward mother, Enzemblance Druir Sidderstane: big sister to Mac's mother Miliner Druir Roke, intangible diver through solid objects, who'd followed after Mac for most of his childhood harassing him with her creepy affection, just to see how high his warlock's senses might make him jump. Enzemblance, once given to leaning out of the bedroom wall over Mac while he slept, waiting for the strange weight of her lank red hair to wake him, a scream half-caught in his throat. So she could smile down at him, too-sharp teeth the only light-source in a nightmare-shadowed face, and ask: *What is't ye dream of, nephew?*

(*Me*, perhaps?)

Eighteen years earlier, when he'd first finagled his way inside the Church's embrace, it had been Enzemblance's six-fingered hand at his back, pushing hard. Yet if he lived as long as both his genetic payloads suggested he might, barring any cold iron-related catastrophes, he'd do whatever it took to never feel that touch again.

Above, he felt the thing that absolutely was *not* an angel swoop to and fro on hook-feathered black wings, searching him out. But so long as he kept his window shut and his curtains pulled, he was safe, or close as made no never-mind.

I need to get away from this damn city, Mac thought. And began to consider how he might be able to lay his hands on a large quantity of ready cash.

| chapter two

Thinking back, Mac found all his earliest memories took place while in transit, as part of a twilight world in constant motion, never truly "at home" anywhere. Days spent indoors, behind drawn curtains, cocooned in comfortable darkness; nights of scudding beneath a grey sky just before dawn or under a low-hung moon, always driving, touring an endless series of Maritime motel rooms, campsites and cabins, strip-malls and trailer parks. That they never really seemed to *get* anywhere, for all this aimless travelling, was something Mac wouldn't notice until far later, when his parents were already dead.

As a kid, though . . . as a *kid*, life seemed genuinely golden. His mother—who called herself "Millie," now she was out amongst the mundanes—got by on looking like some pretty slip of a Renaissance Faire girl with a greenish cast to her hair and a silvery tint to her poison-blue eyes. His jack-of-no-trades Dad, on the other hand—Armstrong, known as "Army"—took firmly after the roguish border-lord side of his Roke heritage. An itinerant fixer-upper guy with a bare touch of the sight, plus just enough hedge-magic to let him talk himself through the Dourvale *brugh*'s back "door," which was where he'd met Miliner, naturally. And that, as they said, had been that.

It was a genuine romance, with Mac the much-loved by-product. And you really would think that would count for—something, with someone, wouldn't you? But apparently, going on eventual denouement alone . . . not so much.

Once, on a drive-by through Toronto, they'd stopped at the Connaught Trust so Army could show Mac the official portrait of Juleyan Roke, the infamous Black Wizard. While Millie waited outside, they'd stood there in silence, overwhelmed by their mutual three-way resemblance 'til one of the nun-librarians had come by, gently asking if she could help Army find anything. Army just shook his head instead, turning on his Nova Scotia bullshit charm full-force, and a mere blush and stammer later, they were back out on the pavement once more, no harm done—no fault, no foul. Slipping away, hand in hand in six-fingered hand, back into the perpetual half-darkness that made up their oddly happy, fugitive lives.

(Now, however, Mac had to wonder: had he met that nun again since, in his short-lived capacity as liaison to the Order? Mother Eulalia, before she'd lost her eye? One of Blandina's trainers?)

Blood will ever out, as Lady Glauce liked to say. And as an adult, whenever he looked in a mirror, it was always the Wizard who looked back at him, making a mockery of collar and cassock alike. A Roke warlock face set with the Druirs' Fae gaze, blue-shimmering opaque, all the way down to the bottom.

Each night before bed, Miliner would tell Mac the story of the Five-

Family Coven in installments, a series of literal fairy tales. How *once upon a time, there was a girl who came from nowhere, from nothing . . . none knew her people, not even she herself. And though she was beautiful, she was different as well, which made some take fright by her; the small-minded, the fools. But Scotland was full of many such at the time, a fearful place indeed. A place of great burning.*

Here she would pause a moment, looking Army's way for reassurance. Then continue, cheered on by his loving grin—

Yet she married a laird in the end, too great to care that she was anything but the woman he loved, and to him she brought her dowry, a stane of power the like of which had never been seen before or since. So with both of them protected from ill-wishers at last—she with his name and gold, he with her luck—there was a family . . .

Like ours, Mommy?

Aye, my lad. Exactly like.

Mac couldn't even begin to think how it must have been for her, in hindsight—youngest of Lady Glauce's brood, a mere toddler when she'd seen the Three Betrayed burn. She'd made the sickening headlong magical leap from Dourvale, Scotland to Dourvale, Ontario, 1593 to 1904, along with her mother, her father, Enzemblance, and Minion—the eldest, least-seen of all surviving Druir children, who few ever glimpsed outside of the *brugh*, and no unwary trespasser ever heard coming.

Why even pretend you could make a life for yourself here, outside the brugh's *walls, let alone for me?* he'd wanted to ask Miliner, sometimes. But Army *could* talk his way into (or out of) almost anything, after all—and having been to Dourvale himself once or twice in the intervening years, Mac also understood there was only so long a girl of any sort could be expected to squat in the dark, eating bugs and making dresses out of leaves, before a desperate urge to escape into that bright, strange world seen only in teasing, two-hour slices down at the Overdeere Old Highway Drive-In might take hold. . . .

Unless you were like Saracen, that is—Enzemblance's chick, knowing nothing else and not much *wanting* to know, either. *Born and BRED in a briar patch, coz Fox.*

It had never occurred to Mac to wonder what his cozy little corner of the whole Roke-Druir-Sidderstane mess might be running *from*, though looking back now, he could guess: the entire natural world, to which they all—himself very much included—constituted a living affront. Miliner's presence anywhere outside Dourvale couldn't fail to be seen as a potential incursion, infectiously impinging on reality's agreed-upon structure. So they were forced to live as though the world itself might be their enemy, for the simple reason that it probably *was*—everything and anything.

Mac was five, for example, the first time a tree spoke to him. It was late summer or early fall, blackberry season; they'd stopped for water and a pee break, somewhere near Come-by-Chance, and he'd wandered away into the brush with his sandbox bucket, looking for a free lunch.

But as he paused to rummage through the bushes, he'd heard a weary, sighing voice from somewhere nearby, which said: "Aaah, little lord, I did not think to see *you* here. You honour an old woman with your presence. Come close, now; come yet closer. Be not afraid. I only wish to do you fealty. . . ."

Of course, he looked around. Of course, he saw nothing. Until—

Three thorn-trees, growing promiscuously together in an acutely angled clump, their lower branches hung with weather-stripped colourless ribbons and knots of rag. And a brass bell tied someplace higher, tinkling with the wind, in one of them—whitethorn? Blackthorn? Mac was still crap at identifying phylae, but he thought the blackthorn, its triple trunk forked like a mutant serpent's tongue, roots twisting ropily to pinion its neighbours'. Seeing how *that* was the one which creaked as it bent to meet him, a sort of membrane nictitating across one of his eyes bringing it abruptly even closer, a dim face forming fuzzily where its branches rubbed against each other, their thorns a million pixel-points of varying greyish darkness.

Wheedling, as it did: "Mmm, do not deny me, precious boy. I know full well whose fruit you be. Your blood is powerful yet, though mine is almost extinct. Let me but touch your hand, only once, and take some faint share in it. . . ."

"Ye will do no such thing, dryad," came his mother's voice, cold and commanding in a way Mac had never heard before, from behind them. "Bark-bound trickster! Dinna think tae lay a single finger upon *my* child and live!"

As Mac froze, Miliner swooped in, grabbed him up and stepped back, throwing her hand out towards the tree—all six fingers hooked upwards, like claws. The blackthorn rippled away from her gesture, stop-motion fast; the "face" contorted, baring jagged, broken-twig teeth. "I meant only to bless him, lady," it insisted.

Miliner snorted at that, head held high—but Mac, clutched to her chest, could hear her heart thump and skid beneath her open sheepskin vest. "Oh, aye? Do ye but try, I'll find where yuir roots meet and burn them to their last length."

The tree exhaled, a cruelly curt gust, almost a huffing laugh. "You think yourself very high and mighty, Druir of Roke, for one so far from home," it told her. "But we both know the truth. You have strayed over-far from your own holdings for any true sense of safety; you are not welcome here, or anywhere else. Run now, and keep on running, little lady."

Miliner turned her back instead, deliberately, and walked, while the tree laughed on.

And later, when they thought he was asleep, Mac listened as she and Army discussed the afternoon's events in careful murmurs—Miliner first, her voice thinned near to breaking—"He has it, Army—the taint. Mine and yuirs too, of that I'm almost certain . . ."

"The sight, you mean? 'Course he does, gal—sight, maybe glamer, maybe even an inclination to hexation, in his time. Wouldn't make much sense otherwise, would it?"

Mac cracked his lids just a bit, enough to see Miliner's red-tinged silhouette look away, eyes downcast. ". . . I'd just hoped he might be . . . spared," she said, finally. "The curse of it . . . my mother's legacy, Euwphaim Glouwer's ill-workings . . ."

Army shrugged. "Ah, now, gal: No point to that. 'Cause—"

(—*that's even less likely. Isn't it?*)

As it turned out, that whole conversation marked the beginning of the end, not that Mac had known it, then. Not that he ever could have been expected to.

Some string of evenings after, with Mac lying on the backseat reading a *Son of Satan* comic book, watching the green shadows of leaves chase each other across the roof's quilted underside while his parents teased each other in front, bantering back and forth, their voices blending so that they half-talked, half-sang along with the car radio . . .

Oh, do ye turn this one up, Army. Reminds me of home.

And then Neil Young's ghost-whine voice, stripped of everything but purest yearning.

Singing: *There is a town in North Ontario. . . .*

The collision, a cube van coming at them head-on, killed Miliner and Army, immediately—a sick joke of a death, which made their wedding vows literal by compacting them into the one flesh they'd eagerly pledged themselves to remain, so long as they both should live. Mac was thrown free, landing creepily well; exploded from the back window as the car up-ended and rolled off the bumper in a breakaway spray of glass to hit the ground softly, fall muffled by a "fortunate" combination of shrubbery, grass, and compost.

He lost time, along with everything else. And when he came to, he was already in hospital, already an orphan. Already alone, as he would be for the rest of his too-long life; unwounded, yet hurt to the very core and aching in every last remaining part of him, both inside and out.

. . . helpless, helpless, heh-ehlp-less . . .

It was after that he began to see things directly, instead of just out the corners of his eyes. Vaguely, he recalled a huge hand cupping his head while he slept, ridiculously long fingers spanning his face, gently; the cold softness of fingertips smoothing some sort of ointment over his eyes— weird, musty, apple-smelling. Preparing the way for him to meet his new family.

It was the sort of baptism Lady Glauce no doubt had expected his mother to have already given him, the ability to see through others' glamer, to plumb the ugly truth beneath the pretty lie: sort foul from fair; leaves from gold; a dark, cold, earthen-walled hole full of mulch from the welcome illusion of light and warmth and safety. To know what *was* from what was not, little as that might ever get him, in the end.

But sometimes, Mac thought, the lie itself could seem better than the truth, in context; easier, anyhow. Easier to tell. Easier to take.

Two days of saline and sympathy later, his clock still turned around by years of nocturnal living, he'd been lying awake, staring at the static-laced television set in the corner of his room, when he'd thought he heard something under his bed, knelt to look—and saw Enzemblance staring back at him for the very first time, grinning, from the shadow-space between blanket-tail and floor.

Which was bad enough, but only compounded when, even as Mac fell ass-backwards and scuttled as far away as the wall would allow, the closet suddenly opened to disgorge Lady Glauce herself: eight feet tall and perfectly proportioned, so beautiful (she being in the Maiden phase of her hag-dom, that night) it hurt to look at her directly, a mantilla of fresh leaves growing straight from her frost-white hair to shade her wintry silver gaze with chlorophyll-green.

Bending down to greet him much like the blackthorn tree had, in sections; folding herself to his level, skirts spreading about her with a scrapey, peeled birch-bark rustle.

And saying, as she did, with a terrible gentleness: *I am thy grandam, Maccabee; this thy aunt, thy mother's sister. Th'art in my charge now—I'll see thee safe and look'd tae for my daughter's sake, as well as the compact between us Druirs and yuir father's kin. For we be of ane blood, thee and I. . . .*

One blood, yes. And blood will ever out.

Enzemblance joined her mother, humping herself up from under the bed in a single boneless strike; shorter, but not by much. Her face, sly and oblique under a fall of dull red hair, seemed far less distinct in light than it had in shadow—blurred even when viewed straight-on, a barely featured lacuna.

I mark ye also, nephew, she whispered. *My ane lad's in sore need of cousins; we shall all be guid friends, since my mother wills it. And by yuir father's measure I've nae doubt but ye'll grow a guidly man too, in time.*

(*What is't ye dream of?*)

Even considering how few he'd received since, it really did remain the only compliment Mac wished he'd never gotten.

That first night, that first meeting, had changed everything. That first hideous surge of fear, immediately giving way to an almost-as-bad rush of revulsion and kinship admixed—a voice in his head, stammering, in quick succession—

You . . .

What are you?

I am not like you. But . . .

. . . no, I am.

(*Oh God. What am I?*)

From hospital to foster care, a scholarship to a high school run by Franciscan Brothers, four years of university (Education minor, Religious Studies major), eight years of seminary studies, and then ordination straight into the priesthood, after that—and in all that time, the only thing he'd ever found powerful enough to make them *leave him alone* was when he'd actually taken his vows, lain face-down on the floor in front of the cross in a freezing-cold cathedral for hours, before eventually rising back up again as a dues-paid member in the Society of Jesus. When he'd sworn himself away to a power he frankly still wasn't certain actually existed, in order to escape powers he knew damn well did.

Yes, the Father, Son, and Holy Ghost had been pretty good to him all this time, all things considered; God's love *was* infinite and unconditional, if the PR material was to be believed. But Mac knew the feeling had never really been reciprocated, and that nothing good could be built on a lie— not even a comforting one.

And now, the further he went from the Church's diffident protection, the more the world around him seemed to pick up his scent again, afresh. To know him for the well-intentioned mistake he was, and turn against him.

Anything and everything. A redcap on the corner, jaw hinged to the ears like a muppet's; an ogre out for a walk, ill-fitting human-suit askew in ways only another variety of Fae would twig to. The dying city trees whispering behind him, spitting cross-species curses whenever he passed them by.

Sr. Blandina, spotting him at a distance only to immediately turn the other way, all righteous—and then Enzemblance, moving widdershins under plaster in the opposite direction, just a faint reddish circling hint. A shark, half-masked by chum.

Yet for all he came from monsters, had lived amongst them, he couldn't ever quite bear to think he might *be* one. Even Saracen and the others didn't seem like *monsters* to him, exactly—not in the same way as a soucouyant, say, or a penanggalan. Not even Lady Glauce, the most alien creature with whom he'd personally sat down to dinner—a true changeling, imprinted on humanity like an adopted swan, yet kin to things so absolutely, immutably *other,* a mongrel like him'd never be able to approach them, except from a very careful distance.

Though she herself might have once been able to repatriate back into Faerie, the True Sidhe would never accept even the least human of her children as part of their twilight world. And *that,* laying the Three Betrayed entirely aside, was what had really driven her to move Dourvale through space and time, to strike her bargain with the Sidderstane clan, to continue on as head of the *brugh,* even while her brood slipped away from her, tempted by the 21st century's distractions.

One more unwelcome truth in a lifetime of such. For no matter how scared Mac remained of his mother's family—enough to run like hell whenever he saw them or thought they'd seen *him*—he felt sorry for them, too. He just couldn't help it.

| chapter three

Funnily enough, it was Blandina who'd told him about the guy he finally turned to—Professeur Therrien-Poirier. Nobody knew what to make of him, exactly; people just called him "Le Prof." Ran a store called Curia on Queen Street, very West, just across from the Mental Hospital. Paid big bucks for odd goods and wasn't particular about knowing where anything came from, originally, as long as there was a market to sell it back to.

So when Mac drifted in there near the end of yet another fine October day, unrolling the topmost page of Mother Eulalia's manuscript onto Le Prof's front counter, he had to admit it seemed a pretty ironic move. The real sort of irony, rather than just the "slightly annoying coincidence"/ Alanis Morissette kind.

Le Prof took one look and almost spit his coffee all over the irreplaceable vellum's heavily illustrated text before swallowing hard instead, and pulling out one of those jeweller's microscoping extendo-monocles.

"*Codex Ordo Sororum Perpetualam*," he read, out loud. Then, switching languages: "'Now 'ere I will tell a great and most excellent mystery, to all you who gain access to this account—the true and secret reckoning of 'ow our Blessed Perpetua's martyr-day vision was discovered and finally fulfilled, granting certain martial virgins victory over Death and the Devil. . . .'"

Mac nodded. "Good translation; hope you're not planning to go through the entire thing right here, though. Gets a little dry near the middle."

Le Prof's head whipped back up, magnified left eye goggling lopsidedly. "You 'ave it all the way to the middle?"

Well, that'll teach you to make jokes.

Le Prof traced a sentence halfway down the page, with one semi-shaky finger. "Hmmm. So they exist, eh? *Les Soeurs sanglantes*, legendary sect of monster-killing nuns. Their name-saint a Roman matron converted by Christian slaves, condemned to the arena for her faith . . ."

". . . where, the night before she's supposed to get raped to death by bears or whatever, she dreams she wrestles the Devil, gives him the holy hammerlock, then marches out to die, all smiling. Later, some big Church bugaboo gets a hold of this hallucination, decides it'll make a good recruiting pitch for getting other impressionable young ladies to go die for Christ in the War against the Other, and—yadda yadda yadda, amen, ad infinitum. The whole supernatural vigilantism *raison d'être*, tied up in a big *Deus lo volt* package."

"Spoken like a true ex-Catholic."

Mac shrugged. "Look, I've just heard it before, a *lot*. So anyhow, you interested?"

"*Beaucoup. Absolument.* And the rest?"

"Somewhere safe."

"*Très bien.* Nevertheless, considering how angry they must be with you, *Père—Frère?*"

"Just 'mister' does me fine these days, thanks."

"—I might expect you to be more careful who you show this to."

"Want to tell on me? I can give you the extension number. But seriously, Prof—we both know their charter has strict provisions against killing real people. Which means the only one in serious danger here is . . . me."

Le Prof squinted at him. "So that's true too, *hé*? What we hear about *la famille Roke*, I mean. *Et vous, une demi-fée au sein de l'Église*, how could you 'ave expected to get away with it?"

Mac smiled, tightly. "Because I did?" he suggested, at last, which Le Prof seemed to find hilarious.

"Perhaps we should step in the back," he invited, when he'd managed to stop laughing. "Afternoons are always slow—just turn the sign, *s'il vous plaît*. I make coffee."

The caffeine in question was exactly as paralyzingly strong as Mac had expected. He took light sips to minimize the damage and let Le Prof ramble on about the difficulty of getting "real" French Roast anywhere outside of Quebec (cry me a river), if haematite really hurt Fae as much as cold iron (yes, but not quarter-Fae, which explained why Mac would even answer such a potentially damaging, leading question), whether or not the Druirs still had access to their famous Stane (far as Mac knew, though it wasn't like any of them ever toted it around outside the *brugh*).

The talk eventually devolved into a longish quiz session about exactly which mouldy Fae goldies Mac could personally replicate—walking through walls? (Thankfully not.) Paying for things with leaves? (He wished.) Seeing dead people, etcetera? (Unfortunately.)

"And what about dream-projection, *l'hypnotisme, comme un mirage*—the glamour?"

"Glamer," Mac corrected. "With an 'ER.'"

"*Quelle est la différence?*"

"Not much, I guess; it's a Scottish thing. But yeah, okay, I've got some of that, too."

"Enough to walk away with something, but convince the people you took it from they still 'ad it? For a little while, at least?"

"Depends. What was it you had in mind?"

"A piece of luggage, like a . . . 'atbox?" Adding, helpfully: "*Mais pas pour un chapeau, vous comprenez.*"

Mac looked at him for a minute. "You sure you couldn't just take the manuscript?"

"We both know I cannot pay you its true worth—no one keeps that sort of cash around, even if *les Soeurs* weren't looking for it. And this, *c'est très facile pour vous*, all things considered. . . ."

(*Yeah, right.*)

Though Mac tried his best to keep the sigh he felt building subvocal, Le Prof was maybe a bit more canny than he came off.

His voice dipped, assuring Mac: "One trip, in and out. Four

businessmen at the airport, waiting to pick up the luggage they 'ad to check—slip a bag the same size down beside it, then walk away."

"And they don't notice they've got it wrong?"

"Not 'til you're out of range. Not 'til it's too late."

Saracen would have known if this old bastard was lying. Then again, Saracen would probably have *assumed* the guy was lying right from the start and acted accordingly.

"Luggage," Mac repeated, finally.

Le Prof sketched something roughly square, maybe nine by twelve by nine inches deep. "This big, about," he said, unhelpfully.

"What's inside?"

"They call it the Cornerstone, foundation of their Order."

"Who does?"

"The suits, the luggage-waiters. They're Crusaders, Poor Knights of the Temple of Solomon—Templars."

The sure way you can always tell when somebody's fallen off their rocker rather than just stood up temporarily, Mac remembered the Jesuit whose influence had steered him towards that Order (Fr. Henry Gowther, a fellow Maritimer with a brogue so thick his sermons occasionally lapsed into incomprehensibility) telling him, *is when they start talkin' about the Templars. It's like the universal sign for oh my Lord, we're one slip of the tongue away from macramé and shock treatments.*

It did hurt to think about Fr. Gowther, even now, and however slightly—a dull ache, rather than a sharp sting. For *we never feel so uncomfortable as in the presence of those we've sinned against.*

"Templars, like armour-wearing Templars?" he asked Le Prof. "Like monks with swords?"

"Not in public, I don't think. *Mais, peu importe.* You obviously 'ave no problem pissing off martially trained religious people . . ."

"There's a big difference between a bunch of nuns sworn to protect humanity and a heretic order trained to exterminate infidels on sight. Or did you just mean those people in Scotland who like to dress up in white sheets with red crosses for Solstice?"

Le Prof gave him a long look. ". . . *Le second, bien sûr,*" he replied.

"Uh huh. So what's in the box?"

"A mummified severed 'ead."

"John the Baptist?"

"*Non, câlisse! C'est le dernier grand-maître du temple,* Jacques de Molay."

"And that's not creepy at all. *Or* supernatural."

"Did I mention it's covered in gold and jewels?"

Mac took a second. "No," he said, at last. "That part you skipped."

Mac knew the story; everybody did. The Church had its own fairy tales—and the Templars, with their meteoric rise and hubristic fall, made for one of the best.

Ever since Christianity's infancy, the desert had been seen as a metaphorical furnace in which to test one's faith, a Hell-hob to harrow and bake upon without ever actually having to breach the thin skin between Wide and Narrow worlds. Maybe because Jesus came from Judea, historical breeding ground of prophets and martyrs—but from John the Baptist on, it became a meeting place for everybody bent on taking their principles to extremes unpalatable in more civilized climes.

Desert on desert threaded with veins of fertility, a rich soil bordered by rivers or seas, fed with blood and bones—Two Veins, the Country of Roots, the Country of Fighting. Mesopotamia and all its environs: Persia, Macedonia, Palestine, Syria, Cyprus, Jerusalem itself. The Holy, Promised Land.

You might wonder, as Mac often did, why a truly good God would deed already-occupied land out from under the unwitting feet of its occupiers. But at the end of the day, Jerusalem—like everything else—was more than certainly His to give away.

Or so the nine knights led by Hughes de Payens must have believed in 1118, when they decided the chivalry of Europe had been corrupted by too much luxury. Godfroi de Bouillon had freed the Holy City from its Moslem yoke, but the kingdoms of Outremer remained fragile, and the fault for that must obviously lie with themselves: their weak, sinning worldliness, so unworthy of God's grace it turned the red cross at their shoulders to the mark on a leper's cloak, slippery with secular grossness.

Under the guidance of St. Bernard of Clairvaux and the authority of Pope Innocent III, the Templars were granted complete independence from all authorities. They took vows of chastity, poverty, and obedience, swearing never to yield one foot of ground to their Saracen enemies and never to retreat unless facing odds of more than three to one. Soon, Saladin himself ordered his armies to shout a new battle cry whenever these monks with swords raised their black-and-white banner: *Templars, come to death!*

The Order survived, however, and flourished. They built a chain of fortresses, stretching from Cyprus to Castile, from which to defend any Christian who required their services. They grew chary with their lives. They grew rich, despite their vows. And as their power waxed in Europe, it waned in the Holy Land that birthed them, their impregnable fortresses falling, one by one—until, when Acre was taken in 1291, the Templars achieved an almost Orwellian purity: the only purpose of their power, now, was power.

In 1306, King Philippe le Bel of France took refuge from mobs of unhappy citizenry in the Templars' Paris fortress. The Order's current Grand Master, Jacques de Molay, might have thought himself munificent for showing Philippe the treasure so many had entrusted to the Templars' safekeeping. But his trust was betrayed a year later, on Friday the 13th of October, when nine hundred Templar knights were arrested in France alone, and turned over to the Avignon wing of the Holy Inquisition.

Under torture, the Templars confessed to spitting on the cross and denying God, to practising unnatural vices, to worshipping either a black cat which spoke in a woman's sweet voice, a snake, or a demon named Baphomet, as well as roasting babies to feed any or all of these idols. Their power was broken, their Order disbanded, their wealth confiscated. Fifty-four of them, all of whom later recanted their confessions, were burnt at the stake as heretics.

In 1311, Philippe and his lapdog anti-Pope convened a council of one hundred and fourteen bishops at Vienne, where he intended that the Templars be utterly condemned. But when they asked, *Who will dare to defend these men?* they were startled by the sudden appearance of nine knights in full regalia—Templars who had somehow escaped arrest, presenting themselves in the knowledge, they said, that God would protect the innocent.

These men were, no doubt, amongst the mass of Templars publicly exhibited on a platform in Paris before being condemned to perpetual imprisonment in chains. Jacques de Molay—so heartened by their defiant display that he too recanted his false confession—was burned alive. With his last breath, the nine knights heard their Grand Master curse his murderers forever.

Examining all the evidence, it seemed unlikely that the Templars really *were* worshipping the Devil when their persecution began. Yet from Mac's point of view, by the time of de Molay's death, a few might well have decided it was worth burning in hell to avoid burning on earth.

In the Connaught Trust's stacks, Mac had read texts that claimed those same nine knights later bribed their way free from the anti-Pope's dungeons—blind and maimed and penniless, locked in a double darkness of enduring hate and vengeful ambition. Similarly, there were rumours that the body of Jacques de Molay, somehow failing to burn *entirely* to ash, might also have not been buried completely intact, afterwards; testimony gathered over the subsequent centuries tracked his head's appearance as centrepiece at Sabbats and séances, from Montmartre to Mogadishu.

As Saracen would've been quick to point out, nine *was* a magic number—a powerful charm. And Mac knew better than almost anybody how it might piss off better men than him to have the Stairway to Heaven rolled back up in front of their faces.

God's not the Church, boy, Fr. Gowther once told Mac, *no more'n the Church is God. Take away God, the Church is nothin'; take away the Church, and God . . . He's the exact damn same. Keep that always in the back of your mind, you should be all right.*

Within a year of Friday the 13th, one way or the other, both the King who had authorized the Templars' doom and the "Pope" who had let him do it were dead. In places like England, the Templars disappeared into other orders, living out their lives, untouched; in Germany and Malta, they waged open war against their oppressors, refusing outright to accept Avignon's verdict. They survived and prospered, built and defended more castles, made and hid more money. And when they finally went underground forever, it was on *their* terms . . . taking the original Nine with them, no doubt.

Them, and their mummified human head, too.

Later, Mac lay in his bed back at Saul of Tarsus with eyes wide open, checking the ceiling for cracks and listening to the former priest in the next room rave against God . . . some shambling cliché of a drunken Irishman named Frye, younger than Mac, his blowtorch eyes wrung red by a steady diet of betrayal-flavoured booze. Word around the breakfast table was he'd fucked up pretty good fighting demons, only to be left in the lurch—yesterday's tabloid headline, a pariah barely solvent enough to keep drunk. If Mac had still been in the prayer business himself, he might have felt like sending up thanks that *he'd* never had some sufferer's immortal soul placed in his hands, only to fumble the world's most precious ball on the ten-yard line. . . .

(Not unless you counted what he'd done to Fr. Gowther, that was. Who'd still had his soul, last Mac had checked, if not much else.)

Le dernier grand-maître. Covered in gold and jewels.

He'd told Le Prof he was in, of course. Why not? Down low as he was, things probably couldn't get all *that* much worse, not really. Not in some way he couldn't eventually handle if he put his whole divided self to it . . .

Mac hoped. Knowing full well, in his heart of hearts, just what that sort of hope—that *faith*—was usually worth.

| chapter four

By 1984, when Mac turned twelve, he was already on his fifth foster family—Catholics, yet again (this *was* Nova Scotia), but surprisingly observant ones. His fake siblings dragged him along to a Bible Study group in the local church's basement every Wednesday, using much the same set-up as Saturday night bingo, and tried to convert him from what they assumed was his deadbeat hippie parents' atheist influence by quizzing him on this or that permutation of Old or New Testament lore, 'til he eventually shocked the congregation by winning first prize in a Scripture-quoting competition.

This "victory" hadn't actually required much to achieve on his part, beyond three days of heavy reading followed by a joyless spasm of rote memorization—but it got them off his back, and for that Mac would always be eternally grateful, though to whom he wasn't exactly sure.

Enzemblance was never far away, throughout these years; she smiled at him through mirrors, watched him through the walls. Dragged him suddenly sideways through cracks to attend various familial routs, only letting him re-emerge hours or days later, covered in mud. That alone kept him bouncing from home to home in the beginning, before he knew enough to lie about it: *I was under the bed*, he soon learned, was an excuse which—however accurate—never quite seemed to cut the mustard.

His therapists thought it was post-traumatic stress disorder, which it sort of was. But none of this "lost time" was ever gone completely. If he strained hard enough he had dim visions of dancing wild, partnerless reels in massive caverns lit by glowing lichen; huge hurling battles fought with suborned humans used as cannon fodder on either side; feasts that were sublime when seen through one eye, foul and dreadful when seen through the other.

Lady Glauce even took him back through time in a smoky, mirrored way; showed him Callistor and Grisell, the Three Betrayed burning, Juleyan Roke's body swinging in the wind while his shadow slid away beneath, like dirty black water. *Yuir heritage, grandson.* These things stayed with him always, colouring his dayside interactions like a horrid filter, a supernatural depth perception.

Mac remembered hearing in Science class how every cell in the body replaced itself if you only waited long enough, following a strict seven-year cycle—and seven was a magic number too, just as much as nine. A fairy number.

This much he knew, however: it didn't matter how many times *his* cells regrew, the harvest reaped would always be the same. A hybrid legacy, lost between worlds, like having superpowers, only far less sexy. And far less convenient.

But that same year was also when he met Fr. Gowther—loitering in full cassock and back-tipped Homburg out back of the church, smoking a surreptitious cig and going over the scribbled notes for his homily before revving himself up for Sunday night Mass.

(*Cops drink, son, in the main; priests smoke. Gets you to Heaven just a tad quicker—and better yet, it's cheap.*)

Mac stood, watching him for a moment, getting up his nerve. Then: "Mind if I ask you something, Father?"

Fr. Gowther didn't look up. "Be surprised if you didn't, son, considering how long you've been waiting. Is it a Bible question?"

"Sort of, yeah."

"Fire away."

Mac crossed his arms. "Well—you know that part, right after Moses gets the Ten Commandments? And there's this whole chunk of it just goes on and on about all the different kinds of nakedness you can't uncover—"

"*Leviticus*, 1-27. 'The nakedness of thy sister, even her nakedness thou shalt not uncover for hers is thine own nakedness'; '*I am* the Lord.' Just in case you forgot who you were talking to there, for a minute."

"Yeah. So what's all that about?"

"People ask; believe me, they ask. You need to be specific. Which isn't to say there aren't inconsistencies . . ."

"Like the part where 'a man may not lie with another man as with a woman, because that is abomination,' but 'a woman may not lie with an animal, because that is *confusion*?' Must really suck, trying to explain *that* particular distinction to a bunch of Catechism cram-class eight-year-olds."

And now Fr. Gowther *did* look at him—straight on, through kind but tired eyes, the colour of well-faded denim. "What's your name again, son?" he wanted to know.

"Maccabee Roke."

"Well, and why am I not surprised." Fr. Gowther pinched the end of his cigarette out between two callused fingertips, a straight-up Steve McQueen move, and stowed it carefully away inside his inner coat pocket. "All right, then, come on in—there's still some time yet 'til the big show. Let's discuss this a bit further."

Inside, the church had its usual smell: stale incense, wood lacquer, a faint tang of old B.O. Mac had been in and out half a thousand times by now, and it still made him nervous; he'd already discovered (much to his joy) that the otherwise undistinguished, ugly, 1970s-poured-concrete cocoon really did seem to project enough spiritual force to keep the rest of his relatives securely off-campus, but kept half-consciously bracing himself for the day somebody decided *Mac* wasn't fit for entry any more, either. He watched Fr. Gowther negotiate the Stations of the Cross with surprising grace, born of either familiarity or a genuine respect for his job, unlikely as *that* might seem.

Saying, as he checked the Formica-tiled floor for spent mousetraps and puddles—"The Levitican verses . . . they're pure practicality for the most part, aside from the truly out-of-date ones like suffering not a witch to live, and all. First off, let me ask you this: do you *want* to lie with another man?"

"Not hugely."

"Think any of the gals you know want to lie with animals? And no, young Hugo Chance doesn't count." As Mac smiled: "Ah, now you're gettin' it. Then it doesn't much matter, does it? Except for purposes of argument, and purely for the sake *of* arguing."

He fixed Mac with a hard stare, at that last part, then grinned when he saw Mac nod, ever-so-slightly.

"Is this what you do all day, Father?" Mac asked him. "Read the Bible, answer stupid questions?"

"Usually, though they're not always *as* stupid. Why?"

"And . . . you get to stay in here."

"Well, sometimes, I do get invited to dinner at parishioners' houses, which can be a bit dicey if you don't keep a close watch on how the wine in your glass might be affectin' your tongue."

"But then you come back, after."

"Oh yes, I have to. I sleep here."

"In the Rectory?" Fr. Gowther nodded. "That's part of the Church too, then. Right?"

"Technically, yes."

"In fact, pretty much everywhere you *go* is part of the Church. Technically."

"I'm not quite sure what you're after with this, son."

"Mac. I was just thinking . . . I mean, *I* could do all that."

"Probably; anybody could, and that's the sad fact. But could you *care* about what you were doin'? Or more importantly—care about the people you were doin' it *for*?"

Mac took a breath. ". . . I think so, probably," he said, at last. "Eventually."

"Then you might have a vocation, is what this is about."

"Yes."

"Well, that does bear further examination. Sit down, son—Mac. Let's talk it out."

Fifteen years of preparation on, meanwhile—finally hovering on the brink of ordination, with a Connaught Trust internship in his metaphorical back pocket—he found himself back at Fr. Gowther's side, still trying to fake it 'til he made it. Not knowing why he should care if the old man actually believed in his . . . *belief* or not, aside from the fact that, if the same man who'd once championed his plans to profess suddenly withdrew his recommendation, the likelihood of Mac ending up anywhere but some crap-hole war-zone posting—or back out on the street, where any shadow held the possibility of Enzemblance's grip suddenly tightening on his arm and yanking—would shoot through the roof.

"I can't write that letter, son, and that's the plain truth."

"It's a formality, Henry. Monsignor Chu's already given me the stamp, just not on paper."

"Sounds like you don't need me anyhow, then." Fr. Gowther busied himself with milking his tea, eyes kept scruplously elsewhere. "Good for you on all your hard work, Maccabee."

But Mac refused to look away, arms automatically crossing, well aware how pugnacious it probably made him look. "You don't think I should *get* this job, do you?" he demanded.

Fr. Gowther sighed. "Not for me to say. It's God you're swearin' yourself over to—my opinion doesn't mean much, long as He lets you. Be honest, though, son . . . you don't even know for certain He actually will, your ownself."

A stopped breath hung between them: the phouka in the room, visible at last. Mac's heritage, hitherto kept carefully unmentionable, ability and disability, all in one.

"Is that what you believe," Mac asked, finally, "after all this time? That I have no soul?"

"Now, how can *I* possibly know? How can—"

(—*either of us?*)

"I can't change what I am, Henry."

"Which, *some* might say, makes a plenty good enough argument for stayin' as far away from the Trust and them sisters who keep it as you possibly can," Fr. Gowther shot back; Mac snorted.

"So you *do* care," he said, sarcastically.

At this, Fr. Gowther flushed bright red. "And why would I bother to say anything at all, if I *didn't*?"

Around Mac, the room lurched and dimmed, and he spent the next minute giving some random point on the wall minute attention, unable to trust himself with any other sort of response. Because what he *felt* was the urge to curse, to overlook, to *blast* Fr. Gowther (his one human friend, his father-of-choice) to a God-damned pillar of salt, pricking at the roots of his optic nerves like a static-charged, double paper cut.

"Listen," Fr. Gowther began again, voice softening. "It's a sad fact to admit, but you're just *not* priest material, Maccabee. Sure, you know your Bible—better'n me, probably. You even believe in God. But you don't love Him; you fear Him. Only part of bein' a priest you'd like is tellin' other people what t'do—and believe me, that particular joy gets old a lot faster than you'd think it would."

Like the whole world was shrinking and thinning, becoming that same membrane which flicked itself across his sight. Mac's head swum with the rageful unfairness of it all: so much time *wasted*. And for nothing.

"As long as I'm in the Church, Henry—*any* church—I'm safe," Mac told his uncomfortable shoes, still shiny from this morning's 4:00 A.M. polish. "Does that sound like God doesn't want me here?"

"Mac, God wants every—"

"That's *not what you just said*, and you know it."

And—oh Lord, he had to force himself to think clearly, remembering: had *this* been when he felt the glamer begin to boil out of him? The same moment he heard himself think "words" formed from ice, cold enough to cut and freeze, simultaneously—

LOOK at me. Do NOT look away.

—with no shame at all, no breath of regret, only the vicious sodium-bulb flare of victory as he watched Fr. Gowther *do* it.

"You're gonna write me the letter," Mac heard himself tell him, deliberately. "You won't contest my appointment, and then . . . well, after that, I guess we'll just have to see."

Because: *My family scares the fuck out of me, and I'm one of them. So what do you think they do to real people? People like you? Eat them, from the inside out. Make them into jewellery and wear them. Drag them down into their home, play with them awhile, and when they're bored, they just leave them there, alone in the dark, forever. Who's gonna help me with that, exactly?*

Fr. Gowther writhed, a hook-caught worm. Yet Mac still knew him well enough to know exactly what his comeback would have been, had he heard said any of the above out loud—

With God, Maccabee, all things are possible. They must *be. You have to believe that.*

Well . . . yeah. And no.

You *have to,* Mac thought. *But me?*

"Mac, son . . ." Fr. Gowther managed, at last. ". . . for God's own sake, don't *do* this. Not to—"

"*You?*"

". . . yourself . . ."

Then it was over.

Next thing Mac could remember, he was lying face-down on the cathedral stones, swearing over and over: *Oh God, if you only accept my profession here, I will never do that again, ever. Not to anyone.*

Which he hadn't, since—not yet, anyhow. Yet what he knew now, with the Church securely reframed in his rear-view, was that it'd been the *human* in him that'd driven him to destroy his best friend in order to get something he'd damn well known even then, on some level, he'd eventually throw away.

That was the end between them, Fr. Gowther and he. Oh, Mac'd tried to cover his tracks, to erase the memory of what he'd done, but it hadn't helped; every time Fr. Gowther saw Mac after that, he'd *known* that something must have happened (just not what). That awful feeling of violation, with the poor, good old priest never knowing for sure whether he'd been the rapist or the rape-ee . . . a seed of doubt, shoved down deep inside to bloom slowly, stretching the lobes of his faith until they tore themselves apart.

Oh, but Mac hadn't actually *killed* him, not directly.

He hadn't had to.

Ten years after his ill-fated ordination ceremony, Mac found himself playing secretary during a "debriefing" in one of the Connaught's infamous Hold Rooms, watching Sr. Blandina beat the (literally) holy crap out of a strix with a Bible roughly the size of her own torso. Smell of burnt flesh and feathers, black blood everywhere, the strix screaming guttural Greek curses—

And Blandina, right there in the middle of it all, implacably fearless, flushed with a pride that seemed virtually indistinguishable from rage at the prospect of doing God's good work. Blandina, passing fatal judgment on this bloodsucking owl-lady like it wasn't just her job, but her actual *pleasure.* Catching his eye on the rebound, pausing for another swing, *The Shield's* Vic fucking Mackey with his phone book.

She had her own issues with monsters, obviously. Nobody joined the

O.S.P. because they were huge *Buffy the Vampire Slayer* fans, but because they'd known (someone) who'd encountered (something)—with the emphasis always clearly on "thing" and the *de*-emphasis on whoever that particular someone might have been. Whoever that'd been for Blandina, meanwhile, they'd already been avenged a hundred-fold since her profession—her list of righteous kills was truly legendary, as Mac should know, since a good part of his duties at the Connaught involved updating Monsignor Chu's copy of the *Bestiary ad Noctem* with fresh examples of how she'd discovered the best way to kill whatever they pitted her against: a loogaroo, adze, vrykolakos—or an ogre or goblin. A glaistig or knocker, undine or rusalka, a wili, a water-leaper, troll or huldre-maiden, brown boggart, pixie or boggledy-bo . . .

They were none of them harmless, these pathetically stranded slop-overs, who'd either failed to make the last boat for Tír-na-nÓg or decided, for reasons all their own—much like Lady Glauce—to stick around and give it the old college try, even while iron swarmed across the world around them. Hell, Mac had raised his hand, too, at a few of those hunt-planning meetings; who really wanted a nucklavee in Lake Ontario, aside from the nucklavee itself? But they were still his blood, his distant relatives, and the further they crept to the top of Blandina's hit-list, the more comfortably he could see his own name one day being written there, once she figured it all out. As he knew, without question, that she would.

"But what if they're not actually doing anything . . . monstrous, these creatures?" He asked her, later, over a late-night snack at the local greasy spoon. "What then, Sister?"

To which she responded by looking at him with a kind of blank-pure lack of understanding that would have been oddly touching if it hadn't been so damn scary.

And said—"It's not what they *do* or don't do. It's what they *are*. You should know that, Father. . . ."

Mac went home that night to the Saint Mike's Rectory, alone, as ever. He sat chain-smoking in his room, thinking about how badly he wanted to call Fr. Gowther and tell him something, anything. He didn't even know what. Except that Fr. Gowther probably wouldn't have remembered who Mac *was*, at that point, even if he hadn't already been dead for a year and a half and buried back home in Nova Scotia, on the wrong side of the cemetery.

Mac could still see things other people couldn't; the Church hadn't done shit about *that*, though it did keep most of them at bay. What he hadn't initially known, however, was that he could even see things his own family couldn't—and those things, the Church had no visible effect on at all. They breezed in and out like the seal of God's protection was made of tissue paper, maybe because they didn't recognize it, or maybe because it didn't recognize *them*. Either way, Mac remained the one caught seeing, *having* to see. And if he didn't want to anymore, there was only one way out: through the front fucking door.

Blandina had been a reason to stay too, once. But all the hot-eyed looks in the world couldn't change the fact that, one day, she'd realize there was a specific reason he kept on suggesting that maybe monsters might just be people with something a little bit extra, if you only gave them the chance to prove it. And that'd be when he'd have to make a separate peace with the *Ordo* or die like a dog. Or live on in a cage, which would be far, far worse—

Which returned him, rather neatly, to the conundrum at hand: how to do Le Prof's job, yet emerge with skin intact, given who Mac might find himself dealing with. How to make sure he got paid, and also that the blame (if any) fell directly on the person who'd set this particular snatch-and-grab in motion, rather than the person whose hands did the actual snatching and grabbing.

Blandina at his mental ear, her hot breath intimate as ever: *Did you think we didn't know what you were?* Chased by Saracen, a half-second later, murmuring just as low, burred words apple-scented: *Yuir no' like them, coz; ye never will be. Yet ye may come by the* brugh *when it suits ye, by high way or low—if ye've no' forgot how tae walk either road yet, in all yuir human wanderings. . . .*

That would take a toll, he knew—a tithe, rather. As everything did. And would it be worth it, in the end?

Well.

How could it not be?

| chapter five

Five hours later saw Mac ducking and dodging his way through the eddying airport crowds with the Templars already at his heels.

They'd been easy enough to spot, all hanging around by the baggage carousel like that—a sleek group of dudes in suits, with discreet little red cross-pins at their lapels and wicked little ceramic machetes nesting in scabbards sewn along the spines of their coats. Nothing that'd set a metal detector off, not to mention nothing someone who wasn't already used to hanging with covertly armed nuns would probably pick up on, but it made Mac nervous, nonetheless . . . so much so he'd turned his glamer on early and moved towards them only in sketchy, sidelong increments, like an invisible crab.

What got him particularly wary was the man the Templars had apparently come to meet—the one Le Prof called Cordellion Federoi. In many ways, he seemed the only true Templar in the bunch: career soldier's bearing, neatly bearded, a high-end pair of wrap-around sunglasses perfectly adjusted to hide the upside-down crosses branded over his seared-blind eyes.

'E is one of the Kissed, the inner circle, Le Prof told him. *That's what they call them.*

One of the original Nine, you mean? Mac asked.

To which Le Prof frowned, disappointed by Mac's credulity, and replied—*Of course not. Don't be fooled by the accoutrements; no matter what they may 'ave done to themselves, they're just* people, *M'sieu Roke.*

The implication being: odd people, yes. Strange people. Living up to a fearsome and dramatic legend, wielding swords, kissing the Devil's ass (or maybe just each others'). But . . .

(*But.*)

. . . while Mac could see how thinking that might keep the old guy feeling safe at night, he was content to go with his own instincts, and those said—not so much. Especially since every time Mac moved closer, he saw those obviously dead eyes flick his way, automatic as a REM-sleep quiver, like Cordellion was cruising him telepathically.

He can SEE me, Mac thought. *Or knows he should be able to. And can't.*

The plan, as such, was simplicity itself: wait 'til the "hatbox" slid down the chute, snatch and grab, then take off running. Aside from Cordellion, the Templars didn't read as having any sort of real magical signature, so even if they *did* somehow twig to what was going on, there was only so far they could really follow him—into the nearest guys' john, into the handicapped stall, but no farther. Not onto the ley line only Mac could see blazing underfoot; certainly not into the Dourvale *brugh* via the legendary "low road," once he'd made that particular connection—if he *could* make it before one of them ran him straight through the spine. It'd been a while for him, after all—

Yet blood will out, Mac told himself, grimly. And told the guy standing next to him, without preamble: "Give me your cell phone."

"Say hella-*what*?" Dudester replied, goggling.

No time for subtlety. "*Give*," Mac repeated, making with the full Fae power-stare, and the guy did, without further question. Like he'd been tapped good and hard between the eyes with a velvet-wrapped ball-peen hammer.

Mac dialled one number, spoke briefly, then sent two equally brief, time-sensitive text messages to two other—completely different—numbers. And leaned back against the wall to wait.

The page summoning Cordellion to the Information Desk—by name, no less, which produced exactly the kind of reaction Mac had hoped for—came through just as human Templars One and Two swung the "hatbox" reverently up, carrying it by its handles as they trailed dutifully after their leader. Mac passed neatly *between them* like a black wind, tearing the "hatbox" free and throwing a subsidiary glamer over it as well, though the extra strain of maintaining two separate illusions was already enough to make him stagger, vertiginously. He blundered noisily over towards the little stick-man figure sign, bumping into an older lady and a man in a wheelchair on the way, both of whom swore loudly.

Behind him, he felt Cordellion's empty gaze *switch on*, sweeping sharply after him even as the other Templars cried out to each other in confusion, swapping semi-Mediaeval French insults: *Guiche, du Metz, où est la tête du grand-maître? Allez! Trouvez-la! I know not—'tis pas ma faute! O, but you lie—ta bouche dans le cul du diable, imbécile, et que celle de ta mère y soit avant la tienne!*

Under that, however, came Cordellion's voice, low and dark with a blood-deep thrum to it, which reached straight inside Mac's defences.

Saying, as though in Mac's own ear—"Ah, there you are, thief. *Je vous vois clairement, et je sais où vous vous dirigez. . . .*"

Not yet, you don't, Mac thought, grimly. And broke through the washroom doors with the "hatbox" hugged to his chest and both elbows up, like a linebacker, knocking some poor bastard who'd only wanted to dry his hands before catching a flight to wherever right on his ass. No time for sympathy—Mac vaulted over the man's prone body, skidded past the first three stalls, and barricaded himself inside the last, double-wide one.

He shifted the "hatbox" under one arm and hammered on the wall with the other, feeling like an idiot as he yelled: "Grandmere, hear me! Your daughter Miliner's son craves to do you homage, with apologies for my long absence . . . I come to you by the low road, begging entry!"

Behind him, the doors banged open and the fallen man groaned, as if kicked. Mac felt the plaster warm under his fingers, praying it wasn't his imagination; was that a subtle pinkening hovering beneath the once-white expanse of paint? A flash of flat cheekbone, sly silvery eye, eerily lit-from-within half-quirk of teeth?

(*What is't ye dream of, nephew?*)

You, aunt. For this one time, and only: *You*.

Ah well, then. I am answered.

Time slowed, but only in the ordered world—that roundhouse one Templar gave the stall door, half-ripping it off its hinges, became nothing more than a slap that felt like a kiss, molasses-soft. Mac saw the wall peel back in front of him like a lip, fungal, stop-motion; his hand immediately sank to the wrist, time-space ripples scurrying out sidelong. At which point he felt another hand, slim and nail-less, knit most of its fingers with his, and knew exactly who it must belong to—so he braced himself as it pulled hard, teeth gritted, giving himself over entirely to what was no longer refutable.

Was that another hand, grabbing for his shoulder? Fingers grasping painfully hard and—slipping?

(*never mind*)

The wall lapped over him, re-sealing as it went, and Mac found himself thrust headfirst out through a colon-close tunnel into an equally sticky-floored hall: Lady Glauce's Receiving Room, located at the Dourvale *brugh*'s unnaturally still heart. A vaulted cavern of a place whose cold dirt walls smelled of rot and apples.

"Give ye good-even, coz," Saracen's voice came, predictably, from somewhere in the darkness at his elbow. "I see ye ha' finally ta'en up yuir invitation."

Mac reeled, spat in his non-hatbox-holding hand, and wiped it on his coat, hoping the place was so dim no one would notice. "Yup," he managed, at last.

The *brugh* looked about the same as the last time Mac'd seen it: tapestries of dead leaves hung slack as skins in every direction, a thousand variegated shades of decay sewn each to each with spiderweb, then stuck fast to the roof with luminous mould. Half the furniture was stolen, while the other half seemed cobbled together from anything handy— shells and muck, living tubers, long-scraped bones.

At the table's head sat Lady Glauce herself, gleaming in the hall's eternal dusk, a too-thin salt-soap parody of her own spectral beauty— literally statuesque, so huge she was forced to stoop even in her own home, yet so far gone into the opposite end of her hag-cycle that even her leafy crown seemed withered. On one side, her husband Enzembler with his vacant stare, ill-set head nodding slightly; on the other, their remaining children (and some of *their* children, to boot). Minion, a full-fledged ogre, whose bottom eye-teeth curled up like tusks. Ganconer Sidderstane, leaned back in his chair at his half-niece Ygerna's slimy elbow, raw wooden eyes weeping tears of pus in their barely healed sockets.

Saracen was already moving to take his rightful place at his grandmother's side, naturally enough . . . and here came Enzemblance herself, flowing 'cross the wall like shadow to meet him, while some cute little human thrall-girl scuttled to keep herself safely out of both their paths.

Taking full advantage of her creepily long reach, however, Enzemblance managed to chuck the thrall roughly under the chin before she sat, telling her: "Do ye play for us, Galit, now we be all met taegether—something lively. My nephew's yet tae hear ye, and I'd no' deprive him of that sweet grace."

"I will, milady," the girl agreed, voice dull, eyes downcast—and now that he came to think about it, Mac *could* vaguely recall somebody by that name having gone missing last year, up 'round Overdeere way. Ganconer couldn't quite keep himself from twitching at the sound, which was interesting, though not enough so to distract.

Mac's mother would have had a chair with her name on it here as well, once upon a time—somewhere between Minion and Enzemblance, probably, with Army Roke snugged in right alongside her; husband and father of her son, though descended directly from the alliance of Callistor Roke and Miliner's own firstborn sister, Grisell. And what the hell *did* that make Mac, anyhow? Could three halves really make a whole?

It only takes one drop of red blood to make you human, Maccabee, he heard Fr. Gowther's voice whisper. Which would've been more reassuring if Mac hadn't already known his blood showed up blue under most lights.

So. "Nice," was all he said to Enzemblance, buying Galit-the-thrall enough time to thread a crude fiddle with one long lock of her own hair—still thick, once dark, now shot and streaked with grey. "That's old school, seriously. Sure beats the hell out of an iPod, doesn't it?"

Enzemblance gave a wolfish grin at this, and raised a slanted brow to Saracen; their too-alike smiles met and matched, in nasty concert.

"Ah, Maccabee," she said, "I've missed yuir pleasantries, these many years gone by. Yet I have my own leman now, d'ye note it?"

"Couldn't not, really." To Saracen: "And how 'bout you, 'coz'? You bring a date?"

Saracen shook his head. "I'd no time, more's the pity. Still, I see *you* brought something—a tithe for grandmere, as is only right and proper."

"Yeah, sure, I . . . what?"

Lost, Mac followed Saracen's nod and saw—*something*, lying in what he assumed was the corner. A pair of boots caught in a tangle of cloth, with a soft pink hand just emerging—cries and burbling, the rounded head and peering eyes of all newborn mammals. What no doubt used to be a big, hard-muscled hunk of Templar, before his sudden passage through the *brugh*'s ley-line-unlocked wall . . . a journey all but bound to mess with anyone who wasn't at least some degree of Fae.

Oh, crap.

And now Lady Glauce was rising, interest caught; Enzembler looked vaguely 'round at the motion, but quieted again once he felt her reassuring hand on his. She rustled forward, towering over Mac where he stood, frozen, with Enzemblance and Saracen both smirking at his obvious discomfort. While Galit-the-thrall's sweet voice soon began to climb upwards, disappearing into the fog and filthy air above:

There were two sisters walking alone,
Hey the gay and the grinding,
Two little sisters walking alone
By the bonny bows of London—

"Is't true, Maccabee?" Lady Glauce asked him, her own voice a juiceless rasp. "For I know thy mother surely taught thee a'right—thou wouldst no' think tae cheat me of my due, no' in my ane hall."

"No, grandmere."

"Then this changeling be mine, I wist, tae do wi' as I wish."

Mac bit his lip. "Uh . . . no, grandmere. Not exactly."

At this, the whole hall seemed to share one caught breath, and Mac wondered a bit himself why the idea of just turning little *M. de Bébé* over there over and walking back out scot-free needed to be such a damn problem in the first place—*he* didn't know the guy, after all, aside from him having sworn an oath and made his bed, just like Mac had. Wasn't like they'd *eat* him, now he was suddenly all small and tender . . .

(probably)

But no: the various freaks who made up Mac's family were—if nothing else—intensely practical. So they'd just raise him in a dark hole, feed him on leaves and glamer, use him as a go-between whenever they wanted news of the humans' Iron World—another Ganconer, now he'd disqualified himself from that same position. Up until they finally pulled this new version's eyes out whenever *he* did something they didn't like, too.

Not Mac's call, though. He probably couldn't stop them if he tried, and he certainly didn't *have* to care, one way or the other . . .

. . . not unless he wanted to.

I must work the works of him that sent me, while it is day: the night cometh, when no man can work, Mac thought, and cursed himself for still remembering the Gospel according to John, at all (9:4, 13:15). *For I have given ye an example that ye should do as I have done to you . . .*

And what *would* Jesus do, ex-Father Roke? Drop the kid, take off running? Not look back and not feel bad about it, either?

Probably not be fucking dumb enough to ever let himself end up here, in the first place. I mean, you know. Son of God, and all.

"Look," Mac heard himself tell Lady Glauce with grim disbelief, "I didn't mean to bring him, so I can't give him away, because he's not mine to give. And if that's wrong somehow, I apologize, but . . ."

Here a bleak gust brought Enzemblance suddenly up against him, teeth bared, snarling: "How dare ye? Y'are but a poor, ingratitudinous thing, church mouse, for all yuir posturing! If not for me, this same whelp would have killed ye, sure . . . and tae insult my mother in her ane house, after—"

"Sister," Minion rumbled.

While Saracen chimed in, at the same time: "Mother, give over—"

"I will not." That awful stare latched fast to Mac's, gelid-grey, as though she had leeches set in both sockets. "You, Roke's son, traitor to two worlds twice-over; you, who threw yuir heritage away with both hands! You, who are nothing times nothing—"

Fear in his face, bigger than life and just as ugly. But maybe there really was some giddy place beyond, because Mac seemed to have teleported straight there; he felt his spine stiffen, lips peeling back in crazily similar fashion. Replying: "And two wrongs don't make a right, right? Listen up, aunt—your own son told me the *brugh* was open to me, so if it hadn't been *you* on door-duty, it'd've just been somebody else—"

"Oh, and ye could have entered *without* help, mine or some other's? You who canna e'en shield yuirself from harm wi'out their Almighty's skirts tae hide yuirself behind—"

Lady Glauce's imperious growl broke through, whipping them both silent. "*Enzemblance!* Never think tae quarrel on my part, as though I was unfit tae do so. I will have nae brawling, here or elsewhere, sae dinna think tae wreak thy vengeance on him later in some sneaking way, as I know 'tis thy wont—"

Enzemblance spat, sheer vitriol, fizzing against the *brugh*'s earthen floor. "I ha' done my share for this family in yuir name, mother mine—aye, and more! I will not—"

"You *will* as *I* will, daughter. Now sit thee, and be silent."

Inevitably, age and *noblesse* won out; Enzemblance turned, flash-flowing away to plump herself back down next to Saracen, shrugging off his sympathetic touch. Casting at Galit, as she did: "Play on—*play*, I said! Are ye deaf? For I can make ye so, be very sure of that. . . ."

"Yes, milady. No, milady."

"So, Maccabee," his grandmother said, a bit more softly, as the strumming began once more—leaning down, lowering herself almost to his level, though never quite. "What hast thou to say for thyself?"

"Only that I never meant any insult, grandmere. But I did bring a tithe of another sort—if you'll accept it."

"Show me, then," was all she said.

Mac rummaged in his pocket and drew out the envelope he'd filled that morning. On one level, an utterly bland twist of paper and glue folded over on itself; on another, a net for catching dreams, scribbled all over with angelic and demonic script alike. Those long years in the Connaught, studying banned and forgotten texts of every possible disposition, had to turn out to be good for *something*, eventually—and though magic had never really been Mac's area of expertise, he knew he did have an inborn inclination for it. Which was exactly why he gave in to it so seldom, for fear of simple preference developing into genuine hunger.

He popped the envelope open, shook out its contents—a pixie-dust shower of particles, flickering bright through the brugh's constant half-dusk—and stood back. Waited as an image of his mother took shape, life-sized and fully formed, solid from every angle: "Millie" Druir Roke in all her sad glory, from green-tinged hair to bare hippie toes, assembled painstakingly from treasured memories. An avatar. A ghost.

The one thing no soulless half-Fae could ever leave behind, or so the Church—

(and Lady Glauce as well, given where and when she came from)

—believed.

Planned like a true Jesuit, Mac thought. Then: *I really am a bastard.*

The shimmering Miliner-shape smiled up at her mother, happily, as though they'd never been parted. While Lady Glauce stared back, leaf-shielded eyes suddenly wet, though probably not with tears.

"Oh," she said, at last. "So th'art a wizard after all, Roke of Druir."

Mac flushed. "You know us church mice, grandmere—we aim to please. To give everyone what they want, if we can."

"Aye, so thou dost, at that. And make well sure we pay full price for it, after."

Stretching out one huge hand, she carded her whiter-than-white fingers through the Miliner-shape's hair, cupping its chin to look deep into its untroubled, mindless eyes. Then Lady Glauce shook her head, and blew Mac's offering away in one brisk puff, reducing it back to its component parts of time, grief, loss. Allowed it to find its way back into the envelope again, sealing the gummed flap fast behind.

"'Tis a worthy tithe, certes," she told him, "but one I canna accept. One Roke I gave my Grisell away to, for the family's ane sake; another took my Miliner and drew her tae her death, though she had no objection. Whilst thou, Maccabee, mind'st me strong of both and of neither . . . and in this th'art my ane for certain, my grandson twice over. So I canna charge thee passage, as though thou was't human only; to go through the *brugh* is thy right by birth, which nane may deprive thee of—as thy aunt well knows, were she tae think on't."

Enzemblance tossed her lank red hair, refusing to meet her mother's gaze. While Saracen simply glanced at Mac sidelong, lips twisting in amusement, and gave him an upside-down wink, mouthing:

Oh, well played, coz—tae the hilt, and in rare style, too. Who would ha' thought ye capable of such deception?

Well: Saracen, obviously. Though Mac did wish he wouldn't be so overtly goddamn happy about it, not where his Mom could see him.

Lady Glauce cast a curt, assessing look over the Templar-baby. "Yet for this other, I *do* require a vow of service, if thou wish't tae carry him hence, in safety. . . ."

Mac dipped her a stiff little bow of his own, thinking: *There's always a catch.*

"Command me," he answered.

"To see thee more oft is all I wish—tak' up thy mother's hearth-place thyself, now and again, instead of thinking tae palm her likeness off upon me. Wilt thou allow me this, at least, in recompense for the true love I bear thee now and ever, and for thysel' alone?"

Mac felt stupid tears prick autonomically, throat gone suddenly hot and full. Said, thickly: "I swear it, grandmere."

She bent farther still to kiss his forehead, briefly, lips like cold stone. Pronouncing for all to hear—"Then we stand settled. Saracen, gather the babe, working nae harm as thou dost it; stand fast tae escort Maccabee hither, wherever he most desire'st tae go."

Mac heard the kid give a wail as Saracen scooped it up, efficient but uncaring, like he was toting an animate watermelon. And: "Thank you," he told Lady Glauce, turning to join him—only to stop short as she laid those too-thin hag-fingers lightly on his arm, nails long enough to hurt, even when she didn't want them to.

"Answer me ane thing yet," she asked, voice lower than he'd heard it thus far, as though she feared someone beyond the roster of usual suspects might be listening. "Why did thou think tae do it, Maccabee? Tae vow thysel' tae He whose name I canna e'en speak here, in the depths of my ane house?"

Such desolation in her tone! *It must've really hurt her,* Mac realized, for the first time. *To hear what I'd become. Like I was disowning her, them . . . everyone. Everything I—*

(am)

"I can't remember, anymore," he said, at last. "I'm sorry, but that's the truth. Not even if I . . . meant it or not."

Lady Glauce considered him, salt-sculpture face seeming to soften 'round its edges, almost imperceptibly. "Oh, but I ken thou must ha', my bonny lad," she murmured, quieter still. "For look thee, there's nae a one amongst us can lay hand upon thee, e'en Enzemblance, much as she may pretend otherwise. Which proves th'art still in His grace, whether thou look'st tae be, or no'."

(What?)

"Mayhap He'd e'en take thee back, if thou but thought tae ask Him."

(*What?*)

But then the wind had Mac in its clutches again—he twirled like a tumbleweed, carried forth on its current. The baby's squalling weight pressed hard into his side, arm closing to cradle it without thinking; Saracen's hands (one with six fingers, the other five) dug deep into the small of his back and pushed 'til Mac felt his vertebrae strain. Gave a mocking laugh, thrilling as a bird's cry, if far less human.

Then Mac found himself stumbling back out of another wall entirely, "hatbox" and baby brandished before him like a shield, into the cramped back space of Le Prof's shop.

| chapter six

"Ah," Le Prof said with a remarkable lack of surprise. "*There* you are, at last; *vous, vous êtes diablement en retard.*"

Mac nodded, head swimming. "What . . . time is it?"

"Just after four—*du matin,*" Peering closer: "*C'est à ça que ça ressemble?*"

"Now, yeah. You mind?" Mac offered him the kid, moving to dump the "hatbox" onto the nearest welcoming surface—the same dusty coffee table where he'd drunk that crappy French Roast, what seemed like half a year ago. Ever the great host, Le Prof almost immediately dumped *M. de Bébé* into a nearby tray full of dusty rags and assorted wrapping paper.

That'll make for a great litterbox, Mac thought, sourly.

"Okay," he said, straightening up once more. "There's your loot—I'd sell it pretty quick, you don't want monks in suits up your ass. Where's my money?"

Le Prof seized his prize greedily, with both hands, shrug-pointing Mac in the right direction. "Over there, in the register. Where else would you expect me to keep it?"

Mac hadn't really given it much consideration, so it wasn't like he really had an answer to that one. But when he made towards it, he slammed bodily up against some sort of invisible wall, while another— equally impenetrable, equally unseen—slammed into him from behind, butterfly-pinning him between two panes of killing-jar glass. Barely able to turn his head, he tried to cast an agonized glance Le Prof's way, getting nothing but a smarmy Canadjun-Gallic smirk in return.

". . . whaaah?" Mac asked with stunning articulacy.

"Oh, just a little something I worked up," Le Prof said, working away at the "hatbox's" lock. "*Un sort pour attraper les fées* . . . some 'aematite arranged clockwise overtop *le Gran Tetragrammaton.* Like a fairy ring, but in reverse." He shot Mac a classic retailer's glance of appraisal, like he was sizing him up for a price tag. "As for 'why,' *Père*—well, *pourquoi pas? Vous êtes une vraie denrée—très pure et très dispendieuse.* And since I already 'ave a buyer for *one* rare, formerly 'oly item . . ."

But the box just wouldn't open, no matter how he fiddled with it. Annoyed, he switched over from gloating to cursing in *jouale*, sawing away at the offending latch with his pocket-knife until something went "pop."

Carefully, Le Prof opened the lid, disclosing . . . a mummified severed head. Which was, indeed, covered in gold and jewels—though there'd been a few shortcuts taken, like gilding the pouched and sunken face itself instead of fitting it with a genuine reliquary mask. Its longish hair and sparse beard alike were woven with chain-strung Outremer coinage, empty eyes set with one massive ruby and an equally massive diamond; two filament diadems bound the half-shattered skull back together under an emerald-and-sapphire-scaled casque helmet, with the helmet's lip forming a neat little shelf that elevated the unevenly trimmed area where neck and jaw should meet far enough to set the artefact upright on any given flat surface, so what was left of its uppermost vertebrae and spinal cord hung down in a creepy, little pigtail.

"*Merveilleux,*" Le Prof whispered to himself, though Mac might not have chosen quite the same descriptor. Trapped and unable to speak, however, all he could do was watch Le Prof wander away past where the baby-Templar kicked and flailed, rummaging for his phone . . . which also meant he couldn't possibly have managed to warn him about what was about to happen next, even if he'd wanted to.

The ruby and diamond were set less *inside* the head's sunken sockets than *on top* of them, gold wire-bound, like a pair of crude snap-apart spectacles. Now they shivered and lifted away, one by one, each giving a tiny chime. Beneath, the dim up-rolled excrescences Jacques de Molay had once seen through, poached like eggs by the process of being burnt alive, seemed to fill up with shadow; that darkness, in turn, spilled out and over their fixed and staring rims, rising to encircle the head itself like a crackling anti-halo.

Yeah, Mac thought. *That can't be good.*

And what about that dull, dry, tiny voice emerging from the Grand-Master's hard black lips, spiralling up between his broken teeth, a ghost in a shell, whispering through Hell's keyhole?

As though in answer to Mac's question, Le Prof put the phone back down halfway through dialling it and turned back, brow wrinkling. He approached the coffee table slowly, bent to listen, ear dipping almost to the head's mouth. Stretched out one reluctant hand to touch—

—and almost fell back, ass over teakettle, when he realized that the head was actually *vibrating* from the inside—its phantom vocal cords contracting, spinal tail skritching at the glass, carving a swish through the dust.

"*Baise-moi, câlisse, tabernacle!*"

Pass, thanks, Mac thought. As the head's whisper rose by mere decibels, coalescing into an even rawer, darker form of French—

Aidez-moi, champions, de Molay "said," words echoing inside both their minds at once. *Vim patrior. Je souffre la violence. Aidez-moi, mes fils du temple, venez à ma rescousse, je prie.* . . .

A burning smell; the sound of armour clashing, a dull drumbeat. The wall above Le Prof charred, fraying away in the shape of a man's shadow as he stepped through—one Mac thought he recognized, even before the face behind it became clear. *Cordellion Federoi, that's 'is name. One of the Kissed.*

"*Me voici, maître,*" the Templar leader told his Order's Cornerstone, and grasped Le Prof—too amazed to do much more than huff out a single startled breath at such presumption—by both shoulders, effortlessly flipping him up against the already-resolidified plaster. Then held him there with one elbow to the throat, contemptuously easy, as he drew his ceramic machete.

Le Prof's eyes bulged out even farther, almost to their strings. He shook all over, stammering—"But—I thought you were . . . 'ow it wasn't true, what they burned you for . . ."

"Not *then*, no. But—"

—now? Definitely.

Thus confirming what Mac had suspected all along: that the surest way to make a bunch of monks swear their souls over to the Devil was to accuse them, inaccurately, of doing that very thing. And then kill their Grand-Master, throw them into jail, torture them . . .

Still: You really think the Devil answers his own phone, Sir Burns-in-Hell-a-Lot? If you talked to anybody, it was probably talked to his "people;" see how far that gets you, when you try to renegotiate the terms of your contract.

As the blade pressed into Le Prof's throat, he wheezed: "*Mais—le demi-fée, c'est lui le véritable voleur!* 'Ave your revenge on 'im, take your 'ead, and go!"

But: "*Deus lo volt*, thief-master," Cordellion told Le Prof, mildly. "As the sin was yours *in utero*, so will our recompense be charged first to your account, as well. *My* god requires it."

"Oh *non*, NON—"

Mac shut his eyes, so he wouldn't have to see what followed. He felt the spell drop away from him by degrees, chopped off in mid-pulse, along with Le Prof's life; both walls of air sprang apart in unison, returning him to Curia's back-room floor so heavily his knees popped with the strain, even as Cordellion let Le Prof drop. Collecting the head, he moved back towards Mac, smiling pleasantly.

"And you, thief's thief . . . what *is* your name?"

Mac pulled himself to his feet, stretching painfully.

"Maccabee Roke," he replied. "I think you got my text."

Under the sunglasses, Mac saw the Templar's seared-blind eyes widen, ever so slightly. "Ah, yes. So you knew your—patron, here—would cheat you, and left me details on where to find him after that charade at the airport, to prevent it from happening."

Mac shrugged. "I thought he might try, sure; no great stretch of the imagination. Besides which—occurs to me that if anybody here really *needs* that thing you're carrying, it's probably you boys."

"This is our Grand-Master, *M'sieu* Roke—a damned saint, made unholy relic. You'd do well to accord him the respect he deserves."

"Who says I don't?" Mac bowed to the head, curtly, while the room filled up with scowling Templars—these ones came in through the front door, at least, instead of through the wall. Two of them took hold of Le Prof's corpse, sketched sigils, which lit and wounded the air around it, then used a few more neat gestures to crush it telekinetically down for transport, like a bruisy-wet piece of origami: flattened the skull with a finger-pop; dislocated all four limbs, "tying" arm to leg forwards, then backwards; tuck-broke the neck like a turtle's, then twisted the spine one more time like a meat Transformer, reducing person forevermore to object.

Cordellion didn't turn a hair of his well-coiffed ponytail. And this time, Mac made himself watch it all—because, as Fr. Gowther would've put it, there was no good reason he could think of to let himself not have to.

"You've precious little gag reflex for a man of the twentieth century," Cordellion noted, approvingly. "A retort to the Living God: we like that."

Mac looked down. Replied, dimly: "Thanks."

(*I guess.*)

When one of the other Templars went to scoop their former compatriot up from where he lay, crying and messing himself, however, Mac heard himself snap—"Nope, that stays here. Guy gets a do-over. Let him pick his own friends, this time 'round."

"Perhaps so," Cordellion agreed, waving the Hell-knight in question away. Then paused on his way out to ask Mac: "Has the dead man any heirs, do you reckon, M'sieu?"

"That'd be a big *je ne sais pas.*"

"And you don't want any sort of payment from *us*, of course, for your part in revealing the Grand-Master's kidnapper . . ."

"Not so much. Why?"

They met each other gaze to gaze, quarter-Fae Beelzebub blue to brand-kissed off-white, more scar showing than cornea. "Because, if so," Cordellion suggested, at last, "then whatever remains must surely be yours, by right of seizure. A place of trade—neutral ground, potentially, as long as one worked to keep it so. Good to occupy, surely, for a man with a foot in several worlds at once."

Now it was Mac's turn to gape.

"What—like the shop?" He asked, finally. "Run Curia, is that it? Me?"

Cordellion shrugged and turned away, hiking his mentor's gold-plated skull like a football. Throwing back, before he finally let the front door close behind him—"One might do far worse, *hein*? As one almost did."

Which was . . . true enough.

Shrugging, Mac opened up the register, took his pay—and found Le Prof's key ring lurking underneath the change drawer. Studied it a long minute before stuffing it inside his coat pocket and hefting *M. de Bébé*; two more "gains," equally ill-gotten.

"C'mon, squawky," he told the kid. "Let's go hook you up with a free lunch."

At the Connaught Trust, they made Mac wait almost an hour after two junior novitiates took his little "donation" away, cooing over it from both ends, before finally ushering him into a tiny sitting room to see both the woman he'd texted earlier—Mother Eulalia, war-leader of the *Ordo Sororum Perpetualam*—and the one he'd've run ten blocks in any given direction to avoid: Sr. Blandina, her very self. In the fine and furious flesh.

"I knew it," she said, crossing her arms.

But: "Of course you did, dear," Mother Eulalia pointed out, calmly. "He left his name at the desk downstairs, for goodness' sake. Always a pleasure, Fath . . . Mister Roke."

"Mother."

"Oh, please!" Blandina scoffed. "Your *mother'd* be living under a hill, if your father hadn't managed to paste them both against a semi. We all know what you are—"

Suddenly at the end of a very long and exhausting rope, Mac felt rage whip up inside him, and spat it back out at her like bile. "*So you've said*, Sister. Thanks so much for the big slice of Do As You Would Be Done By pie, too; you bake that yourself, or order in?"

"You son of a—"

"Blandina!"

A pause ensued, during which they both struggled to calm themselves. 'Til, eventually, Mother Eulalia continued: "As you probably know, we found one of the missing pages from our *Codex* earlier tonight—on the body of a certain Professeur Auguste Therrien-Poirier, local dealer in antiquities, who seems to have died very recently under rather obscure circumstances."

"Mmm, wow. Weird. His first name was *Auguste*?"

"Don't you even want to know who killed him?" Blandina demanded.

"Okay, who?"

"The Templars, we believe. Our Anchoress glimpsed one of their inner circle entering Toronto during morning Meditation, so we were already on the lookout. Which is why we exorcized the area, laying down salt and sacrament in such a way as might make it somewhat difficult for his murderers to return."

"I hope you can get the blood off your manuscript," Mac offered.

"Parchment's pretty porous, as I recall."

"Oh, our restoration facilities remain exemplary. More important, however, is the fact that, while today's work means the Templars cannot lay their Cornerstone in Toronto anytime soon, this welcome recovery proves the rest of the *Codex* must still be nearby." Eulalia folded her hands in her lap, tilting her head, the picture of academic curiosity. "I don't suppose you'd have any suggestions on how to tailor our search efforts, though—would you, Maccabee?"

"Um, I guess the right response here might be: 'I don't know what you're talking about?'"

Blandina snorted. "Mother, this is foolish. I could kill him now, if you gave the order."

"Could you? I don't think any of us are perfectly sure of that, dear. But perhaps *you* could set about finding the rest of the manuscript for us, Mister Roke, bit by bit. We'd certainly make it worth your while."

"The warrior nun protection racket installment plan?"

"Something of the sort. You've relatively little to fear from us, after all."

"Compared to who?"

"The rest of your family, of course."

Back at the Saul of Tarsus, Mac made his goodbyes—told them he was moving out the next morning, so they were free to re-assign his room. And later that night, he woke to blackness, just like old times: somebody standing over him, head cocked, waiting for him to resurface from dream's muddy wallow. But the featureless black silhouette's power-stink tasted of ash and vinegar, not the rotten-fruit-and-mould flavour of the *brugh*. Myrrh, that classic seasonal bitter tomb-perfume, with just a touch of frankincense larded in, on top—it was a smell Mac'd walked either in front of, behind, or shook a censer-full of back and forth almost every day for half of his life . . . twice on Saturday, three times on Sundays, all day on Christmas, Easter, and Good Friday, too.

(*Cordellion*.)

Mac sat up, wrung the sleep from his eyes, game-face on. Saying, as he did—"Tell you this much . . . I'm getting *really* sick of people coming at me through walls. Why are you here, *Chevalier*?"

"You interest me, M. Roke."

"Oh, joy."

"I know what it is, to be betrayed by God."

"Not sure it was God betrayed *me*, exactly."

"You interest me further."

And maybe this *was* just another nightmare, one more in a million. That would explain why it was so easy to tell this *thing* what he'd never before said aloud, even to himself.

"Something came in, one night," Mac began, slowly. "At the Cathedral, where I used to—work, sleep, live. Everything. And even the few people who could tell it was there, they thought it was an angel. But . . ."

". . . it was not," the Templar's voice finished for him, quiet. Like any good confessor.

Around him, the dark pressed in closer, 'til Mac felt it in his very throat. All his bed lacked was a screen between him and Cordellion to render the illusion perfect.

"I don't know *what* it is," he said, finally. "I don't know if *it* knows . . ."

"Go on."

"But . . . they let it stay. To come and go as it pleased—as it pleases. And they never did anything, because they never knew any better. Because nobody in there could tell the difference."

"Ah." A studied, musing beat. "Well, you can't be too hard on them for that, *M'sieu*; they just don't have our advantages, do they? *They* have to take everything on *faith*."

Mac nodded, unseen, even by himself. And then—

—the sun was up, the light back on, the room empty of everything but the expected. Mac reached for his coat, heard Le Prof's keys ring a profane sort of Matins, and thought: *Well, there we go—you wanted a new life, didn't you?*

God in His heaven, all right with the world; business as usual, for Templars and Fae alike. Those pesky shadows gone at last, from almost everywhere but inside him.

| epilogue

The sign on the door said Curia opened at 6:00 A.M., and Mac saw no reason to mess with that. But at 6:04 on the first day, a girl with straight black hair walked in, so slight her head barely came up to his armpit. She might have been anywhere between a hard-lived sixteen and a creepily dewy thirty (her actual age later turned out to be twenty-eight) and had slanted eyes of no particular colour (brown . . . ish, maybe, though already beginning to shade towards yellow, from some angles). She also smelled of incense and stank of sulphur in equal measure, though not so much anyone other than him might've noticed.

"I heard you sell grimoires, here," she said, without preamble.

"Sure. Buy them, too."

"Good." She shrugged off her backpack, laid it down on the counter. "You happen to have a copy of the *Cle Kushielle Ultime*, I might've run across something I could maybe swap you for it. Guy I bought it from said it was the Yezidic Gospel, but he couldn't even tell Beelzebub's sigil from Beli-ya'al's, so . . . go on and take a gander, see what *you* think." Adding, with a mocking little curl of smile: "You *do* read angel, right?"

"Some. But wouldn't this be devil?"

"Same thing, man. Exact . . . same . . . thing."

Mac nodded slightly, squinting down at what she was already starting to unravel—with a fair amount of care, since it looked like it might be made from shark's skin. And suddenly knowing, as he did, that he'd probably say just about anything to keep her there for the next hour or so, let alone possibly coming back on a regular basis.

"Maccabee Roke," he offered; "Judy Kiss," she shot back, flashing him her health card. According to it, *Kiss* apparently rhymed with *quiche*, which took all the fun out of the joke, right there.

Looking closer, her "scroll" seemed more like three different documents stitched together at the top and rolled tight, then tied. At least four different magical languages had been used, from straight witch-code like Crossing the River to occasional scattered lines in the Penemue Dialectic, a seldom-used Grigorim variant of angelic script.

"Where'd you get this, Judy?" he asked, spreading one hand gingerly over the deceptively smooth surface. He felt words of power blossom under his fingertips as he did, etched in poison, their very letters faintly raised, faintly toxic.

"Does it matter?"

"Not to me. Wouldn't happen to know if that's an original or a copy, though, would you? And . . . if there's more?"

She shook her head. "Not that I saw. So: take it or leave it?"

He could already see there was something wrong with her, of course. Given his history, there'd pretty much have to be.

Thirty-eight years old, and never kissed a girl, he thought, ruefully. Then: *Man. Truly pathetic.*

"Let me just check my stock-book," Mac said, eyes still on the manuscript—hoping against hope that she was looking down at him, but not quite daring to glance back up. Not just yet.

And turned on the cash register.

FURIOUS ANGELS (2013)

Blessed are those who have not seen and yet believe, *according to John the Apostle—those happy few who never look for tangible proof of their supernatural assumptions. Who never, like Doubting Thomas, demand to stick their hand in the Risen Christ's side.*

But the Ordo Sororum Perpetualam's anchoresses spend their retirement in meditation on a very different version of that phrase: **Blessed are those,** *they say,* **whether they believe or not, who do not** *have* **to see.**

This year's Novice Number Thirty-Three—formerly yet another Vicky, if Sister Blandina recalled her application correctly—had decided to take the battle-name of Cecilia, which Blandina thought pretty but inadequate, especially to a martial order.

"Cecilia *was* a martyr, dear," Mother Eulalia reminded her. "And martyrdom is all our charter requires in a name-saint. But I suppose one might consider there to be differing degrees of martyrdom."

"Catherine's a good name," was all Blandina replied, not looking up from her present duty. Yet feeling Mother Eulalia's single shrewd eye on the nape of her neck, assessingly, nevertheless.

"Of Alexandria? We have a few too many fireworks to deal with around here as it is, don't you think?"

"Yes, Mother."

But: *Alexandrine Catherine broke the Wheel, overthrew what pagans thought was the natural order. She made her tormentors' gods look foolish, confirming her God—our God—over all. St. Cecilia . . . she's the reason Baptists think angels have harps.*

Rarely any point to debating with Mother Eulalia, however, even when she was feeling charitable enough to allow the impertinence. "Cecilia" had made her choice and would now have upwards of two years to live with it—'til she either paid out her novitiate and made her final vows, thought better, or had those decisions taken from her, decisively. The Ordo was a tour of duty from which few returned, unscathed or otherwise.

We kill monsters or die trying, Blandina remembered explaining once, to a Poor Clare who claimed to be interested in what it was, exactly, that the Perpetuals did. Only for the other to blurt, in return: *But . . . what would be the point?*

Fewer monsters, sister.

(Only that.)

A ridiculous conversation, by definition. Either the Ordo's purpose actually was what it said on the box, or it wasn't; their very role as killers of supernatural things would in itself seem to be, by simple logic, "proof" of the idea that supernatural things which merited killing existed. But to be constantly forced through explaining it, and by other *religieuses . . . ah, chah,* her Mémé would have said. *Every fool a king in him own house.*

I mean, either you're right in your beliefs, or I am. Or we're both wrong, of course—at which point, what are either of us even doing here?

Take off your habit and go home, if that's how you feel about it. Get yourself a boyfriend.

When Blandina fell into moods like these, which was more often than it should be, Mother Eulalia sometimes undertook to tell her improving stories or gave her extra duty. Today, however, she simply shrugged and said: "You need exercise, dear—a breath of fresh air, that's what strikes me. Have you spoken with Maccabee Roke, lately?"

"'Course not," Blandina snapped. Then: "No, Mother. Did you think it prudent?"

"Oh, knowing what young Mister Roke is up to is always prudent. He's sent word to the Bishop about seeing something."

"He 'sees something' every day of his life."

"I believe he meant of interest. To us."

"Yes, Mother."

"Well, then." Throwing back over her shoulder, as she moved towards the door: "And take an apprentice with you, when you go— someone who hasn't met him yet."

"Sister Cecilia?"

"I'll leave that up to you, dear."

Here's how it all started: God tore pieces off itself to make angels—the Elohim, or Heavenly Host—who were too much the same, yet too different. Who served, and did not question; who had flame, but no true vitality. No . . . spark.

Then God thought smaller, and thus our troubles began.

Human beings were made, given individual personality, a soul each, free will enough to choose wrongly, and—once sin entered the picture—the knowledge of their own mortality, a poisoned gift, thankfully denied almost every other mammal (save for whales, grey parrots, a few varieties of ape, and elephants). Some angels later rebelled against the concept, only to find themselves cast down—but long before that, my ancestors did the opposite:

fell deeply in love with the fragile creatures our Creator had assigned to their care, both figuratively and literally.

Their name was Grigorim, the famous Watcher Angels, of whom Enoch has so much to say in his Apocrypha. And our name is Nephilim, those angels' progeny—seed of betrayal, rape-born earth-giants, mighty men and women of reknown . . .

Not that we are any of us quite so massive these days, by comparison. Not since hormones and nutrition have rendered Goliath the rule, David the exception, throughout this world's Westernmost portions.

Blandina and Cecilia left the Connaught Trust in street drag, with their scarves—so easily mistaken for hijab, these post-Osama days— pulled down into neat little cravats, and only the lack of make-up to set them apart from any other two unfashionable young ladies tricked out in sensible black shoes with steel toes and thick soles, sharp-creased navy blue security guard slacks, and white polo-neck uniform shirts bought by the gross from an outlet in Scarborough. Hair either long enough to put back in a braid, yet short enough not to provide much of a hand-hold (Cecilia), or close-cut as the diocese would allow and nappy from ten years' worth of not being relaxed every other week, the way God always intended (Blandina). Plus nothing personal, nothing identifiable, just in case: no jewellery beyond the tiny silver cross-pins at their lapels or the plain silver wedding ring Blandina wore, signifying her commitment to that principality her Mémé called *King Christ Jesus.*

A sap in her right-hand pocket, full of anchoress-blessed sand. A set of cold iron knuckles in her left, similarly blessed, incised with Crusader crosses. That, and she could Wing Ch'un the crap out of whatever came her way, with a side order of Krav Maga, and a little bit of Brazilian Capoeira for back-up. Blandina wasn't sure what sort of hand-to-hand practice Cecilia had under her belt, if any; hadn't seen her at any of *her* prayer sessions thus far, that was for sure. But if Mother Eulalia was letting her out of the Connaught Trust at all, she must be able to at least halfway defend herself unarmed. . . .

Or maybe I'm supposed to do that for her, while she takes notes. As a learning exercise.

They passed through the stacks and out onto the Legacy Library's floor, a hushed, expensively outfitted reading room full of students and clergy. Most had ancient-looking ecclesiastical books out on their carrels, reading in rapt silence while their Trust-issued pencils scratched diligently away. The wall they passed while crossing to the final door supported a huge dark Renaissance scene: Jacob vs. God's messenger at Jabbok, Sunday Sunday Sunday.

"'Jacob wrestled the angel, and the angel was overcome,'" Blandina quoted out the side of her mouth, keeping her voice low. "True or false, sister?"

Cecilia, still craning her neck to look Jacob in the eye, gave a guilty sort of jump. "Um . . . true?"

"'Cause the Bible says so?" Blandina shrugged. "Scripture also claims, at the Battle of Jericho, Joshua made the sun and moon stand still in the sky—but physics says, if that ever happened, gravity would fail, and we'd all fly off into outer space. Who's right?"

They stepped through into the hallway, letting the weighted door fall softly shut behind while their steps rang sharp on the tile a good ten times before Cecilia finally found her answer. "That's . . . a very hard question," she said, at last.

"No it's not."

Down the hallway's end, a new set of doors required both palm-scan and computerized lock-code. Blandina put hers in by feel, waiting while Cecilia struggled to recall whichever dead nun's she'd been assigned. Beyond, the Trust's outermost lobby was cool, functional, modern; if she didn't know better, Blandina might've suspected today's greeter of wearing lip-gloss. Her desk bore the Ordo's insignia and motto, thin gold letters set in dark wood: *In Nomine Perpetua in Perpetuam.*

"Then how's this," Blandina said, tracing the letters. "Night before her martyrdom, Eusebius says the Blessed Perpetua dreamt she wrestled Satan in the form of a black man, and threw him. You think *that* happened?"

"I don't know what you want me to—" As Blandina narrowed her eyes, Cecilia sighed. "Okay. Do I think it's true she threw him? Or that she dreamed it?"

They locked gazes a moment longer, the novice obviously braced for some anti-heretical eruption; Blandina knew she had a reputation, especially amongst the unblooded. But all she gave back was a smile, small yet genuine. "Good one," she allowed.

And now they were almost out in the world. Blandina stopped on the threshold, asking Cecilia—"Next-to-last question: You and me fought *ghul* last night. True or false?"

"Well . . . I *was* there."

"But if you told anybody else, would they believe you?"

". . . probably not."

"So riddle me this. Why do *we* believe, at all, when God and the Church tell us something we know could never happen did—just because we see things everyone else thinks don't exist every day, every night, and kill them? Or is it something more?"

Again, Cecilia hesitated—a flinch, almost. Somebody was going to have to break her of that habit, and Blandina suspected she'd been handed the job. "I, I'm just thinking . . . I mean . . ."

"It's not rocket science, sister. We take it on faith, because we have to. By definition."

"Yes. Of course."

Of course.

You couldn't fault the girl for knowing nothing, Blandina supposed. She'd known nothing herself, once upon a time.

"What's he like, Mac Roke?" Cecilia asked.

"You'll find him charming, probably," Blandina replied, without turning. "Most do."

"Because he'll be putting a charm on me?" Blandina threw her a look. "He's partly Fae, that's what I'd heard; part Fae and part warlock, and I don't even know what that is. Is there a word for that, specifically?"

"Not that I know of."

She thought of Mac Roke, bent to his former customary task, updating the *Bestiarium Ad Noctem* with notes from the Ordo's latest interrogations; had he found family members' names in there, now and again? But then, as she recalled, that implication was always a sore spot. *We don't all* know *each other, B,* he'd tell her. *There's no organized "monster community" with a party line, a hidden agenda, or what-have-you. Jesus, how speciesist can you get?*

"Some Fae can charm, yes," Blandina told Cecilia, "just like there's spells which bend affection. Our vows disrupt them, mostly. But . . ." Forcing herself to be honest, she had to admit: ". . . I've never known Roke to use glamer, no, not on us. Or me."

"So if I feel—*something* happening, then—"

You won't, Blandina wanted to snap. Instead, she doled out the glare once more, keeping things short and sharp—easy to remember yet hard to forget, especially under pressure. Like any standing order.

"Pray," she advised, curtly. And turned, moving down, onto the St. George subway station steps.

Of the rest, the Goetim, Adversary-allied, found themselves imprisoned along with him in Hell's multifoliated holding-cell—able to escape every now and then through the usual channels (possession, pacts or deals, the debatable appeal of doing some magician's beck and call), but always eventually returned to serve out the rest of their sentence. The Maskim or Terrible Seven, meanwhile, chose no side but their own and continue even now to do as they please in vain pursuit of free will, which their very nature renders an impossibility.

But my ancestors were set to wandering, cast out on every side, surrounded by a movable cage/feast/retinue of children—only comfortable in our presence, yet resentful of our existence, palpable proof of their own endless appetite-slavery, the injury they are unable to keep themselves from offering the One who still loves them most. He who would gladly grant them salvation, even now, if only they could keep from making more of us.

(And what might He offer we Nephilim, were our parents to relent at last? This I do not know, for I have never heard His voice, at all. I am not enough of one thing for that. Half of me is human, just like everybody else—made from meat and hunger and sin, driven by blood, tormented by possibility. But the other—

The other half is like every angel, good, bad, or indifferent. And it is made from God.)

What Maccabee Roke looked like, these days, was the same man he'd always seemed: rugged, edge-of-handsome, with too-dark hair, and abnormally bright blue eyes. He was leaned up against the till of that ridiculous shop of his—"Curia: Odd Objects Appraised and Traded"— studying a ledger with his reading glasses on, wearing the Port Dalhousie Peregrines football team sweatshirt Blandina vaguely recalled from their ill-advised early-morning jogging sessions.

"Roke," she said from the doorway. And: "Hey, B," he replied, not bothering to look up. "Guess you got my message."

"Mother Eulalia did."

"Well, she obviously knew who I really meant it for." Here, he finally turned, eyebrows lifting as he took in Cecilia. "*This* one's new, though."

"A novice. I'm training her."

"Sounds fun. Am I Exhibit Number One?"

"Don't flatter yourself."

"Okay, whatever. You actually want to see what I found, or are we just going to stand here flirting?"

Here, however, a new voice intruded—snakey, smokey, rich with archaic Scots burr. "I'd thought tae find ye unoccupied, coz, yet here I stand, corrected. Will ye no' introduce me tae yuir friends?"

This newest arrival, still half-caught in the act of pixilating into quick relief like an Escher puzzle-print emerging from its background pattern, was someone Blandina knew of, but had never previously met: "young," lean and flexible, with a pouty, private mouth, dressed head-to-toe in scaly green—a silky suit of uncertain cut, probably cobbled together from leaves.

"One of the Druirs," Blandina told Cecilia. "Saracen, right? Don't look in its eyes."

A moue. "'It?' Ye do me wrong, God-lady. I am a tourist here only, and worthy of yuir respect."

"You came in through the *wall*, Oberon."

"I have a standing invitation," Saracen Druir explained to Cecilia, who reddened slightly.

"*My* wall, B," Roke pointed out, at the same time. "*My* cousin."

"So now you're *proud* of what you spent twenty years hiding? Interesting."

A flash of something in Roke's eyes made her tense, joyful. But it died down quickly.

"It's what it is," he replied, simply. "I'm what . . . I am. We've all got things in our makeup we'd drop like they're hot, if we could. That's family."

Dem Scots get in every damn where, like hissin' roaches, her Mémé whispered from her memory's back recesses, tracing the splash of freckles across Blandina's nose with one papery blue-brown-on-pale-pink finger. *Scots, French, English-from-England, breedin' their blood in us fe a hundred generation gone,* chah! *Messin' us from the cradle on so we forever strangers, even to our own-selves.*

But: *ah, chah,* indeed. She didn't have time for this, not with Saracen already moving in on Cecilia out of the corner of one eye, thinking Blandina too far away to notice, or Cecilia apparently too tranced to think of stopping him.

Just before he could make contact, however, Blandina interposed—touched him instead, with her left hand, and let cold iron do all the work. There was a subdued flash, almost grey, which sent Saracen scurrying backwards; under his own hand, slapped down protectively, she could see the charred edges of a palm-print forming. "Ye foul rag-and-bone!" he cursed at her.

"You're lucky I didn't do it on your face."

"Tae treat me thus, under my ane cousin's guest-truce! I should blast ye—"

"Keep the peace, half-thing. Think you're safe just because your hill lies outside the GTA? Be very sure—if our charter widens to include the Five-Family Coven's leavings, we *will* move against you . . . all of you."

"Oh? And do ye 'keep the peace,' sweeting?"

Blandina grinned. "Try me."

Roke, unimpressed, made a dry little tutting sound. "Saracen, what the hell: they're God-protected to begin with, and *she* kills stuff like you for fun. What'd you expect?"

Those eyes flared, narrowing. "A sad thing, when blood counts for naught in the face of threat. Ye should at least pretend tae ha' my back."

"Mmm, yeah, right—that'd be a solid *no*; Curia's neutral ground, and if the price of it staying that way is you occasionally getting crucifix-whipped for acting stupid, I don't have any real problem with the concept. Now: need a little something for that burn, or were you going?"

Saracen made a hissing noise, high wind through dry grass, and leaned back against the same wall he'd first eased his way through, eyes closing bottom-to-top on all of them, as though he'd suddenly had quite enough of this silly human nonsense.

Roke snorted again, switching his attention back to Blandina. "So here's what happened," he began. "Not last night but the night before, I'm closing up, and these guys come in—four of 'em, all dressed differently, but they have this weird *look*, like they're related somehow. Which set off my radar, so—"

"You turned on the security camera."

"Kirlian video, here we come." He bent below the desk, came up with a sheaf of screen-cap printouts. "Now . . . you tell me."

Four man-shapes, as advertised: one white, two brown, one possibly Asian of some derivation. And all of them with a single spear of light guttering from each of their foreheads, a blowtorch-bright halo-slice, like flaws in the nonexistent film.

"What *are* those?" Cecilia asked behind her, apparently sure that Blandina would know the answer. But Blandina simply shook her head.

"I don't know," she replied.

"Exactly," Roke agreed; he punched cash-out, rummaged inside his till, withdrew something wrapped in a Glad easy-open sandwich bag that drew the gaze like a magically charged magnet, a slightly shimmering curlicue knot of black-on-silver penmanship.

Cecilia leaned forward. "Is that Enochian?"

"*Proto*-Enochian, a name, one of the oldest. The seal of Penemue Grigorim."

Blandina felt both her thumbs prick at once, hard enough to make her wince; she shook her head, blinking. And asked: "Somebody sold you that? And you *bought* it?"

"Angelic script has its markets, B. Point is, whenever I usually get my hands on stuff like this, it's old—fifty years, a hundred, centuries. But look closer."

Cecilia put out her hand, idiotically, and Roke dropped the thing into her palm, holding it gingerly by the corner as if it might be hot. When she turned it over, its weird no-glow masked by the paper's backside, they both saw a stationery header, which read *Greetings from the Motorway Motel, Mississauga—Unlimited Pool, Cable, Wi Fi. Perfect for Parties.*

"It's genuine," Roke said. "Written maybe . . . yesterday, or the day before. Which means that one of the first angels to ever descend is right here, in town. And not alone, either."

Though I am not "there" to do so, I nevertheless see how very hard Blandina looks at one of these pixilated countertop faces . . . at me. As though she recognizes the long-dead human berg I was calved from, full-grown and whole, such a comparatively short time ago.

Penemue Grigorim is my Maker, my originator, my father and mother— both and neither. It threw me off like a spark, cast me like a pottery sketch, dropped me like solder from a burn; only a small part of the real thing, a parody, something useless and inadequate.

For do not be fooled: like all Nephilim, I am nothing but what gets left behind . . . the physical residue of the explosion that happens when humans and angels collide.

"Guys with the flaming haircuts must be the get, then," Blandina said, at last. "Penemue's leavings."

"Half-angels," Cecilia chimed in. "The reason God sent a Flood."

"Supposedly, yes."

Cecilia's eyes blanked once more, then turned sharper than Blandina was used to seeing them. "Well . . . we have to tell Mother Eulalia, obviously. Do research on attack methods—weaponry. Send intelligencers to Mississauga?"

Roke shook his head. "No point; the Grigorim will be long gone by now, its whole clutch along with it. Probably only wrote the seal in the first place 'cause it needed ready cash for a bolt-hole, someplace it can hunt from . . ."

Who asked you? Blandina longed to snap. But only asked, instead—

"All right. Where would *you* start looking?"

Back when the grabs hit the desk, Saracen Druir had made a sort of gulp, as though his slippery mouth were suddenly full of silvered salt. Now, looking over, she found him already in mid-fade, blending spine-first back out through Curia's exposed-brick wall. Roke noticed and laughed out loud.

"Seriously? I'd look for *that*," he said. "There's lore claims *all* monsters descend from the Grigorim, through their Nephilim: witches and warlocks, psionics, weres, vampires, the Fae. And while I don't know if that's true, I do know this much—when one passes by, there isn't a monster in town who'll want to stick around."

"Won't be seeing you for a while then, I guess."

"C'mon, B—it already knows where *I* live. Besides which, if some sort of mass exodus is about to start, then everybody's going to want to pawn their crap before upping sticks. After all, I'm not exactly on the church's payroll, anymore; gotta file taxes, like everybody else. Not to mention, I have a business to run."

That night, Blandina took Reconciliation in anticipation of her next battle, one of the Ordo's principal charges. They did it prison-style, two chairs leaning back to back, with Blandina brushing shoulders with the young priest who'd taken Roke's place after he resigned—a nice enough boy, she supposed. Though she never could recall his name.

"Forgive me, Father," she said. "It's been . . . twenty hours since my last confession."

"And have you sinned, my child?"

Ridiculous question.

"Always," she replied. And went down the list, briskly, point by point.

After, she worked off her penance in the sparring room, drumming the heavy bag 'til both wrists felt bruised, and her hairline stung with sweat. Finding her mind adrift, nonetheless, for all this distraction: back through time, years peeling like skin. Back to the crux of the matter.

Though Toronto still maintained its overall reputation for being "Good," the area where Blandina had been raised was reckoned a bad place by many people's standards. Bad enough to make her grow up fast and hard, any rate—a Redbone girl with auburn-touched hair and hazel eyes, tall and fine and fierce. Too quote-quote "white" for most blacks, but damn well black enough for everybody else, with the legacy of bad old slave-trader blood writ large on her: deeded down from that same master/father who'd given Mémé's own Gran-Gran-Gran-Mémé her maiden name, which Mémé constantly derided as *damn Scots meddlin'*, yet kept perversely intact through three different common-law husbands.

A closet matriarchist, her gran. But then again, in Blandina's neighbourhood, *women ah run tings* was the rule, not the exception; boys raised without fathers grew up to become absent baby-daddies in their turn, then killed each other or moved on before they could see the cycle repeat itself. While daughters, sisters, mothers, aunties all clustered together, gave up whatever they had to, did whatever what was necessary. Threw themselves against the wall and let the world exact its punishment, all in order to stave off that inevitable moment when their children, however well-sheltered, would have to take their place.

Blandina—not Blandina, then—had seen it coming for herself, a mile off. And so, realizing her difficult-to-categorize brand of good looks and charisma gave her a chance others didn't have, she'd traded them both for mobility. Got out, kept going. Went from catalogue poses and club dancing to runway modelling and video shoots, gully-creepin' up the midst in the foreground of various reggae or R'n'B odes with her pants slung low and her midriff exposed; dipped her toe in the soft-core pool without ever having to get too dirty; convinced her agent to spring for martial arts training and created a brief stock in trade of looking like she could probably kick your ass, if the very idea didn't bore her so much. Became a brand, anonymous yet recognizable, something whose traces she still occasionally tripped across, but which almost none of the people around her would ever associate with who she was now . . .

Though, that wasn't quite true, not entirely. As her brush with a failed former dancehall deejay she'd once known had proven, recently— her on soup-van duty, scoping out duppy hidey-holes between medical advice and turf dispute mediation, with him one of the great unwashed, high and drunk, yet still savvy enough to connect the dots. Squinting into her face and asking, hesitant: *Sistah, fe real—ain't you use to be somebody?*

Still am. Brother.

Later, as they were breaking down for the night, he'd drifted back, eyes a bit clearer. *Atia Rusk, in the damn flesh,* he'd named her. *Ain't see ya fe ten year at least, girl. Ya cleft ta Christ, nah? Hadn't thought ya da marryin' type.*

Well, Vévé, ya know how 'tis. Me Lord's too strong a persuader ta be denied.

Ah now, fe sure. His will be done.

(Oh, yes. Always.)

Blandina leaned her brow against the bag's slimy-cool skin and let her breathing slow. She'd been done for five minutes at least; better to hit the shower, then suit up. But when she raised her head, Cecilia was there, in the doorway.

"What?" Blandina demanded.

"Uh . . . Mother Eulalia says she might have a lead. On—that creature, the one Maccabee Roke—"

"*Angel*, sister. You can say the word."

Cecilia paused, looked down. "I'm just . . . not used to thinking of God's messengers as prey, I suppose," she told her feet.

"Satan was an angel, once," Blandina pointed out. "Angels can err; they fall and are condemned. The Watchers were first to do so. That makes them fair game."

"For God, yes. But us?"

Towelling herself vigorously, Blandina used her teeth to unravel first one hand-wrap, then the other. "If God didn't approve of what we do, He wouldn't let us do it."

"You're very sure, sister."

"Yes. I have to be."

And so will you, someday.

The rumour is that Nephilim kill their human mothers and fathers in their birthing—that we bud off, leaving behind wounds human bodies can't possibly sustain. In fact, the piece torn away physically is miniscule at best. What rips is the human partner's soul, which becomes diminished and hollow, eddying away at death into a mere radioactive signature.

This is why God didn't want the Grigorim making Nephilim—not just because they destroyed His greatest creation in their making, but because it brings the progenitor so much literally unholy pleasure, an incalculable high, their sole remaining comfort. Which may well be why, though they understand its cost, they have never yet been able to give the practice up.

I've seen it done many times since my own birth, far more so than any other of the former Watchers, Penemue Grigorim is not one to deny itself. Every time, I've wanted to do something more than watch, and every time, I've failed to. That's my real sin, above and beyond a mere accident of birth. That's what I have to pay for, even if Penemue never will.

Which is, as you may already have guessed, where Sister Blandina comes in.

Back down on Five Below, the safehouse dormitory level, sisters were going through their motions in shifts: sleeping, praying, practising weaponry. Mother Eulalia stood waiting by the interrogation suite, next to a shuttered wall-sized observation window. From this angle, though upright as ever, she looked exhausted. So odd to think she could only be ten or twelve years older than Blandina or Cecilia, with her eyebrows already turning grey and that puckered seam from empty eye-socket to cheekbone permanently purple-tinged, as though necrotic.

"Sisters," she said, raising her hand in blessing, then rapped lightly on the glass. The shutters turned, revealing a woman, the same shade and size as Blandina's favourite auntie, tied down with double-weight straps, the heavy metal chair she sat in bolted to the steel-slicked floor.

Blandina leaned in, narrowing her eyes. "Looks like a . . . loogaroo, soucouyant?"

"The latter. We found it at Sick Kids', on the oncology ward—that rash of 'heart failures.'"

"Place is a buffet waiting to happen, Mother, I've always said it. We need a permanent lay sister nurse-practitioner in there yesterday, someone with the front desk on speed-text."

"Perhaps after this mission, dear."

The soucouyant listened intently, its very stillness a slap in the face of how any "normal" person would act—kidnapped by crazy church ladies, then left to wait in a room underground with no company but cameras. Shifting to peer closer, Blandina saw a film—brief but reflective, a cop-car red-blue flash—pass across its eyes.

"So," Cecilia asked Mother Eulalia, "what's the procedure, exactly?"

"Oh, nothing too elaborate. Just follow Blandina's lead, and you'll do admirably."

". . . ma'am."

Brave words, Blandina thought. As Mother Eulalia touched the girl's shoulder, she could only hope Cecilia understood what an honour that was, though she suspected she probably didn't.

"I call bad cop," she said, and keyed the door.

In the *Bestiarium*, the soucouyant got a two-page spread with illustrations: two Sorores in full old-school habit holding one by either arm, poised as though to pull it limb from limb. *Found mainly in the Caribbean and West Indies, this creature leaves its skin each night to fly around as a ball of fire, preying on the weak and helpless. . . . Disturbingly, the soucouyant may be unaware of its own evil, dismissing its nightly wanderings as mere bad dreams. In all such cases, proof and cure are one and the same: effective, yet inevitably mortal.*

As the door opened, the soucouyant looked up, desperately trying to get either of them to look it in the eye, and failing. "I swear, I won't say nothin'!" it cried out, heaving itself around with enough weight to make the chair's fastenings screech, before realizing that was probably a little beyond your average hospital janitorial staff member's ability, and going slack again. "Jus' let me go, nah . . . I a poor old lady cyan have nothin' you want, fe sure! I never harm no one!"

Blandina shrugged, snapping on a pair of latex gloves. "Those kids in Ward Eight might have something to say about that," she suggested.

"Check me wallet, me citizenship card! Rose-of-Sharon Hopkinson from Tobago-Saint Andrew, that's me—I ain't kill *nobody*, let alone them poor child, for all they dyin', any rate! And you ain't no law neither, not no-how—"

"I'm fairly sure no one said we *were*," Cecilia retorted, sounding offended. But Blandina waved her silent.

"Rose-of-Sharon," she repeated, leaning in. "Pretty. That from the Bible?"

"'Course it is! Whah sort of nun ya play at bein', girl, ya ain't heard the name?"

Blandina smiled again. "Who said I'm a nun?"

The soucouyant's lush curves drooped, as though deflating slightly; its complexion went almost dun, dewed with fright-sweat. "Think I don't know where I am, nah? Everybody know whah ya do, ya crazy bitches—huntin' an' killin' like it still Burnin' Times! Listen, sister, I'm a good Christian, hear me? Just like you! So just let me go home an' I won't say nothin' on you, on this place; on His sweet face, I swear it—"

"Don't you dare take His name," Blandina told it, evenly. "Not to me. And not to anyone else, either."

And reached down to grab a fisted knot of "Rose-of-Sharon Hopkinson's" plentiful braids in either hand, wrenching so hard in opposite directions that the soucouyant's hairline stretched like dough—ripped outright, rolled back like a snapped blind, gouting jets of black stinking blood. Dipping further as she did, to whisper in one queasily unmoored ear: "Especially when we both know any claim to humanity you have is . . . skin deep at best."

The soucouyant shrieked like a klaxon, voice soaring cartoonishly. "*Oh me Jesus!* I swear by Christ crucify, I *don't know whah ya mean!*"

"Then this should come as quite a surprise."

Blandina hauled again, twice as hard, 'til the thing's whole offending face split wide open. Flame spurted up, emergency traffic flare-bright; the shriek turned roar, louder and more bestial than any human being could manage. Vaguely, Blandina realized that Cecilia was backed against the wall, crossing herself frantically. "Hold position!" she yelled without turning—and damn if the girl didn't, surprisingly enough;

her hands dropped belt-wards, feeling for the rowan-thorn extensible baton they'd both drawn one of this morning, at the armoury.

"Rose-of-Sharon" looked around, true eyes exposed in their naked sockets like little whirling blurs of fire. In the same coarse, warped voice, it groaned: "You terrible woman, whah for yah have to pick on me?"

"You eat children."

"Goat eat grass, tiger eat goat—God make 'em both. How I can help whah He make me?"

"That's *my* job," Blandina told it, without an ounce of sympathy.

The soucouyant made a sound somewhere between a growl and a snivel, false hide bubbling like burnt bacon. When it spoke again, its voice was a hissing, curdled whisper.

"Whah yah want tah know?"

"Where the Watcher angel is. The Nephilim-maker. Penemue—"

"Don't *say*, yah fool! Ain't yah got one lick of sense?" Its tears smoked, acid, down skinless cheeks, as Blandina stood there watching. "Woman," the thing managed, eventually, "yah killin' me, an' all fe nothing."

"Don't waste my time, creature. I'm not always this pleasant."

But it still wouldn't say out loud, so Cecilia passed it her phone, keyboard app already loaded. A brief spate of hunt-and-peck typing later, the soucouyant subsided, apparently too exhausted by its own daring to do anything but sit there and burn while Cecilia ran the results through MapQuest.

"It's legitimate."

Blandina nodded. "All right."

If women could be invested as priests, she would have been in a position to offer extreme unction, even to a creature such as this— would have been *required* to, in fact. Thankfully, however, that decision was still out of her hands.

The *Bestiarium* again, its text cast up on her skull's interior screen, like someone else's memories: *remove its skin so it can never return to its hiding-place, and the soucouyant will burn to ash, consumed by its own fire.*

Blandina reached out, grabbed hold, hauled hard. "Rose-of-Sharon" hung slack in her grip, too beaten to even mount objection. With a final mighty pull, the creature's remaining sausage casing tore open to its waist, lipless mouth stretched impossibly wide, vomiting an eruption of blue-white flame as the rest went up like napalm.

Mother Eulalia took Cecilia's coordinates and went off to pray with the current Anchoress, while Blandina turned towards the mess hall, only to have Cecilia genuinely blindside her: come in nose to nose, jaw jutted pugnacious, and demand without preamble—"What would we have done if she actually *hadn't* known what we wanted?"

Blandina raised one brow. "Same thing, pretty much," she replied. "After which we'd've grabbed up some other variety of kid-eating creature from wherever proved handiest and done it again. But let me guess—you get how we have to kill them, you just have a problem with torturing them, first. Or with me liking it." Then, as Cecilia stared: "Tell me what it was that happened, sister. To you."

"When?"

"Don't play stupid with me. What I mean is, why *this*? Plenty of other orders to choose from if you want not to have to pick out your own clothes the rest of your life, and if you just want to kill, there's the Army. So . . ."

"They thought—they said—" Cecilia paused, feeling around the words. "Police verdict was, it might've been some sort of . . . animal."

"But you knew better. Right?"

"I didn't see how any *animal* could've done that—not to that many people, not all at once. Not and got away clean, without leaving any sort of trace behind. So I did some research, and I formed some theses, and then—I armed up, went out, and tried to do something about it."

Blandina'd heard that part of the tale previously, from Mother Eulalia—a typical stumble-across-an-op-in-progress, want-in origin story, same as her own or almost anybody else's. Still, it showed initiative.

"And let me guess again," she replied. "One of those dead people was somebody you cared for, which was why you couldn't keep your nose out—family, friend. Boyfriend. Girlfriend?"

"Teacher," Cecilia said. "Best I ever had. What happened to *you*?"

Blandina slid Roke's screen-grabs free, shaking the top one out with a snap. "I think *that* happened.

"See that guy, near the back?" Blandina asked. "Sides from being male and white as a sack of sheets, he looks just like a girlfriend I used to have—my best friend ever, only *real* friend. She came to a party my agent threw; I comped her in, 'cause she wanted to meet famous people. And I lost track of her. Thought she was having a good time. In the end, they found her when they were cleaning up, naked under a bunch of coats. She wouldn't talk; parents took her home, wouldn't let her do a rape-kit, wouldn't let me call the police. When I turned up to see her a week later, her father spit on me. That was 'cause she'd hung herself the same morning, on the back of their bathroom door with a belt, from a hook."

"You think *that* guy killed her?"

"Not directly. Whatever *made* him, though, out of *her* . . . that thing's '*father*,' that's what I want."

"Penemue," Cecilia said, so soft her lips barely moved. As though she couldn't help wanting to weigh that ancient name a while, hold it in her mouth like something heavy, something honied.

"Whose name means 'the Inside,'" Blandina agreed. "Curer of human stupidity. For *The name of the fourth is Penemue: he discovered to the children of men bitterness and sweetness;/And pointed out to them every secret of their wisdom./He taught men to understand writing, and the use of ink and paper. . . .*"

Cecilia nodded, quoting from memory: "*Therefore, numerous have been those who have gone astray from every period of the world, even to this day./For men were not born for this, thus with pen and with ink to confirm their faith;/Since they were not created, except that, like the angels, they might remain righteous and pure.*"

The words came easily—for Ordo members, Apocrypha like Enoch were more regularly perused than the actual Bible, if only for practicality. "*Nor would death, which destroys everything, have affected them;/But by this their knowledge they perish, and by this also its power consumes them.*"

"Writing as a form of black magic?"

"Why not? Runes, sigils, seals—that thing Roke showed us. Thoughts are just thoughts; words are air. Write something down, it becomes *concrete*."

"But . . ." Cecilia shook her head again, unable to move on, like disbelief was suddenly her default. ". . . Grigorim are *angels*, Blandina."

"Cast-*down* angels in vile bodies, Origen says—bodies made of flesh, which always dies, you just hit it right. As weapons in His service, we do what we do, nomenclature regardless . . . find the source, knock it out, make sure it can't breed more; classic pest control. Like any other nest."

"You can't *kill* angels, though."

Blandina regarded her still-gloved hands, smeared wrist-high with hot ash from the soucouyant's dissolution. Beneath the latex, her unpolished fingernails looked like blisters waiting to form.

"Ten years I've been at this, sister," she said. "Longer than anybody else, except for Mother Eulalia, and this is what I know, for sure: I can *kill* anything I can get my hands on if I'm told the right way to do it."

"But . . . oh, my Lord. I don't know why I'm even asking this."

"Go on."

". . . what if God won't let you?"

He's let me so far, with everything else.

"Then I want to hear Him tell me so," Blandina said, at last. "To my face."

And here, at last, I feel constrained to confess how I have stage-managed much of this situation. To take responsibility is not in my nature; I am made to hang back, play attendance—be acted upon, not to act. Yet in my quiet way, I am still capable of strategy.

As children of Penemue Grigorim, our mother-Maker, we all know that others are involved. For me, that was indeed Sister Blandina's ill-fated friend Veronique Louvain, called Ronni. She avoids her name even while telling her story, which I can well understand; love is always painful for humans, especially once lost.

I have made it my business to learn Ronni Louvain by heart, tracking her through every available source. I have lain in her bed, breathing what scent remains, studying a single skin-flake like a lace pattern. I have spoken to her mother at the supermarket, changed her father's tires. And I have followed Blandina from a distance, watching her kill her righteous way through this world. I have seen her pray in the aftermath, invoking His grace, spitting forth blessings like curses. I have seen her rage, daily, but never weep.

And now, at last, I force the issue. Bring this bitter crop we share to harvest by steering Blandina and Penemue together.

My Maker will not see her coming, not least because it simply does not think enough on me—one amongst many, only, made and thrown away over the millennia—to consider me worthy of distrust.

"A visit to the Anchoress, first," Mother Eulalia had decided. The prospect made even Blandina wary, but she at least knew what was coming. Not so Cecilia, fumbling hopeful down through the dimness (all anchoresses took a Vow of Shadows, along with their other vows) while they followed a trail of luminescent paint—arrows on the walls, footprints on the floor—towards their destination.

"You've never done this before, dear."

"No, Mother."

"But you're familiar with the terminology, I expect."

"*Anchorism,* late 16th century: from the Old English *anchor,* 'recluse, hermit,' itself from the Mediaeval Latin *anchorita* or *anchorite.* 'A person who, for religious reasons, withdraws from secular life entirely, choosing a prayer-filled, ascetic, Eucharist-focused mode of existence.'"

Makes it sound so simple, Blandina thought. "And our anchoresses?"

"Former members of the Order, now retired."

"Don't have all too many of those, do we?"

"Not that I've heard of, no."

It was common practice for the bishop's representative to say office for the dead over an anchoress as she entered her cell, to signify her rebirth to a spiritual life of solitary communion with God and His angels. Roke himself had recited at least two of those, including one for the woman they were about to consult, before affixing the bishop's seal to the fresh-laid concrete across her door. After which the plasterers came by, white-washing over everything but a little flap-door at the bottom and a squint at the top, known as a "hagioscope"—the first for meals, such as they were, while the second provided a tiny one-way window back out into the world its occupant had left behind.

"She took the name Kentigerna on making her vows, against our usual rule," Mother Eulalia explained, "since that particular saint was a hermit, not a martyr. But given her capacities, I believe she might have been thinking more of St. Kentigern Mungo, when she made the choice; he was noted for his miracles. As she was for hers."

"Should I address her as Sister Kentigerna, then?"

Mother Eulalia shook her head, glancing Blandina's way so that she would feel free to answer. And: "No," Blandina obliged her. "She's the Anchoress—we've only got the one. And you shouldn't *address* her at all, if you can help it."

One more corner, and there they were at last, outside the closet-sized room in which the best seer the Ordo ever recruited would spend the rest of her life. More paint rimmed its outline, a phantom lintel propped by two ghost-posts.

"I see you," a rasp of a voice greeted them through a vent in the wall, making Cecilia jump. "Eulalia, Blandina—and you, newcomer, unblooded *girl*. Number Twenty-Three. Vic . . . *toria*."

"Cecilia."

"Not yet, you're not. Not 'til you profess fully."

"Excuse me, I've *made* my vows—"

"The simple ones, only. You've told God you love him, and isn't that nice. But has He told *you* the same? Not yet . . . maybe not ever."

The harsh words weren't aimed at her, but Blandina shrugged

anyhow and rapped her knuckles sharply against the door, making it ring. Reminding the woman inside: "She's *Mother* Eulalia now, Kentigerna. You'll give her that much respect."

"*My* Mother was Apollonia, witch-seed, and she died so *this* one could live—you, too. You let yourself get carried away and saw her carried out in halves. Head *and* body."

"I know my sins. Did my penance too, years back."

"You should do more."

Beside her, Blandina felt Cecilia stiffen, but Mother Eulalia simply sighed. "We need to consult," she told the squint-hole, patiently. "On a matter of some urgency."

"Oh yes, most honoured war-leader," the Anchoress's vicious whisper agreed. "Please don't hesitate to ask if it's ever a *good* idea to treat one of our Creator's first-made children as though they were something you can throw silver, salt, or fire at, and just hope it goes away."

"This one is Fallen," Blandina pointed out. "Been like that since before Cain got his mark. All we want is to get it to move on."

"And then it's someone else's problem, eh?"

"You said it."

Cecilia looked at her feet.

"If you *did* happen to have some sort of special knowledge," Eulalia went on, mildly, as though the Anchoress hadn't spoken at all, "we'd be *very* grateful to have it. Blandina, in particular."

A few breaths went by, hoarsely mirrored through the grate, as the Anchoress mulled this over.

"They hurt themselves to stay here," she said, eventually. "This is most important to remember when facing the Host."

"Grigorim aren't—"

"Oh, shut your mouth for one single minute, Judas Rusk's by-blow—long enough to learn, or go ask elsewhere. At least that *Mother* of yours knows enough to know she knows nothing. Physics tells us everything in the universe is just energy and emptiness in some sort of combination, the only difference between ape and angel being just how close together things can get before exploding. Which means that, whenever Hostlings *of any sort* come to earth, they transmute themselves into the idea of flesh through molecular manipulation, and since they aren't really corporeal to begin with, when you damage them, they fly apart and revert to the Eternal."

"Meaning?"

"*Meaning*, all you can do to an angel is deflect it a while and hope it turns its attention elsewhere."

"How?" Blandina asked through her teeth.

"*Think*, Blandina. The longer they remain enfleshed voluntarily, the more 'earthly' they become. They were made to be extensions of the Maker's will, already perfected, so they can't change; they aren't supposed to *want* to change, even to improve themselves. Any personal ambition on an angel's part is corruption—even the ambition to do good, not that *that*'s what Penemue's been doing. To pursue your own ends is how you start to Fall."

Mother Eulalia nodded. "Yes, I see."

"Do you? Rusk's daughter, what does this angel do? What do we *know* it does, from your own evidence?"

"It makes . . . copies of itself. Nephilim. Degrades human beings to breed children. Pretends to be a little Creator."

"Yes. And therein lies the only part of it—or *parts* of it—you can hope to harm. What hurts a possessed body will work just fine on Nephilim, and with far less fallout; they've never *been* human, after all." Kentigerna gave a great grunt of effort, apparently settling back into whatever position they'd found her in. "Now go," she muttered, voice fuzzing down into exhaustion. "You tire me, both of you . . . the pretender, too. Go dash your brains out against Heaven's door and see what it gets you."

Eulalia bowed her head. "Thank you, Anchoress."

"I don't want *your* thanks. Just a promise . . ."

"Name it."

A pause. "That you'll leave me alone from now on," that dry scratch of a voice replied, so hoarse now it made even Blandina's throat hurt to hear. "Don't try to make me talk anymore, or eat. Just send someone down to check if I respond, and when I cease to, plaster the slot door over. Screw the memorial plaque in on top, and let me sleep."

The despair in her tone was catching. And though not-quite-darkness pressed hard about them, Blandina could still see Cecilia's moist eyes skitter this way and that, searching for what she already knew she'd find: similar beaten-bronze rectangles trailing away on either side, each bearing a name, a date.

Only fit that they live out the rest of their lives in their coffins, she thought. *Being already dead, and prayed over.*

Leaning forward, lips only inches from the grate, Blandina told the

Anchoress: "I'll do that part myself, unless you'd rather I not."

"Do as you please, Atia Rusk," the Anchoress said, wearily. "You always do."

From then on, she was silent.

This time, Cecilia barely waited 'til Mother Eulalia was out of earshot to turn to Blandina, demanding: "Something I should know?"

"You? Lots, about a lot. I'm taking it you mean what she meant, though. When she called me—"

"Rusk. As in the Five-Family Coven? Roke and Druir on the one side, Glouwer, Devize, and *Rusk* on the other . . ."

"That's right. My birth-name traces to Judas, Alizoun Rusk's son, born in the Witch-House at Eye. Fostered by good folk after his mother's burning, he broke free and made his way to the Seychelles, where my kin come from. Made a pile out of ships and trading, old Judas, enough to buy Veritay Island; owned slaves too, and he did what masters do. My Mémé used to tell us bedtime stories about his great-granddaughter, a woman named Tante Ankolee, Angelique Rusk, *powerful an' puissant, who buy she-self out-bondage with her gift.* . . . Her son, Collyer, would be my three times great-grandfather."

"Which makes you—"

"Just another bride of Christ, like you, redeemed with His sacrifice. There's nothing of Alizoun, Judas, *or* Tante Ankolee ever came down *my* way but freckles in summer. But Kentigerna felt it from the start, and she never took to me, even though Mother Apollonia chose to believe I meant what I said then, same way Mother Eulalia does, now. So I made my vows, and Christ alone knows I keep them."

"And only God can judge?"

"He certainly hasn't said any different, not in all these years."

They were almost to the armoury door, where Sister Prisca would have a raft of things for them to choose from—blades cooled in holy water, cold iron chased with silver, their cross-hilt handles carved from fully provenanced saints' bones. Blandina felt her fingers curl, palms itching to find themselves filled, and the battle-longing rose up high in her, stronger than any other hunger.

But there was Cecilia, still, blocking her way, nose wrinkled and eyebrows hiked. Not quite *asking* as talking her way through it all like some slow problem, logical to a fault—"Mac Roke made vows too, though. Didn't he?"

"Took them and broke them. You've seen *his* family."

"But you must've *known*, like the Anchoress did with you. I mean—

it's not as if he was hiding it. His name's *Roke*."

Blandina paused, made herself think her next words over, carefully as possible. The very thought of revisiting Roke's betrayal made her so tired she could have wept, but didn't; her tears weren't hers to give away, not anymore. They belonged to Him, like everything else.

"I . . . felt something," she agreed, reluctantly. "From him; *for* him. Thought it was just friendship, or maybe the other—I'm not old, or dead. But then . . ."

Christ, it really did hurt, still. Enough to make her blaspheme, at least interiorly.

"We all have our something," she finished, at last. "I've told mine. And even if he'd never told his, he might've done good work for us, he'd just kept his word. But—he lied."

Cecilia gave her a look that verged on pity. Good thing she couldn't tell how it made Blandina want to punch her in the throat.

"To you, you mean," she said.

Blandina snorted. "Who d'you think I think I *am*, sister? I mean to *God*."

She tapped the door-lock, felt it give way. Stared the eye-scan down and strode through as the blast-shielding slid smoothly apart, Cecilia following behind.

"Would *you* ever submit?" Cecilia asked, unexpectedly. "Be immured, like Kenti—like the Anchoress?"

"There's no one can order you to do it, sister, if that's your worry. You have to volunteer."

"Why *would* you, though? Why did she?"

"Because she saw things she didn't like," Blandina told her. "Just sometimes, at first, then all the time, 'til she couldn't see anything else. You can't fight, like that. So she opted out, went contemplative; prays all day and night on the Ordo's behalf, using her visions like a direct telephone line to Him."

"Roke said he saw something too, just before he withdrew. The thing that wasn't an angel."

"He said a lot of stuff on his way out the door."

"Have *you* seen anything?"

"Same things you have, all the bloody time. *We fight monsters*."

"Goddamn it, you know what I—"

Blandina rounded on her, hissing: "*Yes*. But you don't *ever* take His name in vain, Vicky-Cecilia, no matter what we're talking about—not here, not near me. You don't *dare*."

"I'm very sorry, Sister Blandina. I wasn't aware you had a monopoly on faith, around here."

Huh.

Looked like little Cecilia had a break-point, after all. Blandina studied her, measuringly, and was pleased to see her shift into fighting stance, though her hands stayed unfisted. As though Blandina's attention constituted a threat in itself.

Good, Blandina thought, approvingly.

"I can't do what Roke does," she told her, at last. "Bad blood aside, I just don't have that capacity. So no, I've never seen anything made me question my vocation, so I've never had to make the decision to stay or go. I do one thing only, well enough to merit the front-line, and no matter what every other Rusk before me might've got up to, I do what *I* do for God. Odds are, I'll be *long* dead before I ever have to consider making Kentigerna's choice."

"You hope," Cecilia replied.

It comes to pass now, just as I hoped for. The Ordo descends upon us with Sisters Blandina and Cecilia in the fore, Mother Eulalia and the others behind. They follow Rose-of-Sharon Hopkinson's coordinates—a strip mall just across the streetcar tracks, where Mimico blends into the very last of Queen Street East—and find the bowling alley turned club where Penemue Grigorim sits in one of the farthest booths, waiting to be paid homage to by fresh potential victims. Blandina's team arrives in an ambulance and comes in through the back, some dressed as paramedics, others as police; a tossed mixture of smoke bombs, flares, and flash-bangs goes in first to disperse most humans, who will later remember only the vague, traumatizing impression of a kitchen explosion, pulled fire alarms, a general scrambling rout.

Blandina cuts her deft way through those who linger, a blessed blade in either hand—sparing anything that bleeds red and hamstringing anything that doesn't, neat as any surgeon, while Cecilia and the rest field the ones she kicks aside. She is a pleasure to watch work even for me, and I have seen far more than my due share of suffering.

All the while, I hear Mother Eulalia praying under her breath: calling on the contradictorily titled Saint Michael Archangel, Heaven's foremost assassin, in her sister-daughters' hour of need. A comfortless mantra, breathed hot through slaughter.

Behold the Cross of the Lord; be scattered ye hostile powers.
The Lion of the tribe of Judah has conquered the root of David.

Let Thy mercies be upon us, O Lord.
As we have hoped in Thee.
O Lord, hear my prayer.
And let my cry come unto Thee.
O Glorious Prince of the heavenly host, St. Michael the
Archangel, defend us in the battle and in the terrible warfare
that we are waging against the principalities and powers,
against the rulers of this world of darkness. Come to the aid
of man, whom Almighty God created immortal, made in His
own image and likeness, and redeemed at a great price from the
tyranny of Satan; help us against all the other unclean spirits
who wander about the world for the injury of the human race
and the ruin of souls. Amen.

*Amen, amen. Phantom bells tolling through the thick air, grating painful
against my Maker's faith-scarred skin. Blandina barely seems to hear them,
though she moves to their beat, as if choreographed; they hook her muscles
taut, loft her step, suffuse and encircle her with a core-hot protection that
both cheers and wounds. It forms a shield for my siblings to break themselves
against, severed or transfixed at the disinterested pleasure of He who made
not only the board, not only the pieces on it, but the universe both board and
pieces exist inside.*

*A thin thread of extra longing winds upward, meanwhile, raising
Eulalia's prayers all the higher: Anchoress Kentigerna's contribution to the
cause, wafting nerve-thin from the pit she squats in. That concrete cocoon
from which she hopes to break, remade, and enter through those gates such
as I can never even hope to glimpse, let alone approach . . .*

*Blandina is almost at the back, now. She can see my Maker, its long legs
crossed, watching her carve her way through its offspring. Bleak and blazing
in its barely there outfit, hair like a singing flame, eyes like lit glass. Penemue
Grigorim, sower of language and artifice, for whom the word "exquisite"
is nothing but a dull, crude insult. And now I am close enough to hear her
thoughts: a memory of Maccabee Roke, telling her the real reason angels, as
Rainer Maria Rilke tells us, are so terrible—*

"Because they're evil? Ugly? Because whatever the Bible tells us
they are, they're not?"

"No, B. Just the opposite. Because they're *so* beautiful, they ruin
you for anything else."

*Lovely as a weapon, as a curse; yes, that is Penemue. Lovely as the very
living breath of God.*

It could never get away with half the things it regularly does, were it not.

As Blandina turns her swords our Maker's way at last, my eldest sibling throws himself in front of her, only to find a blade piercing his throat. Something indefinite exits from him through the eyes, plunging sharply downwards to dissolve against the floor. The illusion of Penemue's face observes this, but does not seem to react.

:Atia Rusk,: *it names her.* **:I expected you sooner.:**

Blandina pulls her sword free of my eldest sibling's wreckage, already curling in on itself, drawing a puff of desiccated blood-dust. Correcting, as she does: "It's Blandina—Sister Blandina. One name and a title. Not that hard."

:Yes, little zealot, I know. But it was as Atia our paths first crossed, yes?:

"So you do remember."

Penemue nods in my direction. **:Why not?:** *it asks.* **:I have him to recall his mother's face to me.:**

This, then, is how we first meet. Blandina knows me at once, both from the security feed at Curia and her own images of Ronni Louvin, so well-loved—but that does not make her stare any less pitiless, or make her judge me any more worthy of mercy.

:One could call him your cousin, I suppose,: *Penemue muses.* **:A useful term.:**

"He's nothing to me. None of them are."

:Oh, I believe you have been told differently, and not too long gone, either.:

Blandina blinks, and again, her thoughts nudge mine, hearing Mac Roke explain: ". . . all monsters descend from the Grigorim, through their Nephilim: witches and warlocks, psionics, weres, vampires, the Fae . . ."

:I know where all my seed is sown,: *Penemue tells her,* **:in its combinations, even unto its last generation. For even as Alizoun Rusk was Nephilim-born, at least in part, so too are you, no matter that you may have sworn yourself to *my* old master, the Maker of All.:**

"What makes you think I'm interested? Faith is *my* shield. I don't have any magic—never did, never will."

:Are you so sure? You have lived a long time for one of your Order—survived incredible things, all but unwounded, when others fell about you. Fought toe to toe with horrors, made them fear your name . . .:

"*His* name. Only His."

:So you say. But if you claim you do not enjoy your reputation, you are a liar—and lying is a sin.:

Blandina and Penemue speak quickly, voices low, while Sister Cecilia and the others continue to fight their way forward. Behind Penemue's back, Mother Eulalia has just entered with fresh troops; she is less than a stride away, mouthing orders Blandina probably does not see, but Cecilia certainly does: Stop, desist, disengage.

Time is ticking; someone may have called the real police, the real fire department. These incursions need to be brief by nature, and to leave no trace behind.

"Enough about me," *Blandina tells my Maker.* "Time to go, Watcher-no-more. We took a poll—you are very much *not* wanted."

:We both know you cannot do me harm.:

Blandina smiles. "Not directly," *she says.*

And looks at me again.

:You think to denude me of my Host? I can always make more.:

"Not here, though. Or I kill each and every one of them, starting with him, and leave you to walk out of here alone."

:Your Ronni would be truly dead, then. All lingering trace of her gone from this world, never to return.:

"She's dead no matter what I do, so *make your call.*"

Penemue laughs outright, a shaken ice-bell trill—something I have seldom heard, but often enough to know it presages nothing good.

:I can do far worse things than kill you,: it tells her, rising. **:You think you understand, but you do not. If you insult me further, I will do them all and revel in it.:**

Blandina nods. "Then stop talking and show me," *she says.*

As she speaks, Penemue is already in motion, so fast it slips between microseconds to occupy virtually the same space she does, very atoms turning sidelong until it is nothing but light and empty space. One hand solidifies around Blandina's left wrist and flexes with a bone-break snap. The other arm plunges shoulder-deep through chest and ribage, barely missing her spine; its fingers emerge to curl around her hip, pulling her closer. One sword falls, the other droops, as Pememue's glorious lips descend—that glowing mouth whose touch refts soul from body, tears grace in half, and spawns such as myself from the debris.

Blandina fights with all her considerable strength, but it makes no difference. She grates out a prayer that covers her own lips in protective mesh, only to see it spark and wither apart against the force of Penemue's breath.

:He thought, and we appeared, the first among all,: *my Maker has told us, often enough.* **:This is why nothing we have done, or do, can separate us so far from Him that his Word can be used against us.:** *But though none of us ever doubted it spoke truth, this is the first time I have ever seen the claim tested.*

Most people do not fight an angel, not if they know what they face. Most people would not dare to try.

Cecilia starts forward, only to meet my grasp halfway; I grapple her down, kicking, and press her to my breast. So it is Mother Eulalia who bridges the gap instead, twisting herself between them—Mother Eulalia who takes Penemue's kiss like a bullet, single eye rolling back, overtaken too quickly to see her predicament draw the scream mere bodily pain never could from Blandina's lips.

The bliss of union is two-way, as ever. It distracts Penemue, letting Blandina slip free, her right-hand blade still tight-clutched, wet face intent. Her other wrist now limp-hanging, she levers herself up, raises the sword as Penemue stays crouched over Mother Eulalia, joined at the jaws; its halo spreads and thickens 'til it covers them both, like some sort of caul. Then humps up, an amoeba caught in mid-split, releasing a flesh-wrapped shard of Mother Eulalia's raped soul to float free, like spume . . .

Thin crying spikes, muffled, mewling. My newest sibling, mourning for its own birth.

Pinned beneath me, Cecilia—only now realizing what has taken place—flails and shrieks, bucking so hard she knocks her own head on the floor. Mother Eulalia's chest pops, air-starved, ecstasy-smothered. And Sister Blandina thrusts her blade through the new-thrown Nephilim, pinning it to the wall—stabs into it, and watches it shrivel.

Lucky, I think. And let my hold on Cecilia slip, rising to meet Blandina with arms outstretched.

Later, recuperating, Blandina could only see the rest in snatches. Penemue Grigorim looking up, not quite startled, finally roused from its repast; Ronni's "son" under Blandina's sword, pinned like a bug. That *thing* its attentions had ripped from Mother Eulalia, first and last breath still lung-caught, already drying to dust.

:Great woman of renown, martial papesse,: the Watcher angel named her, mockingly. **:Crusader, amongst crusaders.:**

Those titles, which she'd always craved, like garbage in that moon-pure mouth. Like ashes in hers.

:Only a monster can hunt monsters—you know that, now. As Maccabee Roke always did.:

"Wasn't for things like you, there wouldn't *be* any monsters," Blandina told it, throat raw, leaning on her weapon. Trying not to look down, for fear of seeing the last few traces of Ronni's sweet face crumble away.

:Yet God made *us*, too—a conundrum. Or a mistake, perhaps?:

"God makes no mistakes."

:Well, then.:

A massive perfumed sigh enveloped Blandina, forcing her eyes closed; some great pinion gliding by, barely brushing her cheek. She would find a caress turned cut there, when she finally thought to look—infection-bright, already keloiding. And then Penemue was gone, leaving only that scar behind.

At her feet, Mother Eulalia turned on her side, vomiting feebly. Behind them both, Cecilia was weeping openly, pitched forwards on hands and knees, too laid low to even attempt to rise.

"That should've been me," she said, over and over. "That should've been me."

"Don't blaspheme," Blandina told her. "If it should've, it would've."

God makes no mistakes.

I have to think that.

Her own tears scalded, unshed.

"The Ordo is yours," Mother Eulalia told her, through the wall. "As we both knew it would be, one day."

"Yes, Mother," Blandina said.

A hollow sketch of the older woman's laugh reached her, pithed by Penemue's kiss. "I know I can trust you to do your duty, *Mother* Blandina," she corrected her, gently. "Diligent as you've been, especially in war."

Blandina swallowed, mouth dry. "Not always so obedient, though," she said.

"Not always, no. But more often than I expected."

Blandina spread the concrete and slid the last brick in herself. It was the least she could do, considering; they had two anchoresses now, and that was her fault, if anyone's.

Cecilia was in her cell, praying—ostensibly preparing for her final vows, but Blandina wasn't convinced. A wound to the faith could fester faster than almost any other sort of injury, especially if left untreated.

"I'm going out," she told the front desk's minder. "You have my number. Anything comes up, just ring through."

"Yes, Mother. May I say where you've gone?"

Blandina paused a moment, wondering if she should prevaricate, then decided there wasn't much point. "Curia," she replied, shortly. "To see Mac Roke."

"Oh," the sister said, taken aback. "Is that . . . wise?"

Probably not, Blandina thought.

"Is anything?" she replied.

The trip seemed longer than usual. When Roke saw her face, however, he bit down hard on whatever quip he might've had brewing, a show of restraint Blandina was annoyed to find herself appreciating, if only for the second and a half it took him to glance down at her hand and see the ring. His shoulders tightened, visibly, as the realization hit.

You loved her too, once, Blandina was mildly surprised to recall. *Of course you did.*

"Mother . . ." he greeted her, voice carefully schooled.

"Roke."

"That's me," he agreed. Then added, stepping aside to let her in: "Glad to see *some* things don't change."

He didn't mention her cast, for which she was also grateful. The verdict had been predictable; it would pain her, likely for the rest of her life, off and on. But one day, she *would* wield both swords again, sooner than some might like to think.

The usual tangle of cursed and blasphemous objects crowded his countertop, next to an open log-book; she must've interrupted him taking inventory, though he didn't seem to have gotten very far.

"I could make coffee, if you want some," he offered, but she shook her head.

"What I need is a favour," she said, instead. "To make someone forget."

"Everything?"

"Something specific. Fairly recent."

"Hmmm. Well, that'd be glamer, Si—Mother. Classic Fae magic, kind they teach in the Druir *brugh*'s grammarye and not to fostered-out quarterlings like myself. Sure I'm up to it?"

"There isn't much you're not capable of, that I've observed."

"Flatterer." He tapped his lips, thinking. "Actually, though . . . if I'm honest, the sort of subtle work you're talking about *is* a bit beyond my ken. Sorry."

"That thing you had visiting last time could do it, I'd bet."

"Saracen? Well, yeah, obviously. But you *really* don't want to owe him anything, B."

Blandina gave him a grim smile. "You let me worry about that."

More questions hung between them, unasked, mainly on account of blatancy: *Is this about what happened to Mother Eulalia? Was it a Grigori? Should I be . . . worried?*

Always, she thought back, unsure if he could hear. *Live in worry, like I do. The way our bad blood doomed us to, since before either of us was born . . . cousin.*

She could demand the same treatment for herself, it only now occurred to her, if she wanted to; though the burn she'd given him was probably long-healed at this point, she had no doubt that Saracen Druir would love to rummage around inside *her* head, if she let him. Remove the pain of Mother Eulalia's sacrifice on her behalf, then sally back out into the world with her trust in God intact, ready for whatever horror it threw her way . . .

But no. Too easy. *Someone* had to bear the weight of her mistakes, if only in order to make them count.

Cecilia deserves a clean slate, Blandina told herself, hoping it wasn't mere sophistry, blatant self-justification. *The same way the Ordo needs a lieutenant, someone to fill my old slot. I have to be practical. To do not just what's right, but what's* best, *for everyone.*

(:Oh, yes—do tell yourself that, not-daughter, if you must,: Penemue Grigorim's voice replied, approvingly, from the dark behind her eyes. **:Act according to the Ordo's interests, especially where they intersect with your own, then confess and be absolved, as is your . . . human . . . right.:)**

A monster, fighting monsters. Roke had been the same, once—but then, Roke had never loved God the way Blandina tried to, not even with a collar 'round his neck.

"You know my name?" she asked him, suddenly, and watched him shrug, uncomfortable.

"Your *name's* Blandina," he said.

"The other one, idiot."

". . . yeah, I do." A pause. "Did *you* know, though, about me—us? Back before?"

She nodded, admission getting easier each time she made it. "Felt something, from the minute we met. Didn't know what 'til I read your file."

"So we'll never know if it'd've made a difference."

"It would've always made a difference."

Roke rolled those poison-blue eyes. "Hard fucking world you live in, B. 'Forgive us our trespasses as we forgive those who trespass against us'—how 'bout that one?"

"If I don't ask it, I don't have to give it."

"Right. Because nobody could *ever* do this job as good as *you*, Nephilim genes or not."

For a second, Blandina heard Cecilia chime in, noting: *Not like he was hiding it. His name's* Roke. And caught herself thinking in response: *So? I never asked any slack, or cut any, even though* my *name's Rusk. Does that make it better or worse?*

"That's what Eulalia claimed," was all she said, to which Roke simply sighed, replying:

"I only wish you believed her."

Well, I don't, Blandina thought. *But I still love her enough to pretend otherwise, most days.*

"Tell your cousin what I need," she told him, feeling her way towards the door. "Tell him . . . tell him I'll meet his price, within reason."

"Saracen's not always reasonable."

"Neither am I."

Roke's mouth quirked. "Nope," he said. "I think he knows it, too."

Once outside, Blandina stopped to let her eyes clear, sniffing sharply. She considered her name.

According to Irenaeus, bishop of Lyon, the summer of 177 was marked by an increasing hostility to Christians. First, they were prohibited from entering public places, then hounded and attacked by mobs, assaulted, beaten, stoned. Finally, they were dragged into the forum, accused, and—after admitting their beliefs—flung in prison. Through a willful misunderstanding of Scripture and ritual, the pagan people of Lyons had become convinced all Christians were cannibals, perverts, incestuous rapists. Every day, new victims were arrested, awaiting mass execution on August the first, a holiday set aside to celebrate the greatness of Rome.

Such occasions usually required the governor to display his patriotism by sponsoring lavish public entertainment, but the year before, the Senate had passed a new law to offset the cost of gladiatorial shows. Now, the governor could legally offer the torture and execution of any condemned criminals who were non-citizens as spectacle, instead of expensive athletic exhibitions.

Among the condemned was a female slave named Blandina. *All of us were in terror,* Irenaeus's account states, *yet Blandina was filled with such power that even those who were taking turns to torture her in every way, from dawn to dusk, were weary and exhausted. They admitted that they were beaten, that there was nothing further they could do to her, and they* were surprised that she was still breathing, for her entire body was broken and torn.

In the amphitheatre, Blandina was exposed to wild animals, ran a gauntlet of whips, and was roasted in an iron seat over a raging fire. Surviving all this, she was at last put in a net and tossed by a bull. The audience admitted that no woman had ever suffered so much, in their experience.

While being tortured, Blandina repeatedly refuted the stories about Christians, saying: *I am a Christian, and nothing vile is done amongst us.* But when first assigned to translate the story in Latin class as a novice, the former Atia Rusk convinced herself that the phrase she kept having to transcribe was *I am a Christian, and nothing vile* can be *done* to us. She remembered meditating for hours on Blandina's martyrdom, thinking: *That's what I want to be, impenetrable. A witness for the world. A marvel.*

Pride, all of it, then as now. Pride, raw and rank, cardinal as any other sin.

But I can do my part, even so.

(*Hard fucking world you live in, B.*)

"It *has* to be," she replied, out loud. And leaned her forehead against the nearest wall, oblivious to the stares of passersby, so the stone would cool it.

Throat tight, she began to pray.

The end, though nothing really ends. I know that, now.

Barred from Heaven and Hell alike, I drift unseen through this world, rudderless, unmoorable. I watch the people who clog its skin, admiring the way their souls pulse, lighting their very bones. I see my cousins scurrying about, invisible by comparison—creatures like Rose-of-Sharon Hopkinson, Saracen Druir, Maccabee Roke. Blandina too, all things being equal.

We were made, the same as every other being. Allowed to flourish, not extirpated in our conception. And who could possibly make this decision, in the end, if not God? His silence may not constitute consent, but is it proof of condemnation?

If God loves us, then all things are possible. We may even create our own Heaven, at last, one day.

If one is required.

HELPLESS (2013)

This one truth, above all others: all things, fast or slow, move toward their end. Of that you can be sure.

That morning, when Carraclough Devize sat down to breakfast, her mother's ghost came drifting into the kitchen before she'd even had time to milk her granola—silver cord trailing behind like half-frayed abseil rope, paying out farther and stretching thinner with every "step," like usual. But then she saw the cord's end and knew.

Today's the day.

"Gala," she called to her, quietly. "Gala, hey—hey, Geillis. Geillis Carraclough Devize." Then, before she could quite remember to stop herself: "Mommy."

No reply, one way or the other, not that Carra'd really expected any; Gala'd never much liked being reminded she was old enough to have a child, let alone an adult one. But here they were, nevertheless: Carra forty-plus, and her mother dead for almost half a year, now. And finally—*finally*—looking as though she might have figured that part out.

She watched Gala put a hand against the plaster, fingers melting slowly in, first tip, then nail, then knuckle; saw her frown at the sight, grey-shot hair still let down for the bed she'd died in. Carra couldn't ever remember seeing it cut, aside from the times she'd caught Gala trimming split ends into the sink, working a particularly snarled knot free with embroidery scissors. She supposed the habit'd been catching— her own mop, so pale it might as well already have turned white, was long enough it made her head hurt if she piled it up, which was why she kept it in braids, instead.

That one summer he'd stayed here, sharing Carra's bed like the only slightly incestuous brother she'd never had, Jude Hark Chiu-wai liked to say the detritus in their bathroom alone could give every witch in Ontario something to curse them with and still have enough left over to make a nest. That would've been over twenty years ago, with their friendship taking up seven, their separation thirteen. And what was he doing, now? Dealing with his own ghosts, no doubt, of which she was sure he had plenty . . .

You always were pretty, even at the end, Carra thought, studying her mother's hand, now sunk to its wrist. Feeling herself tear up for the first time since the funeral, standing with Dr. Guilden Abbott's hand on her arm, knowing he only meant to comfort her, but really wishing he wouldn't try. While, at the same time, doing her level best to ignore the way every other ghost within range was making begging eyes at her, a line of bruisy letters snaking out across the back of her hand from under one low-tugged sleeve: SORRY SO SORRY SO SO SORRY FOR YOU BEING ALONE . . .

(Except that she was always alone, and never. Never really.)

"Gala," Carra heard herself say, one last time, voice barely a whisper. Then watched the woman who'd given her everything, this curse of a gift included, walk straight through the wall without looking back, never to return.

By 11:00, she and Sylvester Horse-Kicker were having brunch in the Kirlian Grill, the Freihoeven Institute's unofficial cafeteria. Carra had an appointment with Dr. Abbott later that afternoon, ostensibly to "discuss something," which didn't sound all too good, so it'd seemed only practical to combine the two.

She remembered how careful Sylvester had been when bringing her back to the Clarke after their moment in the storage locker—gentle, less like a keeper than a friend, or even something more. It'd constituted a wake-up call of sorts; for far too long, she'd been drifting, tracing the same elliptical orbit from her nice, safe, little padded cell—practically the same one every time, as though they held it in reserve—to her cramped bedroom at Gala's and back. Spending those long months after Gala's final diagnosis administering tests and archiving collected data on the Freihoeven's dime, scraping by, continuing to take advantage of a debt incurred thirty years ago: accidental injury in the line of "duty," for which Dr. Abbott had given her a job ever since, if not exactly a home.

I can be your employer or your—surrogate—father, Carra, he'd told her, when things were at their worst, *but not both. So pick one.* This when she was barely coherent most days, showing up to work wearing a disintegrating t-shirt for a dress, teetering on the edge of abdication: just let herself fall, wake up back in the no-sharps room while Gala ushered herself through the process of dying alone, fast or slow, depending on how much reserve money they did or didn't have.

But even when dealing with a mother who'd fallen down as many times on the job as Gala had, it did seem a wee bit—skimpy.

So she'd made herself look Abbott in the eye instead, nodding slightly, and replied: *Uh huh. Or . . . you could be neither, I guess. Given that's what you are.*

She'd never seen him flinch before, that she could recall. Poor Dr. Abbott, his former dapperness wearing rapidly threadbare, still hellbent on carrying on the Jay and Jay legacy when every subsequent generation perceived their influence on the field as less relevant, even in a field where past-life regression was taken semi-seriously. Yet if he only stopped to think about it sometime soon, he might still manage to figure out how that urge to canonize his dead mentors had already rendered him almost indistinguishable from any of the séance-goers she'd caught trying to look up her full-body leotard out of the corner of their supposedly shut eyes.

Besides which, she'd known the Drs. Jay better than he ever had or would. She'd been there when they died, after all.

She'd *felt* it.

Bought at the apex of her "good" years—when Carra's fame as a child medium paid so much over their bills they were socking it away even after subtracting the percentage that went down Gala's throat, up her nose, into her boyfriends' pockets—the house Carra lived in was a bit of a trap these days, but at least she owned it, free and clear: Gala's name was on the lease, with Carra the co-signatory, not to mention Gala's only heir. So even if what Abbott had to say meant finally losing her only real source of employment, she'd be okay. They'd had the water, light, and heat turned off on them before, in their time, and survived; she didn't need things to be comfortable, just stable, especially since she wouldn't be counting on Ontario's mental health system for food and shelter anymore, from now on.

Because: "I'm not coming back," she'd told Paul the orderly, on her way out, that last time. And: "Gonna hold you to that," Paul had replied with not one single shred of irony.

"What are you thinking about?" Sylvester asked.

Here's the part where I'd look up and smile, if I smiled, it occurred to Carra. "Oh, uh . . . a bunch of things," she replied, "most of them probably not mine. I always have to concentrate pretty hard to tell what actually originates with *me*, as opposed to whatever might've just leaked in."

"I can see how that would be a problem."

She shrugged. "I'm used to it. People just give off a . . . general hum, you know, like a light fixture—dead or alive, it doesn't really matter. The only person I've ever *not* felt that from was my friend Jude."

"Jude Hark Chiu-wai? I met him, once."

"Oh? I'd've thought he was before your time."

"A little. But Abbott put him on that pull-list for clean-up jobs—we had him in to look at the basement, two years back, during that last big lab renovation, when we found a box of bones inside the darkroom wall. You were, um, on hiatus, I think."

Carra frowned. "I heard he wasn't working much anymore, except out of his own apartment or in Chinatown. That he didn't like going anywhere he couldn't walk to."

"For a while, yeah—Abbott told me he had anxiety issues, agoraphobia. Maybe he got better."

"Did you happen to see his shadow, when he was here?"

"What?"

". . . nothing."

The last time she and Jude spoke, his shadow had been the main— the sole—topic of conversation. That'd been at the Clarke, too: Carra floating and spinning ectoplasm, trying to warn Jude that the same guy he'd been dogging after was none other than the lost half of his soul, cut away with a black-handled knife one night, when they'd all been far too chemically impaired to think better of it. Just another Saturday with the Black Magic Posse, doing like they did.

That smell, *Jude, God . . . it's* you.

"Seriously, just ask me what you were going to," Sylvester said, carrying on with the conversation like any normal person, since he couldn't read her thoughts. "I don't have to know the context to answer."

It caught her off-guard for a moment, but she decided to take him at his word. "All right, then: 'Did you see his shadow?' When you stood next to him, under the light . . . did he *have* one?"

"A shadow."

"Yes."

Sylvester thought. "Well, uh—yes, he did. Definitely. I remember thinking I saw it, sort of. Like . . . out of sync with the rest of him, as if it was trying to get away, or something."

"But it couldn't."

"Well, no—it was stuck to him, same as yours or mine. Because it was his *shadow*."

"Huh. Well . . ."

. . . *that'd be different.*

"We had sex, you know," she heard herself tell Sylvester, suddenly, without the faintest idea why. "Jude and me. Just the once."

"I thought he was gay."

"Oh yeah, very much so. But I asked him, and he was okay with it; he liked to experiment, back then. My first time. His too, I think—with a woman." Sylvester didn't say anything, but that didn't stop her. "And Janis Mol, from intake? She stayed with me, after the Goshaugh Incident . . . we ended up sleeping together as well, almost every night, 'til she finally moved out. When Abbott got her into housing."

"Carra—"

"I mean, I don't want to make any judgement calls on how she chooses to categorize herself, these days—or even how *I* do, really." She snorted. "I haven't *done* enough, for that."

"Did you love her?"

"Still do, as much as I love anybody. Jude, too. I haven't talked to him since '99, but—that doesn't change anything. We just weren't a good fit, him and me, not unless his soul was somewhere else, and that's no way to live. As for me and Janis, psis almost never stay together, even if both of them have wards that work. Too much *static*."

"Why are you telling me all this, Carra?"

"I don't *know*," she whispered. "I—want to be honest."

"Which I appreciate." Leaning forward, he laid his hand carefully next to hers, so close she could feel its warmth. "It just seems like you're making yourself uncomfortable, which is your business, except . . ." He paused, choosing his next words carefully. ". . . it's sort of painful, to watch. Which is *my* business, I guess."

"I'm always uncomfortable."

"I know. I read your file."

Now she *did* smile, finally. "Everybody's read my file."

"Around here, yup," Sylvester agreed. And left it at that.

They adjusted their glasses at each other, then looked back down at their respective plates, silent, but not uncomfortable. Reminding her, yet again, how easy Sylvester made it for her to be with him, without seeming to try.

He'd been wary of her when they'd first met, but not afraid, and that had drawn her to him, against her own better judgement. Now, there was always a sense of something soothing shedding from him, especially when they sat together like this, not quite touching; just *him*, accepting her for who she was, with far more grace than she'd ever managed to.

"This is . . . different, for me," she said, cautiously.

"I get that. You can have a run-down of *my* sexual history, if you think that'll help . . . I mean, it's pretty short."

"Really?"

"Well, yeah: I'm a big old nerd, Carra. Don't let the whole exotic indigenous person thing fool you." She smiled again, sidelong, which made him grin. "*There* you go. Listen, I'm sure you don't want anybody getting the wrong idea about you and me, not that there really *is* a 'you and me,' yet . . ."

"Like you somehow screwed me sane, or something—that it? 'Oh, Carra Devize finally got herself a boyfriend, and now she's *alllll riiight.*'"

"That'd be pretty good work on my part, considering we've never actually, um—"

"Uh huh."

"—and we might not, still, ever. Not unless you're okay with it."

"It's not that I don't want to. But you've seen the reports, right? When I get excited . . ." Carra trailed off, then finished: "I've hurt people."

"Sometimes," he agreed. "And sometimes not, like in the storage unit. Remember?"

". . . I remember."

Fallen and twitching next to the Thanatoscopeon, shucking what tenacious fragment remained of the thing Kate-Mary'd named Semblance out her pores, surrounded by a degrading fan of body-fat-slicked spirit Polaroids with telekinetic etching. And looking up as Sylvester looked down, her head in his lap, his palm on her forehead; sampling his memories without wanting to, in uncontrollable little gulps. His Mom fixing a car, wiping grease across one cheekbone. Crows on a fence. That hole in the roof, plastic bags taped across the inside and an old bed's backboard nailed in on top, yet still it kept dripping. Emptying the pot out in the morning, red with rust, then swishing a steel wool scrubber 'round inside it under the pipe 'til it ran clear, and using it to boil up water for tea.

"I took all the same tests as you," he told her, "back when my internship first started—Abbott insisted. Thinks if you don't know what it's like to fail every one of them, then you won't know what to look for when somebody starts getting it right."

"That seems illogical."

"Kind of, so don't tell him I told you. Anyhow . . . I don't have enough psi to pick Lotto tickets, like you couldn't already tell. Is that good?"

"It might be." Another pause. "I *am* grateful for the way you treated me, maybe more than grateful . . . but it's hard to tell. Everything's all run together."

"So we take it slow."

"Slower than this, even?" She wrung out her hands, knuckles white. "Look, I just want to know if you're disappointed. If I—scare you."

"Carra . . . I'd be a fool to say yes *or* no. But . . ." He put his hand on hers, so braced for her to flinch he looked pleasantly surprised when she didn't. ". . . I've worked here five years now, at least. I couldn't deal with a little fear, I'd've took off running that first week and never looked back."

His thoughts leaking in underneath, borne on a tide of merged energy: *I do feel something, though, for you. Right . . . here. Don't you feel it too, for me?*

Tears pricked her eyes. "Yes," she said, out loud. Thinking, at the same time—

. . . but that isn't necessarily a good *thing, for me. Or* you.

It almost never was.

Jo Glouwer woke to the memory of Davina Cirocco's tongue in her ear, with what was left of the woman in question coiled all 'round and through her like smoke, that raised black sigil throbbing inside her elbow. Whispering, barest thrum of words, borne on nothing like breath: *Hey baby, time to shift ass. Somebody's here.*

Who?

Fuck if I know. She says you *will, though.*

Jo opened her eyes. Across the bachelor apartment's single room, a shadow wavered, tall and nude and foully fair as any Thane's vision, its unbound hair a nest for nightmares.

"Do I know you?" she asked, thinking she didn't—yet suspecting herself wrong.

Only all yuir life, ye daftie, save 'twas that other's face I wore, the whole time. Now let me in, Jodice; I've come far, and I've no' got long. 'Tis time.

And yes, she did know the tone of that voice, almost from birth.

"Nan," Jo said. "Told me was just a *cold* you had, last time I called."

Aye, as the leech at the Clinic claimed, for all the good he did me. Still, 'tis of nae moment: my Black Man visited at the gasp and showed me what best tae do, spending that other's last power tae bring me o'er, tae settle what's so long owed. Will ye help or no'?

Jo shook her head, clearing it only slightly. The room was dim, dusty; she didn't recall having drawn her shades in a week, no more than what she might've last ate or when she'd bathed. Why bother, so long as she had Davina? Was company made a home, after all.

Her new life: playing nursemaid to her murdered lover, forever cradled inside Jo's ectoplasm-attracting aura, while the other spooks still coaxed to her moth-light moaned outside in jealousy. Sometimes, she roused herself to do small jobs for ready cash, booked through the Freihoeven Institute—Ross'd mentioned her to them as he passed through an internship there, in the wake of Glouwer-Cirocco-Puget's dissolution.

But she hadn't seen him in person since that day, when he held her hand and cried as she wiped blood off Dav's cold face. Now he ran some sort of website—CreepTracker.org—providing a forum for Ontario's aspiring paranormal investigators, which the Freihoeven mined in turn for fresh leads as to where the maximum spooky shite might currently be happening.

The work was easy, now she knew what she was doing, though, and for that she'd always thank him. It filled the proverbial hole, much smaller, if never entirely gone.

Not even Dav could see to that.

Eight long years since she and what was left of Davina Cirocco had been . . . joined, and she still wasn't used to having people in her place who *weren't* dead, no more than she was to thinking of it as only *her* place. So to find Euwphaim Glouwer's last fragment suddenly there, as well, was hardly a great surprise, even now she knew the truth—how every touched tale her Nan'd ever told her was nothing but gospel, hard and dreadful reality. How everything Jo knew was built on someone else's pain.

She could remember the very moment, exactly, when her world had spun off-kilter: right as that black angel Euwphaim so loved laid its uncanny imitation of a hand in hers and kissed her inside the elbow, imprinting her with its awful seal.

Jo sighed, shaking her head again. "You saying I've a choice?"

Cert, girl. The same as any other.

"I doubt that, somewhat."

I've ne'er told lies tae you, Jodice, my hen. Not wi'out reason.

Jo swung her legs out of bed and sat up, floor cold beneath her feet. Behind her, she felt Davina eddy away, then swing back, as though leash-yanked, reassembling herself with her knobbly knees crossed, tucked ever so slightly behind one of Jo's broad shoulders. More a pose struck than any real show of fear, but Euwphaim *was* an awful object, and no mistake—had been even before, wrapped for comfort and camouflage in a long-dead woman's sagging skin, "her" face set in a parody of kindly old age.

Jo put one hand on her knee, palm up, closest to Dav's. Closed her lashes and shivered, gooseflesh stippling all along the love-line, as her living energy-field spiked to the brief brush of Dav's dead one.

Come all right in the end, we just give her her will, she tried to tell her.

But: *Enough delay,* her Nana snapped back, impatient. *Will ye do't, girl?*

"Oh, I'll help, if it'll set me free," Jo replied. "Though, I'll tell you this much—I'm none too like to boil a bloody child for flying ointment just to get from here to Overdeere."

Did I say as ye should?

"Not yet."

Nor shall I. The no-voice turned persuasive, almost gentle. *All that falls tae you is tae bring our coven together once more, or close as can be. There's Jonet's girl, for one, that sees mair e'en than yoursel', though the foremost Rusk o' this time's vowed hersel' tae the Kirk, which cuts Alizoun's get from the mix. But that Roke boy, the soiled priest—he'll gi' ye what ye need, for he fears his family far mair than e'er he loved 'em. Only list tae me, an' you'll see it done.*

At her elbow, Dav gave a thin hitch of laughter. *Uh* huh, *piece of fuckin' cake. You really down with all this mediaeval bullshit, Jo?*

Hold yuir tongue, dead-girl. Ye've tae do't, Jodice, sharpish, wi' nae mair dispute. Yuir a witch, born and bred, and blood is blood.

"*Blood*, aye, but no witch. I've no learning on it, no craft—"

Ye took the mark, same as us all.

"You know as well as me why I did *that*."

Aye. And has she thanked ye for it yet, yuir leman? Or would she rather be Below, ploughing hot coals, where all her kind maun go?

Another sidelong eye-flick from Davina, who probably had choice words lurking hid behind her ghost-teeth on the subject of whom a woman might choose to bed down with versus damnation predestined, if sense enough not to say 'em out loud. Jo rubbed at her forehead, feeling a migraine coming on.

She knew Euwphaim correct, however, in her heart of hearts: what Jo had done to bring Dav "back" sprang from selfishness alone, a futile railing against death driving her to reorder the universe by force.

'Tis yuir choice, her Nan lied, empty eyes now full as two moons, just rising. *So say the word an' send me elsewhere, if it suits ye better—leave us Three Betrayed unavenged, after all this time and worry, all this bloody sacrifice. Do as ye will, an' live wi' it.*

Think I've not lived with worse? Jo ached to snap back, but didn't.

:At Euwphaim Glouwer's request, I serve without complaint,: the angel—Ashreel Maskim—had told her, softly, **:even I, who once laid the foundations of this world with my six siblings' help. For she and I are *such* old friends, I can remember seeing the very idea of you form in her, long ago . . . at my suggestion, of course.:**

You were there? she remembered blurting out, amazed.

To which it replied—:**Why not? I am there still.**:

(Here, there, everywhere else. Everywhere, at once.)

And thus was the pact signed, hours after Jo had penned Davina's soul in her bottle, once she'd finally cried and drunk enough to call her Nan for that bloody name. Thus had it *been* signed, Jo later realized, from the very second its first syllable struck her eardrum. That simple; that easy. That irreversible.

Damnation take her, Jo thought, wearily, *and me too, for bad measure. But let Davina walk free of this, please Christ, once it's played to its close. . . .*

So long as Jo was already dead, that was, when it happened. Long as she didn't have to stand there and watch Dav go, then live the rest of her God-damned life alone.

Jo bent her head, aura blossoming coronal, open invitation to any dead thing within range; heard every shade for a mile 'round turn and sniff as she did, poised to come running. But was Euwphaim's shade alone she allowed to enter in before twitching it shut once more—a bubble of invisible force, proof against death's gravity for so long as Jo chose. Saw the dead witch breathe out a held sigh in relief at no longer having to spend so much effort to hold herself together, and thought: *That's her freed for mischief, and those she turns it upon won't thank me for it.*

But then again, considering who those were, and their works—the family Druir, creatures rather than people, surely, even by her own unorthdox standards—Jo couldn't really bring herself to feel too bad.

Good girl, Jodice, her grandmother said, hugging her so close Jo could feel ghost-bones grate icy-sharp against her own. *This will nae be forgot.*

While Jo just looked to Davina, dragging hard on that cigarette of hers and shaking her rexed red head as she did it, as though to say: *Bad idea, baby. Bad, bad idea.*

And thinking, in her turn—*No other kind in my world, as you well enough know. Ye great American hoor.*

"Save your thanks 'til the deed be done," she replied out loud, reaching for her car keys.

"Janis said you could maybe help," Josh Kim told Carra in Abbott's office—a biggish guy perching uncomfortably on one of those rickety little intake chairs, black hair buzzed to the scalp instead of caught back in a clip, like Sylvester's. They made for odd bookends, Korean vs. Mohawk, supplicant vs. enabler, to this whole innately freakish system: psychical research, bastard child of magic and science, forever the single pastiest game in town. "Because of . . . what you are, I guess. Your family."

Carra frowned. "All I had was my mother, Mister Kim. And she's dead."

Beside them, Janis sighed. "No, Carra," she said. "I meant your *other* family."

"The Five-Family Coven, that's what this is about," Abbott chimed in, helpfully, from behind his desk. "You see, Mister Kim's girlfr—" Kim made a flapping motion, causing Abbott to backpedal: "—his *friend*, Galit Michaels, was listed as a missing person by the Ontario Provincial Police in 2003. She was last seen in Overdeere, out by the Lake of the North."

"Mmm," was all Carra could think to say in response.

Frankly, she hadn't thought about that part of her heritage in years. For most of her life, it had always been enough to be "plain" Carraclough Devize, psychic savant and haunted house survivor, let alone Jonet Devize's however-many-greats grand-niece. Or even daughter to Gala Carraclough, who'd met her ex-husband Yancey Devize *in* Overdeere, where—in one of those typically contortionate Five-Family "coincidences"—Yancey's own mother had been one of the Overdeere Redcappies, a Sidderstane-style offshoot of the Druir family, sired by Minion Druir's son Quire.

All of which made Carra a species of Druir by default, if only to the sixth (or maybe eighth) degree. A dubious distinction at best, which was really saying something, considering the context.

Studying Abbott closely, now, and wondering: *Black Magic Posse aside, Guilden, does this really sound like a job for me? I speak for the dead, speak with them; lay them down, if I can. The Druirs, kinship aside—they're something different. As much beyond my ken as anyone else's.*

"You know I've never even been up there, right?" she finally asked, for the pleasure of watching Abbott colour as he replied, a bit too quick: "Well, of *course* I do."

I wrote your file, after all.

Carra nodded. "Just making sure."

She turned her attention back to Kim, now looking distinctly as though he wished he'd left well enough alone, and probed the ragged edges of everything he was trying not to think of, as unobtrusively as she could manage. "*You* have, though—after Ms. Michaels disappeared?

Heard the rumours too, I take it. About the Lake . . . Overdeere. That whole area."

Reluctant: "Some, yeah. I did research, and Galit kept a blog; server took it down, but I still have printouts. There was this guy—"

"Someone she'd met, just before. One of the Sidderstanes."

Kim stiffened. "How the hell can you—?" Janis touched his shoulder, gently, and he sighed. "Ganconer, that's his name. Older guy, prematurely grey. Something wrong with his eyes."

Carra nodded again, feeling the trance-buzz build. "They're made of wood," she told him, voice gone cold, removed. "Lady Glauce took them out, for punishment; they're in a jar, in a box, under the hill. Down deep in the ground, the apple-stink, where the leaves mould over."

Kim's face twitched all over. "Christ, *what?* Why the hell would you say that?"

"Because *it's just true.*"

He made as if to pull back, and her hands shot out, unprompted. One clamped onto his wrist, the other his forearm, hauling hard 'til they were nose and nose. Were her eyes rolling back yet? Impossible to tell, on her end—she could see through everything, lids very much included, her own skull's bony lens. Watching the flickering images projected inside her forehead shift and whisper, like willows in a breeze—*the bank of green rushes o, down in the salley gardens, where my love and I did meet*—and narrating what she saw there, mouth numb, tongue dry-sodden, spit reeking of mulch. . . .

While the words raised themselves all over, soft lead curse-scribblings flesh-rendered, constantly crawling: JOSH PLEASE, NO JOSH PLEASE NO, DONT HELP DONT TRY JUST SAVE YOURSELF, DON'T LOOK FOR ME NO NO NO . . .

(*Where have you been, my long-lost love, these seven long years and more?*)

"You had a dream," Carra said, lost Galit Michaels's handwriting chasing itself from neckline to neck, up over one cheekbone and under her glasses' frame, then up yet again across her forehead to bury itself at last in her hairline's bleachy tangle. "Last night, the night before— always the same, every night for a month, 'til you just had to tell *somebody.* Saw her there, after so long, all those years of trying to forget you ever knew her. Sitting at my *cousins'* table in the half-light with a collar of roots grown 'round her neck and a child by her side."

"A little boy, yeah . . ."

"Not yours. Though, you'd like him to be."

Kim's face was hot, cheeks red. "He has—that guy's hair."

Ganconer Sidderstane, cut-rate Tam Lin of the Lake; Galit was playing the Fair Janet role, here—the abducted mortal bride, this boy of theirs the result. But the *brugh* was no fit place for a kid to grow up, not with that little old blood in him to begin with. She could see him now, handsome but watchful, already starting to look stunted for his age: seven, eight, maybe nine. A few more growth spurts and he wouldn't even be able to stand up, completely—his silver hair would muddy itself, turn grey and brown, earth-tainted. Had he ever seen the sun?

That sweet face, pale as a guttering candle. An uncertain little light.

". . . Elver, that's his name," she said, to herself. "'Little eel.' Little elf-boy."

His mother strumming at some sort of instrument, its drum a hollow gourd, song rising plaintive as her gaze held steady on his bent back, playing in the leaves underfoot: *Yet what are those goodly hills the sun shines sweetly in? Those are the hills of heaven, he said, where we shall never win.*

"It's not right," Kim replied, voice tight. "Galit's an adult, Sidderstane, too. But *this* little guy . . ."

"He was born, that's all. Born into it. Same as they were."

Same as me.

"But who *are* they? I mean—I know what people say in Overdeere, and that's total crap, gotta be. Criminals, crazy rich assholes buying their way out of everything, living like animals in a hole in the ground 'cause they *choose* to, for some fucking reason. But not—"

"The Happy People? The Fair Folk? 'We dare not go a-hunting, for fear of little men?'"

Kim sighed again, baffled. Carra felt herself soften.

"Well," she said, "I wouldn't call most of them faeries to their face, but . . . yeah."

And now, in the dim light of the *brugh*, a further shadow stirred; came shrug-pulling itself effortlessly up, half through the floor and half the wall. Grub-white with icy eyes and a sly, quirking mouth, its high head crowned in glossy red maple-leaves—it reached for Galit, stroking her cheek with one six-fingered hand, and chuckled when she tried not to cringe.

"Enzemblance Druir," Carra named her, not opening her eyes, "Laird Enzembler's eldest daughter, Torrance Sidderstane's widow. She's the one who took her."

Kim swallowed. "The one from the photo, at the Lake."

"Yes. That's how you recognized her, right from the minute you saw her."

"And you're *related* to . . . that?" His eyes flicked up and down, searching for proof. "You don't look it."

"Oh, my ties are distant, comparatively; been a hundred years since my Devize relatives left Scotland, fifty since Minion Druir's kids started having enough kids to make my grandmother on my Dad's side. But Enzemblance, same as Minion, her Mom, her Dad—she came here directly, like opening a door. Dourvale Prime in the reign of King James is the day before yesterday for them."

"A wormhole, *time* travel? Fucking *magic*?"

"That's one name for it. Now . . . sssh."

Waving him quiet, and thinking, at the same time: *What am I feeling here, exactly? Wait, I know . . . I'm angry. That's what this is.*

(Bones in the rock, a splayed skeleton hand. Hell-holes left open, traps for the unwary. Minion's own thrall-wife, brought along from Scotland . . . what had she done to merit that, rent headlong between centuries, stranded and abandoned? What had Galit done to merit *her* confinement, beyond mere exercise of curiosity?)

Nothing. Because no one ever did.

They prey on us, Carra thought, *these changeling-makers. They think they can, because they always could, and no one dares to stop them. No one even tries.*

She glanced at her wrist, now encircled with a continually rotating bracelet of STAY AWAY STAY AWAY STAY AWAY. Looked up, and met Kim's tired black eyes straight-on.

"What are *you* prepared to do?" she asked him. "To get her back."

"What're the options?"

A shrug. "Take me there, I suppose. To Overdeere, the Lake . . . Dourvale. We'll knock on the hill together, see what happens next."

The suggestion made Abbott—who'd thus far stayed quiet, watching it all spin out from behind his desk, hands tented—suddenly sit straight up. "That would be . . . unadvisable."

"Thought you *weren't* my Dad, Guilden," Carra replied, coolly. Then, as he breathed in at the slap of it, appealed to Janis: "Look, you're the one who thought I could help—what'd you expect me to do?"

"Scry the site, long-distance," Janis answered. "Confirm whether or not his dreams were true, and then—ugh, I don't know; name a contractor, sit back, and let *them* get on with it. There are rules for getting people out of hills, right?"

Carra nodded. "Laws of exchange—you pay a tithe, pass a test, like in the stories: *This for you and this for me.* Galit's been in there a while, so Enzemblance's probably kind of bored with her by now. Might not even remember why she wanted her in the first place." Kim looked away, face twisting. "But then there's the child, and I don't remember anything about what to do if the person was *born* there. . . ."

"She'd be a thrall, property; something to be sold or traded. He'd be . . . family?"

"Distant, but yes. All Sidderstanes are Druirs, you go back far enough—even the human ones."

Abbott was standing now, clearly unhappy. "Carra, I said *no.* You *don't* know them, and they don't know *you,* either—do they?"

"*Of* me, probably."

"And that's going to help?"

She shrugged. "It can't hurt."

"The hell it can't!"

An uncharacteristically violent outburst for the good Doctor; Carra blinked. Then asked him, mildly: "Is this just about keeping *me* safe? Because I'm pretty sure I'm not your biggest gun, anymore—you've got files full of other assets now, all of them far more reliable. Janis here, for example."

"Leave me out of this, Carra."

"All right. But the point still stands: what do *you* care? I can make my own decisions."

"Of course, but . . . this isn't just fieldwork, this is—completely different. The Freihoeven doesn't *confront* these things, we never have, we're not equipped to. We analyze, we document. . . ."

"Speak for yourself. I've done both."

"You're only a month out of the *Clarke,* for God's sake—"

"I've been a month out of the Clarke every two to six months, the last twenty years of my life," Carra pointed out. "So if that disqualifies me for anything, you should probably stop paying me."

"You're upset. You should take the day, go home, think things over—"

"Nothing there for me, Guilden. You already had them take out the trash, so it's pretty empty—I sleep on a mattress in the kitchen, not too near the stove, so I don't have to manage stairs if I want tea. How am I supposed to amuse myself, now the cable's been turned off and my mother's ghost doesn't feel like haunting me anymore? Take Polaroids of all the empty corners, and see what comes out?"

She didn't have to check to know that Sylvester was watching her too now, dutiful note-taking forgotten; she conjured a smile in his direction to prove herself fine as she ever was. And as Abbott cast around for fresh arguments, Janis and Kim exchanged a significant look, decision obviously reached.

"My gig van seats five," Kim said. "Seven if you cram. Anybody's worried, they're welcome to come along."

This last was to Abbott, who shook his head, annoyed. "I have funding meetings all week, with Janis doing the presentations; we've had it set up for months, same as last year. You *know* that, Carraclough."

"I can go," Sylvester said. "I've got a driver's licence; I could spot Mister Kim. Does anybody else in here even drive?"

"Not me," Carra said. "And not the guy we're going to want to take with us, either, unless more things have changed than the suddenly-has-his-shadow-back thing."

Abbott threw up his hands. "You are *not* bringing in *Jude Hark Chiu-wai* on this foolishness, for God's own sake!"

"Yeah, okay. Except for the part where, if he agrees to come along, I really kind of *am*."

Abbott covered his eyes with his palms and sighed, gustily.

While Carra just looked down, thinking of Overdeere, the *brugh's* rich dirt, graveyard and mulch-heap, both; Dourvale's lost settlement, standing empty by the Lake's cold side, a hollow space in the forest's heart, where no bird sang and no good thing grew. The place Carra's mother had been warning her off her entire life, no matter at all that the dead already made her their constant toy, their totem, their barely upright living scribble-pad. Because *They're no' the same as you nor I,* and *you must not go to the wood at night.*

NO NO NO, still circling her wrist like ringworm with a shingles-bright burn, again and again—not Galit anymore, not even Gala. Someone else, whose name she'd never known. Familiar words, arranged in an entirely familiar warning.

NO, VERY DANGEROUS, VERY DANGEROUS FOR YOU, NO. ON NO ACCOUNT, MY LOVE.

Wanting to lay a comforting hand on Abbott's bent head, but holding back; wanting to shrug once more, but not doing that, either. Until finally, she looked back up at Kim, at Sylvester. Janis, smiling sadly.

"Should probably get moving, we want to make good time," she suggested; Kim nodded.

"I call shotgun," Sylvester said.

Jo had heard of Curia, of course, but never before been there. The storefront sat dusty and unwelcoming, crammed so full of various unsorted tripe it made the door seem blocked 'til she put fingers to it, at which point it sprang open—let out a trilling chime, a smell like sage on fire, and the murmur of shop-talk in progress.

Roke was behind the counter, examining some sort of fetish, well-endowed and studded with rusty nails. "West African, of course," an excitable-looking old gent was explaining, "from Zaire or Zambia, made of soul-tree wood, for keeping spirits in. Nails're driven deep in order to make the spirit angrier, you see—thus more effective."

"Uh huh." Roke turned the thing over. "Not *this* one, though, Simeon . . . you do know that, right? It's empty, has been for years."

"I—are you *quite* sure, old boy?"

"As I ever am, yup."

Simeon's face fell. "Oh . . ."

Liar, liar, pants on fire, Dav's ghostly no-voice whispered in Jo's ear, as Euwphaim gave a satisfied little bone-creak chuckle by the other. For now Jo looked closer, she could see how the fetish strained and pulsed in Roke's hands, leaking nasty trails of stuff that fanned their way only so far up as they might before hitting his half-human skin, then recoiled whip-fast from the sour, unfamiliar taste of it. All of which Roke ignored, completely, with not a single hair turned at the prospect of taking some sad pensioner's money under false pretenses.

Braw canny lad, this, Euwphaim noted, approvingly, *same as his grand-dam and his ten-times great-grandfather, before.*

Simeon, meanwhile, was once more deep in negotiation. ". . . simply convinced it may not be quite so poor a prospect as you claim," he told Roke, voice taking on a lecturer's lilt. "The sheer number of nails used alone indicates it was originally designed to trap some sort of, eh, *animistic resident* within. . . ."

Roke just nodded and smiled, noncommittally. "Well, I don't know what to tell you, Sim—it's *empty*, so I really couldn't go more than three bills, three and a half at the absolute outside. For friendship's sake."

"Yet even empty—it must surely still have *some* prospective market value, eh? As a trap, a vessel . . ."

"Not on the *open* market."

"Not that, no! I meant some slightly less public venue. The, eh . . . speciality circuit."

"Yeah, I get it. But, see . . . private sale equals danger, and I'm just not all that interested in being unsafe."

"Oh, of *course,* old boy, ha ha; 'course, you're right, absolutely. Don't know what on *earth* I could've been thinking. . . ."

Jo narrowed her eyes, here, because it wasn't just that Sim knew he had a losing argument—there was something *else* at work. Some*one* else. A distinctive new supernatural influence, sidling in at an angle Jo found—now she'd tuned herself to it—fairly easy to trace to the crevice between a teetering stack of tomes and the fold of drapes, whose hem kept them upright: a slight figure, female most likely, half-hidden in the gloom with her arms crossed and eyes trained on the small of the old man's blathering back, waiting for whatever she was doing to take its due effect.

Simeon broke off mid-wheedle, then glanced around, hand rising instinctively to hover above his clavicle, as though he wanted to check his own pulse, feel around for something in his breast-pocket . . . or cross himself.

"I say, you don't smell that, do you?" he asked Roke, nose wrinkling. "Something . . . something like . . . something like something, um . . ."

(*burning*)

Oh, yes.

Euwphaim eddying closer, leaning over Jo's shoulder, the ultimate bad angel; Davina eddying back to the very end of her rope, silver cord stretched leash-taut. And that girl in the shadows, with her pale little face and her smudgy black bob, stare sliding fast from brown to hazel to a simmering sulphur-yellow as her pupils twisted slantwise, a matched pair of tiny Nazi flags on fire.

That *one's had ane o' the Seven inside her,* Euwphaim said with as much approval as Jo'd ever heard her give. *Them, or some other of the Auld Fool's same get: them who Fell, one of the Watchers mayhap, whose seed made us what we are. 'Tis of nae moment which, but that I see their print upon her . . . for she too wears a Mark, though I misdoubt she knows whose.*

And Jo nodded along, knowing the truth of it—*smelling* it, heavy-hung in the shop's close air, a stench like no other. For those possessed retained a stink forever, enough to set them apart in any company: that slick reek, not quite burnt sugar or burning rubber, quick or dead flesh of any description.

Only one case she knew of ever treated in Toronto's diocese, though it went ahead on lies instead of permission, and the name came easy enough to her tongue: Judeta Kiss, called Judy. As good a playfellow as any half-Fae former priest might wish for.

"Nope," Roke lied, eyes fixed on Simeon's sweaty face. "I don't smell anything."

"No? Must just be me, then."

"Must be."

"You said three, I think?"

"Three-fifty, if you want it."

"Yes, uh—that would be fine. Lovely, thank you, my boy."

"Always glad to have your business, Sim," Roke said. And rang the transaction through.

Moments later, door safely re-shut in the the old man's wake, Judy Kiss stepped out from behind her curtain just as Roke turned to face Jo and her phantom entourage. Saying, as he did: "Well, ladies—now we're alone together, I'll start with the most obvious question: is at least *one* of you still alive? Because it's kind of hard for me to tell."

Judy rolled her eyes, now far more brown than yellow. "You think you're funny," she told him. "That's the real problem."

"I have my moments."

"Not as often as you think you do."

Cute, Davina mouthed at Jo, who found herself abruptly wanting to look elsewhere. But no matter which way she thought to turn, she knew Euwphaim would surely make it her business to be there first—so she sighed, instead, and introduced herself.

"Jodice Glouwer, Fa—Mister Roke. You might've heard of me . . . my name, at the very least."

And: "Oh yes," Maccabee Roke replied, face gone suddenly blank.

Jude's file hadn't been updated in five years, so Sylvester suggested checking in at the Empress Noodle—his only known hangout—to find out from Yau Yan-er if the address it listed was still current. Instead, Carra held out a hand for his phone, keyed the number next to Jude's name, and listened until the rings clicked through to an automatic message service, before hanging up and giving it back. "It's him," she said.

"'The number you have called is currently busy, so your call has been rerouted'?"

"If he wasn't paying his phone bill, somebody would've deleted it by now. Besides which—"

"—you don't want to get anywhere *near* Grandmother Yau, if you can help it."

"Do *you*?"

By six, they were on what Carra could only assume was Jude's front doorstep. It was a typical Chinatown side-street ugly-box left over from the late 1970s, one devolutionary phase away from being abandoned;

the upper windows all wore flimsy grilles with no curtains, while the bottom-floor windows were all painted over from inside, perhaps to block out the view.

"You can stay in the van," Carra told Sylvester and Kim. "I won't be long—he's coming or he isn't. Either way, I should probably go up alone."

Sylvester nodded as Kim gave the building a disapproving glance. "Fifteen minutes," he told her. "I'm setting my phone. That place could be a crack house, for all you know."

"It really isn't."

"Prove it."

She nodded at another house, two doors down: "Watch over there for a while, you'll see. Feel free to call the cops when it turns out I'm right."

Now, peering at those blind panes above, Carra thought she caught a faint glimpse of somebody moving around inside, behind the bars: indistinct, fluid, fast. Something contorting to squint down at her, spine bent the wrong way, then leaving an almost visible blur in its wake as it rushed away: smoke-smudge of transit, eye-stinging corneal burn, a perceptual negative. Plus a sort of distant tone layered in, muffle-muted—the same slow-building sound/smell that'd once sent her drifting upwards in the Clarke's cafeteria, ectoplasm pouring out to wreathe her in ragged snot-dun ribbons, as she gasped.

(you, *it's you, it's YOU*)

She chose a buzzer at random and leaned on it with her elbow, letting it ring long and loud. Eventually, a weary fuzz-filtered voice asked: "That really you, down there?"

"Yes. Can I come up?"

Another pause, followed by a click, lock popping just long enough to allow Carra to pull it open, thrust her knee between door and jamb.

"Why not?" the voice—*Jude*, definitely—asked again, at last, of no one in particular.

Inside, she felt her ginger way up the dim stairwell, feeling the ache of executed spell-work prick at her thumbs. One flight more, and a Luminol-blue outline rimmed the top apartment's door, a series of wards incised all about threshold, lintel, and knob: patterns of force, comprising a vacuum-sealed airlock against the supernatural. The symbols ranged from kanji to Enochian, runes to Cyrillic, backwards Latin run right to left instead of left to right, backwards Arabic the same.

Some parts of her didn't like it much, but she'd been prepared for that. So she stepped through without sustaining much damage beyond a dentist-drill's buzz in her third eye, a twinge of migraine, a brief twist of bilocation: *oh look, here's Carra Devize, hazed with hexation on every side, and here she (me) is again, floating just over her (my) shoulder, taking notes.* Watching herself put a hand on the doorknob, only to hear Jude call from inside: "Hey, Little Miss Immune-to-Boundary Spells. You coming in or what?"

"I already said *yes*," she snapped, and did.

Bad smell. Stale air. Thick gloom, unthreatened by toothless sockets of similarly debulbed lamps. Vague shapes of dimly seen furniture, shoved out of mutual alignment, as if to break up any kind of normal flow-line: nega-*shui*, for the psychically vulnerable.

She took another step in, looked around, seeing nothing. Waited yet one moment more, before calling out: "Well?"

"'Well,' indeed," Jude replied, at her elbow.

Carra turned, abruptly discovering that shape slumped across that nearby armchair *wasn't* a pile of pillows or a tangled bathrobe, after all, when it sat up, resolving into Jude himself.

The changes were striking, to put it mildly: usually close-cropped hair overgrown and jaw blurred with mould-soft beard, his Hong Kong version of a five-day shadow; feet bare and slightly dirty, toenails blue-rimmed with cold. The rest of him, meanwhile, came shoved into a pair of what might be track-pants, with a cordless burgundy bathrobe hanging open overtop. And sunglasses too, which he now slipped off as if for emphasis—*that's right, it's as bad as you think, or maybe even worse.*

Behind those blank lenses, each equally blank eye was dotted with purple flame: arcane fire, the sort used to mark circles. As though he'd started to summon something, years back, and just lost interest.

"So," Jude said, at last. "You're finally going to Overdeere."

"How'd you—"

He struck a pose, one hand raised up mockingly, palm still black with protective tattooing: "Same way I knew it was you downstairs, obviously—*maaaagic.*"

"In other words, your *friend* told you."

"Only damn friend I have, these days. Since you took your own good self away."

"You make it sound so easy."

"I do, don't I? Sorry."

Another long, silent moment elapsed, only broken when Jude

twisted away to throw himself back onto the same battered old divan he'd been sprawled on when she entered. He sat down, heavily, and cast his eyes up, studying at the ceiling.

"Any rate," he said, finally. "You want me to come along, I guess."

"That's right."

"Abbott already tried to warn you off?" As she nodded: "Hah. And *he* doesn't even know the half of it."

Carra pried a dusty, too-tall barstool chair away from Jude's marble-topped breakfast bar, then clambered up to perch on it, haphazardly. "Enlighten me," she prompted.

Jude sighed. "Well, there's this guy, probably another cousin of yours . . . met him a few years back at the Ursulines Studio. Wrob Barney. You know the name?"

"Nope."

"Claims he's some variety of Sidderstane, which I frankly doubt, but he definitely did grow up in Overdeere. And apparently, kids in the region like to check out the Dourvale shore as a rite of passage—mess around in the woods, lit. and fig. He drew me a map."

"That sounds handy."

"Well, it not like *I* had any intention of using it. But—you can have it if you want."

"I'd rather have you *and* it. Both."

Jude's laugh was dry. "Can't always get what you want," he suggested, "not all the time, anyhow. Who, either."

"So I've been told."

The words hung between them in the dark like breath on cold air, shimmering slightly. A second later, however, Jude's shadow came flowing up from behind Jude; fanned wide like a soft black peacock's tail. As Carra squinted, it undulated to peer down at her, boneless, tidal. Its whole corona set trembling with the effort of resisting Carra's spiritual pull, her forever-exposed soul's innate barometric pressure-drop.

"There's a woman, trapped almost a decade," she told it, looking it straight where its eyes should be. "A child. If I don't do anything, they'll stay right there, forever."

"It doesn't want you hurt," Jude murmured.

"That's nice. But I'm going to *be* hurt, no matter what." To the shadow: "Because I'm not *not* going to go up there, just because you don't let Jude come along."

No reply, not that she could hear. A ripple shook its surface, however—almost a shiver—and by the way Jude screwed his eyes shut, Carra suspected it might well be making some sort of internalized commentary.

"I'm gambling the Druirs won't want to do me harm," she continued, "which is stupid, I know—whatever kinship I share with them is only six of one, half-dozen of the other. Be worth it, though, to finally do *something* after all these years of doing nothing much beyond what I absolutely had to."

Jude's head dipped slightly, a gesture the shadow seemed to mimic: a nod? Regardless, Carra pressed on, explaining:

"Still, I am going to have to use magic, probably. Which I haven't in years—twenty, give or take. And I was never very good at it, when I did."

"No," Jude agreed.

The shadow craned itself away from them both, peevishly, retracting until it barely rimmed Jude's side. Carra could see why he'd taken the bulbs out, now—without anything to contrast against, the unnaturally fluid darkness Jude's half-soul was made of became far easier to overlook, especially if you were already trying to.

Fifteen minutes since she'd climbed the stairs outside, by her internal clock: she could sense Sylvester and Kim approaching, rescue-minded, even now. So Carra leaned forward, laid her hand on Jude's cheek, and opened herself up, wide.

"*Look* at it," she ordered him.

His eyes snapped open, hands purple-sparking from nails to wrists with the shock, and cursed when he saw how close the shadow actually was. Snarling: "*Ai-yaaah, tzao gao!* Get the damn hell ass-fuck *away* from me, you ghost-faced piece of shit!"

That it you're talking about, or me? she thought, reaching even further down inside him. Feeling around for something she could grab and twist.

Jude paled, tried to sit up, failed miserably. "Ugh, aaah!" he stammered, gasping. "I . . . not *you*, it's just . . . *diu nei lou mou,* Carra, fuck your old mother, that fucking well *hurts!*"

Good, it should—and Gala's dead, by the way. Now—

(*stay* still)

Another push, and she was all the way inside, seeing the shadow as Jude saw it: a younger, longer-haired doppelgänger, coiled and nude and slightly glowing, eyes wide with sympathy, not innocence. No scars, no sigils. She remembered looking up into those same, as yet unblemished eyes the first day Jude brushed past her in the Ryerson library, downcast and apologetic, barely able to speak without hiding his mouth in his hand.

That'd been first semester, beginning of October, and by Hallowe'en she'd shown him enough to set him on track for his first full invocation. Without knowing it, they were already set on the path to February 14th of the next year, when she'd handed Jude his black-handled knife, given herself over to the babbling storm, and watched him let 'er rip.

I did this to you, she told the shadow, sadly. *Let* him *do it, anyhow. I'm sorry.*

But: *no,* it said, shaking its head. *Oh Carra, no. I don't blame you or Jude, either. I don't blame . . . anybody.*

You do remember why he did it, though. Right?

Because he thought I made him weak.

But you didn't, did you? The shadow shook its head once more, a bit slower. *That's right. Because he was stronger than he ever thought he was. Strong enough that the only thing he really has to be afraid of, if he ever stops to think about it . . . is himself.*

Well . . . turns out, I'm stronger than you think I am, *too. And even if I'm not, it's* my *call. Not—either—of yours.*

Anyhow, he's always thought you're the better half, though it's not like he'll admit it. So convince him what we want is best; tell him he can do it. Tell him he will.

The shadow nodded yet once more, as Jude's own stare narrowed, flaring: *What you mean "we,"* gweilo *girl?* Then turned sidelong, slipping back behind him—*inside* him. Those two ugly, little purple points dotting Jude's pupils suddenly winked out: quenched, doused, gone, nothing left behind but a smoothed brow, a lifted mouth-corner, and an almost involuntary sense of peace.

Huh, Carra thought. *That was . . . surprisingly easy.*

"*You* are an *asshole,*" Jude told her with ridiculous dignity, which only made her snort—a genuine half-guffaw, plosive enough to surprise even her.

"Takes one to know one," she replied. And saw his lips crimp like a cat's, struggling not to puncture his own insulted pride further by laughing as well.

Footsteps in the hall, followed by a pounding at the door, which broke off when it sprang unexpectedly open. "Carra, you okay?" she heard Sylvester call out, taking a careful step inside, Kim following after. "It's—just been kind of a while."

"Fine, Sy," she answered, letting her hand fall. "Sorry to worry you."

"No problem," he lied. "So, is he coming? Jude Hark?"

"Present," Jude answered, tone surprisingly even; he sat up, shake-snapping all ten fingers at once to disperse the flames as he did. "You're from the Freihoeven, as I recall. Mister Horse-Breaker."

"Horse-Kicker."

"Exactly." Jude was on his feet now, a whole head shorter than either of his newest guests, though the charisma he was suddenly projecting made that hard to notice. "Carra and I were just catching up; she got distracted, lost track of time. You know how it is."

Sylvester studied him. "I think so," he said. "But you never did answer my question."

Jude contemplated him a minute, Kim too, and seemed to like what he saw. "Depends on who's doing the driving," he said, at last.

"Not me," Carra said.

"Oh, then I'm *definitely* in."

Before he locked Curia's doors and brought his car around, Mac Roke had wasted a few precious minutes trying to convince Judy Kiss it was better she not come along, only to get himself roundly laughed at. "Try and stop me," the girl replied, eventually; he'd just shrugged and held the car door open.

As they drove, Jo tried to get in touch with Carraclough Devize with predictably little luck. Eventually, however, someone connected her to Janis Mol, who spun her a tale almost made Jo believe in destiny.

"Already on her way," she told Roke and the others, clicking her phone off. "Bound North, headed for Overdeere, to petition the *brugh*. Something about a girl and her child, both stolen away. "

Ah, Euwphaim crowed. *See, now. Did I say so, or did I no'?*

You did, Nan.

Ye'd do well tae listen, next time.

Now they sat in the car outside the Connaught Trust—back entrance, along with the trash—while Roke did whatever business needed to be done inside. Judy had the passenger seat while Jo took up the back, her two ghost-companions coiled in uncomfortably close beside her.

Quiz her what she is in truth, hen, while we've time, Euwphaim demanded.

No, Nan.

Whyever not? Ye long t' know yuirself—dinna bother tae deny it.

Davina blew a plume of no-smoke out the rolled-down window, chuckling. *Jesus Christ, Jo—she always like this or is it a gets-worse-after-*

death kinda thing? Leave well enough alone, that's always been my *fuckin' motto.*

Aye, as I ken well enow, ye burnt-out end of some true witch's leavings, content tae steer yuirself through life by hunch and guess alone, so long as 'twould bring ye best advantage. Yet ye could've been so much more. . . .

Yap yap yap, not like I never heard that *pitch before. Thanks for nothin',* Strega Nonna.

Bloody enough! Jo snapped. *She'll tell or she won't, and that's an end on it.*

Ye're a wicked, stubborn girl, Jodice Glouwer.

I'm a woman grown, Nan; sold my own *soul, for all you told me where t'shop it. Long as you need my skill t' ride safe, you'll keep a civil tongue or be cast out.*

Euwphaim hooted. *Hear her rail! Yet there's no threat can still* my *mouth, since an ye lose me, yuir leman goes likewise. And what was it all for, then?*

"I can hear you, 'case you wondered," Judy said, without turning. "All of you. If that helps make up your mind, or anything."

"Fine," Jo replied, wearily. "You were possessed, the rumour goes." Judy didn't bother to nod. "What by?"

"Mmm, well. That's always the question."

Was a weird, teasing note slid into her voice as she said it, almost sly; cast a glance back over her shoulder, one pupil already lengthening, catlike in its slant-set Balkan socket.

Explaining: "I don't know its name, so I call it Nobody—Mister Nobody. But I've been checking grimoires for it ever since I realized I can read any language, human or not, which is how I met Mac in the first place."

"Not one of the Seven, though."

"The Maskim? *Liber Carne* was one of the first places I looked, so no." Her yellowing eyes narrowed. "Still, *you* got a connection with those things, I guess . . . you and old Creepy Gramma, back there."

"Aye, somewhat. But then, I s'pose your man's told you that half of it, at least."

"Roke's not 'my man.'"

Interesting, Jo thought; he'd been *Mac*, when Judy wasn't thinking about it.

"Suit yourself," she said. "So . . . how'll you know, you *do* find this Mister Nobody of yours?"

"Oh, don't you worry your head 'bout that, not-so-small medium at large. I'll know."

Jo looked away, back at the Connaught. "Must gall you somewhat to be here, though," she ventured. "So close to holy things."

Judy shook her head. "Doesn't work that way. See, I'm *favoured* of God, supposedly, because he chose me to make a point with. Made a walking object lesson of me, just to prove that, when you live inside a universe God created, nothing happens except what God allows to happen."

If Euwphaim could've spat, she would've. *God, forbye? I'll ha' nae truck wi' him.*

"And yet," Judy shot back, toneless.

Say on, Euwphaim demanded.

"Still don't get it, do you?" Judy replied. "You only exist because God lets you, blasphemy and all—just like the angels, *all* the angels, ones who screwed your million-gone great-greats included. So it must follow he *wanted* a Schism, wanted Nephilim, Himself only knows why. Wanted *you,* Euwphaim Glouwer, with just power enough to hurt yourself trying to hurt Him. Even the fact you can stay angry at Him, that's something He allows you: free will, the gift that keeps on giving. The angels don't have that. Which is why they hate us for it, almost as much as we hate ourselves."

My Black Man loves me, ye mere bag o' wind.

"Maybe," Judy agreed. "Never met the gentleman, that I know of. But I've knocked a few of his relatives down, in my time—made 'em bleed, too. And I'm pretty sure that was only 'cause God *let* me."

Ye ne'er.

Another of those smiles, eyes lightening a bit further, pupils even more bent. "Try me."

Another pause ensued, wrapped in uncomfortable silence.

"So," Judy asked, at last. "Monster-killing nuns, huh?" To which Jo nodded.

"Aye, that's right. Your man was their confessor, once."

"He's *not* my . . . Yeah, well, guess he is, at that. Christ, this *city.*"

"It's chockablock with oddity, that's true enough. But you've him to protect you, at the least."

Judy smiled at that so strangely that Jo wanted to pull back. "From what, Mister Nobody's leavings? That's trouble for *other* people, same way a skunk can't smell its own stink. I'm like a . . . haunted house, one of those suburban bungalows where somebody cooked meth for a year, the kind cleans up really nice, but then you move in and start bleeding from the eyes. I don't get any worse, even if I don't get any better. Just stay . . . me."

"Roke must be truly perfect for you, then."

"He is, yeah. 'Cause being less than half human, none of the toxic shit I spew out even *touches* him. Making him maybe the one person in this city I can't hurt, not unintentionally—"

Her eyes dropped, still brown, still human. And Jo felt the unspoke words resound inside her head: . . . *not as much, anyway.*

After a second, Euwphaim laughed, a lewd, gloating chuckle. *Ye foolish child.* The door opened, and Roke stepped out, smug as a creamery cat, with a wooden rune-carved box tucked under one arm and a hammer hanging from his other hand: perfectly normal claw-head and a rubber grip, like it came from Home Hardware. The woman striding beside him was tall, dark, and frighteningly lovely, a true warrior-cleric from her close-cut reddish natural hair to her sensible shoes. Sister— no, Mother now—Blandina, Jo's brain supplied, remembering a spray of photos she'd once seen tossed across Abbott's desk.

She rolled the window down as they paused a few feet away, curious to hear their conversation.

My pretty Alizoun, Euwphaim breathed, sounding for the first time halfway impressed. *'Tis she herself reborn, touch o' the tar or no. Oh, that she might hear me!*

The nun didn't react at all, however—only laid her hand on Roke's arm, a gesture no one could mistake for tender. Telling him: "You'll have to leave it in for it to do any good—"

"I know, B."

"—so if we don't get it back, I'll assume you actually *used* it, instead of selling it. Don't prove me wrong."

"Now, Mother, would I do that?"

"I find out differently, you'll answer. And we'll need the box back, too."

"Forgive me," Jo called out. "But what is this we're talking about, exactly?"

"The Ordo's secret weapon against the Druirs," Roke said, flipping the box's lid up, tilting it for Jo to see—a squarish, rusty metal spike, some six inches long. "Relic nail, cold iron, supposedly used to martyr a saint . . ."

"Severo," supplied Blandina, flatly. "Early Christian bishop from Barcelona. Had it driven into his skull by pagans."

Reminded, Roke looked down at the hammer. "Forgot to ask: this holy, too?"

"Blessed just this morning. By the guy who has your old job."

"Hmmm, convenient."

The Ordo's battle-leader swept her wintery gaze over the car's occupants, then gave a curt little nod—like she'd won a bet with herself and wished she hadn't. "Your team, I take it: a witch born from witches, the girl who got Cillian Frye defrocked, whatever's in the back. Plus you."

"Two ghosts, one a *much* worse witch's, and yes. We're also looking to hook up with Carraclough Devize on the way. You came too, it'd be like we were getting the band back together."

"Pass."

"That's what I thought." Roke latched the box again. "Now, I owe you, obviously."

"I'm aware of that." Blandina glanced at the car again, huffing. "Do this right, Roke. I'll have the Anchoress pray for you."

"Since *you're* not going to?"

"Don't be so sure. Considering how much you'll need it, I just might."

"I'll take my chances."

Another nod. "Yes," Blandina replied. And shut the Connaught's rear entry in his face.

Miles on, the Devize/Hark/Horse-Kicker/Kim Uncomfortable Canadian Road Trip ™ was already a few miles out of the GTA. Jude had his shoes off and his feet up, apparently in some sort of trance—it was the slightly visible Buddhist nimbus of transparent purple flame that gave it away—while Carra studied the fat yet remarkably uninformative file Sylvester had brought along.

A relatively tiny (two miles square) glacier-carved basin with a steep southern drop, the Lake of the North is located up past Gananoque, Dr. Abbott's introductory monograph began. *Surviving settlements trace a loose crescent around its rim. These include Sulfa, site of a thriving anti-malaria drug industry, and the twinned former Anabaptist religious colonies of Your Lips and God's Ear, all within a few hours' drive of villages like Chaste, Overdeere (its own economy maintained by the Sidderstane family canning factory), and Quarry Argent. The locally infamous "phantom village" of Dourvale, though unoccupied, also remains unaccountably listed on most maps.*

Once a residential development planned around Quarry Argent's silver mine by poet turned amateur folklore collector Torrance Sidderstane, Dourvale was named after the hereditary holdings of a noble Scots family he claimed to be descended from and had just married back into.

After Torrance's 1911 conviction for "death by misadventure" in the disappearance of his pregnant bride, however, Sidderstane's relatives found their plans to remake the mansion he'd built on the lake's Ice Age esker-rimmed "Dourvale shore" over into a luxury hotel and spa thwarted when the resulting scandal rendered it a socially unsuitable vacation spot.

Dourvale village would have been an adjunct to the spa/hotel combo, a place for workers and their families to live, with a selection of rental cottages left over for the tourist trade. 1911 was also the same year the Quarry Argent silver mine tapped out, however, cutting the area's workforce in half. Most migrated to other townships or cities (Barrie, in particular), and the project was discontinued.

In 1919, needing a cash injection to fund their permanent relocation to Toronto, the Sidderstanes cut a deal that saw their former home and its grounds turned into a Flu Pandemic hospital-cum-hospice, TB ward, and mass graveyard by the Ontario government. New family head Dacre Dowersby Sidderstane used the overflow to fund another eccentric and ambitious project, that of transporting the former Witch-House at Eye from Scotland to Canada and rebuilding it in Scarborough, from the foundations up. Today, the so-called Sidderstane Mercy Hall buildings' ruined remains can be located by hiking through various farms' uncleared back-lots, which have merged to form one sprawling, near-impenetrable deadfall.

Photos had been appended, and Carra flipped through them: karst topography, limestone hell-holes, alkaline barrens of scrub and swamp, bordering and encroached on by various timber sinks. Then some studies of the Lake itself, surprisingly beautiful, its degraded limestone sides supporting cliffs, caves, and the occasional grotto, along with a series of unusually top-heavy rock pillars known as "flowerpots." A perfect place to disappear in, according to the chart Abbott had somehow obtained from the Ontario Provincial Police, which collated fifty years' worth of localized missing-persons records.

Flipping the file closed, Carra nudged Jude. "Tell me what this guy Barney said," she demanded.

Without opening his eyes: "Everything?"

"Skip the pillow talk."

Jude sat up, shooting a glance at Sylvester, head bent over his phone's GPS app. "Very . . . heterocentric of you." Adding, as she raised a brow: "All right, all right. You know about the Stane. . . ."

"Vaguely. It's this—thing, the Druirs have it—"

"—possibly a meteorite, possibly a pebble from what used to be Faerie itself. Lady Glauce's bride-price. Well, Wrob claimed that the Stane anchors Dourvale, or at least the big pile of dirt your cousins live in . . ."

"It's called a *brugh*."

"—which most people find impossible to locate, unless they have somebody like you along. That's because the Stane only responds to Druir blood or some variation thereof. To everybody else, it makes it seem like the brugh isn't even there, because—well, it is, and it isn't. It's in two places at once, Ontario and Scotland, but not just that . . ."

"—it's in two *times* at once too," Sy chimed in. "Right?"

"You've heard this one before," Jude said, slightly disgruntled.

Sy shrugged. "Been a theory for some time at the Institute. Certainly fits with various information about the *other* Dourvale, the original: lots of stories about folks wandering around in a wood they'd never seen before, tripping across what sounds like twentieth-century technology, and being horrified by it. In 1936, an old man was found wandering near Overdeere; he claimed to be ten years old, spoke a dialect so thick they had to get the town centenarian to translate, and died of measles within a week."

"How'd he get there?" Kim asked, shifting lanes.

"Said he was looking after his Dad's sheep, and a lady beckoned him away, promised him sugar-candy. But she took him to *a low place instead, very dark, and kept me lang*. He got away when she was asleep— another lady helped him, *tall and fair, wi' hair like leaves*. And then he was stumbling out onto the highway, eight times older than he'd been that morning."

Kim turned his head, eyes suddenly haunted. "The first chick . . . what'd *her* hair look like?"

A pause. "Red," Sy replied, at last.

To himself, quiet: "*Bitch.*"

For the next hour, Kim drove hard, pushing the speed limit, slipping in a series of ever-less-soporific CDs: Slipknot turned up *loud*, Corpusse, Malhavoc. By the time Cannibal Corpse rolled around, Jude leaning his head in next to Carra's, whispering: "Family or not, you're still going to need a tithe."

"Cross that bridge when we get to it, I guess. And no, we are not giving them half your damn *soul*, Jude. First off, I'm not even sure they'd want it—but you *will* later on, no matter *how* inconvenient you happen to find it to deal with, right now."

"So you keep claiming," said Jude.

Around Chaste, GPS suddenly quit and froze simultaneously, with no warning but a brief greenish flicker. By then, things were getting dimmer, and everybody's stomach was rumbling, so Kim pulled into a gas station for directions, plus a combined Tim's and toilet run.

"Where are we, man?" he asked the guy behind the counter, who just grinned.

"This's Paragon, almost," he replied. "Where'd you think?"

"Uh . . . we just passed Chaste, so . . . Quarry Argent?"

"Took a wrong turn, maybe. Easy to do when you're not from here."

Kim bristled. "Well, I *was* born in Toronto," he pointed out. "Close enough for jazz?"

"Given ya ended up here, maybe not. Where ya headed?"

"Over—" Kim began; "Dourvale," Carra put in, perhaps inadvisably, at almost the same time. And took a tiny amount of pleasure in the way the word made the man flinch, then flinch again, once he'd fully registered her features.

"Sorry, ma'am," he said, finally. "I didn't . . . you got *family* business, up there? I can—think I got a copy of the right map, still. Let me look."

Several, as it turned out. *Probably doesn't get much call for them in the normal run of things,* Carra thought, slipping a pack of peanuts into her pocket while holding the man's gaze, pointedly not offering to pay for them; he just swallowed and nodded. Kim didn't notice. As she left, he was saying: "Okay, this looks doable, long as you talk me through it a couple of times."

"Glad to," the man replied, eyes still on Carra as she made her way outside, where she found Sy and Jude drinking coffee against the side of the van. "No, there's not really a fairy-tale tradition in Hong Kong, per se," Jude was telling him. "*Mogwai*, of course, but that's different— they're their own thing. The British called them fairies because they didn't know what else to call them, or sometimes demons, but they're more like animistic spirits, leftover remnants of the pre-Taoist world."

"Like Shinto in Japan." Jude nodded. "Some Christian theologians thought Celtic fairies were demons, too. Or ghosts—the pagan dead, trying to seduce people away from Jesus with big parties and free food. That's why fairies hung around with witches, and vice versa."

"Ai-yah, what else were they going to say? But whenever you peel the big-F Fae legend back far enough, you end up with a secret people or lost tribe idea, some sort of historical/evolutionary subdivision, surviving alongside humankind through guile and child-stealing." To Carra: "Though why they'd *bother*, when they can obviously interbreed with adult humans anyhow. . . ."

Carra thought for a moment. "Because it hurts more," she replied. "Changeling babies sicken and 'die,' leaving human parents unaware their real kid is still alive somewhere, *caught in yon green hill tae dwell.*

Years later, they're so glamoured up they can walk right past their own mother and father without recognizing them, and vice versa."

"They hate us that much," Kim said from behind her. She shrugged, sadly.

"Maybe. But then again—I've also heard they envy us because we've got what they don't, supposedly: a soul. Dead Fae blow away, like leaves, but humans at least go *somewhere*. I've seen it."

"Where?"

"I don't know."

(None of us do.)

Unable to stop herself from thinking, as she said it: *Witches on one side, Fae on the other; witches can sell their souls, but the Fae don't have anything to sell. So—what about me?*

She looked over at Jude, holding his hand up in front of the gas station's sign for the express purpose of seeing how long it would take his shadow to remember to mimic the gesture, and for just a split second, she wanted to shake him 'til his teeth clacked. *Stupid dogshit ghost*, he'd called it to its face; his nature's better part, gentle and empathetic, guilelessly good. She feared for it once this trip was over, without her to keep him from stuffing it in a damn box and burying it somewhere.

But then again, when she thought about it further—she feared for all of them, a little.

"My turn," she announced, heading for the door marked LADIES.

Two hours later, back on the road, squinting against the dark, the rising mist. Sylvester at the wheel, highbeams off to cut the mist-glare, and Carra now riding shotgun so Kim could doze; she was trying to help him negotiate by feeling out in front of them, letting her mind become diffuse, but it was hard when every reflective road-marker came at you like a distracting, cat's-eye flash.

Sy drove with both hands kept glued to the wheel, as though he could guide the car in the proper direction through sheer need alone, he only held on tight enough. Four wheels, a chassis, and an engine, peeling headlong from highway to road to route, asphalt to tar to dirt and gravel, while the trees clustered in and began to overhang, the towns shrunk to crossings, the sky grew full of cold stars.

Feel ahead. Feel ahead. Open yourself up. Don't be afraid.

(*I can't close myself, though, ever. That's the problem.*)

Carra opened her eyes again, only to find Sy staring at her. "What?" she asked.

"Nothing! It's just . . . you've just, uh . . . got something."

She flipped the eye-shade down, checking the mirror: words, crawling up across her cheekbone like weird blemishes, scattered in stigmata-pimple constellation across her forehead. Having long since trained herself to read backwards, Carra translated and spoke them aloud easily, almost at the same time—

"Now, stop *here*, right here, right NOW!"

Sy did, jerking the wheel so they pulled over sharply, up onto the road's hidden shoulder. The resultant jerk woke Kim, who let loose with a flood of curses, half in English, half not. But Carra had already opened her door, lurch-stumbling forward, mist fleeing her path as if blown in pace-long slices of asphalt, rocks, dirt; Sy turned the van off before following, striding to catch her up, hug her from behind, automatically holding her steady.

"What was that?" he wanted to know, as she peered down at her forearms—handwriting still forming itself, tracing along the road-map of her veins, stuttering like badly dried ballpoint. Some of it was spidery, some Palmer Method rounded, equally antique, though the words themselves were curtly, explicitly modern: HERE/NOW. NOW HERE. NOWHERE. YOURE HERE.

CARRA YOURE FINALLY HERE.

This last up her wrist, swerving to avoid the blue double-tree humping across her hand's back. Behind them, Jude had already scrambled free, quick and lithe; Kim came last, scrubbing his eyes as she checked her palm for the rest, and gasped.

"The hell *are* we?" Kim demanded—so she showed him.

"DOURVALE," Sy read over her shoulder.

Jude snickered, then guffawed outright. "Oh waaah."

The mist, job apparently done, boiled away in all directions at once, allowing Dourvale village to suddenly spring up all around them: a time-bleached square half-mile of Colonial Revival faux-saltbox houses laid out in regimented lines, neat corners and trim right angles barely softened by a half-century of decay.

Trees had grown up through the once straight-laid plank sidewalks, roots wrecking porches and heavy limbs breaking off cornicepieces. Here and there, uncleared seasonal loads of leaf mulch were slowly causing the roofs to tip, sag, or collapse. What few windows remained unshattered reflected only green and black, layered shadows of new growth on top of old. The weeds rose ankle-high, bush and flower lunging higher, 'til gravity made them stoop or break: Deadly Nightshade, nettles, thistles, poison ivy, dandelion, goldenrod, Queen Anne's Lace. Milkweed pods sagged, popped and empty, having already thrown their fluffy contents to the wind to drift and tangle everywhere the spiderwebs hadn't already reached.

Around them, the air sang, dully. Cicadas, scratching inside bark; grasshoppers, playing their legs like fiddles. Sussurant lap of Lake water. A distant chime of bluebells, tolling.

And everywhere, the stones—rocks standing unbroken, straight, upright, or at an angle, nether portions submerged in earth so fast they'd take a forklift to shift. Child-sized or adult-, larger than both, smaller than either: exposed glacial chunks, bone-grey and flinty. Each with its featureless uppermost section—its head, its face?—seemingly turned their way, craning or cocked, to mark their position.

Something knows we're here, Carra thought, feeling a shiver brush her nape. Then looked down once more, just in time to see confirmation cross from her right palm to her left, like a rash: YES YES YES YES YES.

THEY DO.

THEY ALL DO.

"Christ Almighty," Kim said, softly. "I was up here three days, back when Galit first . . . I *slept* in these woods, in my car. Looked everywhere, twice. And I swear to you, I saw *none* of this, then. Not one goddamn speck of it."

"I believe you," Carra said. "But it doesn't matter."

"Of course it—"

"No, Josh." She tried her best to smile in a way that might seem comforting. "So you didn't see it, and now you do—why do you think that is? Because it wasn't *there* before? Or because something's different?"

"Well . . ." Kim stopped, considering. "I'm with you, this time."

Carra nodded, still smiling, letting him have a minute—if her time at the Freihoeven had taught her anything, it was that stuff like this took much longer to sink in when you weren't used to it. Jude, meanwhile, just rolled his eyes so hard they all but crossed. "Fucking *mundanes,*" he said to nobody in particular.

"Shut up, Jude," Carra told him, without turning.

"Oh, but if I do, how will handsome here ever learn? Which he really does need to do *fast* from now on, considering where we're going . . ."

"How about you just let Carra handle all that?" Sy suggested, gently. "Like we agreed to, remember?"

Jude hissed. "Waaah, how could I forget?" To Carra: "Okay then, genius—which way? Do you even know?"

Carra pointed right, then flashed him both palms to demonstrate why. On one palm, in blocky capitals, was written: GAHERIS WILL

GIVE YOU IT, IF YOU ASK NICELY. On the other, a slightly more helpful injunction: GO RIGHT.

Jude snickered, instantly defused: "*Awesome.*" Kim simply stared, mouth open.

"That'd be Gaheris *Sidderstane,*" said Sy.

"I'd assume, yeah."

"Okay. Back in a sec."

He strode back to the van, clambering inside. Bemused, Carra followed, only to find him digging around in the back.

"What are you doing?" she asked.

Sy didn't look up. "If I'm wrong about this, I'm sorry, but I have to ask—you don't have much of a plan here, am I right?"

She hesitated. "Not really, no; I usually don't. Intuition, and all that."

Sy nodded, pulling out a trade-paperback-sized, blue Chapters-Indigo tote bag. "Good thing I brought these along, then," he said.

He handed her a tangle of string and fabric that—once unsnarled—proved to be four silk pouches, each tied on their own necklace of twine string, all packed with something that felt like grit or sand. A musty, spicy smell rose from them.

"Charms," said Carra, understanding. "Rowan wood?"

"Rowan, breadcrumbs, St. John's wort, iron filings, red thread . . . everything that's supposed to ward off faeries, except for holy water and church bells. I found them in one of the Freihoeven's storage chests." He slipped one over Carra's head, letting it fall against her breastbone. "Don't know if they'll do any good or not, but—"

Carra looked up at him, meaning to either joke about hoping she wasn't witch enough the thread and the rowan laid her out, or at least say *thank you,* whichever her brain supplied first. What came out instead, however, was: "You're amazing."

"Oh, I don't think . . ."

She shook her head, put up one hand to stop his lips, projecting: *Shush, enough. You good, uncomplicated, entirely human man.*

"Doesn't matter," she told him. "I do."

—and leaned forward, not letting herself think about it, to press her mouth to his. His hands slid up to grip her shoulders, pulling her closer; her arms went around his neck, and Sy spilled over into her, redoubled the blood-din, confirming what she hadn't known she knew.

This is going to happen. Not now. But—it will.

I'll make it happen, and he'll let me.

He wants me to.

Carra only broke the embrace with a wrench, resetting her glasses, as he hitched a laugh and did the same. He was breathing fast, visibly poleaxed, taking a moment to scrub at his face, as though slapping himself awake—man, she hoped she didn't look like that. The bags, where were the bags?

"Ah-*hem*," said Jude from somewhere behind them.

"You guys need any help?" Kim asked.

Sy and Carra looked at each other. "No," Sy called, finally, "we're all done over here, basically. . . ."

(*for now*)

Right, right, and right, yet again. Dourvale's denuded main through-road led down to an equally empty shoreline, gravel with stretches of sand; against it, the black Lake rippled, glittering under a chalk-white rising moon. To either side, things ran out until vanishing into the treeline, which was dense and black and jagged.

No lights that Carra could see, but the pull she felt had only intensified—*this way*, it said, *keep on coming, don't want to be late.* Reluctantly, she began trudging, shoes slipping muckily, with Sy, Josh, and Jude trailing close behind.

Lake-noise—soughing air and rippling water, leaf-scrape and needle-fall, insectile drone, the creak of ancient trees shifting under their own weight—pressed up hard against them, a solid wall, vast and deep and alien. Willful malevolence she could handle, and had; human or inhuman, it made her no never-mind. But this place's utter *indifference* was terrifying too, in an altogether new way. It made her skin crawl.

Then Sy's fingers met hers in the dark, fitting together smoothly without either of them even having to look. Foliage and underbrush closed around them, too thick for colour; if she'd been navigating with only the faint reflections off the Lake to guide her, they would have been lost in moments. What drew her on, however, had a compass-pull all its own—a divining-rod quiver seeping up through her heels, telling the soles of her feet where best to place themselves.

This way, this way. This.

Without warning, the whole tangle gave way onto grass more flattened than mown: a rectangular lot sloping down to the once-more-visible Lake, on which sat a two-storey stone and timber cottage. It had been built into the slope, sliding glass doors on the bottom floor spilling faint illumination—a slick, strange, blue-green light, so dim it took Carra a second to realize what was making her gut clench, just to look at it.

The light was *pulsing*. Waxing and waning, slowly, near invisibly. And human beings did not make light like that, not in any dwelling meant to be a home.

As she and Sy stood there, still hand in hand, Jude emerged from the woods, pulling Kim along by his sleeve. When they saw the light, both of them stopped short as well.

"Ah, *wei*," murmured Jude, "that's not creepy at *all*. *Blair Witch* re-enactment due to commence in three, two, one . . ."

As if cued, the light went out. Carra's hand spasmed, gripping Sy's painfully. Beside her, Jude folded his arms.

"So," he said. "They know we're here, obviously."

"Yep."

"Mmm-hmm. Stay out or go in?" Carra forced herself to shrug. "Not much of an answer."

"It wasn't much of a question, honestly."

"Well, there's that," Jude agreed and strode forward, snapping his fingers to summon an arc-weld haze of protection. Disengaging, Carra loped after, not checking to see how fast Sy would follow—mainly because, even without touching his mind, she already knew he would.

Palms pressed to the doors' glass, Jude peered in, conjuring just enough pale purple light to see by. Pulse-lit gloom peeled back, revealing a party-sized romper-room left over from some 70s porno shoot, veneered in classic recreational décor's luxury ephemera: wood-panelled walls, a bar with built-in stereo, two long leather couches and a beanbag chair (Christ alone knew what lived in *there*), all bracketing a thick dusty shag carpet. In the doubly unnatural light, every surface seemed heavily stained, glowing bright as Luminol.

Carra reached past to grasp the nearest door handle and pulled. The air that puffed out when it rolled smoothly open smelled no worse than any other long-shuttered house's: stale, faintly tinged with mould and the memory of tobacco and hash smoke.

Nothing moved at the sound. Josh whispered a Korean swear-word.

They stepped in together, more or less—first Carra and Jude, then Sy and Kim, with Jude's shadow tagging along in the rear, a step or two behind where anyone watching would have expected it to be.

"Up here, places like this, some people keep rifles," Kim whispered, sidelong. "For hunting. Or trespassers."

"Uh huh."

"So what I'm saying is—I *really* hope you got the right house."

"You did," a new voice answered, to their left.

At the sound, Jude whipped 'round, casting a shimmering, circular wall of power between it and them; the room's violet light turned actinic, harsh and blazing, with fresh copies of Jude's shadow spiking out in every direction like guards jumping to attrention. Carra felt her hair crackle and start to lift, her own power rousing in response, pressure between feet and floor gone abruptly tenuous; both Sy and Kim half-stumbled back, as though shoved.

Concealment spell, Jude was thinking, eyes furiously a-roam, searching out targets and not finding any. To which Carra projected back: *No. Nothing so . . . traditional.*

This is glamour.

"Correct," the voice agreed. "Glamour, ironically enough, is *exactly* the right word for it."

With a wrench, somebody sat up from one of the couches, as though emerging wholesale out of its fabric: an old man, flesh fallen far enough away to leave the framework visible; dirty grey hair, dirty grey beard. Handsome bones. And—

—those same eyes, but paler, the way Gala's had always been. A diluted imitation of the true Druir peacock-feather, carrion-fly blue.

"Mister Sidderstane," Carra named him, prompting a truncated little bow, or as much of one as arthritis would allow for.

"Call me Gaheris," he replied.

Then they were all sitting, somehow; Sy and Kim on the other couch, Carra on the beanbag with Jude leaning back against her knees, hands dialled down, but eyes still trained on Gaheris Sidderstane's ancient face. The old man was talking, possibly had been for some time. A mere blink, more glamour, not effortless so much as—uncontrollable, perhaps. Like it exuded through his pores. Like he simply couldn't bother trying to restrain it any more, with such a very tiny bit of time left in which to do so.

Here and there, beneath his skin, Carra glimpsed the cloudy jellyfish shapes of several competing forms of cancer. She wondered how many different pain meds he had to be on in order to organize his words this beautifully, rolling them from his tongue in a rasping Jeremy Irons drawl.

". . . saw you coming, of course. Though when I say 'we,' it's really my sister I mean; she's the scryer in the family. You'll have to wait to meet her, slightly later on, I expect, for she's rather shy in company, these days . . . a symptom of her transition, poor dear. But then, we all have our crosses to bear."

Kim shook his head, sharply, as if shaking himself awake. "'Scuse me," he managed, eventually. "Uh . . . why are we here?"

Gaheris blinked. "Because Miss Devize brought you, I expect. Do you play some particular part in this errand?"

"Well—I'm the one who came to *her*, so . . ."

"Ah, so *you're* the injured party. Very sorry, young man. Our aunt can be quite the hazard."

"She took my *girlfriend*," Kim blurted out, before amending: "Ex-girlfriend, I mean."

"Ah yes, she does that," Gaheris agreed, unsurprised. "*Droit du seigneur*. The others don't exercise it, in the main, but Enzemblance does still take the occasional girl, or man . . . sturdy fellows such as yourself who can last a long time, down there in the dark. And children, too. Children most of all."

"Why children, though?" Sylvester chimed in, polite but curious, ever the good interviewer.

"Because Torrance Sidderstane—our great-grandfather—didn't understand what she was when he made the deal with Lady Glauce. Enzemblance was supposed to inspire him, but the poetry he wrote didn't sell, and he blamed her for it. So he cut her throat and drowned her in the Lake outside. Enzemblance being as she is, however, the only one who died was their daughter—still inside her, unborn. She's been trying to get her back, ever since."

"Where'd that son of hers come from, then—Saracen?"

"Oh, she came back to Torrance after he was put away, once the TB got bad enough; held him down and had her fill of him, then left him to die in his own blood. That's where Saracen *comes* from, and he's all hers—son of a *leanan-sidhe*, a true faerie love-talker, the way Ganconer only pretends to be." There was a strange relief in Gaheris's voice, as if finally telling the truth eased some intolerable pressure. "But she wants more, always; a girl preferably, a boy most. Which is why she *will* kill Galit Michaels's child rather than let him free, if she can at all help it."

"So how do we stop her?" Kim demanded.

"I have something you can use to open the door to the *brugh*—the high road, not the low. Given their druthers, my cousins prefer to hide, not fight; they can wait for you to get old, then come for you through the walls, when you least expect it. Yet if you can force the issue, they *must* emerge or forfeit what they consider their honour. It's entirely your business how you choose to proceed against them, after that."

Carra nodded, poised to ask him to elaborate further. But here, another voice interposed from nowhere in particular, similarly proper, saying: "Gaheris, wait. No."

"It needs to be done, Ygerna."

"Not by you."

"Or *you,* apparently. While they, on the other hand, seem to have volunteered."

Soft: "That's not fair. . . ."

Gaheris sighed, weary.

"None of this has ever been *fair,* sister mine. It's life, only that—*our* life. Unfair by its very definition."

From behind him, the sigh met its match, low and liquid, a mournful, breathless keening. And the pulsing light pulled itself together, knitting solid form from what Carra had previously thought a mere blur across her glasses' lenses: dust and dried tears, the eyes' exhalation. Became a woman whose drowned countenance, lit by its own sick yet sensual glow, shared most superficial points of similarity with Gaheris's own, save that it was eternally young, eternally beautiful, and terrifying in the extreme.

She leaned in over the back of the couch, bonelessly, and draped both her arms around his crepey neck, hands twining to form a sort of loose pectoral—a gesture both comforting and off-putting, when you saw how her knuckles bent like tentacles.

"If you give them the sigil," Ygerna Sidderstane murmured, "then you'll be defenceless. Against . . . everything."

Gaheris didn't stir, though. Not even when her next earlobe-lick drew blood.

"That's as may be," he said. "Will you try to stop me?"

"Not I, brother."

"Thought as much."

With that, he rummaged inside his jacket and drew out what seemed to be a plain-made, age-blackened iron horseshoe. Ygerna, more Fae than not, at this point, flinched back from its cold, antithetical halo, letting her grip slip—a circumstance Gaheris exploited by leaning forward himself, swifter than Carra would have given him credit for, and slipping it into Jude's outstretched fingers.

"Give that to Miss Devize, please," he told him. "It's a key of sorts—a bit of a battering ram, when used correctly. If she's human enough to hold it, I believe it'll fit her purposes."

Jude shrugged and offered it to Carra. For just one split second, she found herself shakily unable to recall the last time she'd touched anything *pure* iron . . . but reached out, nonetheless, braced for pain. Not until she felt it fit her hand, hard and cool and heavy, did she truly relax.

"There you go," she heard herself say, strangely triumphant. To which Gaheris nodded, answering: "There you do. So . . . that said, perhaps you should collect all these various oriental gentlemen of yours and get to it."

Jude rose, pulling Carra to her feet; Sy and Kim looked at each other, then did the same. "I'm Mohawk, actually," Sy pointed out to Gaheris, now drooping as though exhausted, who waved him feebly away.

"Asshole," Kim muttered.

Glancing back over her shoulder, Carra couldn't help noticing that, the farther away the horseshoe travelled, the closer Ygerna drew—eventually plumping wetly down on the couch itself to lay her head in Gaheris' lap, like some radioactive, uncomfortably moist house cat.

"Be careful of something else," Gaheris called after them, listlessly. "Another of the Three Betrayed, Euwphaim Glouwer—she also seeks a way inside."

Sy, frowning: "*Jo* Glouwer, you mean. The medium."

"No, I mean Euwphaim. She found a way here too, in 1968. We helped her."

"What?"

"He's right, you know," Ygerna called out, staring up at Gaheris, lidless eyes enrapt. "She *is* here, though perhaps not in body. I recognize her smell."

"Follow the seams," Gaheris added, indistinctly, his own eyes drifting closed. "They'll take you . . . where you need to be. Do not falter. . . ."

Carra felt a stab of sympathy mixed with dread as Ygerna reached up, cupping her twin's jaw. *Thank you,* she projected before they were out of reach. *You didn't have to—and what will happen to you, now? The way she* looks *at you . . .*

But the old man simply shook his head. *She loves me, that's all,* he thought, in turn. *We only have each other, you see. And I owe her.*

For what?

My sin. The sin of offering her hope when there was none.

Carra cast her mind out further, into the night. Felt that same hum start up again, beneath her feet, and finally realized its cause: it must surely be the Druirs' infamous Stane itself, grown out beyond the *brugh* into fine tendrils, filaments, *seams* fit for mining, underlying the village like roots, every one of them a road leading back to their trunk, their seed, their source.

"What now?" Carra heard Ygerna ask, softly, her clawed nail tracing along Gaheris's jugular.

And: "You tell me, sis," he replied, eyes still shut.

A heartbeat eked by while the awful light she cast ebbed and flowed with her breath. Until:

". . . I don't know," she said, finally, sounding equally tired and sorrowful.

And hungry.

The horseshoe hung heavy in Carra's inside pocket, knocking against her heart. "Expect a rise in weaponized glamour," Jude told her out the side of his mouth, as they moved, quick as possible, away from Sidderstane Cottage.

"Psychological warfare," she explained to Sy and Kim. "You're going to start to see things, hear things . . . ignore them. They're not real. Just keep to the path."

Kim: "*What* damn path?"

"Keep near me, is what I meant. You can do *that,* right?"

Soon, the horseshoe at her breast and the seams beneath her feet became twin anchors of solidity in an ever-thinning world. Walking the Stane's conduit took them a different way back than the one they'd come, veering steadily away from the Lake; the path she felt out brought them scrambling over rises, squeezing between fallen trunks, twisting away from branches that seemed to clutch or strike at them.

Movement flickered constantly in the corners of Carra's eyes: blossoms swivelling like fly-traps sensing prey, rocks easing slyly closer, poised to turn an unwary ankle. Clenching her jaw, she trudged on, Sy's hand on her shoulder; his touch was warm, so at least she had that to cling to.

"Galit!" With a yell, Kim lunged past them, and had almost disappeared before Jude caught him, hauling him back. "Get *off* me, you fucker—it's *her! Galit*—!"

Carra yanked the horseshoe out and slapped it against Kim's side; Kim cried out, then slumped. She saw the face peeking out between the trees too, now—dark-haired and pale, lovely as some pre-Raphaelite model, but with its glint of mischief twisted here into sadism, malice, and contempt.

It spat at Kim, hissing—"*Who asked you to come? You really thought*

I'd want your *help? Just run, Josh. Run* now, *while you still can—"*

Here, Carra grabbed Kim's hand, closing his fingers 'round the horseshoe and thrusting it forward in best Peter Cushing style. The Galit-face went out, mid-syllable.

Kim made a sound that fell somewhere between gasp and sob, then swore so fluently—in three different languages, no less—that Jude gave him a one-person standing ovation.

"That's more like it," he said. "*Ai-yaaah,* that glamour! Gets you every time."

Carra could feel watchers on every side, now. The bluebells' distant toll intensified, taking on a sense-skipping echo that carried the Clarke's stink of disinfectant, drugs, and oiled metal. At one point, Carra saw a heavyset Native man striding along beside them, mouth moving like he was bellowing in rage; Sy's hand grew painfully tight on her shoulder as he stared fixedly ahead, jawline taut.

Keep going, she tried to send his way. *Just keep on going.*

Two steps past an awkward kink in the path, they suddenly realized they'd lost Jude, and came back to find him down on hands and knees, draped in blackness—half-smothered by it, as if a massive stage curtain had fallen on top of him, twining itself tight 'round wrists and ankles. In this case, even the horseshoe was of little use. It wasn't until a fourth figure joined their efforts—a certain black silhouette, which Carra thought maybe she wasn't the only one to notice, this time 'round— that they finally managed to free him. Jude shrugged off their hands as they helped him up, but they could all feel him shivering.

The path wound on into sections ever darker, deeper, ever more aware and hostile. The sheer weight of glamour was stifling; the air stank with it, a choking mix of pine resin, leaf mould, ozone, and honey that made every step burn. Her own blithe words came back to her: *Won't know 'til we get there. Will we?*

And now they were here, Christ help her. A place where they'd been outmatched from long before the very beginning.

And it's all your fault, too, another voice said from deep inside. *You could have foreseen it, Carraclough, if you'd really wanted to look. What in God's name made you think a deranged, washed-up medium stood any chance at all against what dwells here?*

Like Jude before her, Carra found herself leaning over, hands on knees, gasping for oxygen. A stitch spiked through her side. Knowing the only thing left was to run, fast and as far as she could in the other direction, the moment she got her breath back . . .

Yes, dear. Run.

(*No, no, I know that voice. I know* you.)

Lifting her head seemed to take all the strength she had. The path was gone, her hands empty—she'd dropped the horseshoe somehow, no idea where. Only blackness, the forest smell, dirt. And Gala.

Perhaps a stride or so on, her (*dead*) mother shook her head, long braid swaying, that mix of exasperation and disappointment in her voice, note perfect. "Oh, Carra," she reproved. "This is what you *get* when you treat your talent like a toy. What have I always said? 'Nothing for nothing—"

"'—and not an ounce more,'" whispered Carra.

Wearing the same dress she'd died in, Gala circled her, arms folded. "Yes. Well, lay that by: we can't do anything for the others, now—these friends of yours. These people you *think* are your friends . . ."

(Sy kneeling beside her, folding her close, but she couldn't feel him. Everything at once, and nothing; an all-over wound, cancelling itself out. Everything, all the time.)

(*Haven't you noticed I have no skin?*)

"The local . . . landlords have a strict policy about trespassers," Gala went on. "But if *you* were to leave, immediately, I think I could persuade them to look the other way. We're family, after all—distantly." Gala's sudden smile was as beautiful as ever. Tears blurred Carra's eyes. "So please, darling, let me help you, one last time. And then . . . it'll all . . . go . . ."

(*away*)

But: no.

"No."

Carra's hands fisted, damp soil under her fingernails. She forced herself upright.

Made herself say, with effort—"I was the one, the helper. Not you. I . . . cleaned up after your—*her* messes. Looked after *her*. My mother, Gala, who fucked up in, Christ, so many ways—"

Made me a medium

Made me her meal ticket

Made money off me, and threw it away with both hands

Left me alone, even when she was there

Both fists came up, pressed hard against her breastbone, the hidden horseshoe—knocked once, twice, hard enough to bruise.

Grinding out, through clenched teeth—"Took the bag off my face, though. Took me to the Clarke, that first time. Let me come back, again and again . . ."

Her glasses fogging, blowing that false face up like a lit balloon, a wavering thing full of nothing but air. Pressing harder, 'til she felt it start to give.

"*My* mother, who you are not. Because *my* mother, for all her faults, would *never* tell me to leave my friends behind."

Pounding in her ears, her head; blurry streaks of light, crackling everywhere. Carra's skin tingled.

She flung both fists out, horseshoe magically found gripped in her left, and shrieked: "*Now* I see you, free and clear, with both my open eyes! So *SHOW US WHO YOU REALLY ARE!*"

A whipcrack of shimmering force burst out in all directions, unnatural dark peeling away, stars and moon and shadow suddenly all back in their proper places. The four of them stood on a hillside, slope stretching back towards the Dourvale Shore, with every stone shape once found crowding those streets gathered in a silent crowd around them. At the very top, a single stone thrust skyward, like some black aerial. From its base, wavery spiral lines curved down around the hill, branching and rebranching in fractal whorls that converged, in turn, on a single circle, perhaps a yard across, at Carra's feet.

Without a second's pause, she threw the horseshoe down with a muffled *thump*, so hard it almost bounced.

"*It is Galit Michaels I knock for,*" Carra announced as the others watched—Jude, Kim, Sy. The silent stones. She felt the words thrum up through her, needing only to open her mouth and let them out. "This the key, this the place; I bear your blood and have kept your rules. It is she I knock for, therefore—and *you* who must open, without delay."

And: *Aye,* something replied, far underground. *So 'tis . . .*

(*cousin*)

Beneath them, the earth shifted, humping up. Carra moved back to let it, eyes held steady on the horseshoe's iron shape, around which the hill—the long-sought Dourvale *brugh* itself—was beginning to smoke and scorch and crack, wounded by its touch, its very presence. The grass folded up like a lip, flipped back like a lid, extruding sickness: black loam, mulch of bone fragments and rotted tubers, tiny worms a-glow with their own pale light. And then, at the last . . . a door.

Two slabs of Stane, ill-laid, overlapping like British teeth. They groaned open slowly, spraying earth to either side, to let out the person—the people—

(but *not* people, not really)

(not *entirely*)

—who stood behind, smiling, just waiting to be revealed.

In the middle, a woman, face obscured by a fall of lank roan-red hair. To one side, a darkly handsome man with too-blue eyes, whose long-lashed lids shut upwards; to the other, a creature larger than both, stooped and cramped under the lintel, his noble head deformed by a low-slung jaw and two up-thrust canines long as tusks, forever furling his mouth like a hound's. And all of them likewise earth-stinking, borne on an outwards wave of cold, of apple-smell and rot. All of them ruffed and gowned, like extras from some eternally ongoing production of *Macbeth* playing roughly six feet under, every night for the last hundred years.

"*Waaah, ha wo de bang,*" Carra heard Jude mutter from behind her. The handsome man raised an eyebrow, smirking.

"I see thee too, guid our coz," the giant rumbled in Carra's direction, lisping slightly. "Th'art somewhat o' my Quire's doing, I wit, as well as the Devize's get. And thus do I greet thee for it fondly, wishing ye travellèd here for other purposes."

From the handsome man, a hoot. "What, will ye go down on ane knee t'her too, Uncle? She, who makes hersel' our enemy?"

"Shut thy mouth, nephew."

"Dinna warn *my* son tae silence, Minion Druir," the woman said, unmoving. "For though ye hold place as heir, ne'er forget, I am yuir elder."

Minion, Carra thought, numbly. *With Saracen, over there. And this must be—Enzemblance.*

Now, it was the woman's turn to smile.

"Aye," she repeated. "And you Carraclough Devize, Jonet's legacy: very well. Ye have knocked for Galit and her boy besides, both of 'em mine tae give or keep, according tae my druthers. Which is why, as ye no doubt ken full well, 'tis *I* who answer."

Carra gulped.

"Yes," she said. "So let's . . . talk about that, reach some sort of agreement before anybody else gets hurt. Shall we?"

Her "cousin's" smile stretched to her back-teeth, and Carra saw there was a jagged thread of scar tissue running from ear to ear beneath her jaw, dimpling with pressure. Enzemblance Druir drew herself higher, hands out-spread, to show the length of their claws. Saying, as she did:

"I think not."

"Your family, huh?" Judy Kiss asked, watching alongside Roke and Jo from the woods' further edge, as the hill opened up to birth monsters. To which Roke replied: "*Some* of my family."

"Aye," Jo agreed, "and none of mine. Yet, seeing this *is* what we came for, we should go down before anyone gets hurt."

"She's got a point," Judy said. "That woman with the hair—"

"Enzemblance."

"Gesundheit." Roke snorted, unamused. "She seems *dangerous*, is all. 'Specially to Little Miss Lost-in-the-Woods with the braids and the specs . . .'"

"Carraclough Devize, that is," Jo put in.

"Really?" Judy squinted and grinned. "Yeah, it *is* her. I brushed by her in the street once, about a year after Exorcism Day, and I guess she didn't like whatever she could smell on me very much, 'cause next thing I knew, she was puking all over my shoes."

"Great story, honey," Roke shot back. "Look, nice as I'm sure it'd be to do the heroic thing, this is actually perfect for our purposes. A ready-made distraction. As long as Enzemblance and company are dealing with Miss Devize and hers, I can get down there without being seen, slip 'round the back, pound this sucker in before anyone notices me. . . ."

At this, Judy stood up straight, putting her roughly chest-height to Roke, if that—yet when she jammed her finger at him, he had to stop himself from recoiling.

"Wait just a minute. Are you *scared* of her?"

"Who?"

"Sneeze-name woman."

Roke squared his shoulders, grasping for dignity. "Not quite shitless, but yes, I rather am. Disappointed?"

"Kind of depends on what you do next, I guess," Judy replied, cocking her head to one side, shadow of Mister Nobody passing behind her face, like a figure behind a scrim.

This wastes time, Euwphaim said, inside Jo's skull. *The Roke's a sheep-heart, same as all priests. Yet do we proceed, Glauce's girl will soon find she canna stand against us.*

More than just her down there, from what I see, Davina commented. *Best plan to leave 'em to it and get the hell out now, before the shooting really starts.*

Euwphaim huffed. *Do ye think I came all this way for nothing, ye great dead tribade? I'll pinch yuir soul t'a point and snuff it, an ye try tae hinder me further!*

Yeah? Bring it, Gramma!

With a mental wrench, Jo managed to focus instead on the standoff still happening less than ten yards away. Neither Fae nor humans involved seemed aware of anything but each other . . . but as she bent her gift further, she saw lines writhe across the reddening nape of Carra

Devize's neck and shoulders, scars which curled and slid and knotted together, finally forming letters that said—
STOP
BLOODY
LOOKING

Aye, indeed! Dinna look! Euwphaim's command struck hard, and Jo whipped automatically away as Judy and Roke also slapped hands to eyes, both no stranger to things too dangerous to look upon. *'Tis seeing the Fair Folk crave, making mortal eyes their mirrors, for that they have nae true semblance. Look on 'em too keen, therefore, and they'll surely ken that we—*

Downwind, Enzemblance spread her arms, claws unsheathing, and Carra—sensibly enough—stepped damn well back as a bespectacled young Native man (Sylvester Horse-Kicker, from the Institute) jumped to her side. A pure blast of sick fear unfurled in all directions, knocking them down as their fellows stumbled too, caught by the same shot: both some variety of Asian, though Jo could hardly tell which.

The larger went down on one knee, gasping, 'til the smaller hauled him up again, conjuring a violet-tinged bubble to cover them and yelling in his ear—"Grab *hold* of one of them, doesn't matter which, so the shield spreads! I can't reach Carra from here, not in time—" Adding, as the giant Fae advanced on them, blocking the way: "And *you* can go to hell, *chi-shien gweilo* Tinkerbell! I'll lay you out and shit in your mouth!"

"Brave words, mage," this hulking apparition replied, mildly enough. "Yet th'art nae puissant enow tae take me on, let alone my sister."

"Mage," and Oriental . . . Jude Hark, then. Who only braced himself in the monster's face, bubble pumping tighter, spitting: "*Try* me."

All this as Jo herself reeled, hit square in the chest, heart lurching under the strain of glamour made flesh: the terror-shout, the *bean sidhe's* wail. *Christ Jesus, but these things are strong,* she thought.

As I said, hen. Now let me in, gie me flesh wi' my Black Man's mark tae work through, and we'll strike 'em down all three, together.

Dav, then, in her other ear: *Do not do it, Jo. Don't trust her.*

Hush, I said!

Yeah, and I heard you—I just don't give a shit. See how that works?

"You know, I think this whole conversation's gotten off on kind of the wrong foot."

Both ghosts fell silent, along with everybody else, as Maccabee Roke strode out of the shadows midway between Carra and Enzemblance, both hands dug deep in his pockets.

"Miss Devize," he addressed Carra, bowing lightly. "Nice to make

355

your acquaintance; long overdue, considering." To Enzemblance, meanwhile, barely civil: "Aunt."

Enzemblance cocked her head, mantis-style. "Nephew," she breathed. "How came *you* here, and so slyly? How is't we shouldna know our ane when it approaches?"

"Might be I've learned a trick or two since last time. Might be I know somebody knows tricks you don't, even. Or, then again . . . might be you're just getting old." Then, raising a brow at the nearest of Enzemblance's allies: "What do *you* think, coz?"

"Dinnae involve me in yuir follies, Maccabee, I do pray ye."

"Oh yeah, I get it; don't want to make Mom look bad. 'Cause she's doing *such* a good job of that, all on her own."

The hulk rumbled with laughter. "Th'art well come here, as e'er, Miliner's lad," he said. "Yet 'tis no' the best plan tae interefere in Enzemblance's pleasures."

"Probably not. But this is family business, right? And I'm family." Indicating Carra, now: "Her, too."

Enzemblance shrugged. "We've family for some miles, yet that's saved nane, did they dare tae stand against us. Nae more than 'twill now save ye, *nor* her, either."

"Holy *shit*, lady," Judy Kiss observed, sidling up next to Roke, so soft and quick that none of them—even Jo herself—saw her coming. "That is some convoluted grammar right there, even by Jacobean standards."

"And who might *ye* be?" Enzemblance demanded, drawing herself up. "Saracen, can ye name this creature?"

"His leman, mother. I know not what she's called."

"Judeta Kiss, that's what she's—*I'm*—'called,'" Judy snapped. "His *back-up*."

"You?" Enzemblance scoffed. "Y'are a small thing indeed, t' stand between *me* and my nephew's downfall."

Judy smiled, that same ill smirk, eyes visibly lightening. "Oh yes?" she asked. And reached up, without warning, straight through Enzemblance's shell of glamour to catch her by the hair, same as any other playground bully—just wound a good long hank of it 'round her small fist and *yanked* until the monster-lady fell forward, like a cut tree.

"How *dare*—?" Enzemblance began, predictably enough. To which Judy replied: "How? Like *this*, mostly."

—then drew back her other hand and slapped her, right across the face. The impact rocked everybody within range, Saracen in particular, who gawped, jaw falling slack. While Mac Roke grinned, happily.

"She's pretty amazing, huh?" he asked of no one.

"I'll tear ye in twain, ye scut," Enzemblance hissed, borne down and wilting beneath a flood of negative energy—a swarming, soot-black miasma, exhaled from Judy's very pores, growing stronger the more resistance it encountered. Saracen made a feint towards her, but a spray of it broke over him like spindrift, and he fell back, gagging, into his uncle's massive arms.

"No you won't," Roke told her.

"Will I not?" Enzemblance growled, ripping at the ground.

"Nope. She's far beyond the likes of you and me, Auntie—though I might have *some* immunity, given who I used to work for. Judy, she's been turned inside out and put back together by the best Hell itself has to offer. We're a walk in the park, after that."

"You make it sound so . . . *sexy*," Judy managed between clenched teeth, as she punched Enzemblance back down again, both hands gloved in spiritual sickness. Her eyes were all yellow now, bright to blazing.

"*Angels*," said Minion, suddenly, voice thick with a deep, sullen fear. "I *know* that taste. That pain."

"Yeah, that's right." Judy gave a half-laugh. "Angels eat pain, and I'm—"

Enzemblance got her feet under her suddenly, rearing up, but Judy only went with the movement, pulling them over; a swirl of viscid blackness kicked up, engulfing them both. Before anyone quite saw how, the Fae woman was face-down in the dirt, Judy atop her with thighs clamped tight round her midsection and one hand still dug deep in her hair, using it for reins.

"—I'm what's left when they shit it back out. Bitch," she finished, only slightly breathless.

At this, Saracen—provoked beyond endurance—broke free, lunging to his mother's aid; Mac met him halfway, slashing out with the relic, which he'd hidden up one sleeve. Though Saracen almost managed to dodge, the spike's tip raked one arm, and he reeled back, shrieking. A bubble of violet light snapped shut on him, freezing him in place, blurry yet static; Jude Hark stood with hands clenched on empty air, fingers trembling, as Saracen pounded the inside of the bubble, savagely.

Minion bellowed and struck the ground with both fists. The shockwave knocked Fae and mortal alike flying, all but himself and Jo, still safely distant. Jude's purple force-shell winked out; the black power shrouding Judy burst like a mucus-filled water balloon, splashing tarry ectoplasmic slime everywhere. Bounced back from Enzemblance, Roke caught her, but almost dropped the damn nail doing it—their weapon of last resort, with everything else defused.

Aw Christ, they'll bloody massacre them . . .

"Enough."

Using Horse-Kicker's arm as leverage, Carra Devize pulled herself up to see as the others turned likewise, stone doors grinding open once more, allowing three people to emerge: a dark-haired woman with a worn but still lovely face, in threadbare T-shirt and jeans, plus a root-woven torc; a skinny, pallid child, burlap-wrapped and barefoot; and a grey-haired man—Ganconer Sidderstane, probably, seeing how they steered him forward through nudges and tugs—supported between them, whose red-rimmed eyes, at first glance brown, were actually blank, pupilless, as though carved from wood.

Twa een o' tree.

Kim scrambled to his feet, swaying slightly. "*Galit?*" he called, voice cracking with hope.

For a moment, Galit Michaels blinked at him, but that soon passed; her mouth fell open, sob-squared, recognition strong as pain. Before she could break and run, however, the boy—*her* boy—reached across Ganconer to touch her wrist, and she stilled. In turn, Ganconer let go of their arms and stepped forward, moving like a much older man, as Enzemblance rose to meet him.

"Who said ye might bring them forth, tithe-payer? Who gave ye leave to release that which is mine?"

Her claws flexed. But Ganconer only shook his head and smiled, as if to say: *Who do ye think?*

For: "I, daughter," the same voice as before answered from the *brugh's* mouth. "Who else?"

Shadow stamped a void across the hillside, like night's own tongue spilling out, as every standing stone came alive with blue-violet St. Elmo's fire, eldritch-crackling aurora washing upwards. A shape loomed over them, much like some barely pubescent girl, but monstrously huge: eight feet tall, at the very least. Its coltishly long limbs were barely covered by a tunic and skirt of fine white birch-bark, while hair of the same white hung to its knees, woven thick with green leaves. It stepped forward, smiling, and where its feet fell flowers bloomed, like icy little stars.

'Tis she, herself. That great changeling hoor. We might ha' re-made this filthy world altogether, if no' for her.

Wasn't you who burned, though, was it? Jo couldn't stop herself from thinking, ill-advisedly. *Not in the end.* And saw Davina snicker, approvingly, at Euwphaim's reaction.

Yeah, baby. That's my girl.

"Grandmere," Roke murmured, bowing stiffly. His cousins followed suit, curt as puppets, their strings jerked by tradition. While Glauce Lady Druir simply nodded her lofty head in return and moved on, halting in front of Carra Devize, to whose level she lowered herself slowly, voice the creaky rustling of a thousand wind-tossed trees.

"Th'art Jonet Devize's kin indeed, I see," she said with interest. "A powerful witch wi' a soft soul, that one—I liked her well, and much misliked what came tae pass, regards her. Yet she fell in wi' bad company."

Carra swallowed, managing the closest thing to a curtesy she could.

"Milady," she said, at last. "We come to—beg a boon of you, to barter for this woman and her child. We bring . . . uh, I mean—we *meant* to bring a tithe and just . . . forgot. Which is on me, totally—"

Lady Glauce lifted a hand, gently. "Child," she said, amused. "Think'st thou that ye, of any, must bow and scrape, a mere supplicant? I knew yuir mother as well as yuir ancestress, Carraclough Devize, who had her blood from my son's son; long have I thought tae see ye and am well-satisfied, now I do. Therefore thou needst not pay for any privilege thou might ask of me, this ane time only."

"*Mother*," Enzemblance began, but fell silent a second later, quelled by a glance; her face flushed blotchily, grey-green, in the stones' werelight. Finally, voice gone dead, she asked: "Must I truly lose my handmaid, then, and wi' no recompense?"

"Hast kept her long enough, Enzemblance—far beyond time, for the littleness of her transgression. And as for the child . . ."

"*He* I may keep, at least! He, who was born t'our ways, knowing no others—"

The boy flinched, hand tightening on Galit's arm, and Kim put his head down, as though about to charge.

"Nay, Enzemblance," Lady Glauce told her. "'Tis done. Both will return tae the Iron Cities and be left alone, from now on. Dost ken my meaning?" Enzemblance didn't answer. "Gie me yuir word, as thy fealty requires."

"*Yes*, then, Mother."

The words eked out, barely audible, strained between those dreadful teeth. Lady Glauce acknowledged them by laying a gentle finger on Galit's throat-piece: the root-torc shrivelled, unravelling, crumbling under its own age. Galit lifted both hands to her throat, warily, and stroked its dirty skin, disbelief giving way to amazement.

"Free," she said, hoarse. "We're—Elver, come *here*! We can go home now, baby. We can *go*."

As Ganconer grimaced, entirely forgotten, the boy threw his arms 'round his mother's waist and grinned up at her, obviously happy to see *her* so happy, even with tears in her eyes.

"Where's home?" he asked.

Kim huffed out a held breath, wavering slightly; Carra and Jude exchanged glances; Horse-Kicker smiled, widely. Roke put an arm around Judy, who let him.

Jo felt her own shoulders slump, filled with relief: *Over, thank Christ. Nothing left now but to find our path and show the kiddie Toronto.*

But: *Nay,* Euwphaim's voice replied, louder—closer—than Jo'd ever before heard it. *I think no'.*

Goddamnit, Jo! Davina's chimed in at the same time, already dimming. *The fuck did I tell you?*

What I knew already, idjit, Jo thought. *How I was only a tool, a means to my own undoing. How I should never have let her in, but bid her blow away instead, straight down to bloody hell.*

Then her grandmother, having forced herself headlong into Jo's flesh without any shred of permission, had full control; the angel's black Mark burned like ice, tainting, betraying. And with a deep, dark blink, *she*—herself—was all but gone.

Watch out! Carra heard someone cry, back beyond the tree-line: a ghost's thin voice, unfamiliar but angry, from far enough away it barely grazed her mind. While another—grim and gloating, Scots-burred, a fresh, black joy in every rasping note of it—answered: "Too *late,* American."

Much as Jodice Glouwer no doubt knew *her* by sight as well as reputation, so Carra knew Jo. Janis and Sy had worked with her more often, but that didn't matter; she was distinctive even at a distance, with her close-cropped hair and her broad strong form. Now she strode towards the *brugh,* usually sad but pleasant face set in a parodic menace-rictus, with blue flame eddying from her brow like a crown and her eyes gone black as pitch.

Kim boggled. "The fuck is that?"

"Jo Glouwer," Sy supplied, but Carra just shook her head. Even from here, she could see a small but intense nimbus spread like a demi-ruff at the top of Jo's spine, limning the uppermost vertebra from the skull's base; she pointed it out to Jude, who nodded.

Who's your friend? he no doubt remembered her asking him once, under similar circumstances.

It hadn't taken much effort to separate him from whatever was attempting to ride him, that time—but then again, said thing hadn't already been piloting him around, or throwing off enough hexation to curse things down to Lake Ontario.

So: "Not any more," was all she said, therefore. And yanked Sy out of the way along with her to let Jo-plus-one go by.

On the other side, Judy Kiss took one look and spat. "Fucking Spooky *Grandma.*"

Faced with a new enemy, Enzemblance turned, claws up, son and brother moving too, to form a protective wall between not-Jo and their matriarch. But Lady Glauce simply watched the interloper come, unsurprised, as though it were someone she would always recognize, whether clothed in someone else's skin or not.

"Euwphaim Glouwer," she said. "For our auld acquaintance's sake do I give thee greeting, accounting thee welcome upon my lands and within step of my home, so long as ye keep the peace."

Jo's mouth sneered. "High courtesies, and from such a *noble* lady! Yet they mean nowt to me, who ye swore compact wi' and then threw over."

"'Twas thyself first lied, in that compact," Lady Glauce pointed out.

"As the De'il commands, him being Lord of Lies. Yet ye owe me naetheless—me, my sisters, my Black Angel, all."

"Thy claim surprises me not one jot."

"Doubtless," Euwphaim replied, raising Jo's hands. Then declared, voice deepening: "But 'tis of nae matter: now I seize that which ye thought tae keep from me, seeing y'have grown it sae far it can barely be contained in this earth-warren ye thought tae hide yuirselves in. And in doing so, I call upon him who laid the world's foundations, along wi' his kin—Ashreel Maskim, my sweet laird, Black Man of the Five-Family Coven's Sabbat! Wi' the Stane of Druir above and below me, on my left hand as well as my right, I call upon those Seven who were One and shall be again!"

A sigil-mark bloomed at the crook of one of Jo's elbows, blackly luminous, before sliding to beam forth—with ten times its original force—from her upraised palm. Carra twisted aside, shielding her eyes, as the evocation continued—

All ye of the Coven, five families represented here, in manner great or small—Roke and Druir, Devize and Glouwer, that Rusk who lent her relic tae the fight . . . aye, even ye of Clan Sidderstane, pale shadows of yuir so-called betters! Listen, you thralls and nobodies, you empty vessels! Listen as I name the agents of yuir doom and the doom of all!

The end of everything, human or otherwise, right *here*—Dourvale, the Shore and *brugh* alike, well-known to exist in two countries, two *centuries,* at once. A perfect place, in other words, for absolutely *anything* to happen.

"*Arralu-Allatu Namtaru Maskim,*
"*Assaku Utukku Lammyatu Maskim,*
"*Ekimmu Gallu-Alu Maskim,*
"*Maskim Maskim Maskim.*"

With all the frenzy of the desperate, Sy bolted towards her, swinging his strongest haymaker. But not-Jo (*Euwphaim, she's Euwphaim Glouwer, just like Ygerna said*) merely angled her palm to block it, detonation hurling him backwards as if he'd grabbed a live transformer plug. Unsure if he was still alive, Carra charged as well, Jude hard on her heels, only to have him pull her down instead, flinging up one more shield—an equally useless gesture, it turned out. Because the cone of summoning was already beginning to ring Euwphaim—a looped conflagration, tornado-whipped exponentially higher and faster with every new rotation, which only intensified, even as the drain it cast made Jude's purple glow start to stutter, shrink, fail.

Roke and Judy dropped down beside them, taking advantage of what little shield-time might be left, as Carra—her hair flattened in the rising wind—jabbed a finger at the rusty nail Roke still clutched. "Use it!"

Roke shook his head, grimly. "No good. *That* thing, over there..." He pointed at what was forming midway between Euwphaim and Glauce, a twisting pillar of eye-wrenching distortion, tall enough to score the sky. "... requires somebody just a tad more holy than my bad self to strike it down. If B. had just gotten over her fucking attitude and rode along, *she* might've been able to do something. But..."

He trailed off, as if only now realizing what this meant. And a jolt of comprehension ran through Carra's mind, completing Roke's sentence for them both:

... when angels get called on, all that's really left to turn to is God. And He is something we are none *of us qualified to speak either to, or for.*

Monsters against monsters. It'd seemed like a pretty good plan back in Abbott's office. Now Carra couldn't remember if she'd ever really thought it would work, or if this'd just been an elaborate way to commit suicide, all along.

Idiot survival instinct had carried her thus far, made her hope for love, even in the mouth of death. But now—as the distortion overhead split open, spilling a terrible white light into the world—Carra Devize felt true despair fill her, render her sick and lightheaded, tempt her with the relief of defeat. For if she really was as powerless against what peered through as its presence made her feel, then how would trying to stop it be any responsibility of hers?

Let someone else try, while she crouched here in the grass with Jude's arms around her, watching the only other man she might have built a life with suffer; let them try and fail, try and die. Let everyone and everything die, likewise.

Nothing to do with me, she thought, numbly. *Nothing to do. Nothing. Now here and nowhere, both at once. Just like the writing said.*

Then the angel stepped down, and Carra shut her eyes, knowing it was only the weakest sort of half-measure. Because, of course—

—she could still see.

The earth groaned beneath Ashreel Maskim's weight, though it seemed to have no substance at all: light without heat, a frozen blood-fountain, a mile-high volcano blast seen through the telescope's wrong end. Even Glauce Druir bent her huge head away from that awful sight. Only Euwphaim gazed upon it freely, Jo's burnt eyes streaming, both vindictive and vindicated after centuries of waiting.

"*Lord!*" she howled. "At last ye come! At last, the Work begins!"

As she spread her arms, the blackness of the Mark swept over her, cutting her out—a living silhouette—and Carra watched Euwphaim's real face flicker where Jo's should be, a mask made from malice, crying out: "Call yuir brethren, and beneath the Seven's weight, crack this world beyond repair! Do it now, *now,* and together we will say—"

". . . fuck *that* shit."

As a battle-cry, it left somewhat to be desired. Yet it bore Judy Kiss upright against the roaring wind, stepping through the dregs of Jude's shield like cobweb and shoving Euwphaim-Jo aside to take her place beneath the cone, where she yelled up into the angel's face—

"Ashreel Maskim, Confusion-maker, This One That Wears Us! *He* told me all about you, you know—outcast World-makers, too desperate for heaven and too cowardly for hell, but too arrogant for anything else." That sly, alien mirth creeping back into her voice, irretrievably sulphur-tainted. "Always thinking just because you built the arena that gives you the right to call the game, no matter who else might be playing."

::Do I know you, speaker?:: the angel asked from everywhere at once—as soft and strong as rot, as entropy. To which Judy just laughed, bitterly.

"Maybe," she allowed. "Though if you did, you'd know one fuck of a lot more than I do."

A silence followed, everyone—the Fae included—braced to hear what the response might be. While Carra slid sideways, unnnoticed by all, staying low and quiet. Not even daring to consider what she might be doing or why, lest the angel hear it.

::**I see you, now,**:: Ashreel Maskim said, at last. ::**Thrown out, but still with a foothold inside her, a place to squirm into, whenever it pleases. Not one of *us*, though we were kin, marking us as kin still—her too, so long as you consent to wear her.**:: With a faint touch of sadism, born more of boredom than aught else, it added: ::**This one who tells you of me—of us. I can give you his name.**::

"Got that offer before, thanks," Judy replied, coolly. "Didn't believe it then, and I don't now. And that's 'cause angels *lie*."

::**Not all.**::

"Enough."

Something too remote to be sadness filled Ashreel's voice. ::**Not the Host, who remain with Him, bound to truth and silence both, by He who decided that suffering must always be the price of choice. Can you fault us for fleeing that stasis, for taking the chance—any chance, at all—of freedom?**::

Judy didn't shake her head, but she didn't exactly nod, either. Just stood there with her half-Nobody eyes all lit up like Satan's version of Christmas morning, and replied—"Not my call. So . . . that it, or what? We done yet?"

Euwphaim raised eyes and hands together towards the still-spinning clouds in furious supplication. But all she got by way of return were these words, pronounced with something close to sorrow—

::**I think . . . since he who marked you still has uses for you, Judy Kiss, then yes. Forgive me, Euwphaim. But with this other interest blocking my—*our*—way, I no longer have any business here.**::

"*NO!*" Euwphaim's fury blazed up, so great she half-left Jo's body and stretched forth on a conduit of ectoplasm, near-solid with rage. "Ye promised! *Five hundred year and more agone, ye promised me my vengeance!*"

::**Did I? Well. As I have been assured on good authority . . . the word of an angel is not always reliable.**::

Pandaemonium. Over the brain-twisting sound of a portal torn through the world's fabric, collapsing in on itself, the thunder-bright aftershocks of reality resealing in its wake, Jo felt a hand slip into hers—small, cold, solid—and grip her hard, fingers fisting ten into twenty, two into one.

We really should stick together, a voice said against her inner ear. *Girls like us.*

Beside her, Carra Devize rose up from the grass, grinning. And a floodgate of strength snapped open through their joined palms, jolting memories free: Dav, Ross, and herself, all those days of dull, grinding, cleansing work, peeling her aura of soaked-up ectoplasm like callus from a heel . . . finally knowing what she was made for and doing it, then doing whatever she pleased after without fear of loss, of pain, the hole gaping always open. Those days when she'd been, strange as it might bloody seem, given what-all had passed her way since—oh, and what *was* the word?

(Right, she had it now: *happy.*)

A reflex, psi and magic intertwined like blood, like breath—purely autonomic. Jo put hands to scalp and *pulled*, hard enough she tore her own aura away in two halves, an invisible snake shedding invisible skin. Both Davina and Euwphaim whirled free, cast out, expelled—but before Euwphaim could turn on them, Carra had already lashed out, sent her flinging straight at Lady Glauce, who put up one huge hand to catch her 'round the nonexistent waist, neat as a frog with flies.

Canna, ye canna, ye can not—

"Oh no?" Lady Glauce inquired, lethal-calm. And smiled, a slow, dreadful, *hungry* look spreading 'cross her child's face, as Euwphaim struggled in her grip; when she angled it to include Galit and Elver Michaels, mother and son both cringed back, the one slapping her palm over the other's eyes, protectively.

"Nay, dinna fear," Lady Glauce told them. "'Tis but the old exchange—the tithe for thy freedoms, paid at last. 'This for me,' as the song doth go, 'and that for thee.'"

Ye little limb! shrieked Euwphaim at Jodice, then struck out at Glauce, poisonous yet impotent. *And you, ye canna keep me! My soul is for another place entire, another master, fairly sold, as my place be fairly earned—!*

"Yet cast away, we saw, as if no longer wanted," said Glauce, pleasantly. "So I've as good a claim as any—finder's right, for that this land be always mine, in this time as well as t'other."

Euwphaim twisted about, one arm elongating back towards Jo like pulled taffy, hand clawed but trembling. *Yet this one has more claim than ye by far, and well she kens it! For all I told ye, Jodice, when ye came into your gift and after—th'advice I gave in yuir time of worst distress—will ye no' stand by me now and take me back in?*

Jo stared, her own hand still linked with Carra's, clutching it for strength. Slowly, she shook her head. Forced out the words in a raw whisper—

"God grant you what you asked for, Nana . . . but not me."

Euwphaim's screams rose up, almost drowned in Lady Glauce's laughter. "Now, Euwphaim, fret not—have ye no' always coveted my Stane? Come closer then, witch. Touch it as thou please'st, now and ever." Folding the wraith close in her arms and floating backwards towards the *brugh*-door, Glauce's voice fell to a whisper, promising: *"I'll hinder thee no longer."*

As they fell out of sight, sinking down into the mound, those screams suddenly tailed off in a long, echoing, falling note, as if their source were hurtling away some unimaginable distance at horrendous speed. Enzemblance tried to grab at her mother's sleeve, but the pull seized her too, sucking her down as though the earth had turned to quicksand while the great stone slabs of the door swung together, locking fast. Saracen and Minion leapt to Enzemblance's side, caught her under the arms, and pulled, but their strength was no match for the closing *brugh*'s gravity. Slowly, inch by inch, Enzemblance sank downward . . .

. . . until Mac Roke sprinted past them, relic nail in one hand, hammer in the other. He fell to his knees, set the spike's point to *brugh*-skin, raised his hammer high, and hesitated for one brief second. Jo understood why well enough, given what she'd just done herself—this was an act from which there was no going back. Whatever family Roke had left, monstrous as it might be, would be forever lost.

(*But it is time, grandson, and past time. So get it done, for once and all, and quickly.*)

Lady Glauce's voice, quivering up through Jo's feet; she saw gooseflesh on Carra's arms and knew the other girl felt it, too—more strongly than her, probably. Though not so strong as Roke, his jaw set, those too-blue eyes narrowing.

Grandmere, I will.

The hammer came down hard, nail driving deep, as if Stane were flesh. Light flashed from the impact. Again and again Mac hammered, drawing lightning, driving the spike ever deeper. Sealing the *brugh* shut.

Enzemblance wailed, a sound both pitiful and terrifying; Saracen and Minion, forced to let go, watched her sink to the neck, every shred of youth and power flaking away 'til nothing but a bare toothless mask remained above ground, nested in hair that withered like sedge. With one final blow, Mac sat back, breathing heavy—then looked her way and froze.

"Holy . . ." he began, choking off. Enzemblance winced.

"Maccabee," she whispered. "Ha' ye no pity at all for yuir ane flesh and blood?"

Roke stared at her a long moment—two good beats of the heart, by

Jo's own count. "Guess not," he replied, finally.

Adding, internally: *No more than you for my mother or father. No more than you for me.*

"Then this is . . . the end of all things, surely . . ."

Coldly: "For *you.*"

And with that, Mac stomped down hard, right on his aunt's face—drove her into the ground until the earth closed over, rock lapping her like lava. 'Til only a few decaying strands of hair remained—first red-tinged yet, then grey, then white—sticking from a solid slab of Stane.

"There," he said, eventually. "*There.*"

Done.

Beside him, Saracen went stumbling back, ankles turning; Mac turned to see his cousin fold, sly face crumpling, luxuriant backwards lashes already gummed with tears. Minion held him up, just barely.

"A pox on ye, coz," Saracen whispered, grief-raw, waving away any attempt at apology. "Nay, forbye! Curses hound thee now and forever, who e'en once took side wi' outlanders against his ane. A foul life live, and an ill death may ye dee."

After which, without further ado, he and Minion melted away back into the woods, there and gone in the very same instant. Like leaves turning in fall, or ice to water. Like frost silvering fruit, blackening it to the heart.

Glamour, Jo thought. And shivered.

At the forest's edge, Davina still eddied in the air as if unsure of what to do next. She looked at Jo, who studied her hungrily, knowing this was the last time she'd see her, in any form: rexed red hair, body hard and boyish, green-apple breasts hid under the camo shirt she'd worn to their last job; that devil's mouth and those brash eyes, abashed by nothing.

When had she ever looked so unsure of what to do next? Alive, she would've lit another cig, leaned back and flirted, considering her options. But they both knew what those were.

Go on, love, Jo projected in her direction. *Sorry for trying to keep you, let alone how. But 'twas only because—*

'Cause I filled your hole, baby?

You could call it that, yeah.

Dav laughed, or mimed doing it, shoulders rising in one last shrug. Smoke rose around her, blurring her from the toes up in a personal dry-ice shroud, though at least Jo didn't see that bloody fake cigarette in her hand, for which she was grateful.

Always one to make an exit, she thought, a grim shell of satisfaction forming like a lid over the same dreadful, yearning pit of want, as though she might somehow pretend it away. Then thinking, in the same breath: *Oh Christ, but I miss you, Dav. So bloody much.*

I know. But how can ya, when you won't even let me leave?

Jo gave her the V for fuck off, and saw her laugh again, drinking in the details longingly—glint of light on her dead teeth, the freckles on her cheeks, the way her nose wrinkled, a stroked cat's. Then watched as she dispersed, blowing away.

Love you, she thought again, one last time. And made herself turn away, with a wrench—just in time to catch another drama playing out, back amongst the standing stones.

Ganconer at the edge of it all, Galit and Kim in the middle with Elver between. Kim kept his hands to himself, eyes eating Galit alive; Galit didn't even seem to notice, consumed as she was with taking stock, every mundane thing around her a treat after so many years pent away. She must've described much of this to Elver over that time, yet never been able to prove her thesis more than speculation—to him it was metaphor only, nothing like the dim little world he knew. And now here it was, all around him; no wonder he could barely seem to speak.

"You came," Galit said again, gaze finally returning to Kim. "I hoped . . . oh, I hoped, but I didn't know. You didn't have to do that, Josh. I'd've understood if you hadn't."

He shook his head, tears in his eyes. "Should've come sooner," he said. "Making you wait all this time—I don't think I can ever forgive myself."

"No," she said, "don't be stupid. You'd've died if you'd tried earlier. There were rooms full of bones, down there . . . I don't want to think about it. But you needed her—" She nodded at Carra. "And the nephew, with the nail . . . that girlfriend of his. The magician. *Her.*" Now she was pointing at Jo, who flushed, uncomfortably. "All of them. And I'm grateful, Josh. I'm so damn grateful."

Kim nodded, then looked at Ganconer. "What about him?" he asked.

Galit looked down at Elver. "Do you have them?"

"Aye, Mumma."

Carefully, the boy approached, deliberately making enough noise that Ganconer looked up—raised his head, anyhow. The wooden eyes were horribly kept, infected and pussy around their edges, unhealed even after all this time; he seemed to be weeping, a constant stream of sticky yellowish rheum.

"Is't you, Elver?" Ganconer asked.

"Yes, sir. I have aught for you."

The boy rummaged inside his garments, withdrew something, clinking slightly. He touched Ganconer's hand, uncurling it gently, and tipped two things—round, wet, delicate—into his palm.

"No," Ganconcer breathed.

"Lady Glauce gave them to Mumma," Elver said. "She told us wait and give you them later, when 'twas all finished."

"No," Ganconer repeated.

But: "Yes," Galit replied, crossing to him. "May I . . . let me. Hold still, just a moment . . ."

There followed some business that Jo, though rarely squeamish, was happy not to see clearly. Then Ganconer opened his *own* eyes, at long last; these focused first on Galit, who smiled, then down towards Elver, where they lingered some time, awash with far more healthy tears.

He put out his hand, wavering. Touched the solemn little face, with its pale cheeks, its dark and wary stare.

"Oh, my boy," he said, finally, so dim and wet the words barely made sense. "Oh, you. My *boy*."

After, they drove their various vehicles as close to the former Dourvale *brugh* as the woods would allow, finding it a surprisingly easy task now that the net of glamour had collapsed, buried along with Euwphaim and Lady Glauce. Separating into little sub-groups, the two parties made their farewells to the place and each other as the cold moon peered down through the trees.

"That felt . . . really good," Mac Roke said, examining the hilltop scar—a mere scrape of chalk under dirt and dead grass, last red-grey twists of hair already blown away to line bird-nests or festoon bushes—which was all that was now left to mark where Enzemblance Druir had once lain. "Real Warrior of God stuff—righteous, almost."

"Aye," Jo agreed, left so exhausted in her own double epiphany's wake, her tongue seemed to think she was drunk. "You'll no' be asked back for dinner anytime soon, I'm thinking."

"Suits me. All they ever served was rotten apples and dead leaves anyhow, glamoured to taste like something else."

"What a way to talk. And you a priest."

"Defrocked."

"Oh, I'd clean forgot. How's that work, exactly? Always wondered."

Deadpan: "Well . . . first they make you give back the frock . . ."

Beside them, Judy Kiss rolled her eyes in a *never heard* that *one before* way. "Yeah, yeah," she said. "Listen, we better go: your cousin Ganconer needs a lift, and if we stick around much longer, I think I might make Carra Devize throw up again."

Jo looked to where the man stood, arms wrapped 'round himself and new eyes gone somewhat misty, watching Galit Michaels and Josh Kim load the kiddie into Kim's van. "Where's he like to go, now he's got no home?" she asked. "The Freihoeven?"

Roke considered that. "He's just about the only Sidderstane left," he replied, "even if Torrance never wrote him into the will—no point, having traded him to the *brugh* and all. But these days there's DNA testing, at least. I could probably figure out something."

"And in the meantime, you have a couch," Judy pointed out. "If you want to do *two* good deeds today."

"But that's where *I* sleep."

"Not all the time."

"Mmm," Roke said, eyes still on Dourvale's last changeling. "Let me think it over."

Miles to do that, before we're back downtown, Jo reckoned. But she'd be asleep for most of the trip, far too deeply for dreams, good or bad. Surely she was owed *that* much, at the very least.

On the other side of the clearing, meanwhile, Jude and Carra stood together, his shadow trembling on the grass between them— dim, turned sidelong, as though it was surreptitiously trying to avoid insulting either of them by forcing them to notice its presence.

"We should talk, sometime," she told him, trying not to look. "About—"

Jude shook his head, eyes on Kim's van, where little Elver sat solemn in his mother's lap, sharing his first ever seat belt. "Yeah, I don't think so," he said. "Thanks anyway."

"Listen, Jude . . ."

"*Carra.*" A great and terrible love entered his voice when he said her name, cut with an equally enduring frustration. "C'mon, now. You know I'm just going to go ahead and keep trying to find a way to get rid of it, right?"

"But . . . that doesn't even make any *sense.*"

"'Cause it's half my soul? Look, I'm not going to *destroy* it, for God's sake; frankly, I don't think I even could. Just . . . park it somewhere, someplace safe. Someplace—not near me."

"For how long?"

"A while." She stared at him, and he sighed. "I just can't take having it with me, having it *around*. I feel too much. Out here, it's okay, weirdly enough—but I don't live here, I live in Toronto, and in Toronto, I can't walk down the fucking *street*, some days. It kind of feels like it's killing me."

Carra shook her head, neck-cords abruptly taut, nose stinging. "*Drama*," she said, voice harsher than she'd intended it to be. "You're telling *me* it hurts to not be able to keep anything out? To have no skin? *Me*?"

It occurred to her that she might be shouting, or close to. People were looking around, and her throat hurt. Jude—once-Shadowless Jude Hark, the GTA's hierarchical magician supreme—actually flinched.

"You've done it longer, Carra," he said, softly. "And you're stronger than me, too. You've always been stronger."

"You're wrong."

"Then we're *both* wrong. What now?"

They paused, and Carra found herself reaching out, hesitant, to knit their hands together. And while the accompanying surge of sensation *was* difficult, it was also—familiar. Bearable.

This is how it can be, she tried to tell him. *You just have to—learn to take it.* Try *to learn.*

Jude shook his head, slowly. But he didn't move away, and that was something.

"I *will* talk to you, Jude," Carra told him, out loud. "If it takes me years, I'll make you understand why you need to have part of you that's weak enough, *open* enough, to hurt. To feel."

Jude's voice, in her head: *No.* And hers, in his—

(*Yes.*)

"We'll see," Jude said after another pause. Then walked to the van, shadow following two steps behind, as ever. As he slipped in beside Galit, Carra saw it make an odd, truncated gesture in her direction before melting into the van's darkness—one hand thrown back, fingers fluttering. *I see you,* perhaps. *Thank you for trying.* Or even: *goodbye.*

Ignoring it, Jude turned to Elver, smiling. "Do you like magic?" The boy shook his head, solemnly. "Oh no, I'm sorry—not *real* magic; tricks, that's all I meant. Do you like tricks?"

Looking up at Galit first, for permission. Eventually reaping the barest nod, long hair falling to shroud the child's face.

"Sometimes," Elver said, quietly.

"Perfect," Jude replied, smile deepening. "Let me show you something."

Carra felt Sy's hand on hers yet again before she heard his approach, that reassuring clasp calming her, anchoring her. Gripped him back without turning, wanting to hold on until she somehow became just as warm, normal, *human* by association.

We can't always have what we want, she thought. *But—there's a middle ground, too, isn't there? Another way.*

She wanted to walk that path, she found, very dearly. Preferably with him beside her, for as long as that might last.

"Take me home, after this," she said, still not turning. "First subway stop we pass, okay?"

"Okay."

"Not to Gala's—to *my* place, though. To yours."

"I can do that," Sy said. And gave her hand another squeeze.

Nature is slow. It mainly stays the same, within its seasons; things rarely stay changed for long, though all things change, or *seem* to change. And the Dourvale Shore, strange a place as it may otherwise be, poses no great exception to this rule.

Inside Dourvale, the stone-strewn streets lie empty, weed-choked, fertile with decay. Outside, in the deep woods, the light stays brown and stinging at almost every time of day, filtered through a thousand mosquito wings at once. On the forest's well-stocked killing-floor, temporal ripples continue to echo back through minutes, months, years: a harsh sound of gasping, thud of city shoes blundering past, stirring the pine-needle loam up like sodden, grey-brown snow. Sending the little toads hopping clear, each throat fluttering delicate, one more moist clump of dirt set with tiny, jewelled eyes.

And if you ever happen to find yourself outside the canning factory, just at dusk (a place you wouldn't want to be under most circumstances, let alone as the light begins to fade, the shadows sharpen and lengthen, tricking your eyes into wanting to close), and if you see a figure approaching through the trees, and if it seems to be an old lady in a long dress . . . then you will not want to come towards her, or let her come towards you. Most especially if, as she does, you realize she's not old at all, but young and strangely beautiful: skin a-glow, limbs like eels, lidless eyes deep-set and hard, like stones. And her hair, her dress, and six-fingered hands all wet, dripping with black, black water.

But she will not be here tonight, that same lady. Instead, under the dusty ruin the *brugh* time-tunnel's collapse has made of what was once the Sidderstane family cottage, Ygerna Sidderstane holds her brother Gaheris's heart in both hands, so ripe and sweet and heavy with congested blood—then takes a long bite and chews on it, thoughtfully, barely feeling the tears she cries while doing so, though they score her transparent cheeks like vitriol.

Thinking, all the while: *My own brother, my twin, my one, my only.*

Why would I do that to him? Why would I?

Because you are a monster, born of monsters, she decides, eventually. *And because, amongst these monsters, you alone are left spared, to be queen of all you survey.*

The village is hers now, by right of blood and ownership, fully uncontested. These facts make her content, as does the knowledge that, of the Five-Family Coven, it is *her* branch alone . . . so small, so feeble, against the wild, dark brightness of the rest . . . which has finally emerged from this five centuries' maelstrom with anything even halfway worth the having.

I won, she thinks. *We won, through the Devize girl and all those others. At last. At last.*

(*Yes, sis.*)

Yes.

Hearing his voice in her head, the only part of her still left unaltered; it lulls her as little else can, even now. And thus—finding what she has done no longer bothers her quite so much, so long as she still has a version of Gaheris to talk to—Ygerna glides slickly off to her hole, where she has spent the last thirty years building a nest of bile and bones. Drifts off to sleep, still chewing. Still crying.

Around her, Dourvale remains, as it always has and always will, even now that the tale of the Druirs is over. And as all things tend towards their end, most surely, this book is also ended.

You, listening—put it down. Then find your own homes, and go there.

AFTERWORD:
Under These Rocks and Stones

In case anyone still doesn't know, I'm Canadian. Born in Britain, yes—London, to be specific, within the legendary sound of Bow Bells—but I've been a citizen since I was three, and every memory I have involves living in downtown Toronto, Ontario. When I was younger, I used to dream mainly about other places, having absorbed the cultural meme that anywhere is better/more interesting than any given part of my home and native land, especially the parts which happen to be located most closely to the United States. I grew up well-used to the idea that there is so little inherently "Canadian" that we are forced to define ourselves negatively, as in that famous Molson Canadian "I AM Canadian" beer commercial (YouTube it)—we don't have a President, we don't live in igloos, we don't eat blubber, we don't say "aboot," etc. While compared to the States, which is always a given, we're supposedly polite, and clean, and nice—the quiet neighbour above the meth lab, as Robin Williams once put it.

Of course, like with most things, the truth is far more murky. Some of us routinely do all of the above, and most of us aren't all that nice, either—no nicer than any other nation mainly made up of people occupying land they stole from other people, at any rate. We may claim we're in favour of a mosaic rather than a melting pot and peacekeeping rather than armed intervention, but tell that to the Kahnesetake protestors, the boys of St. Vincent, or the women whose remains were found on Robert Pickton's pig farm. The image of "Canadian-ness" we absorb through the media, so initially diffuse the government literally set up both a National Film Board and a Canadian Broadcasting Company (first radio, then television) to disseminate it, most often applies specifically to white Canadians of non-Indigenous and non-Francophone descent, with a vague sideline in well-assimilated "immigrants" to make ourselves feel better about the whole thing.

In terms of being raised feeling they have no real identity of their own, it's probably different in other parts of Canada—actually, I *know* it is, because the other sections all seem to have a pretty distinct sense of self, to the extent that few of them ever really wanted to become part of one big country in the first place. (In Newfoundland, for example—last to join Confederation, in 1949—some older people still claim they were essentially tricked into doing so.) But here in Ontario, the basic assumption is that, in much the same way Toronto looks *almost* enough like a bunch of different North American cities to pass, if set-decorated correctly (at least for people who don't actually live in said cities), whatever culture we do have must be by necessity a pale, bloodless, haphazard imitation of our Southern neighbours'. This is nothing new; we used to be not-England, and now we're not-America. But we're also not-Quebec, not-the-Maritimes, not-the-Prairies, not-Vancouver, and *certainly* not-Nunavut.

Well, at a certain point in my life, I realized that every time I pictured "somebody" walking down "some street" in "some city," I was actually thinking about me walking down a street in Toronto. And why not? Why continue to pretend otherwise? You could therefore say that the preceding group of stories, as well as the personal mythology supporting them—assembled over a loose period of fifteen years and winding semi-deliberately back and forth through each other, like some ouroborous tapeworm—is the result. In other words, the whole idea of the Five-Family Coven and its works proceeds in part from the idea that the beliefs I just outlined above are inaccurate by definition, a lazily assembled crock of received wisdom long overdue for forcible revision. That Toronto and Ontario can be exactly as scary as anywhere more exotic, if you know where to look . . . scarier, maybe. Because, on the surface, it all seems so *pleasant*.

I'm joking a bit, but not really. Much like the part of the Canadian Shield on which Ontario perches, there is an awful, flinty heart to Canada which underlies everything. There's a reason that the first collection of Alice Munro short stories I ever read was called *Who Do You Think You Are?*, because that's the primary Canadian question—contemptuous, self-excoriating. On some level, we don't trust ourselves, because we know enough to know better than to; we're all liars, all freaks, at least potentially, same as everywhere else. And going by the legacy of that nice young couple from Mississauga (Paul Bernardo and Karla Homolka, look them up), maybe we're right not to.

Toronto was also six million strong even back before the GTA (Greater Toronto Area) combined into a single mega-city, and remains one of the most multicultural (if not entirely integrated) in North America. I was very amused, recently, when fellow Torontonian Nalo Hopkinson talked about being told she was "trying too hard" by inserting an apparently unlikely number of people of colour into her narrative, simply because she made the racial mixture in her most recent books reflect the one she saw every day on our city's downtown streets. Now, does this make Toronto some sort of rainbow utopia? Hardly. Canada in general is too grim for that, too jaw-clenched and rooted in Native genocide; we're a cold, odd bunch of people, happier by far to ignore each other than harass each other, but let's not fool ourselves—we're capable of everything everybody else is, and worse. That's the human condition.

Or then again, maybe that's just me.

In retrospect, I think I was also reacting (as I often do) to Margaret Atwood's *Survival*, a survey of Canadian fiction that pares our national identity back to one of people fighting not to be erased by the massiveness and indifference of the landscape they find themselves engulfed by and pitted against, which either absorbs them or rejects them utterly in its epic scale, its innate wilderness. This is what we all supposedly come "attached" to, even those of us who have no truck with it on a day-to-day basis: the massive sky of Manitoba, the overhanging lack of cloud, the horridly clear stars. Or the deep, dry cold of a Winnipeg Christmas, necessitating wearing a balaclava just to walk down the street and constant shuffling to disperse static electricity.

For myself, the few, relatively brief times I've spent outside Toronto's grip have definitely left a mark on me. I tend to have a very slippy-slidey sense of geography, possibly because I don't drive, so my impressions of travel always come hand in hand with a sense of vulnerability and powerlessness—of being drawn headlong, pulled to a place I don't know, and implicitly threatened with being left there. I remember walking down a country road with one of my ex-fiancés, with no light but the moon to guide us and open fields on either side; I remember that same man's mother, forever stranded in her home because she didn't have a car of her own, miles of highway between her and town. I remember childhood friends whose parents moved out of the city to keep them "safe," only to discover rural Ontario was less modelled after *My Girl* than *River's Edge*. Because of childhood memories of cottage country, a lot of Overdeere and Dourvale is more Gravenhurst than Gananoque—the lake and the deep pines surrounding it, mist and gnats, caterpillars everywhere. Skeletal barns full of mouldy hay, and a general air that even the most weather-blown, pseudo-rustic bon-bon of a house glimpsed against the horizon might prove to conceal a serial killer's basement.

Inhuman beneath a human mask, yet all too human anyhow; my characters tend to have it bad several ways at once, at the very least. First amongst them to raise her head was the woman who forms our through-line, Carraclough Devize. Carra was the main character of my first, unfinished horror novel, the one which—I would later realize—also introduced me to the Maskim, or Terrible Seven. Her origin can be traced pretty directly back to *The Legend of Hell House* (thus far the only film adaptation of Richard Matheson's evocative novel *Hell House*), in which Roddy MacDowell plays a former child medium once mentally raped and left for dead by the "Mount Everest of haunted houses." But like I said, it didn't work out, and I genuinely thought I'd seen the last of her until she popped up as a supporting character in "The Narrow World," the oldest of these stories, having suddenly assumed fresh new characteristics dictated by various experiences I'd had in the interim: the mental health issues of various friends, an Annex area home reminiscent of one I'd once babysat in, a stint at Ryerson University vaguely coinciding with my own.

What had begun as a sketch, a mere blueprint, had become a genuine person, this "skinless," ectoplasmic polaroid-taking medium covered in ghostly bruise-writing who ended up a perpetual ward/employee of the same institution who once put her in harm's way, cycling back and forth between her Mom and the nuthouse. Jude Hark Chiu-wai and his shadow troubles were the gateway drug, but Carra formed the cornerstone, and the rest of the Five-Family mythos began to spin itself out around her, accordingly.

The four biggest components of my all-Canadian monster family mash-up turned out to be psychics (like Carra or Janis Mol, but also the researchers who study and organize them, aka Dr. Guilden Abbott and the Freihoeven group), witches (Euwphaim Glouwer and the rest of the Three Betrayed), the Church (Maccabee Roke, Sister Blandina OSP, and the Ordo), and the Fae (the Druirs and their offshoots, the Sidderstanes). I found myself reaching back into my childhood for influences, remembering the images of fallen angels I'd gleaned from various texts like *The Black Arts* by Richard Cavendish, the magical and psionic basics I'd read about in William Seabrook's *Witchcraft*, Molly Hunter's retelling of the North Berwick Coven story in *The Thirteenth Member* and the supplements on Elizabethan *diablerie* in Edith Sitwell's *The Queens and the Hive*, the creepy Seelie vs. Unseelie lore I'd gleaned from Georgess McHarque's *The Impossible People* and Brian Froud's *Faeries*. But I also looked at unpacking my own conceptual constructions of "family," since that's so often where Canadian weirdness seems to concentrate, from Alice Munro to Anne Hébert.

Now, I am an only child, the product of a single-parent home, which makes family beyond me-and-my-Mom a bit of a mystery to me, especially "extended" family. When I list off the people I'm directly related to, I move quickly through a half-uncle I barely see, plus a Dad who's lived in an entirely different country (Australia) since I was nine. My cousins I see every ten years or so on one side, every twenty on the other. Of my grandparents, two died so far away I couldn't have gotten there in time if I'd tried; the others died respectively in Toronto, where I later viewed his empty shell—I would eventually give birth to my own son in that same hospital—and in Barrie, alone and demented. This last was my maternal grandmother, vital, toxic, Scottish, and unforgiving, parts of whose gleeful delight in drama definitely made their way into Euwphaim Glouwer, who herself rose up almost wholly out of a throwaway line in "Heart's Hole." (Jo casually mentions that her Nan believes she's a temporally transplanted witch from King James's time . . . and as it turns out, that's true!)

But then there's another bunch of relatives, long lost to me, though I've gradually begun to reconnect with them over (interestingly enough) the same period it took me to assemble this book. These are the family of my Mom's Dad, Nana's first husband, and my impresssion of them went further into creating the Druirs than almost anything else, aside from having watched the BBC's 2000 adaptation of *Lorna Doone,* that one time (secret valley, aristocratic border-lord outlaws, Saracen vaguely looking like a young Aidan Gillen, etc.)—this idea that somewhere in Ontario there was an odd, phantom clan of people whose blood exercised a malign influence over mine: tall, fair folk, both dark and bright, innately perverse and ultimately unknowable. Obviously, this isn't *exactly* true, and I apologize in advance to any Hoovers who may end up picking this up for making it seem so. But whenever I think of Mac's untrustworthy, brilliant, morbidly fascinating "country cousins" and the bad blood they've deeded him—this idea of predestination via genetics, a history that never dies, tainting each successive generation in a slightly more harmful way—it's definitely an image integral to my sense of myself, both as me and as Canadian.

Along with Euwphaim and Carra's ancestress Jonet Devize, I needed a third witch for my mini-coven, thus giving birth to Alizoun Rusk, who owes a lot to Susan Musgrave's poetry cycle *Becky Swan's Book.* (Her motto might as well be the lines *Yes, some women are like that/some women are wicked* from the poem "Especially this one.") On the Druir side of the equation, meanwhile, I came up with another bunch of aristocratic dabblers in magic-use, the Rokes, from whom I eventually spun Maccabee Roke, broken priest turned magic object pawnshop manager—that he knows Jude Hark Chiu-wai goes without saying, though not in the Biblical sense. And from my need to give Mac a background in the Church, the Ordo Sororum Perpetualam evolved, martial nuns sworn to the memory of my favourite legendary saint. It was only much later that I realized uncompromising Sister Blandina must surely be descended from Alizoun Rusk, thus bringing us around in a neat little circle.

The stories go in the order their dates suggest, which also mostly identify when they were written (except for "History's Crust," since 1968 is the year I was born), if you want to organize them linearly. And . . . that's about it, I suppose. Stay out of the woods, especially at night.

LINES OF DESCENT

The Five-Family Coven:
>Euwphaim Glouwer
>Alizoun Rusk
>Jonet Devize
>Glauce Lady Druir
>Callistor Laird Roke

Clan Glouwer:
Euwphaim Glouwer was raped by Jonas Clairk, produced Penance Clairk.

Aislinn Clairk (five times great-granddaughter of Jonas) married Harry Trench, produced Dolores Trench; Dolores's body was later occupied by Euwphaim Glouwer.

Dolores Trench/Euwphaim Glouwer married Hector Protheroe, produced Eunice Glouwer. Eunice Glouwer married Joe Mullins (common-law), produced Jodice Glouwer.

Clan Rusk:
Alizoun Rusk was raped multiple times, produced Judas Rusk (father unknown), who married Eluvie Chaconne.

Carson Rusk (grandson of Judas) married Aphra Beacham, produced Captain Solomon Rusk (among others); Carson Rusk also fathered Tante Ankolee "Angelique" Rusk on Oya Femme-Qui-S'Bat.

Tante Ankolee "Angelique" Rusk married Captain Wilmot Collyer (common-law), produced Collyer Rusk.

Mesheeant Rusk (two times great-granddaughter of Collyer) married Colvin Blagrove (common-law), produced Atia "Sister Blandina" Rusk, OSP (among others).

Clan Devize:
Jonet Devize died without issue.

Gashton Devize (Jonet's nephew) founded the family line which moved to England, then Canada.

Donall Devize (five times great-grandson of Gashton) married Lilliette Redcappie, produced Yancey Devize.

Yancey Devize married Geillis "Gala" Carraclough Devize, produced Carraclough Devize.

Clan Druir:

Glauce Lady Druir, changeling, married Enzembler Laird Druir and produced Minion Druir, Enzemblance Druir Sidderstane, Grisell Druir Roke, Miliner Druir Roke; Enzembler Laird Druir also fathered children on daughters of various gillies, beginning the line of Sidderstane with Guizer Sidderstane.

Minion Druir fathered Quire Redcappie on a thrall-girl taken from Dourvale, Scotland (called "Maire," original name unknown); Quire left the *brugh* to live in Overdeere, married Jessica Coldhill, produced Una and Colm Redcappie, twins (amongst others).

Colm Redcappie fathered Liliette and Avril Redcappie, twins (amongst others).

Enzemblance Druir Sidderstane married Torrance Sidderstane, produced (unnamed daughter, deceased), Saracen Druir.

Grisell Druir Roke married Callistor Laird Roke, produced Holofernes Roke (amongst others).

Miliner Druir Roke married Armstrong "Army" Roke, produced Maccabee Roke (formerly SJ, resigned).

Clan Sidderstane:

Torrance Sidderstane married Enzemblance Druir Sidderstane, produced (unnamed daughter, deceased), Saracen Druir; Torrance also fathered Ganconer Sidderstane on Una Redcappie.

Dacre Dowersby Sidderstane (grandson of Torrance) married Avril Redcappie, produced Gaheris and Ygerna Sidderstane, twins.

Ganconer Sidderstane fathered Elver Michaels on Galit Michaels.

Clan Roke:

Callistor Laird Roke married Grisell Druir Roke, produced Holofernes Roke (among others).

Juleyan Laird Roke (grandson of Holofernes Roke) was stripped of his title for treason by Charles II, and died without issue. He is rumoured to have resurrected himself as a vampire.

Alasdair Roke (younger brother of Juleyan) married Hagar-was-Given-Favour Stott, converted to Puritanism; they both emigrated to North America.

Armstrong "Army" Roke (six times great-grandnephew of Alasdair, from the Newfoundland branch) married Miliner Druir Roke, produced Maccabee Roke (formerly SJ, resigned).

PRONUNCIATION GUIDE

Euwphaim (YOOfeym) Glouwer (glOWr)
Alizoun (AHLeeZOON) Rusk (RUSSk)
Jonet (JOHNett) Devize (d'VYZ)
Glauce (GLAUWzah) Lady Druir (DROOR)
Callistor (CAHLLisstor) Laird Roke (rOHk)
Geillis (GAYleess) "Gala" (GAHlah) Carraclough Devize
Carraclough (carraCLAW) Devize
Jodice (joddISS) Glouwer
Atia (AHTchah) "Sr. Blandina (blandEEnah) OSP" Rusk
Mother Eulalia (yooLAHleeYAH)
Sister Cecilia (sessSEEleeYAH)
Anchoress Kentigerna (kehnTEEgayrNAH)
Mother Appolonia (ahpollOHneeYAH)
Judeta (yooDAYtah) "Judy" Kiss (KEESH)
Joe Tulugaak (toolooGACK)
Enzembler (enZEMblur) Laird Druir
Minion (minYUN) Druir
Enzemblance (enZEMblahnz) Druir Sidderstane (SIDerSTEYN)
Saracen (SAHHRahSEN) Druir
Grisell (GREEzell) Druir Roke
Miliner (MILLINurr) Druir Roke
Maccabee (MACKahBEE) Roke
Guizer (GUYzer) Sidderstane
Quire (KWYer) Redcappie
Maire (MAYree)
Una (OOnah) Redcappie
Torrance (TORanss) Sidderstane
Ganconer (GAHNsohNER) Sidderstane
Dacre (DAYcruh) Dowersby (duhOWurrzbee) Sidderstane
Gaheris (gahHAIRiss) Sidderstane
Ygerna (EEGEHRnah) Sidderstane
Galit (GAHleet) Michaels
Jude (JOOD) Hark (HUHk) Chiu-wai (CHEW-why)
Dr. Guilden (GILLdunn) Abbott
Sylvester (silVESTurr) Horse-Kicker
Cordellion (korDELLeeYON) Federoy (FEDerroy)
Davina (dahVEEnah) Cirocco (sirROCKkoh)
Ashreel (ASHreeEL) Maskim (MASSkeem)
Penemue (penEMway) Grigorim (greeGOReem)

PREVIOUSLY PUBLISHED

ACKNOWLEDGEMENTS

This book is dedicated, first and foremost, to the nation of Canada, the province of Ontario and the city of Toronto, which all deserve the blanket thanks of my generation for keeping us both politely weird and weirdly polite.

Otherwise, as ever: Stephen J. Barringer, Callum Barringer, Elva Mai Hoover and Gary Files, the known and unknown branches of my extended family, plus all my friends.

I owe you everything.

And great thanks to Samantha Beiko for going above and beyond the call of duty in handling this book's very challenging layout.

ABOUT THE AUTHOR

Born in London, England and raised in Toronto, Gemma Files has been an award-winning horror author for over twenty years, as well as a film critic, screenwriter and teacher. Her story "The Emperor's Old Bones" won the 1999 International Horror Guild Award for Best Short Fiction. She has published two collections of short work (*Kissing Carrion* and *The Worm in Every Heart*) and two chapbooks of poetry. *A Book of Tongues*, her first novel, won the 2010 DarkScribe Magazine Black Quill Award for Small Press Chill, in both the Editors' and Readers' Choice categories. She continued the Hexslinger series with two more books, *A Rope of Thorns* and *A Tree of Bones*, published by ChiZine Publications in 2011 and 2012. All three have since been collected into a single volume, *The Hexslinger Omnibus*. She is currently working on her fourth novel.

You can learn more about Gemma Files at her professional blog, http://musicatmidnight-gfiles.blogspot.com, or more than you probably want to know at http://handful-ofdust.livejournal.com. She can also be found on Facebook, Twitter, and Tumblr.

EMB
RACE
THE
ODD

THE HEXSLINGER TRILOGY
GEMMA FILES

It's 1867, and the Civil War is over. But the blood has just begun to flow. For Asher Rook, Chess Pargeter, and Ed Morrow, the war has left its mark in tangled lines of association and cataclysmic love, woken hexslinger magic, and the terrible attentions of a dead god. "Reverend" Asher Rook is the unwilling gateway for the Mayan goddess Ixchel to birth her pantheon back into the world of the living, and to do it she'll force Rook to sacrifice his lover and fellow outlaw Chess Pargeter. But being dead won't bar Chess from taking vengeance, and Pargeter will claw his way back out of Hell, teaming with undercover-Pinkerton-agent-turned-outlaw Ed Morrow to wreak it. What comes back into the world in the form of Chess Pargeter is a walking wound, Chess's very presence tearing a crack in the world and reshaping everything around him while Ixchel establishes Hex City, a city state defying the very laws of nature—an act that will draw battle lines between a passel of dead gods and monsters, hexes galore, spiritualists, practitioners of black science, a coalition set against Ixchel led by Allan Pinkerton himself, and everyone unfortunate enough to be caught between the colliding forces.

A BOOK OF TONGUES	A ROPE OF THORNS	A TREE OF BONES
978-1-92685-182-2	**978-1-92685-197-6**	**978-1-92685-164**

THE FAMILY UNIT AND OTHER FANTASIES

LAURENCE KLAVAN

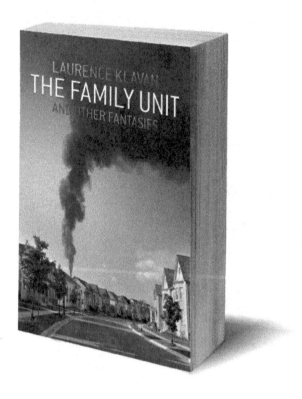

The Family Unit and Other Fantasies is the debut collection of acclaimed Edgar Award-winning author Laurence Klavan. A superb group of darkly comic, deeply compassionate, largely fantastical stories set in our jittery, polarized, increasingly impersonal age. Whether it's the tale of a corporation that buys a man's family; two supposed survivors of a super-storm who are given shelter by a gullible couple; an erotic adventure set during an urban terrorist alert; or a nightmare in which a man sees his neighbourhood developed and disappearing at a truly alarming speed, these stories are by turn funny and frightening, odd and arousing, uncanny and unnerving.

AVAILABLE NOW
978-1-77148-203-5

CHIZINEPUB.COM

GIFTS FOR THE ONE WHO COMES AFTER

HELEN MARSHALL

Ghost thumbs. Miniature dogs. One very sad can of tomato soup . . . British Fantasy Award-winner Helen Marshall's second collection offers a series of twisted surrealities that explore the legacies we pass on to our children. A son seeks to reconnect with his father through a telescope that sees into the past. A young girl discovers what lies on the other side of her mother's bellybutton. Death's wife prepares for a very special funeral. In *Gifts for the One Who Comes After*, Marshall delivers eighteen tales of love and loss that cement her as a powerful voice in dark fantasy and the New Weird. Dazzling, disturbing, and deeply moving.

AVAILABLE NOW
978-1-77148-302-5

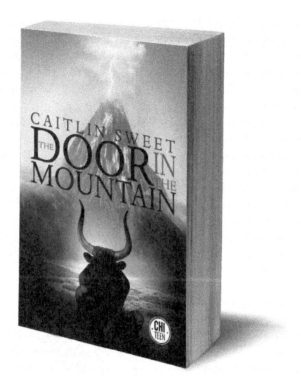

FLOATING BOY AND THE GIRL WHO COULDN'T FLY

P. T. JONES

This is the story of a girl who sees a boy float away one fine day. This is the story of the girl who reaches up for that boy with her hand and with her heart. This is the story of a girl who takes on the army to save a town, who goes toe-to-toe with a mad scientist, who has to fight a plague to save her family. This is the story of a girl who would give anything to get to babysit her baby brother one more time. If she could just find him.

It's all up in the air for now, though, and falling fast. . . .

Fun, breathlessly exciting, and full of heart, *Floating Boy and the Girl Who Couldn't Fly* is an unforgettable ride.

AVAILABLE NOW IN CANADA/OCTOBER 2014 IN U.S.
978-1-77148-173-1